EARTHLING!

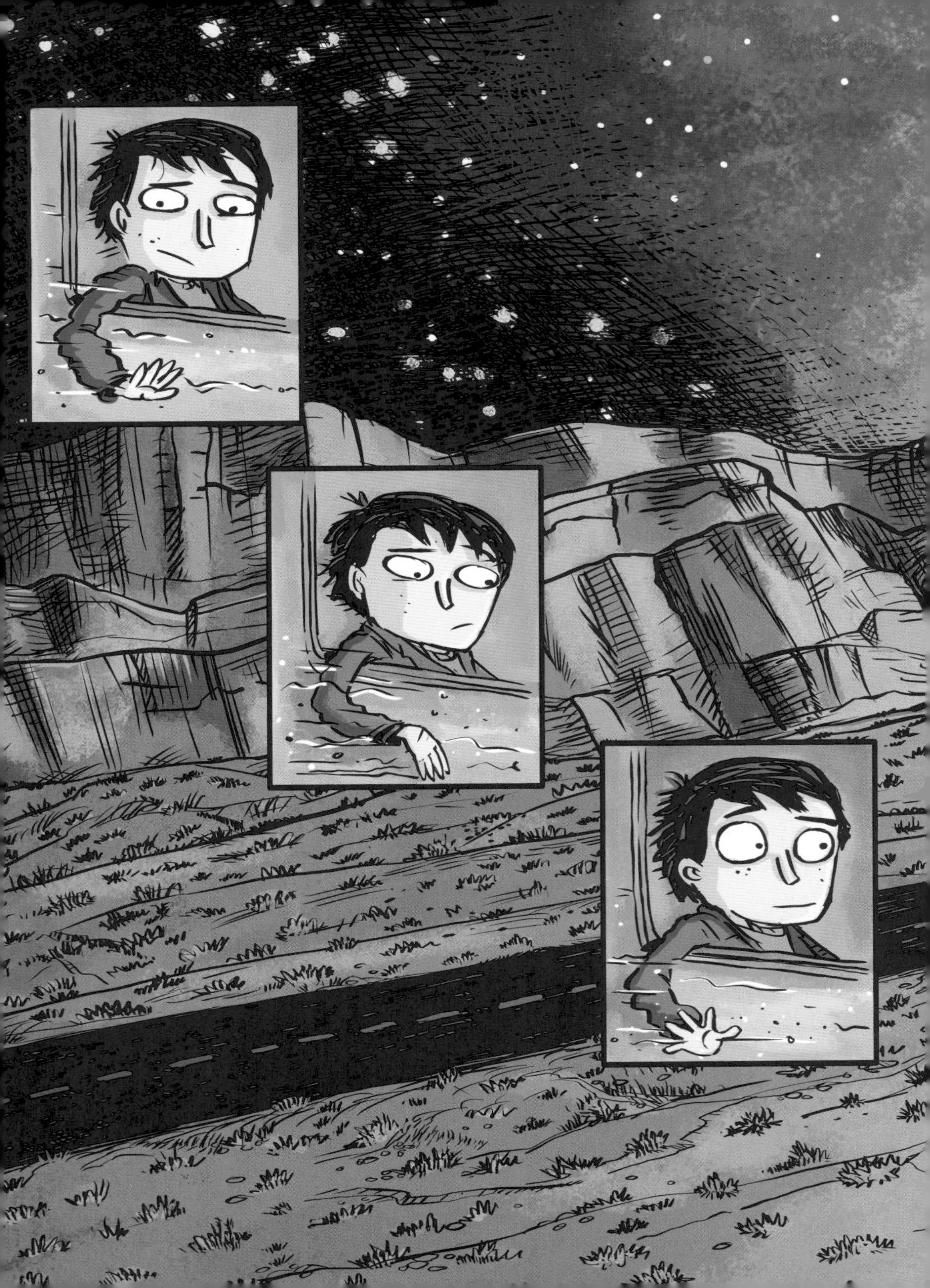

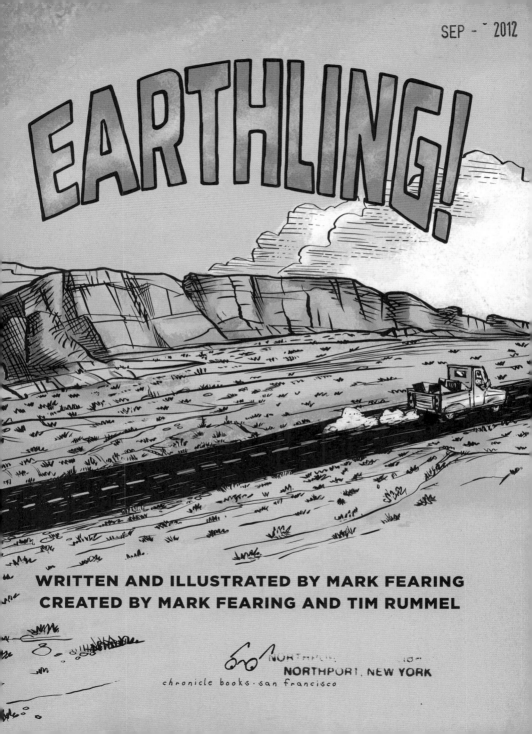

EARTHLING!

WRITTEN AND ILLUSTRATED BY MARK FEARING
CREATED BY MARK FEARING AND TIM RUMMEL

chronicle books · san francisco

CHAPTER 1

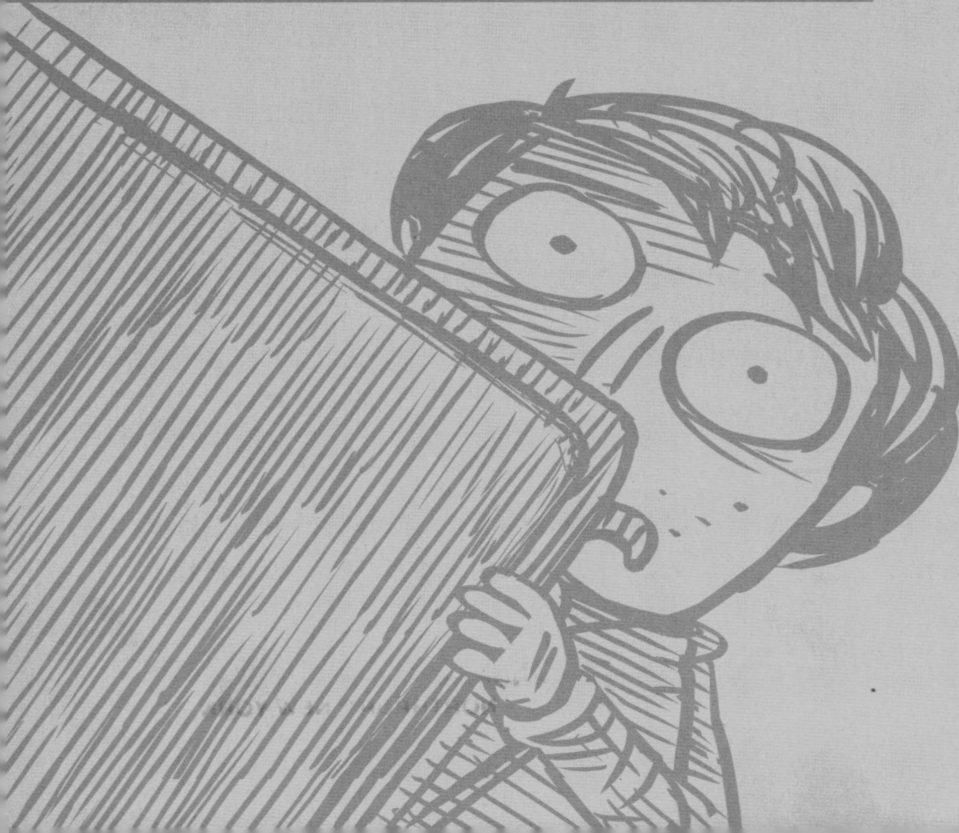

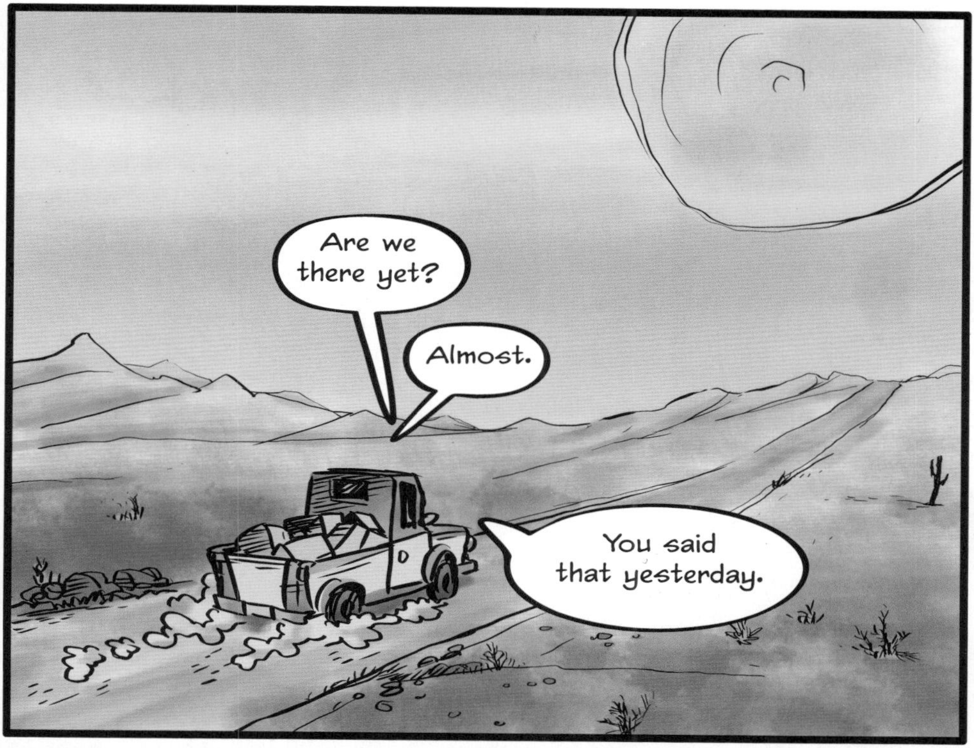
Are we there yet?
Almost.
You said that yesterday.

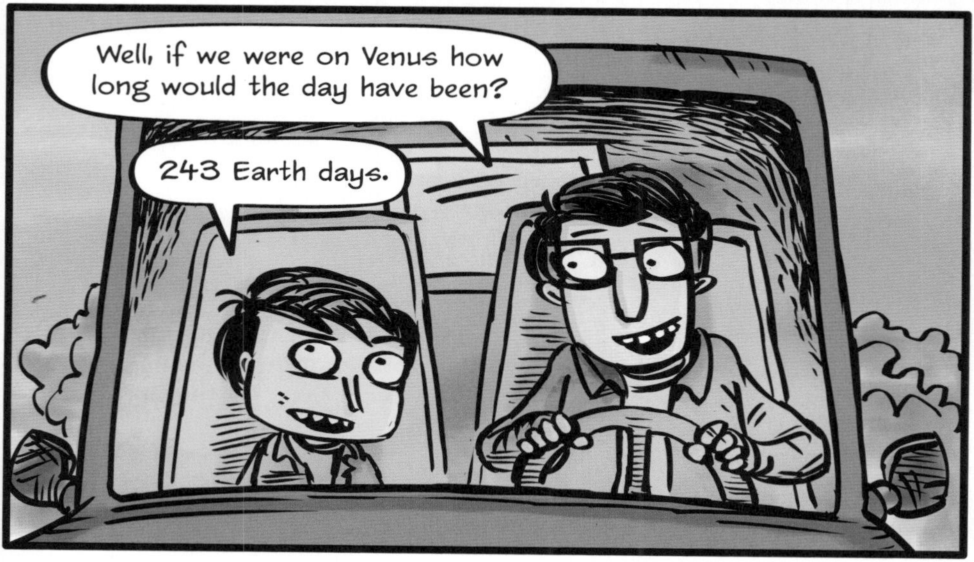
Well, if we were on Venus how long would the day have been?
243 Earth days.

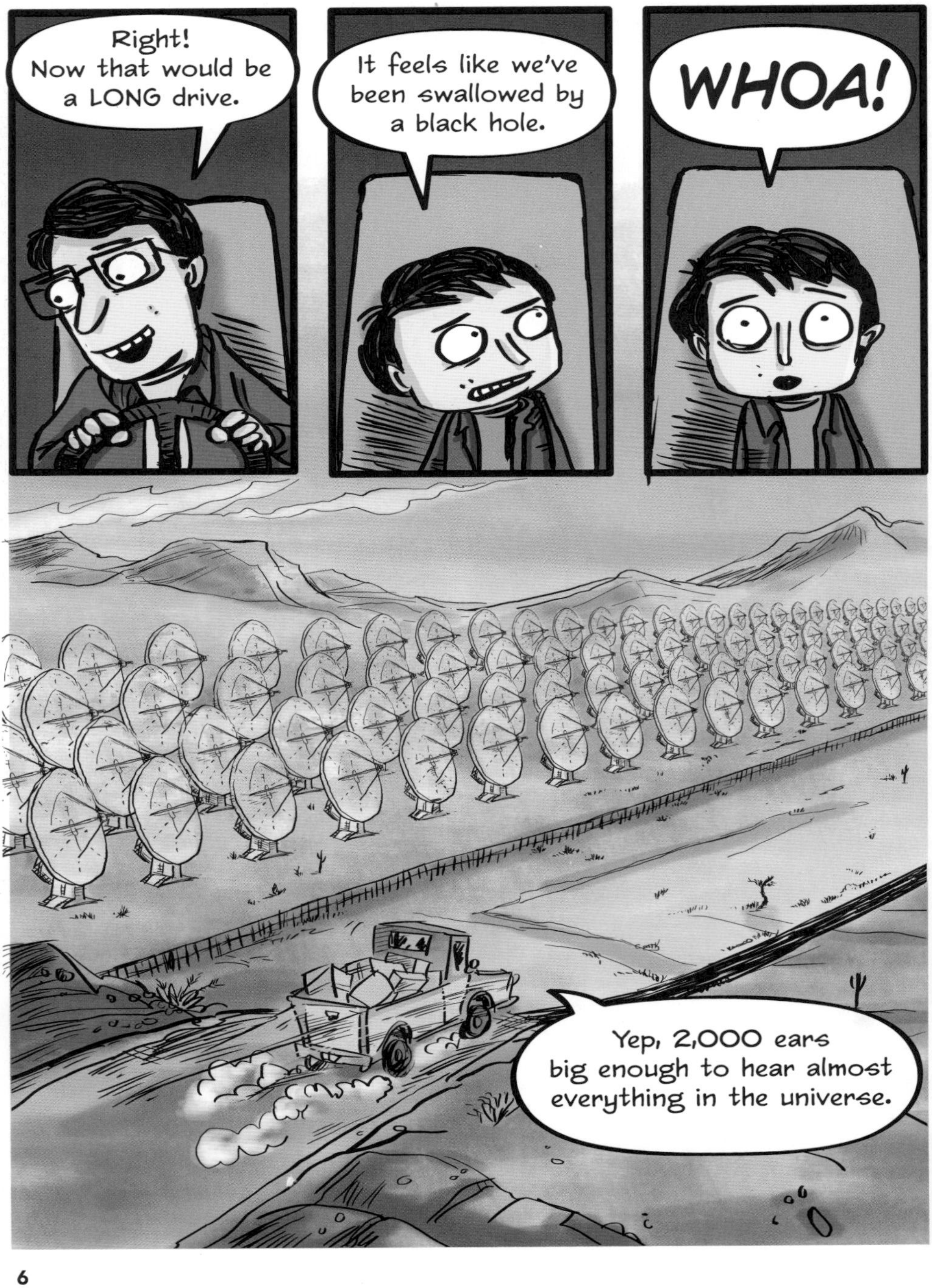
Right! Now that would be a LONG drive.
It feels like we've been swallowed by a black hole.
WHOA!
Yep, 2,000 ears big enough to hear almost everything in the universe.

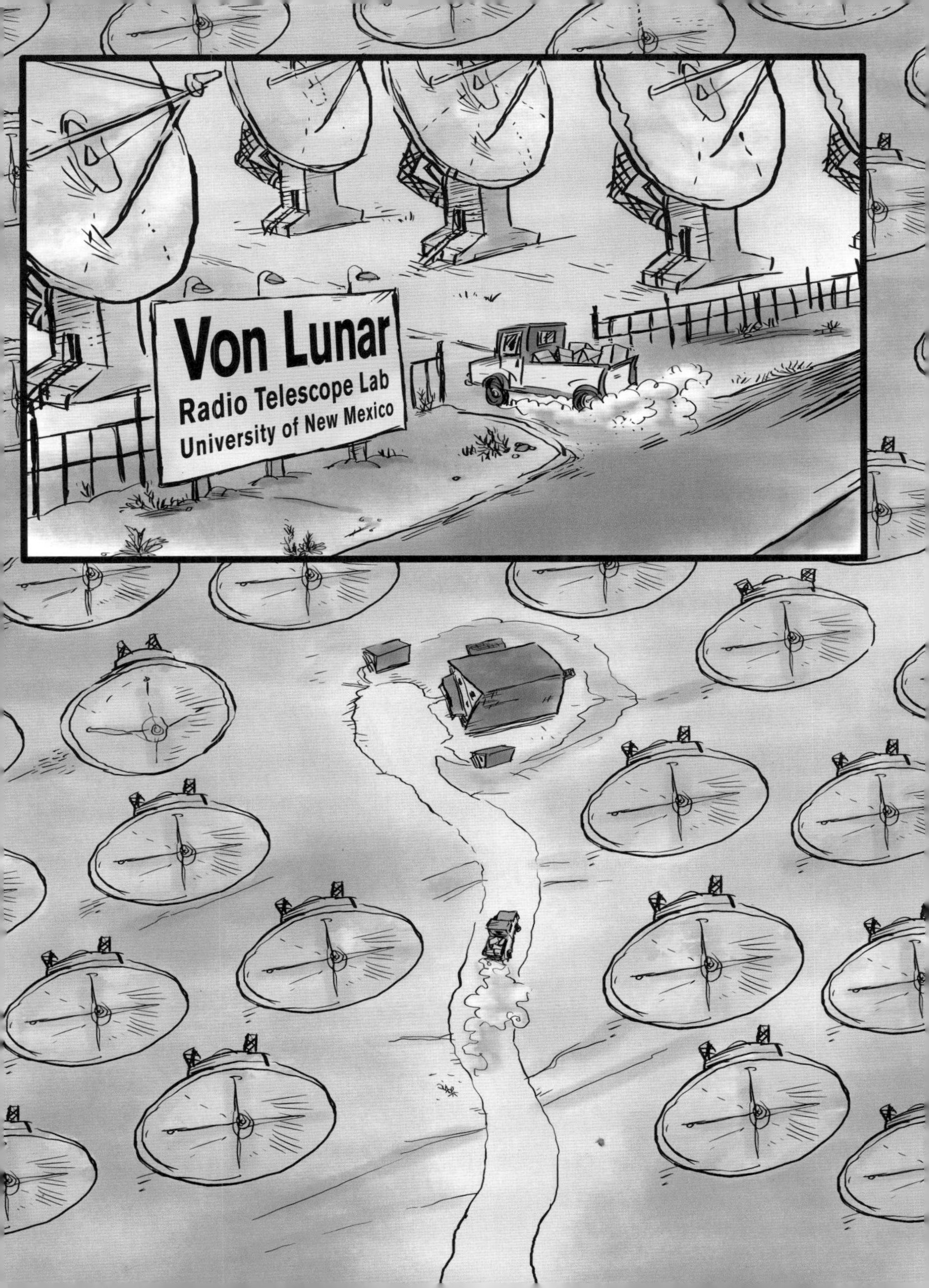
Von Lunar
Radio Telescope Lab
University of New Mexico

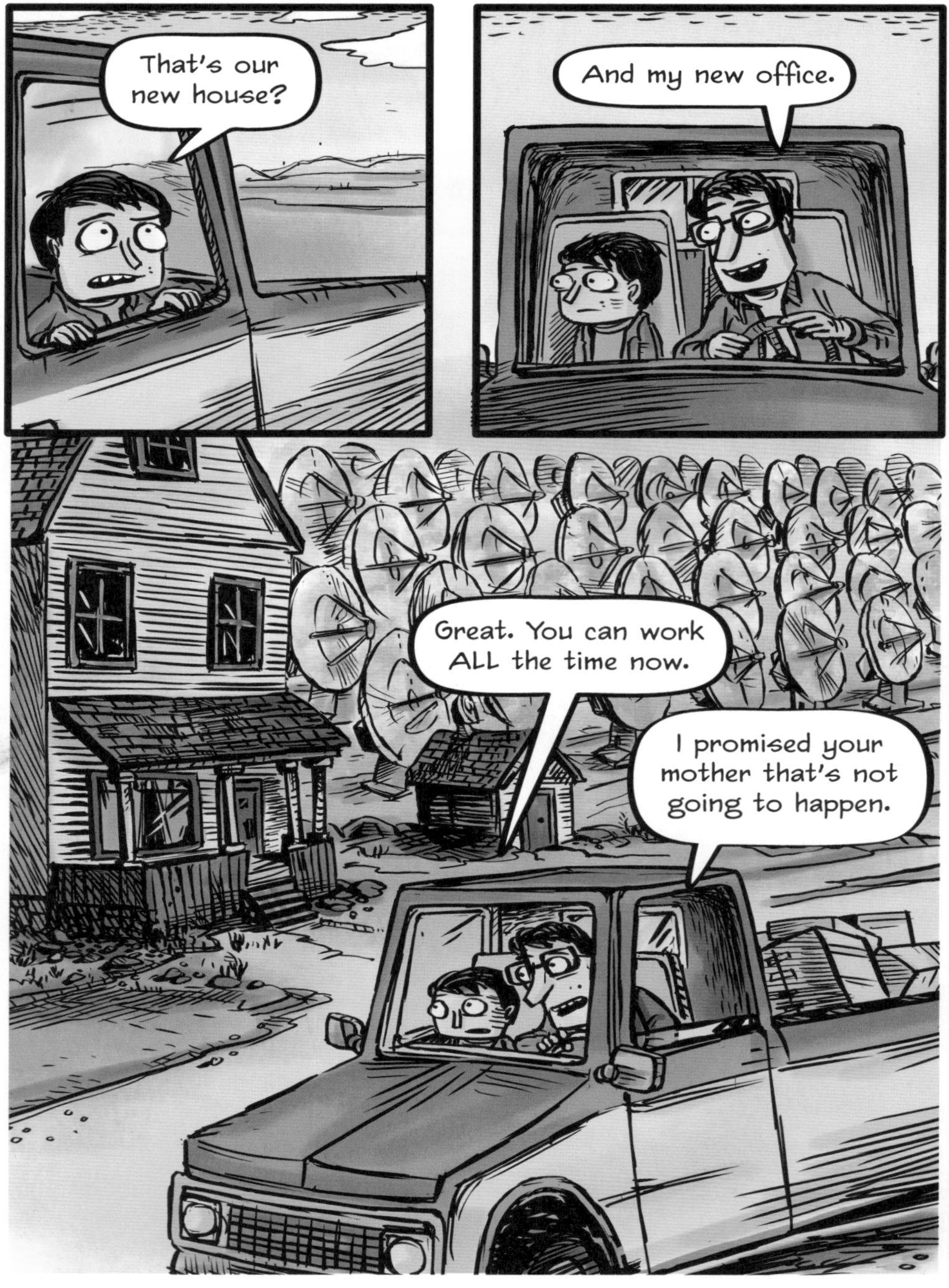
That's our new house?
And my new office.
Great. You can work ALL the time now.
I promised your mother that's not going to happen.

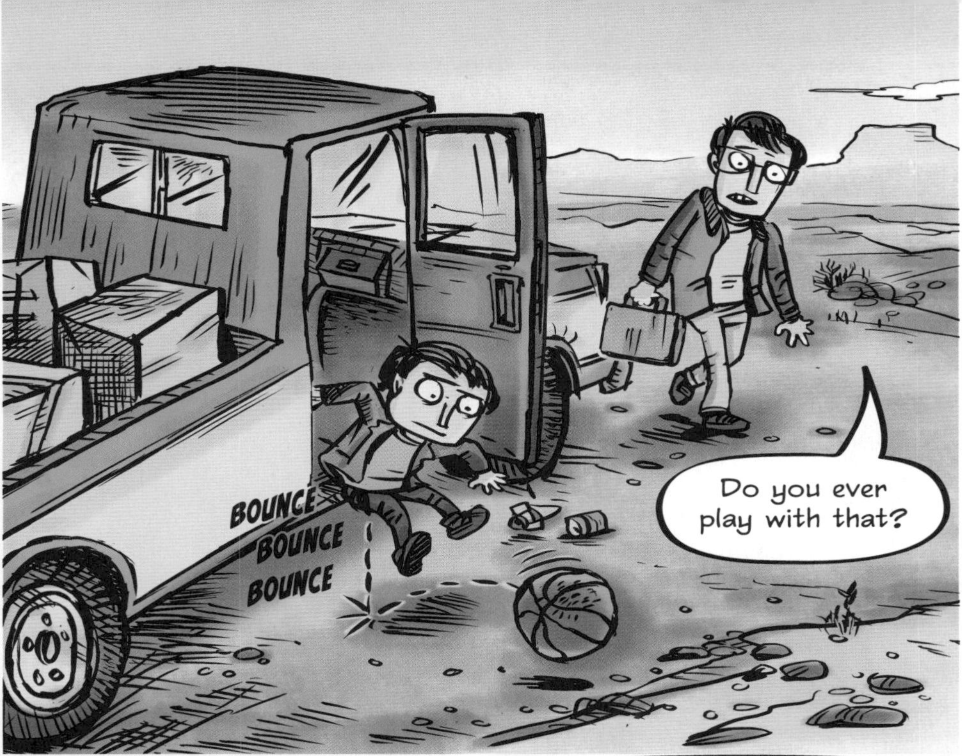
BOUNCE
BOUNCE
BOUNCE
Do you ever play with that?

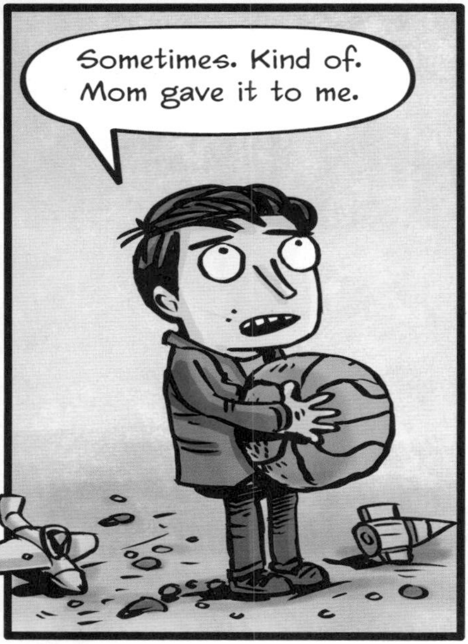
Sometimes. Kind of. Mom gave it to me.

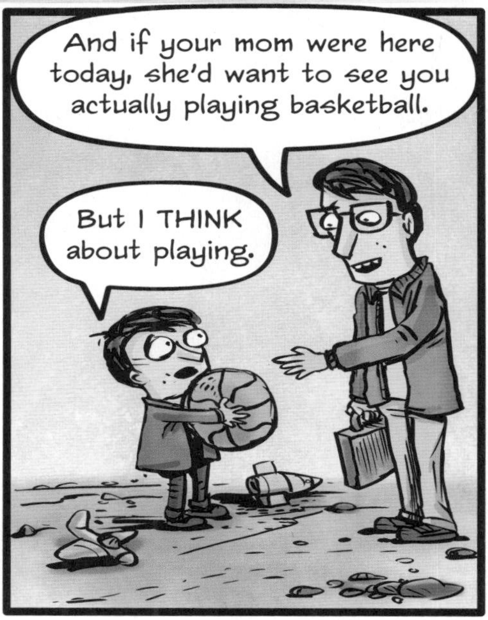
And if your mom were here today, she'd want to see you actually playing basketball.
But I THINK about playing.

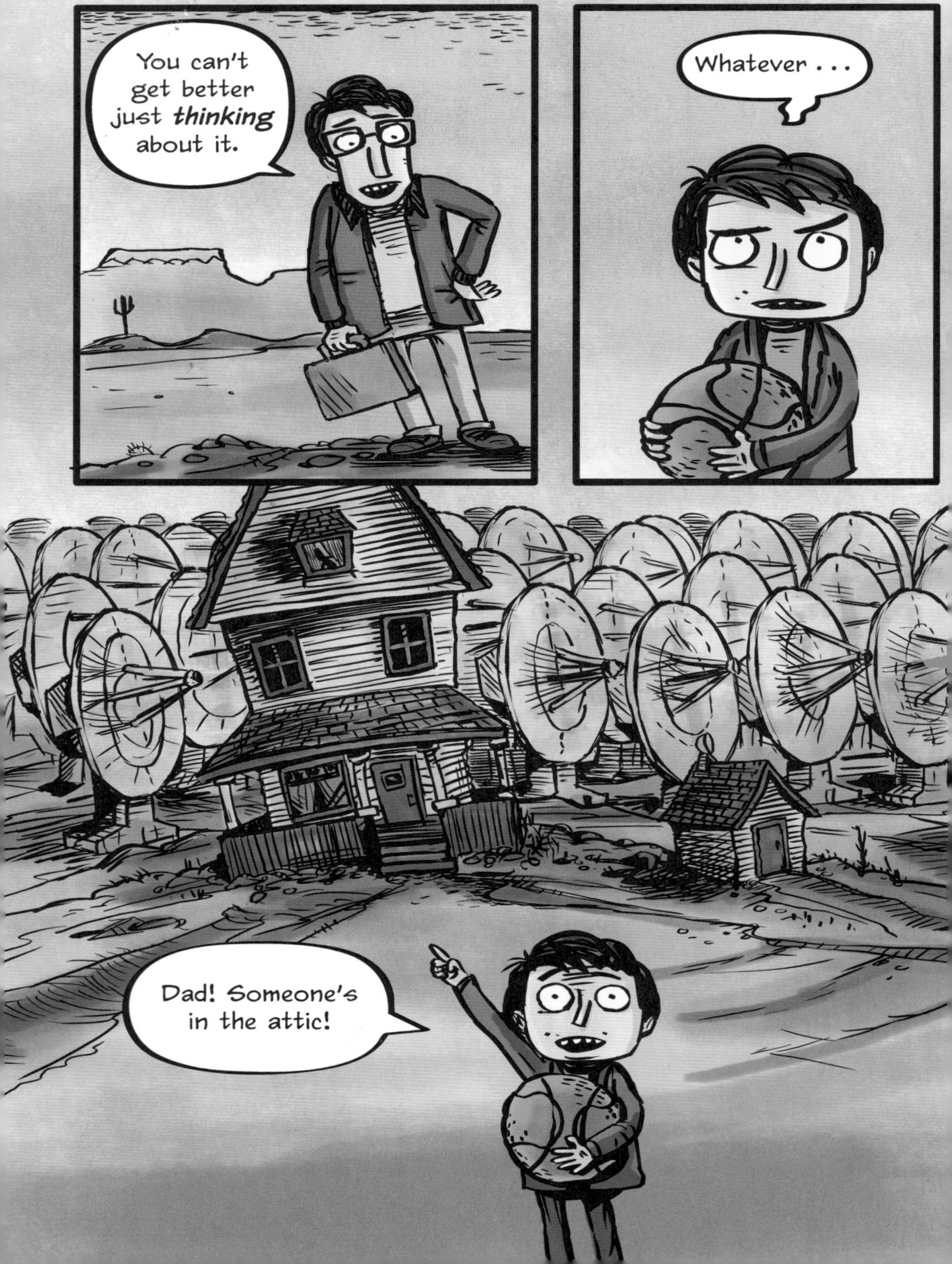
You can't get better just *thinking* about it.
Whatever . . .
Dad! Someone's in the attic!

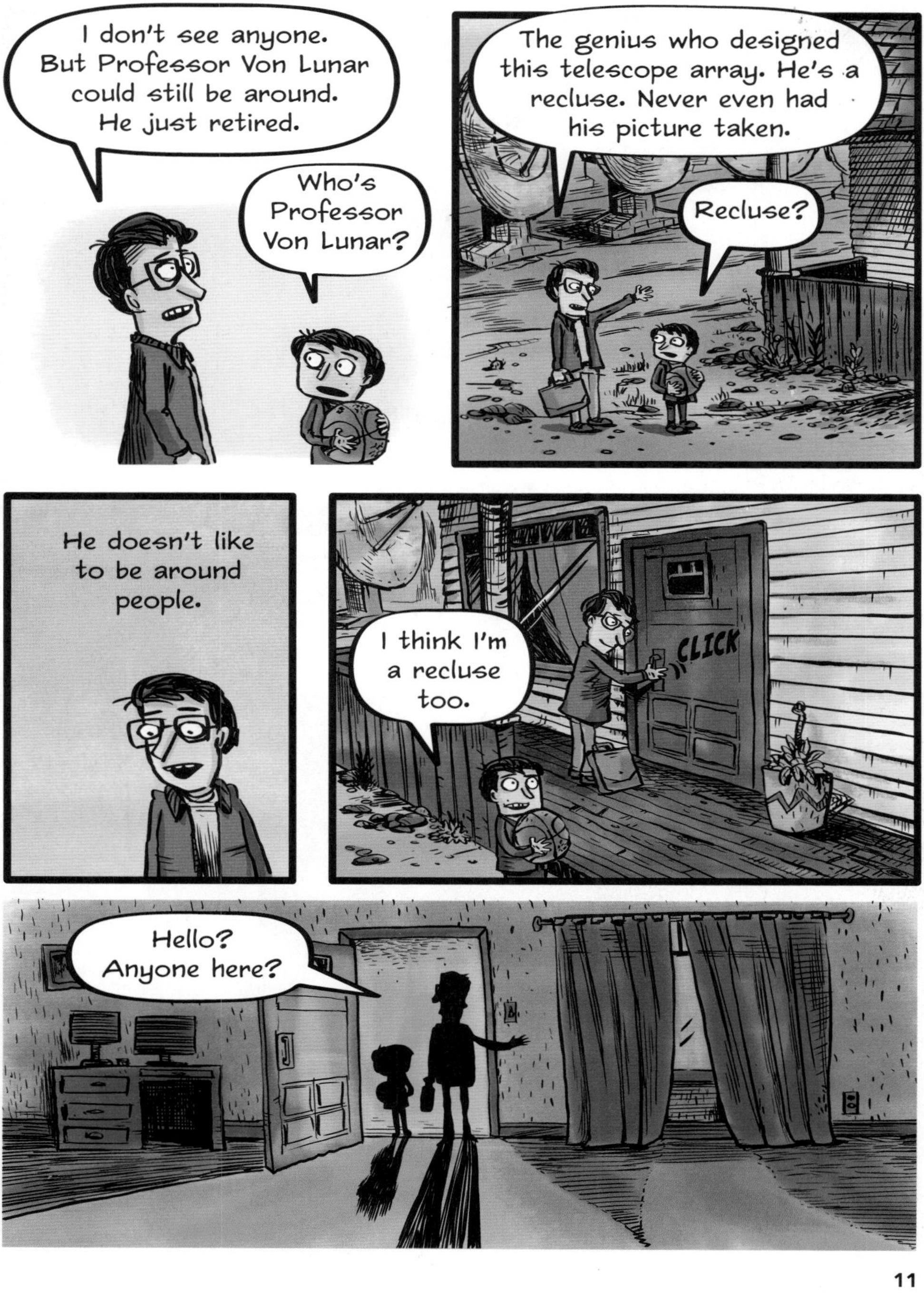
I don't see anyone. But Professor Von Lunar could still be around. He just retired.
Who's Professor Von Lunar?
The genius who designed this telescope array. He's a recluse. Never even had his picture taken.
Recluse?
He doesn't like to be around people.
I think I'm a recluse too.
CLICK
Hello? Anyone here?

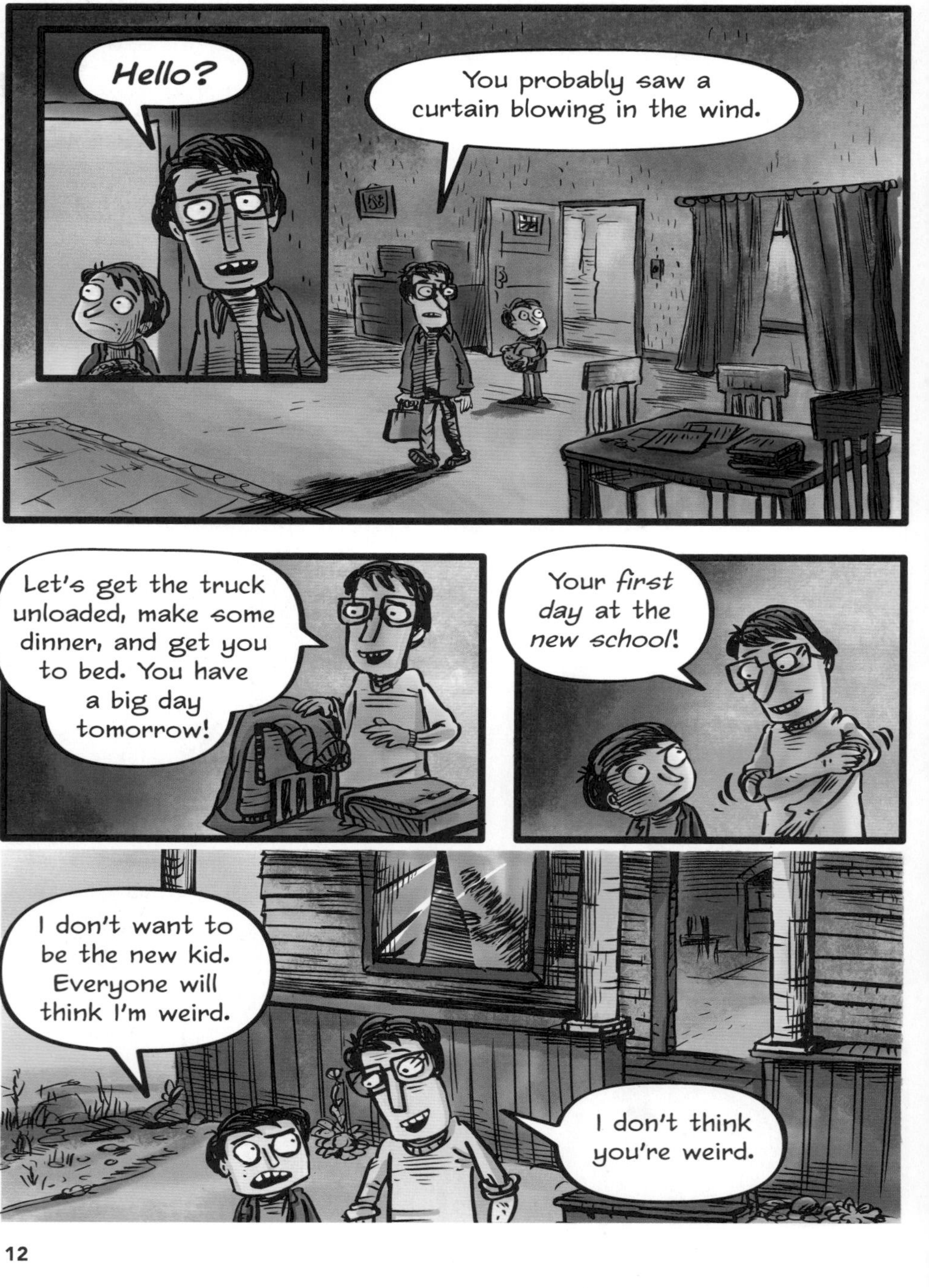
Hello?
You probably saw a curtain blowing in the wind.
Let's get the truck unloaded, make some dinner, and get you to bed. You have a big day tomorrow!
Your *first day* at the *new school*!
I don't want to be the new kid. Everyone will think I'm weird.
I don't think you're weird.

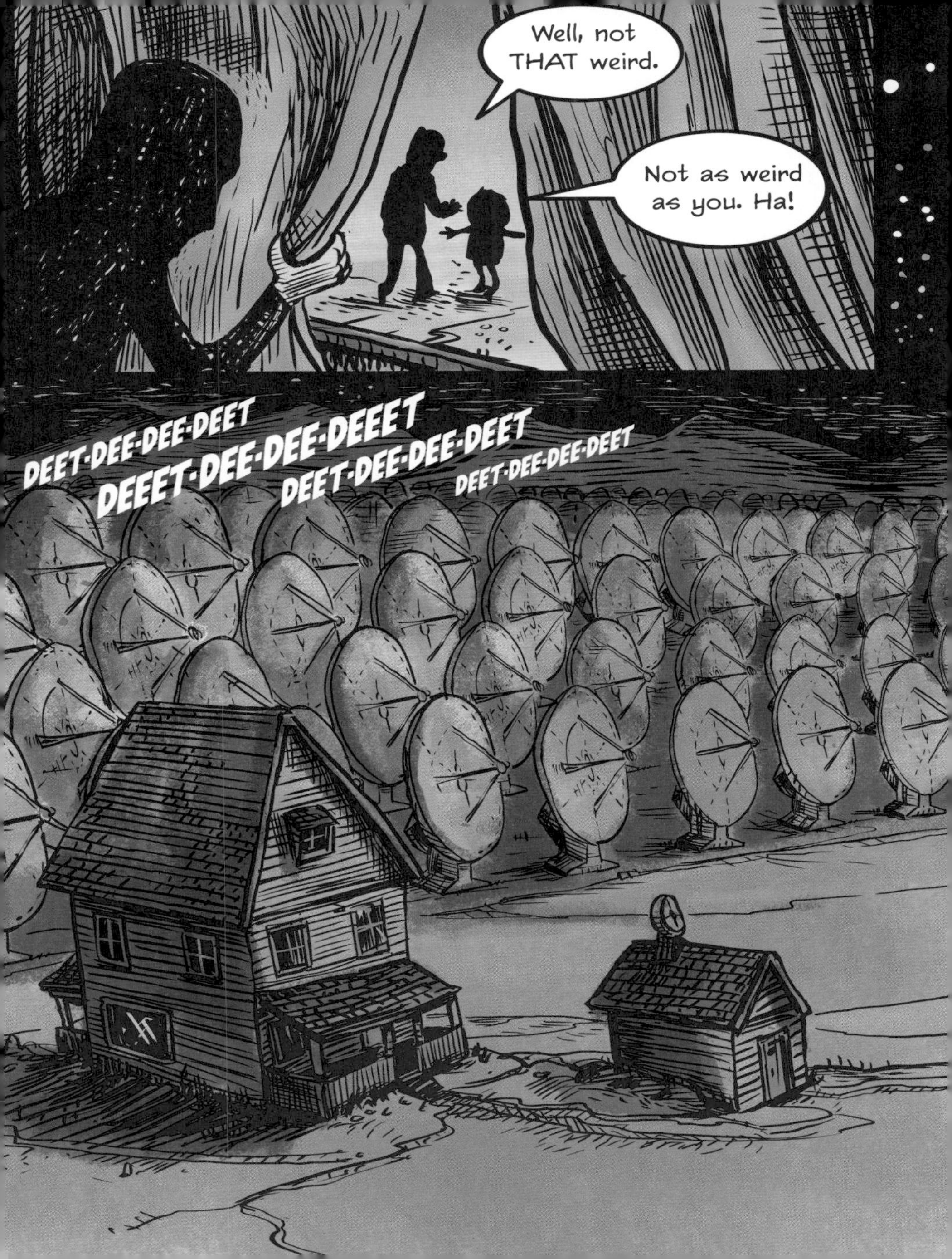
Well, not THAT weird.
Not as weird as you. Ha!
DEET-DEE-DEE-DEET
DEEET-DEE-DEE-DEEET
DEET-DEE-DEE-DEET
DEET-DEE-DEE-DEET

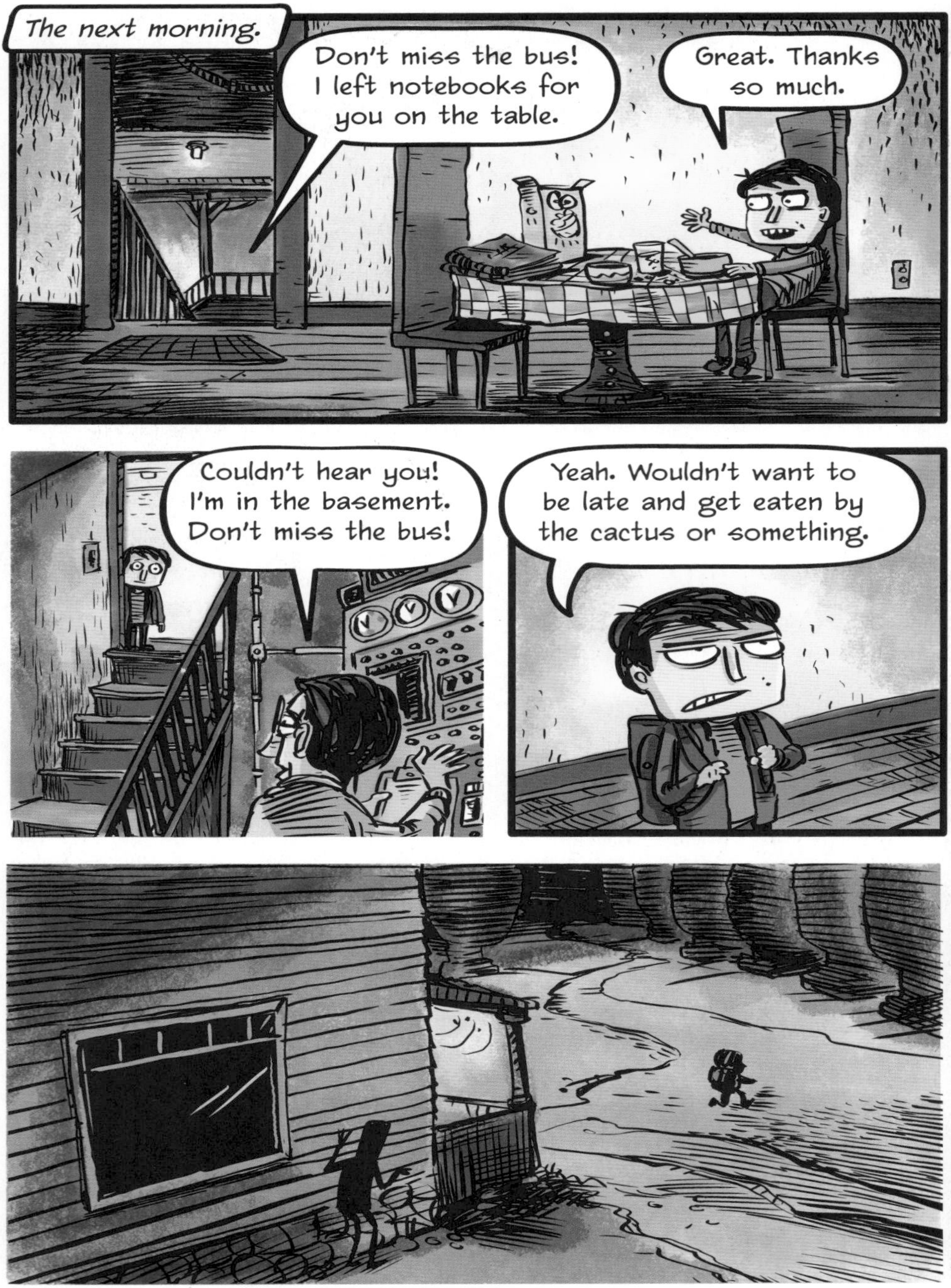
The next morning.
Don't miss the bus! I left notebooks for you on the table.
Great. Thanks so much.
Couldn't hear you! I'm in the basement. Don't miss the bus!
Yeah. Wouldn't want to be late and get eaten by the cactus or something.

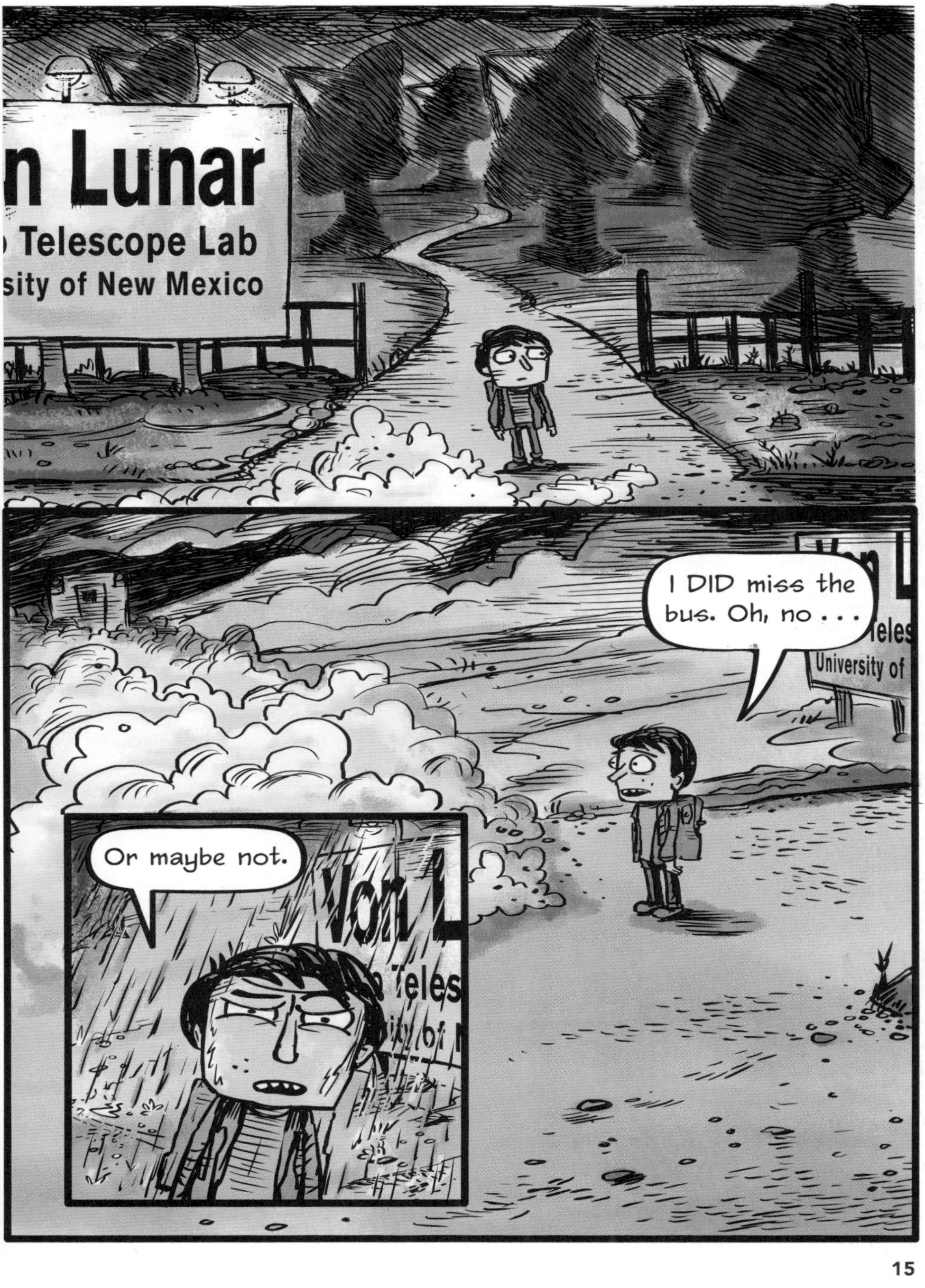
n Lunar
Telescope Lab
sity of New Mexico
I DID miss the bus. Oh, no . . .
Or maybe not.

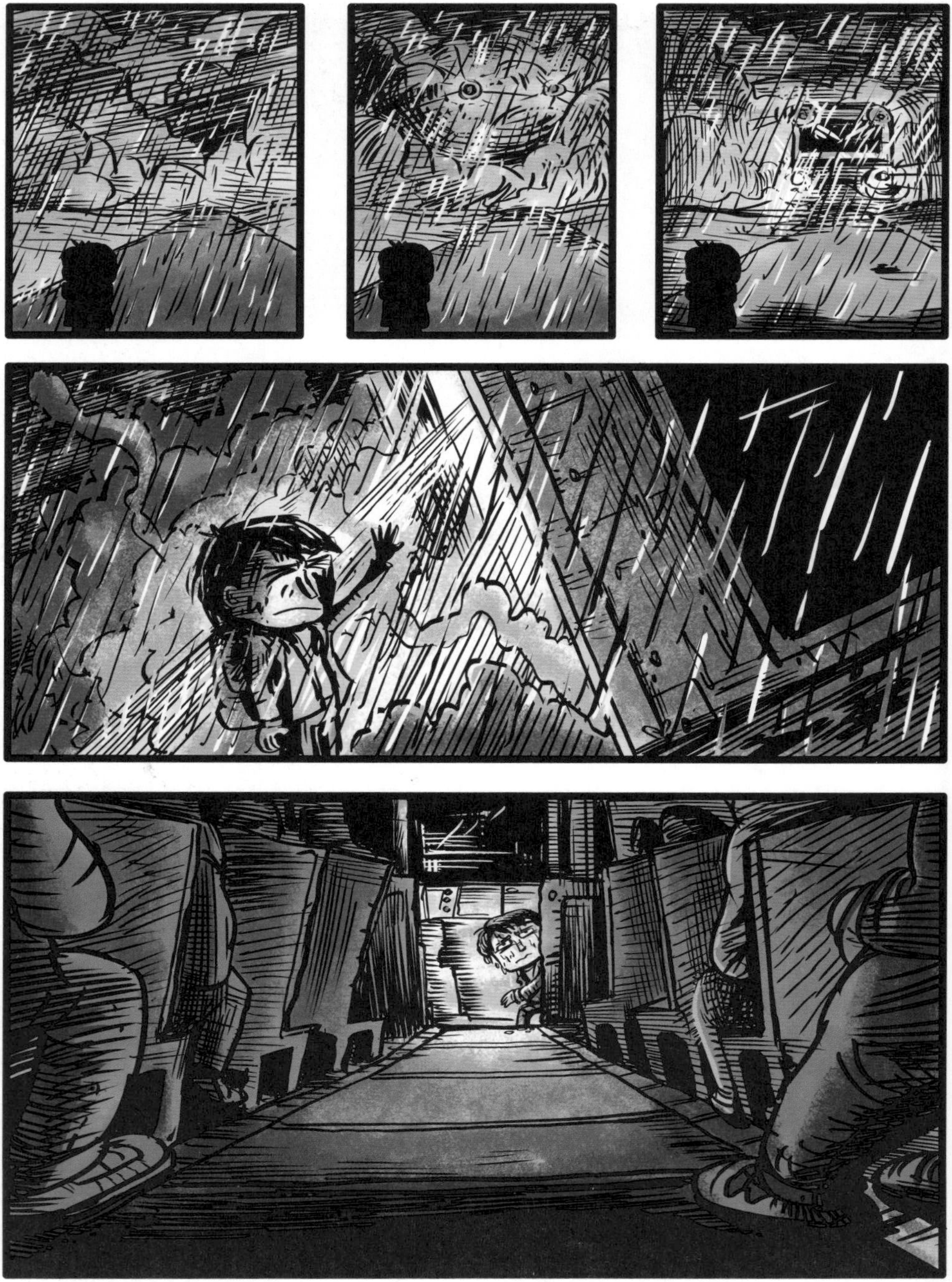

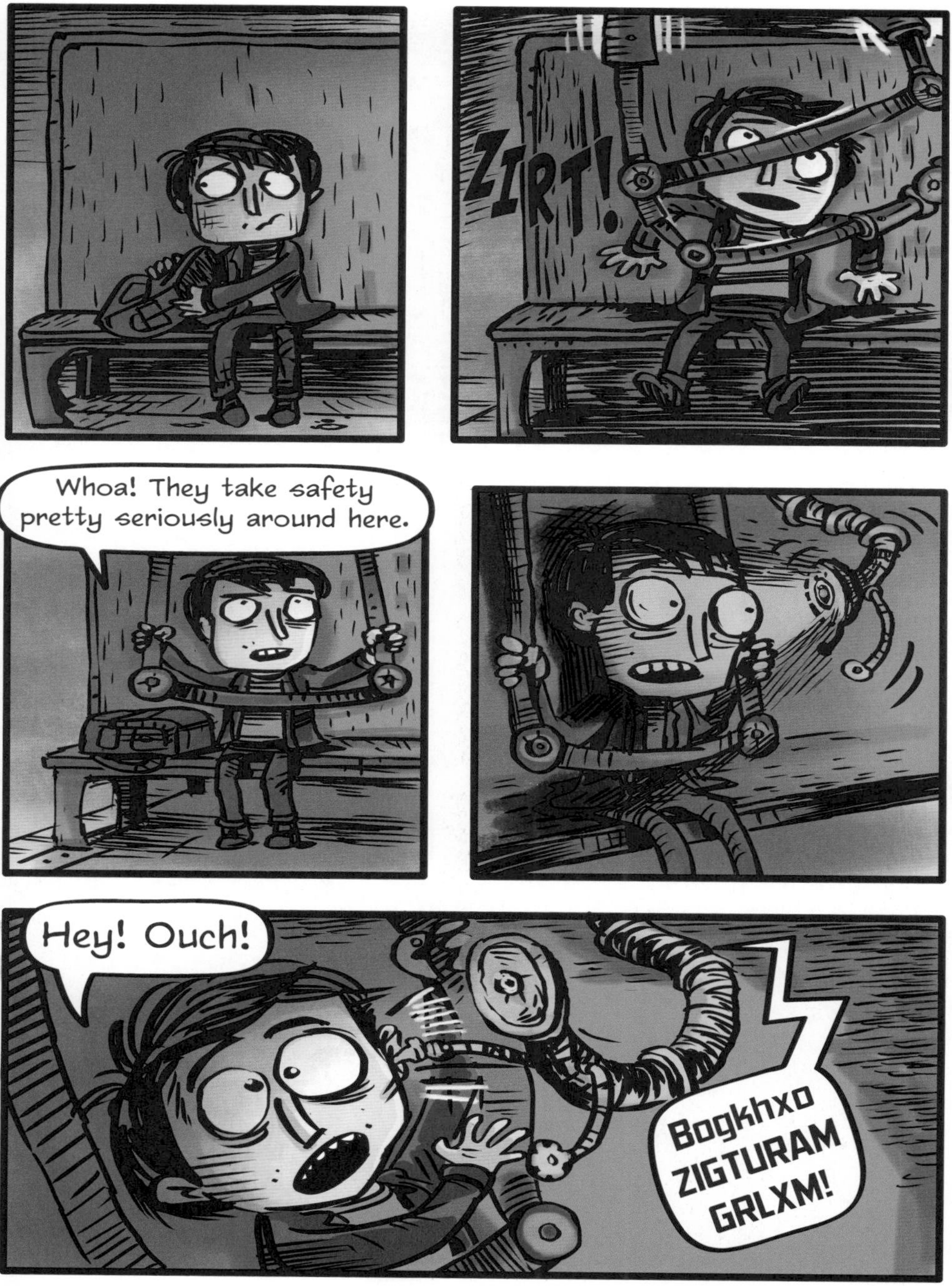
ZIRT!
Whoa! They take safety pretty seriously around here.
Hey! Ouch!
Bogkhxo ZIGTURAM GRLXM!

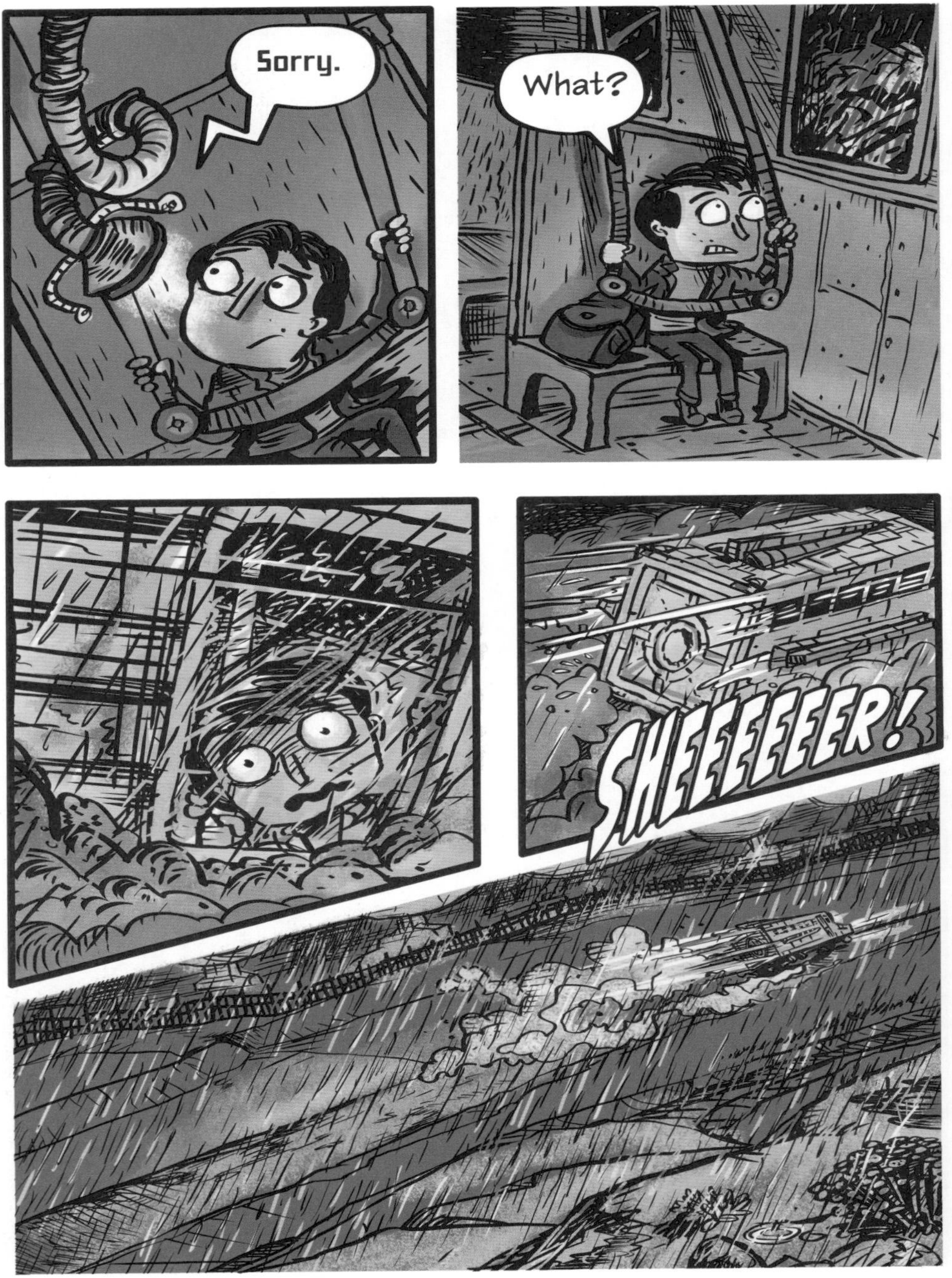

Sorry.
What?
SHEEEEEER!

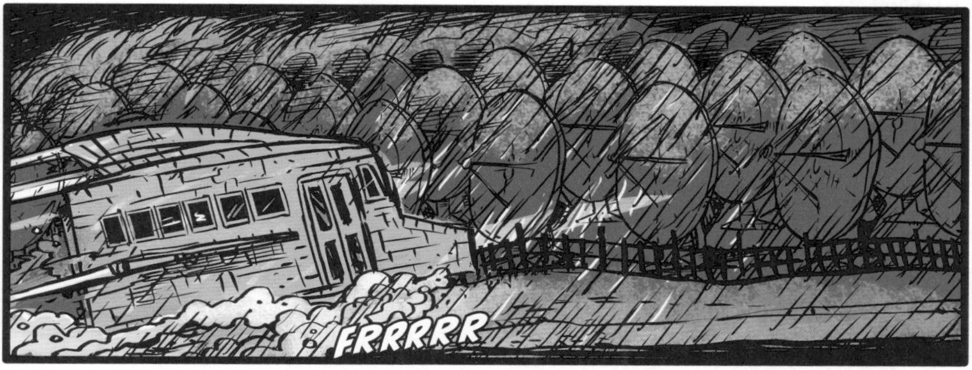
FRRRRR

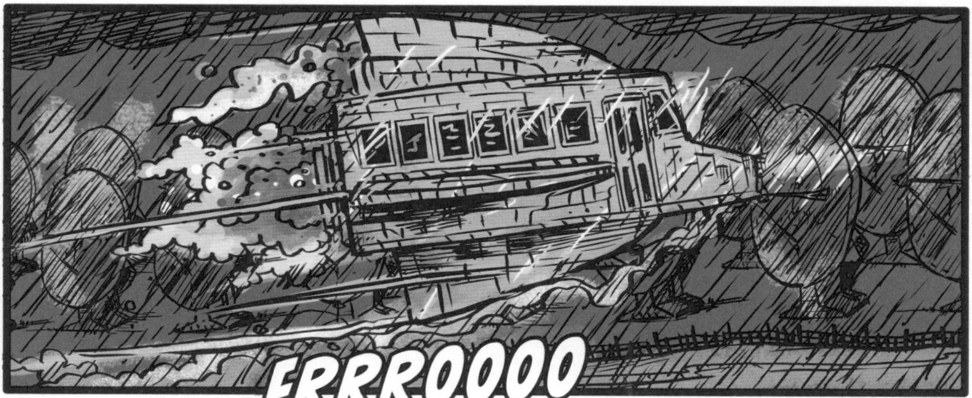
FRRROOOO

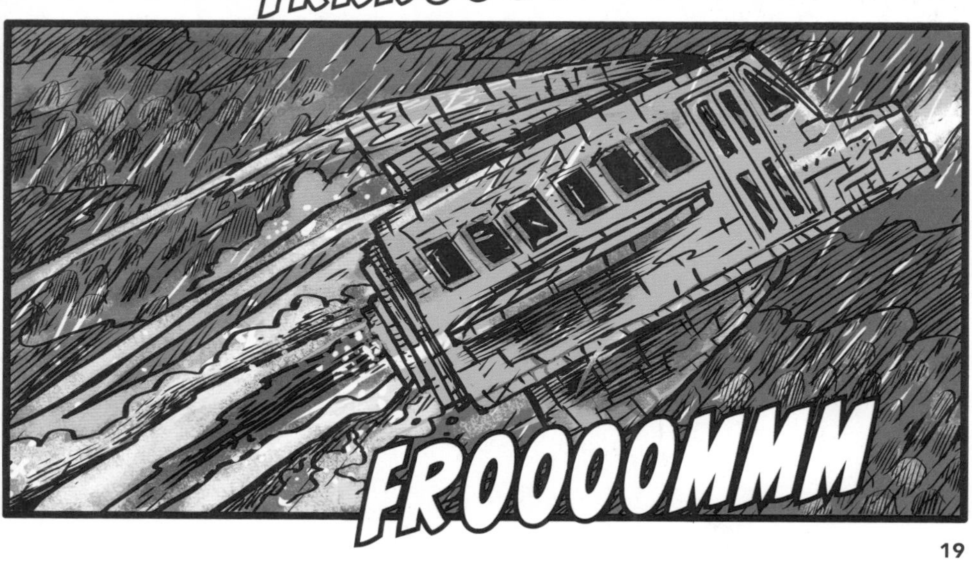
FROOOOMMM

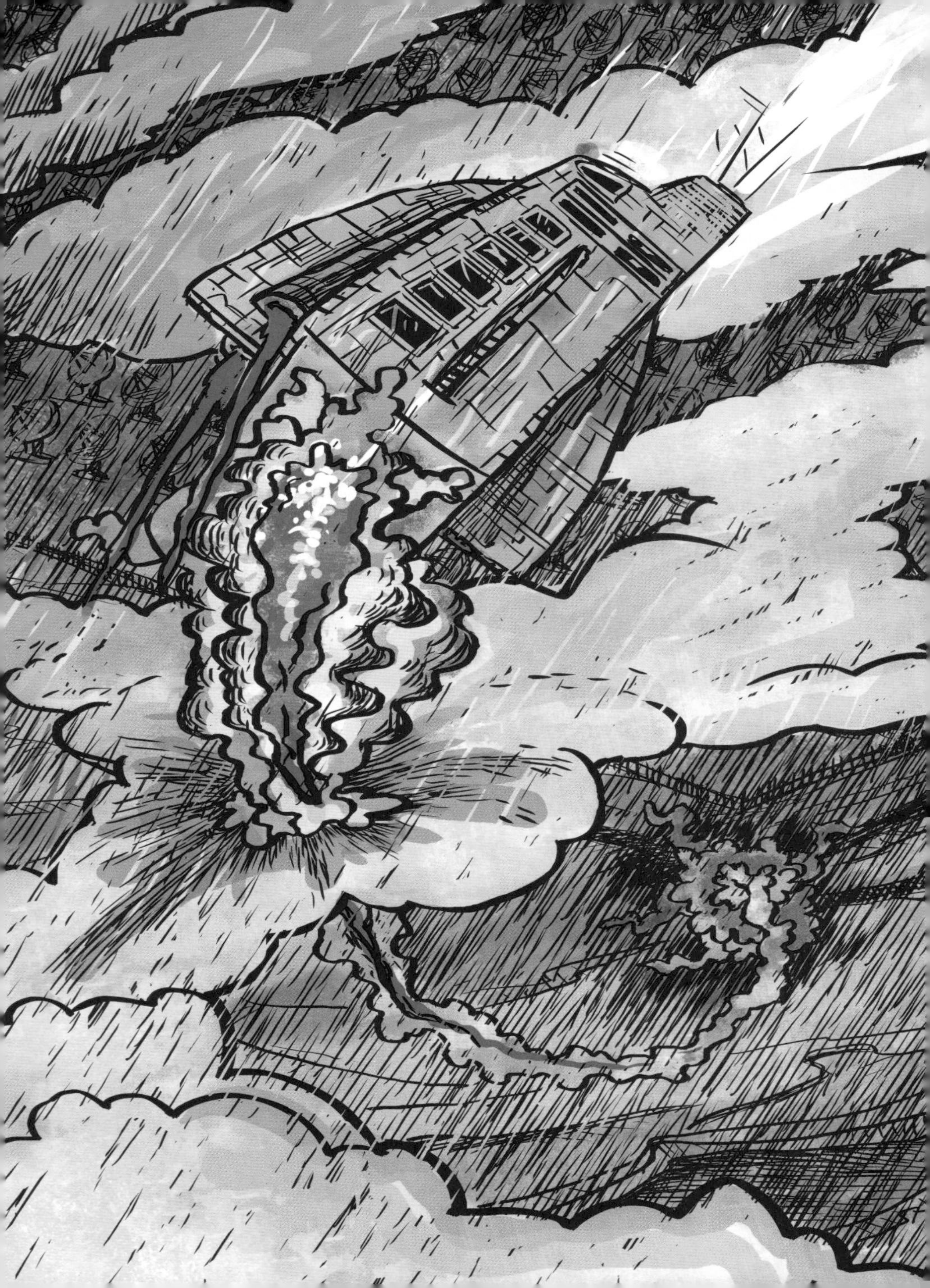

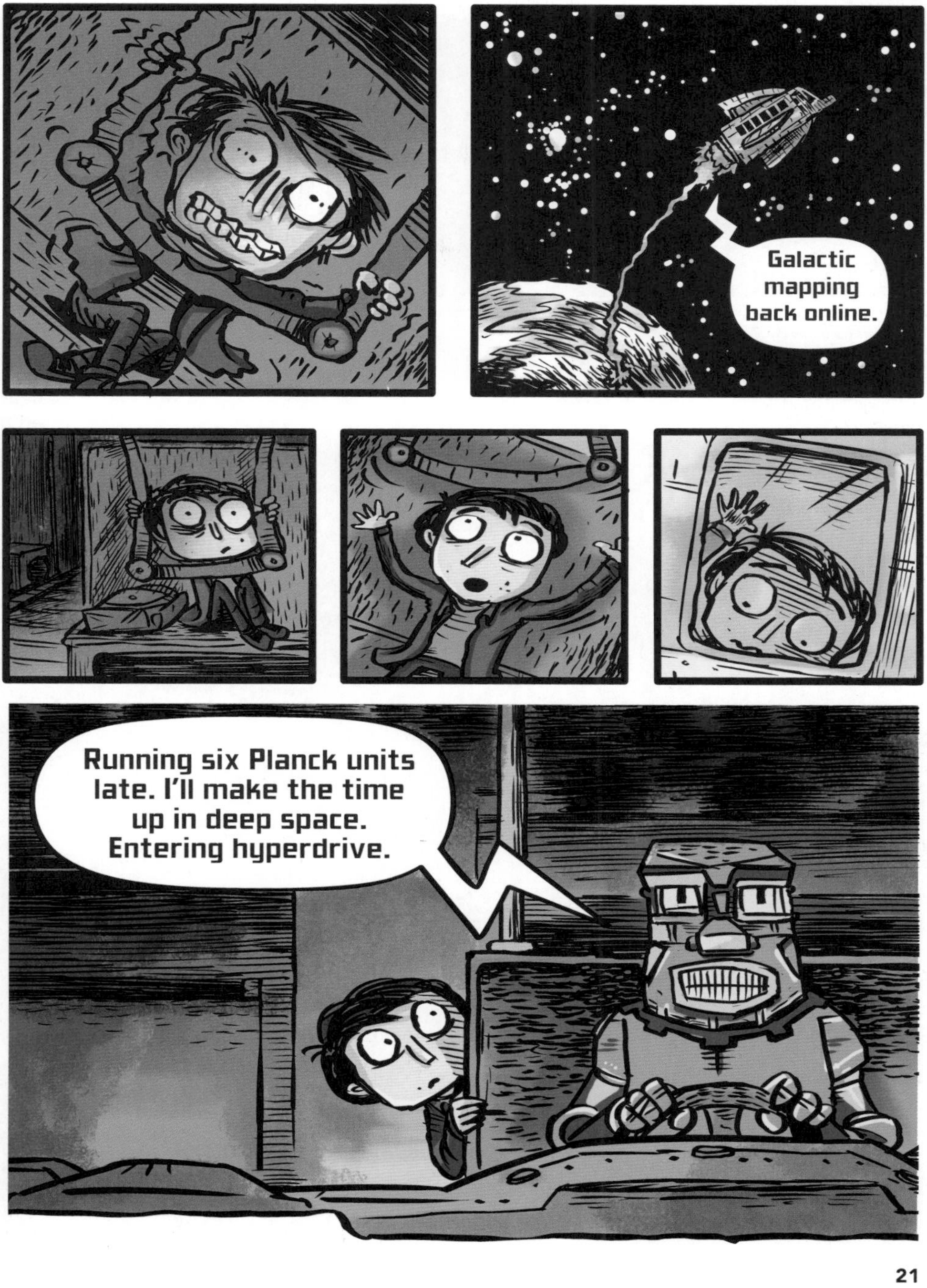
Galactic mapping back online.
Running six Planck units late. I'll make the time up in deep space. Entering hyperdrive.

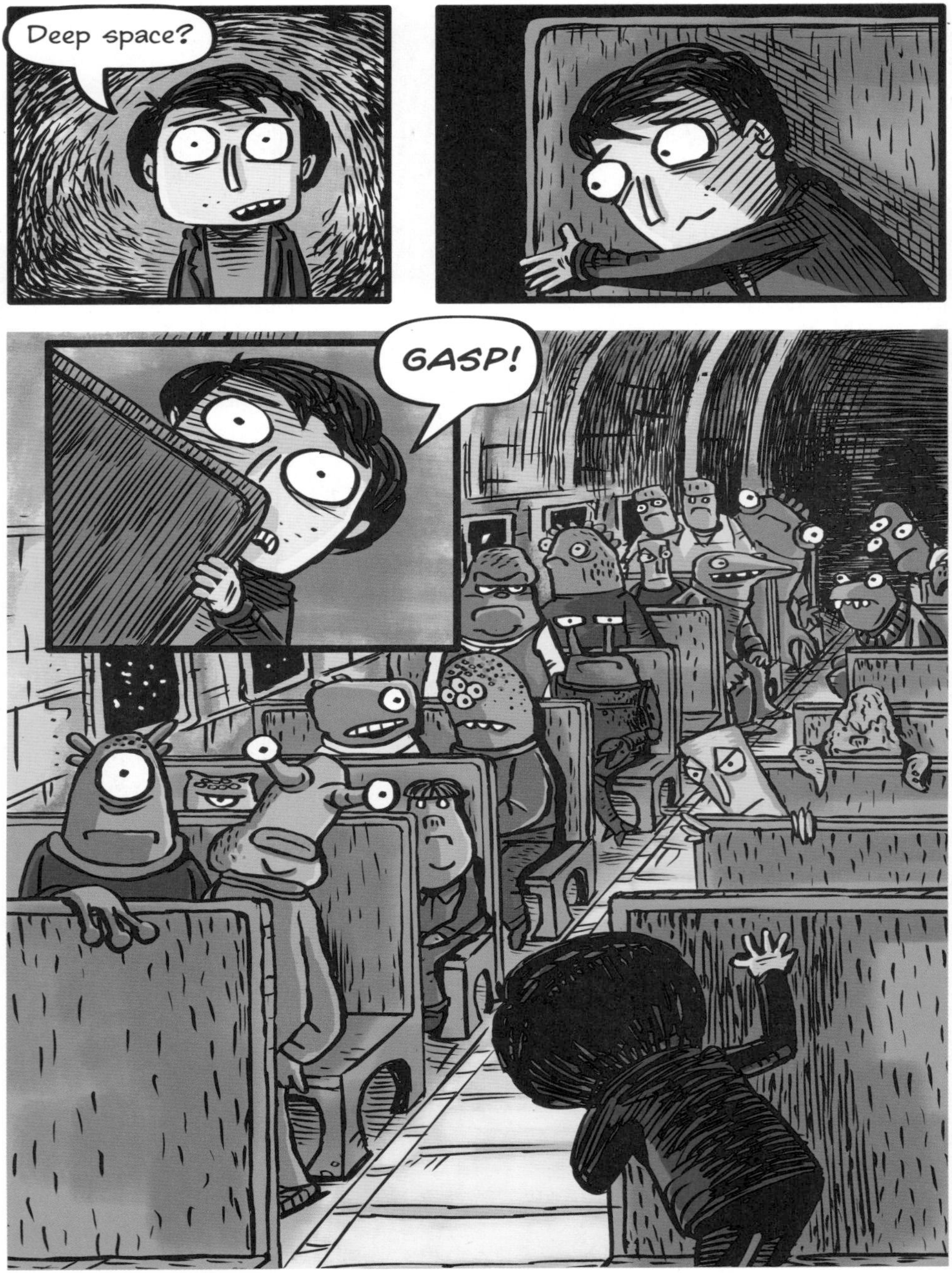
Deep space?
GASP!

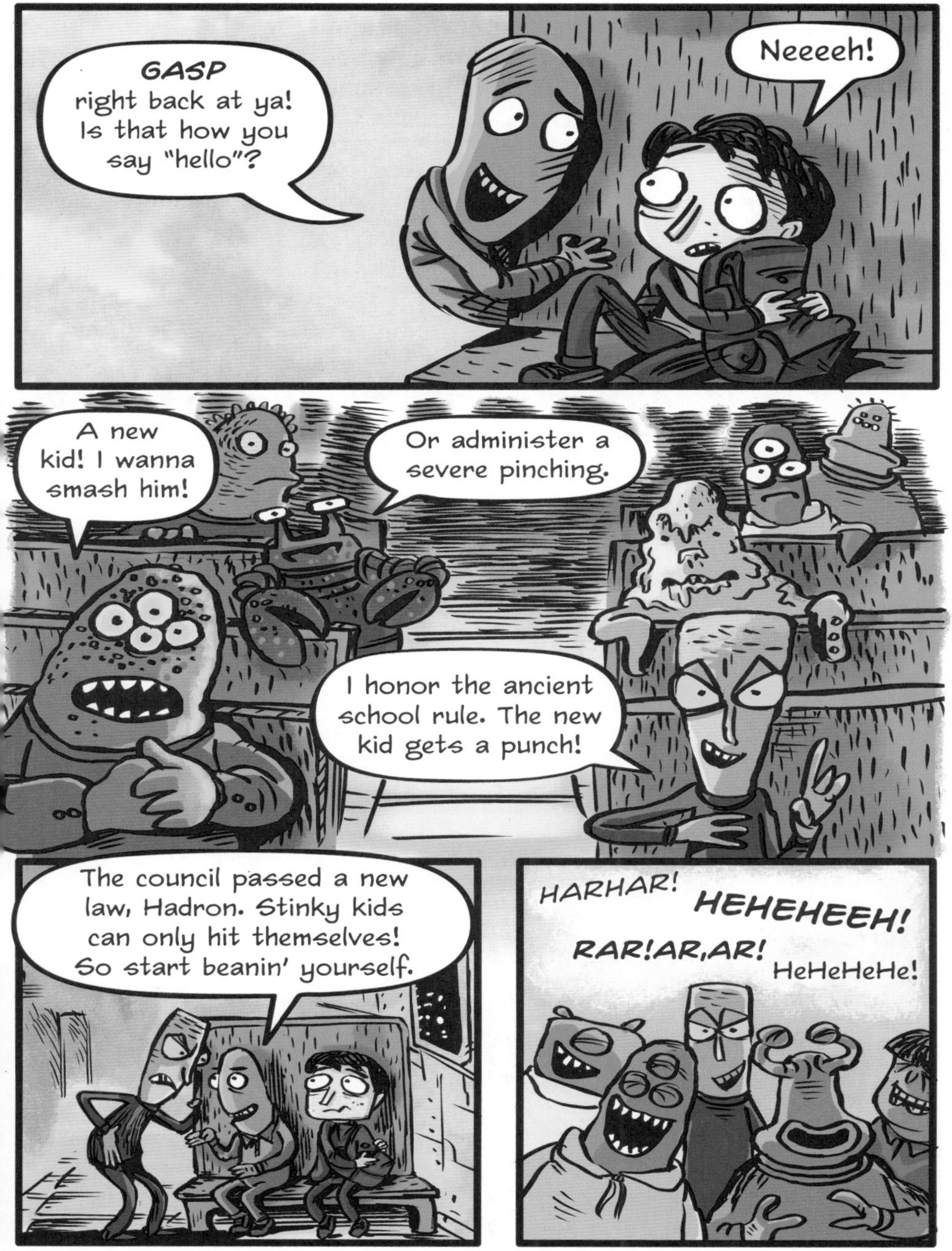
GASP right back at ya! Is that how you say "hello"?
Neeeeh!
A new kid! I wanna smash him!
Or administer a severe pinching.
I honor the ancient school rule. The new kid gets a punch!
The council passed a new law, Hadron. Stinky kids can only hit themselves! So start beanin' yourself.
HARHAR!
HEHEHEEEH!
RAR!AR,AR!
HeHeHeHe!

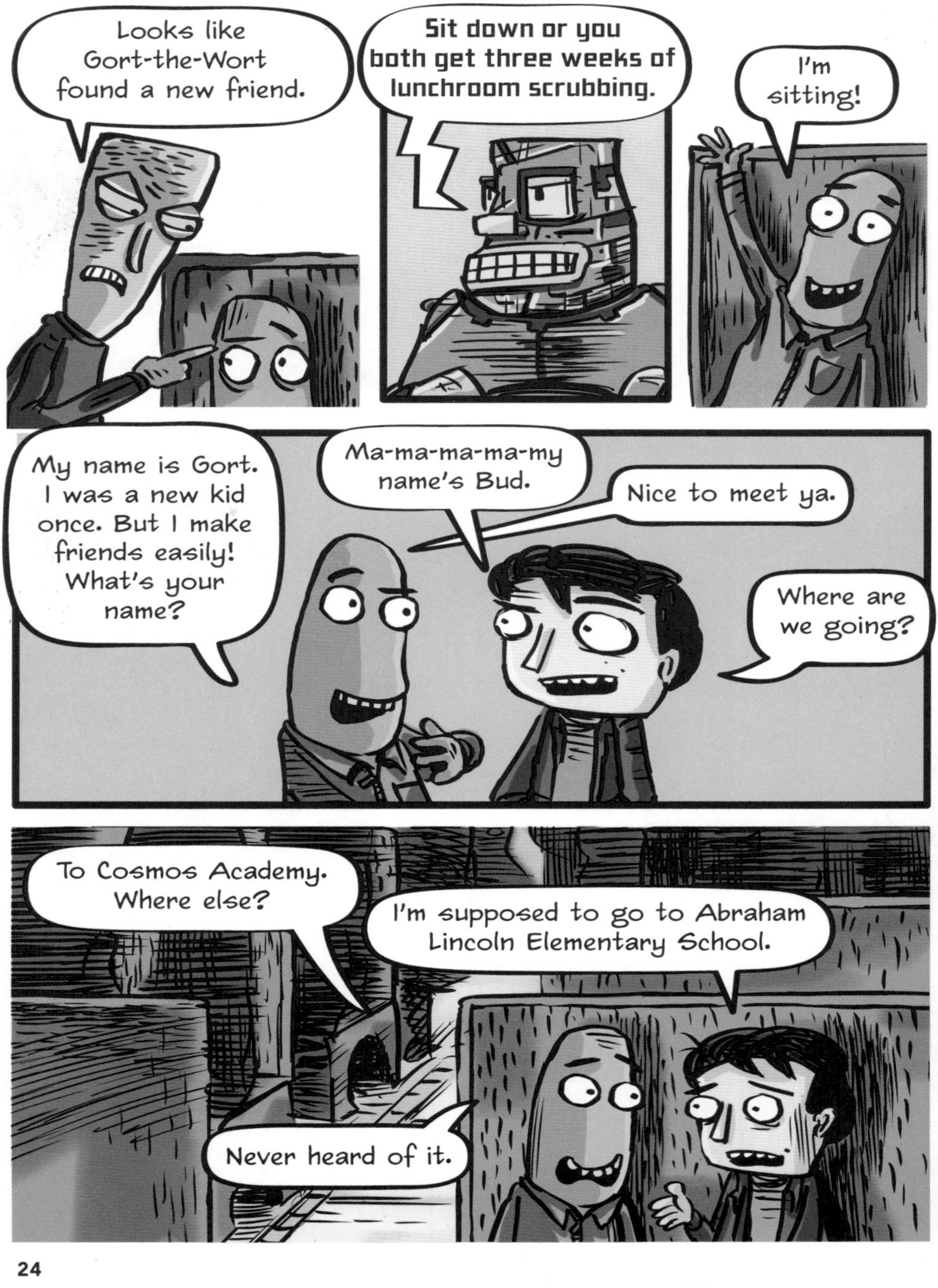
Looks like Gort-the-Wort found a new friend.
Sit down or you both get three weeks of lunchroom scrubbing.
I'm sitting!
My name is Gort. I was a new kid once. But I make friends easily! What's your name?
Ma-ma-ma-ma-my name's Bud.
Nice to meet ya.
Where are we going?
To Cosmos Academy. Where else?
I'm supposed to go to Abraham Lincoln Elementary School.
Never heard of it.

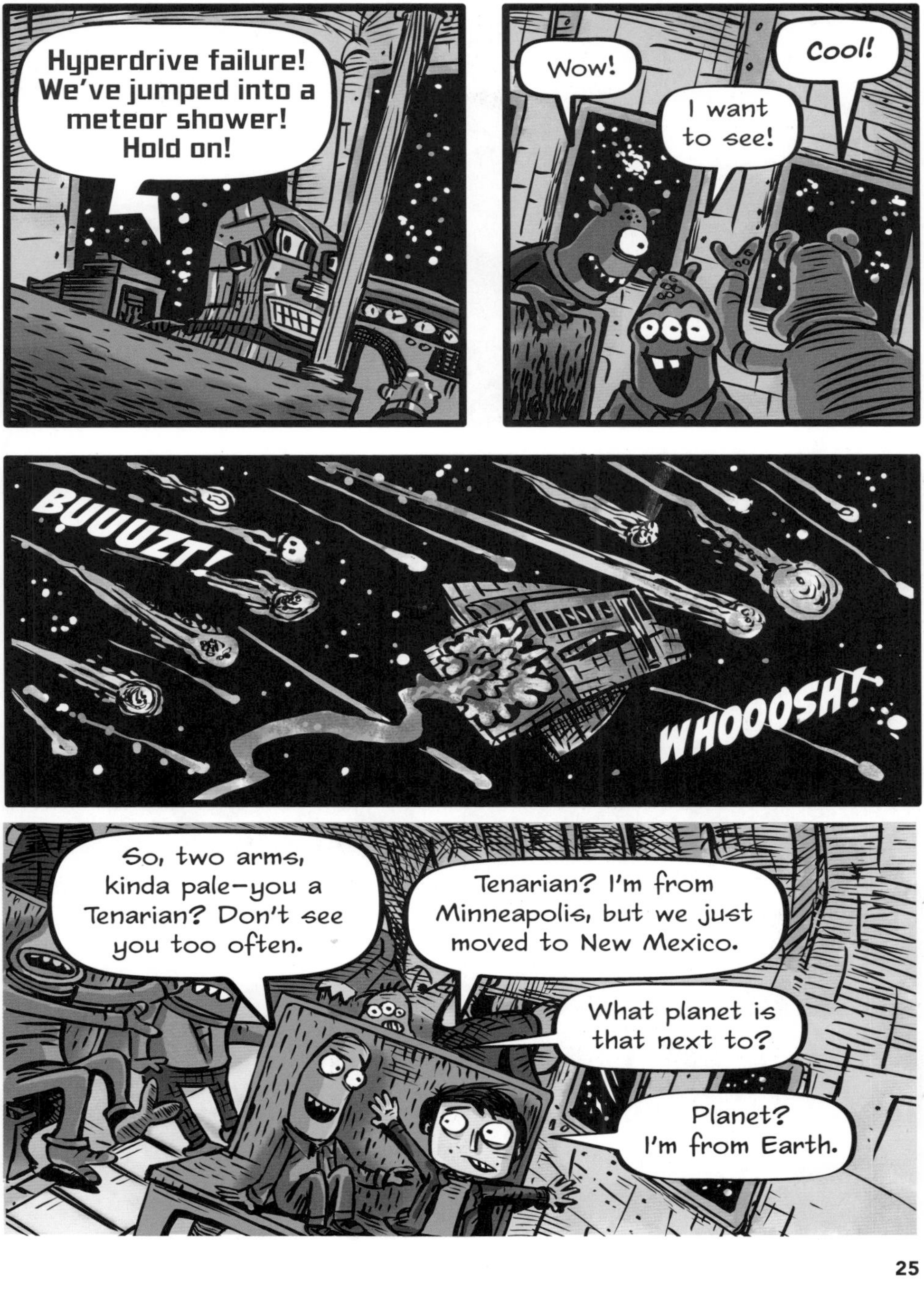
Hyperdrive failure! We've jumped into a meteor shower! Hold on!
Wow!
I want to see!
Cool!
BUUUZT!
WHOOOSH!
So, two arms, kinda pale—you a Tenarian? Don't see you too often.
Tenarian? I'm from Minneapolis, but we just moved to New Mexico.
What planet is that next to?
Planet? I'm from Earth.

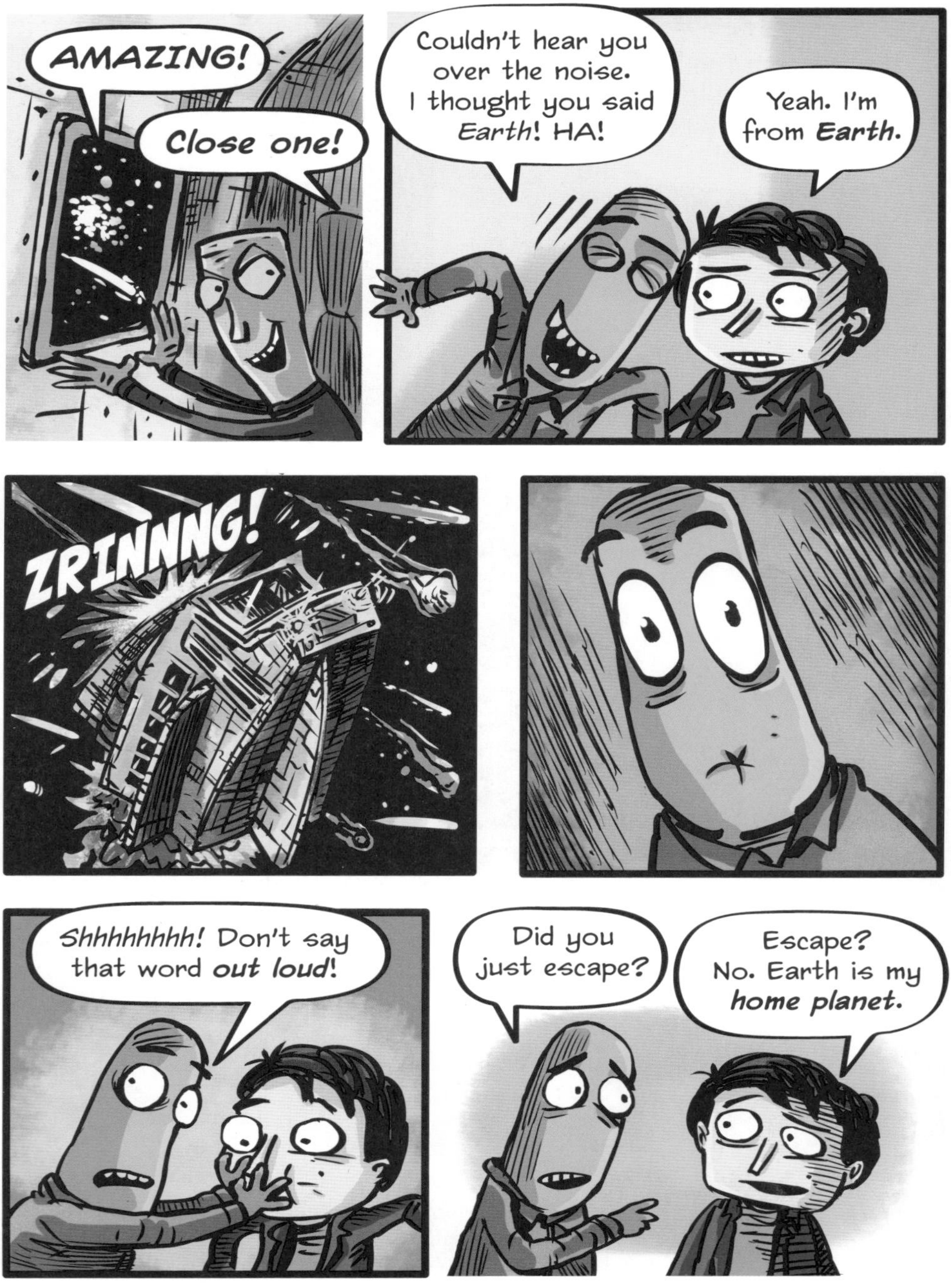
AMAZING!
Close one!
Couldn't hear you over the noise. I thought you said Earth! HA!
Yeah. I'm from Earth.
ZRINNNG!
Shhhhhhhh! Don't say that word out loud!
Did you just escape?
Escape? No. Earth is my home planet.

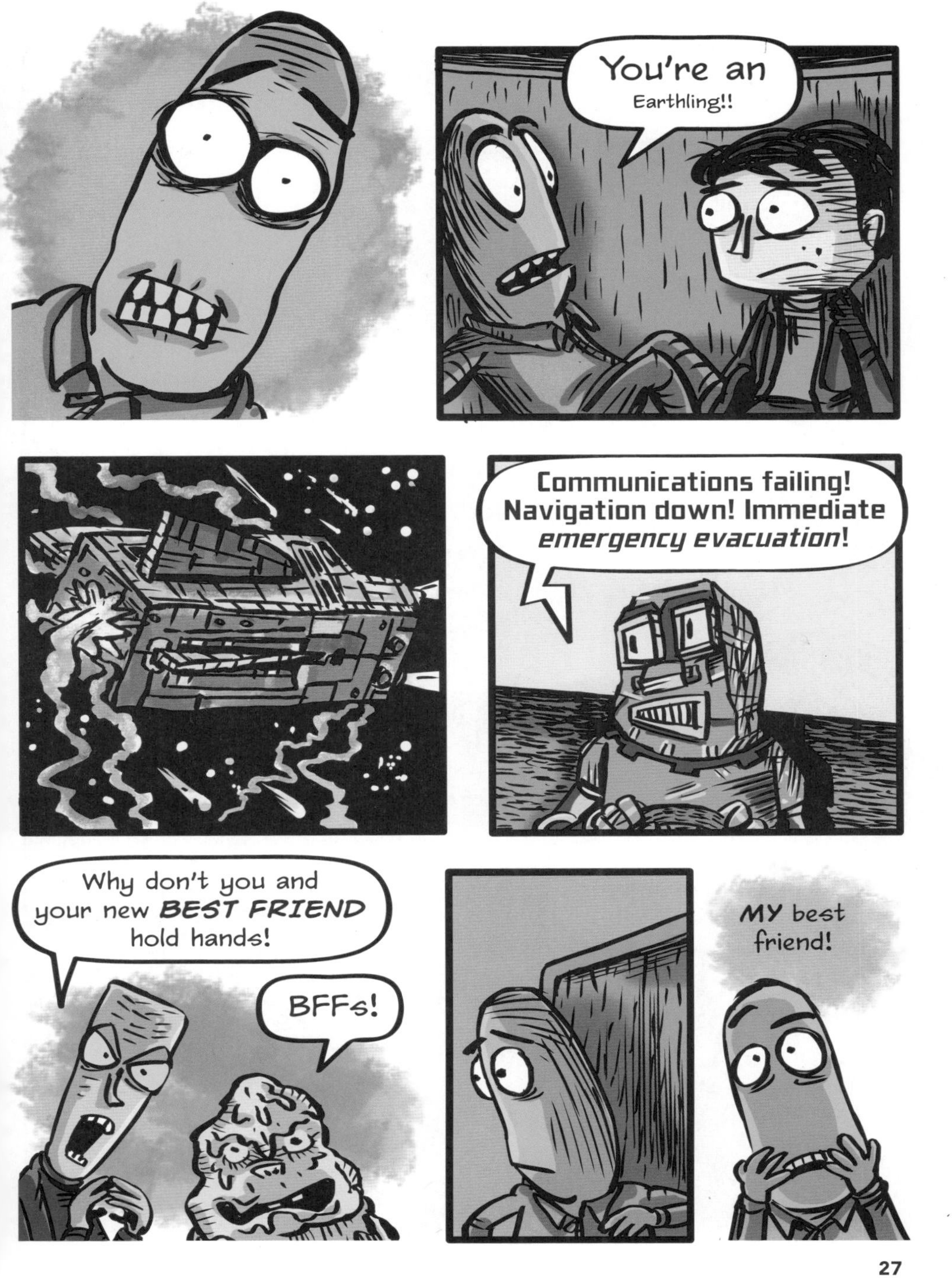
You're an Earthling!!
Communications failing! Navigation down! Immediate *emergency evacuation*!
Why don't you and your new **BEST FRIEND** hold hands!
BFFs!
MY best friend!

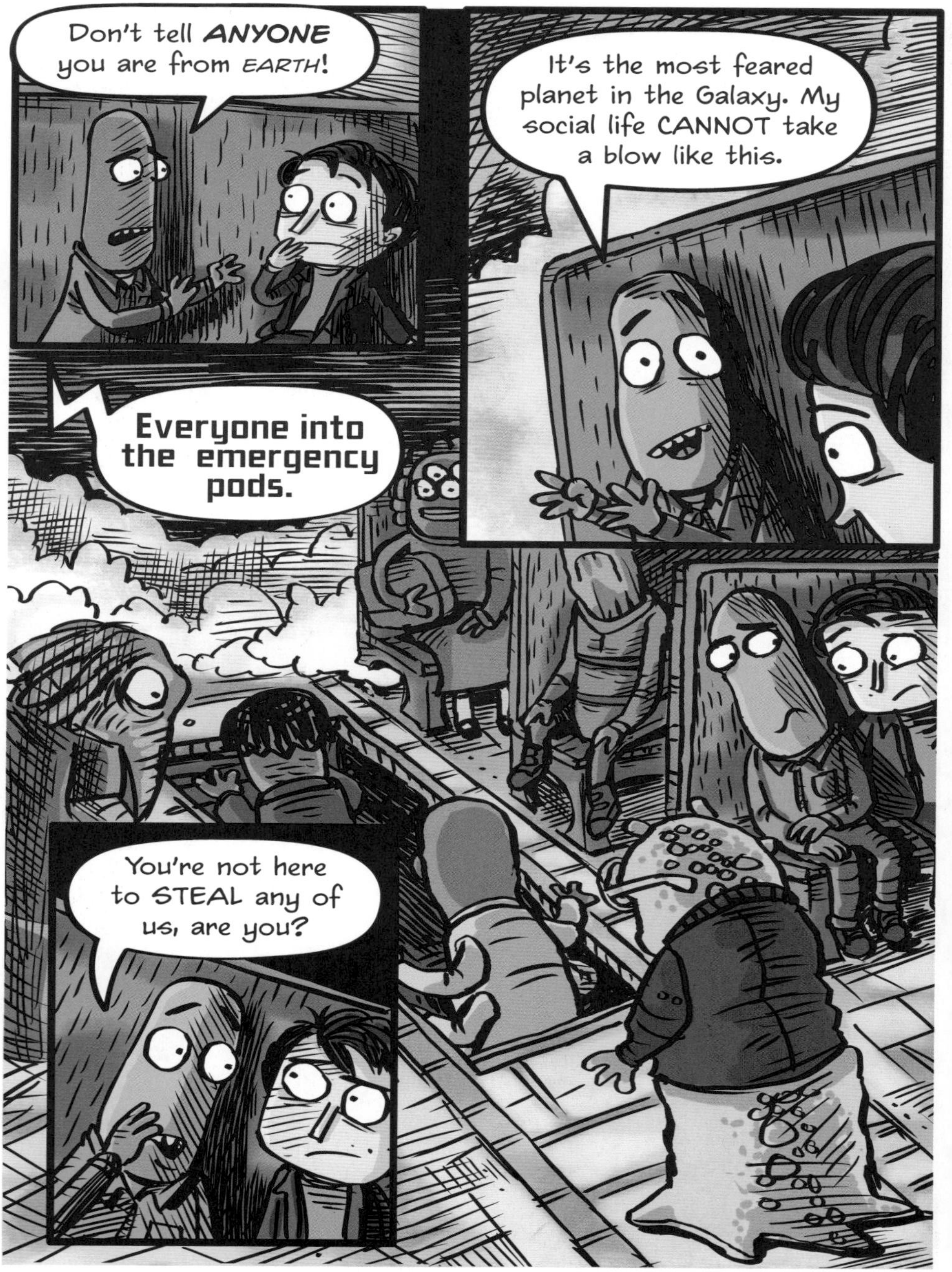
Don't tell ANYONE you are from EARTH!
It's the most feared planet in the Galaxy. My social life CANNOT take a blow like this.
Everyone into the emergency pods.
You're not here to STEAL any of us, are you?

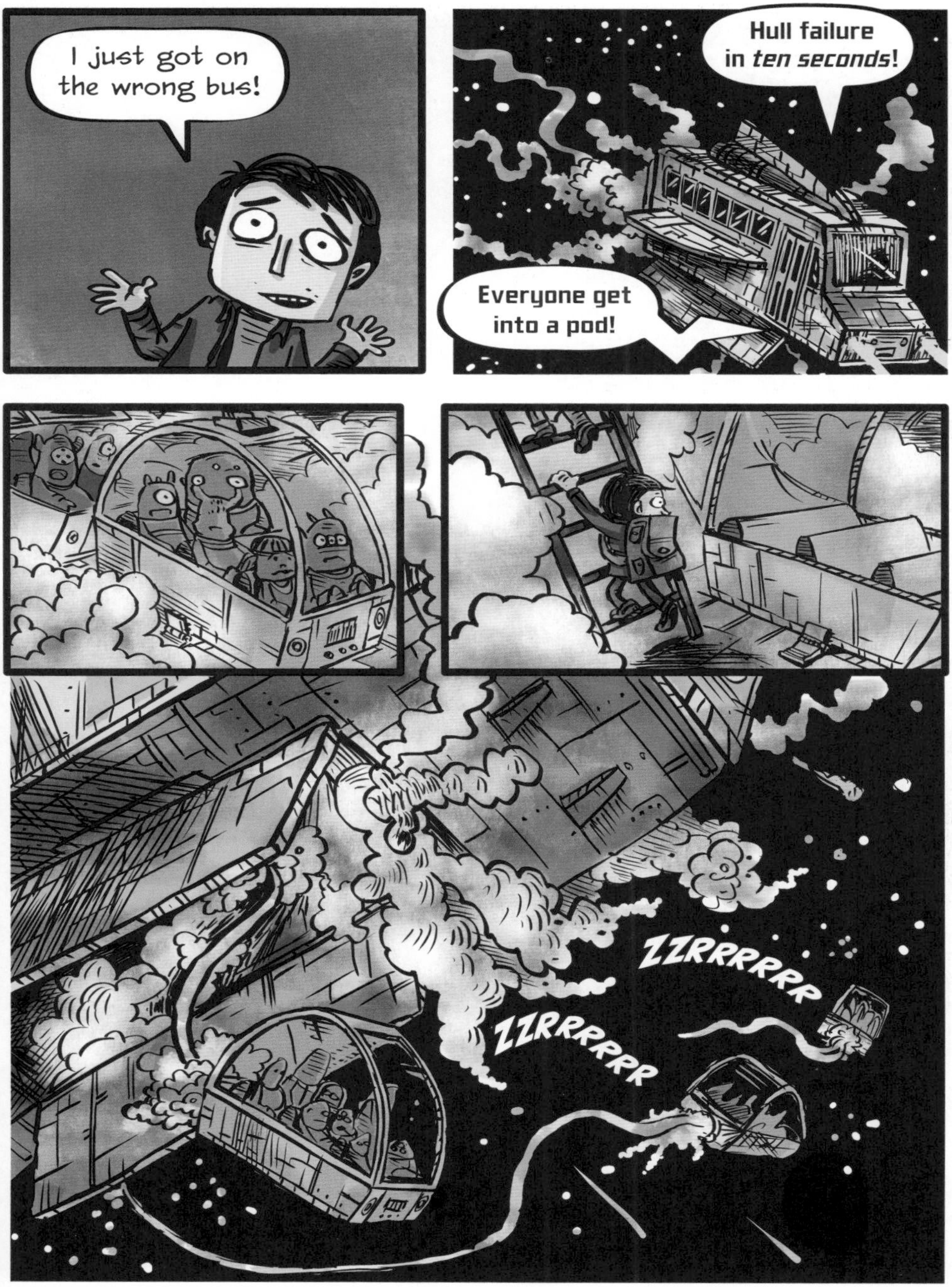
I just got on the wrong bus!
Hull failure in *ten seconds*!
Everyone get into a pod!
ZZRRRRRRR
ZZRRRRRR

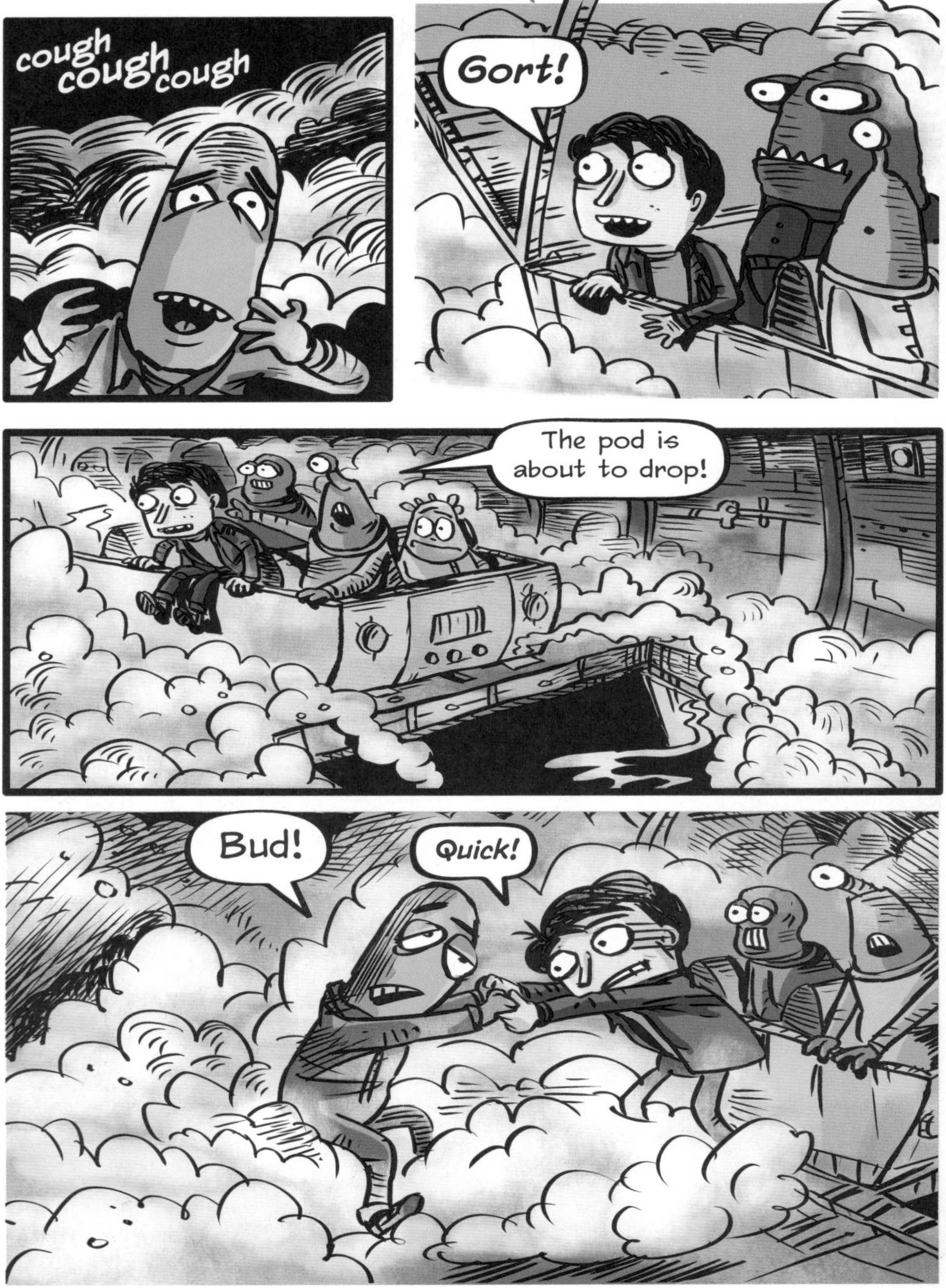
cough cough cough
Gort!
The pod is about to drop!
Bud!
Quick!

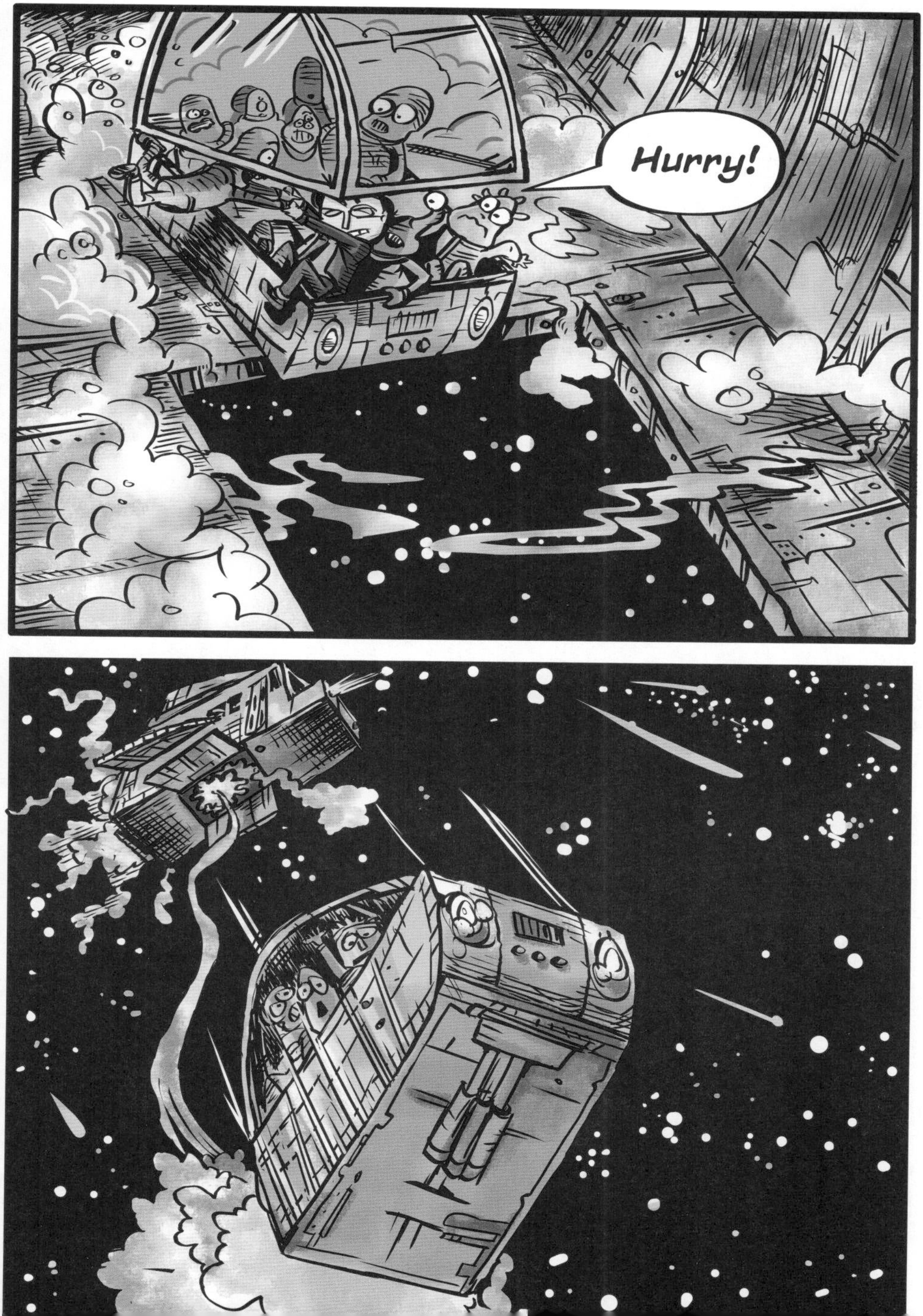
Hurry!

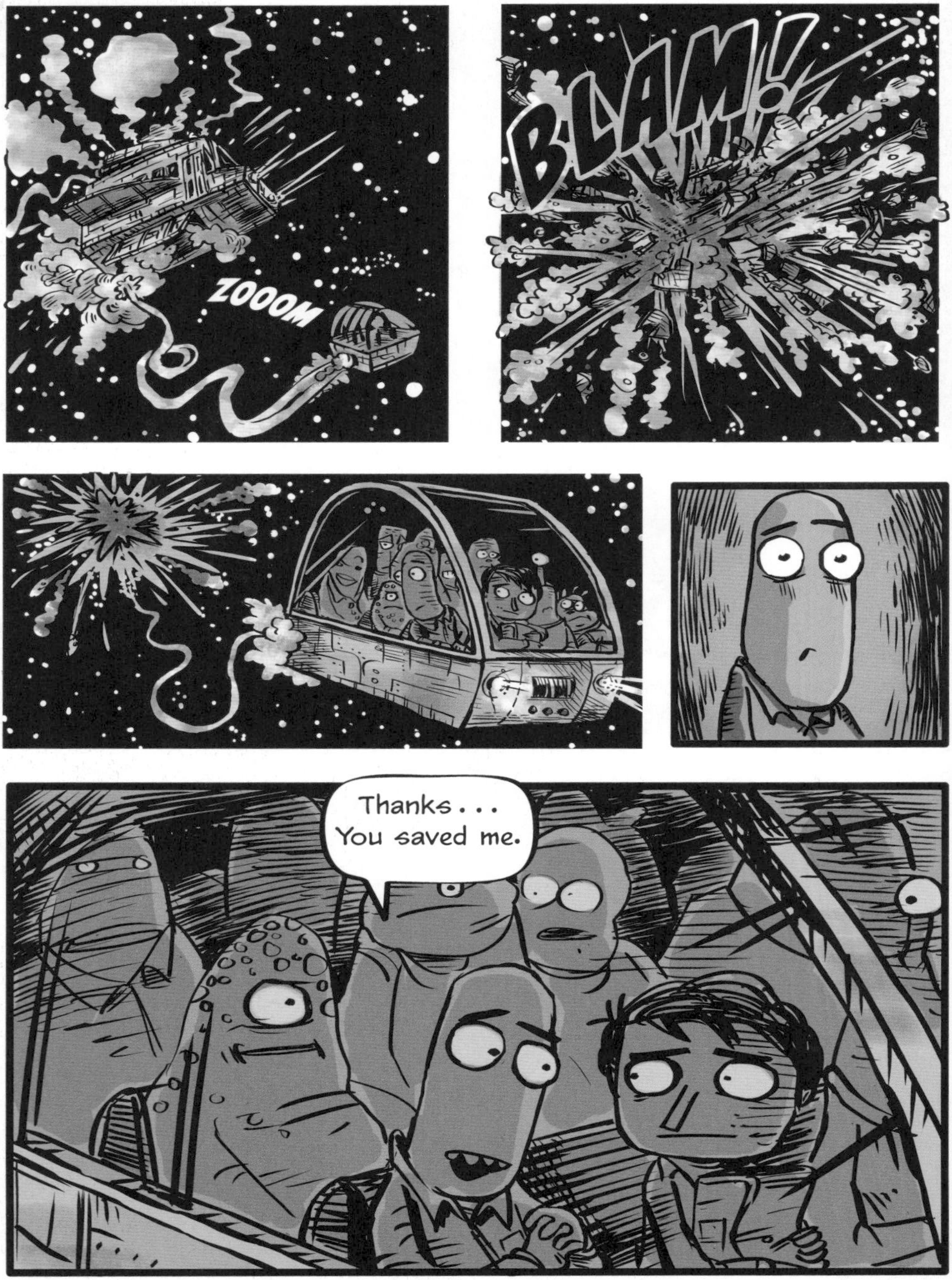
ZOOOM
BLAM!
Thanks . . .
You saved me.

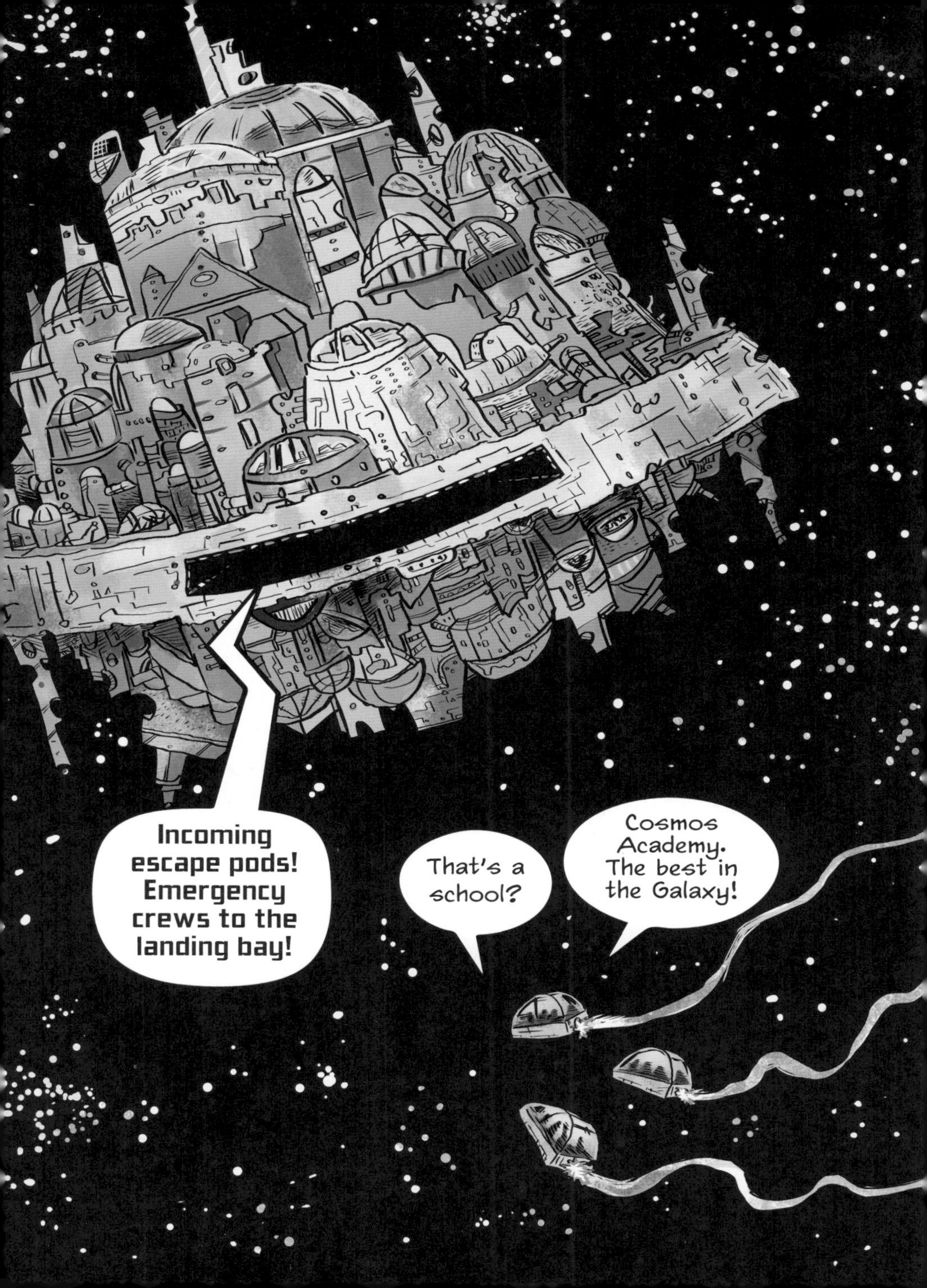
Incoming escape pods! Emergency crews to the landing bay!
That's a school?
Cosmos Academy. The best in the Galaxy!

CHAPTER 2

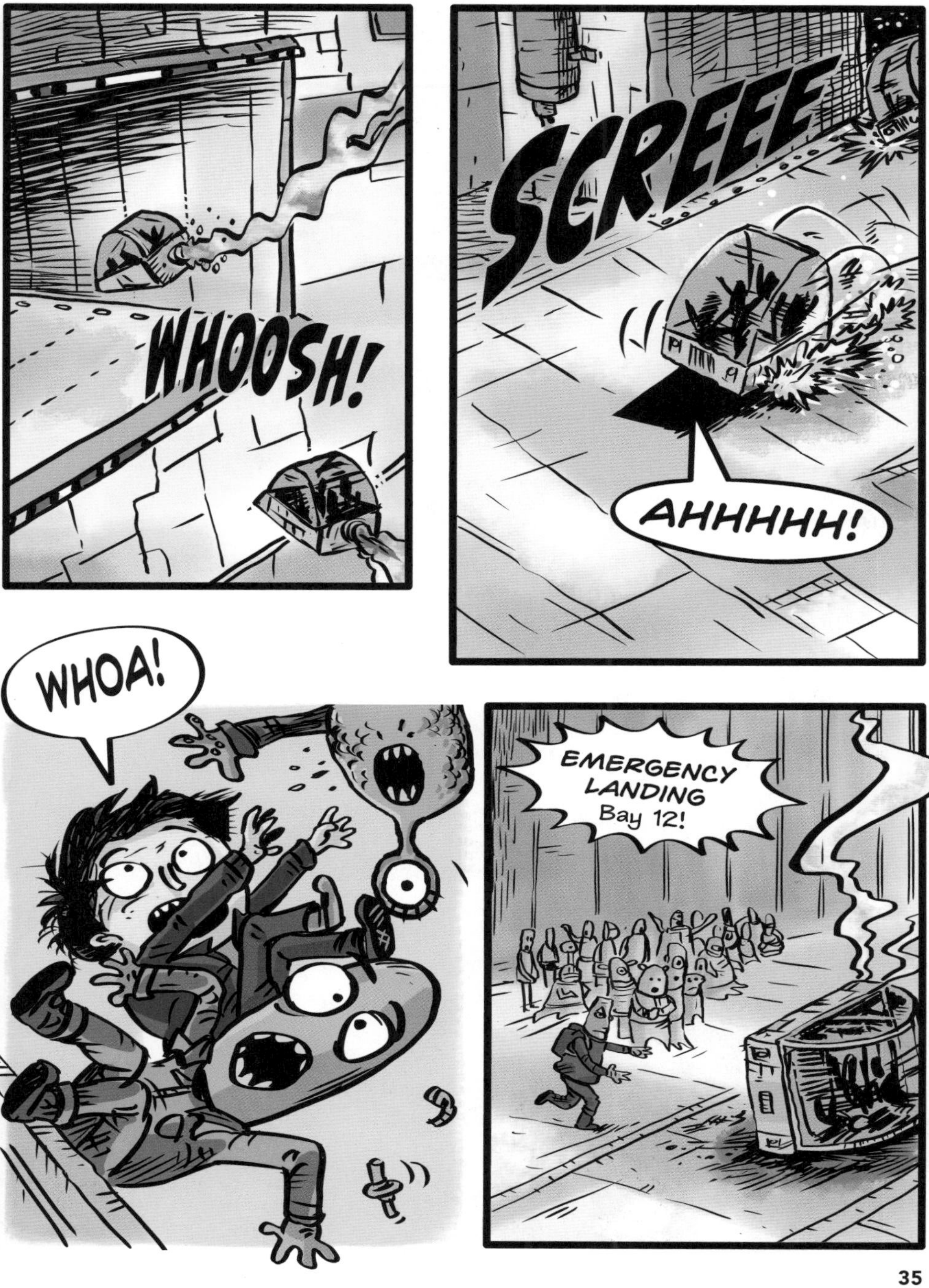
WHOOSH!
SCREEEE
AHHHHH!
WHOA!
EMERGENCY LANDING Bay 12!

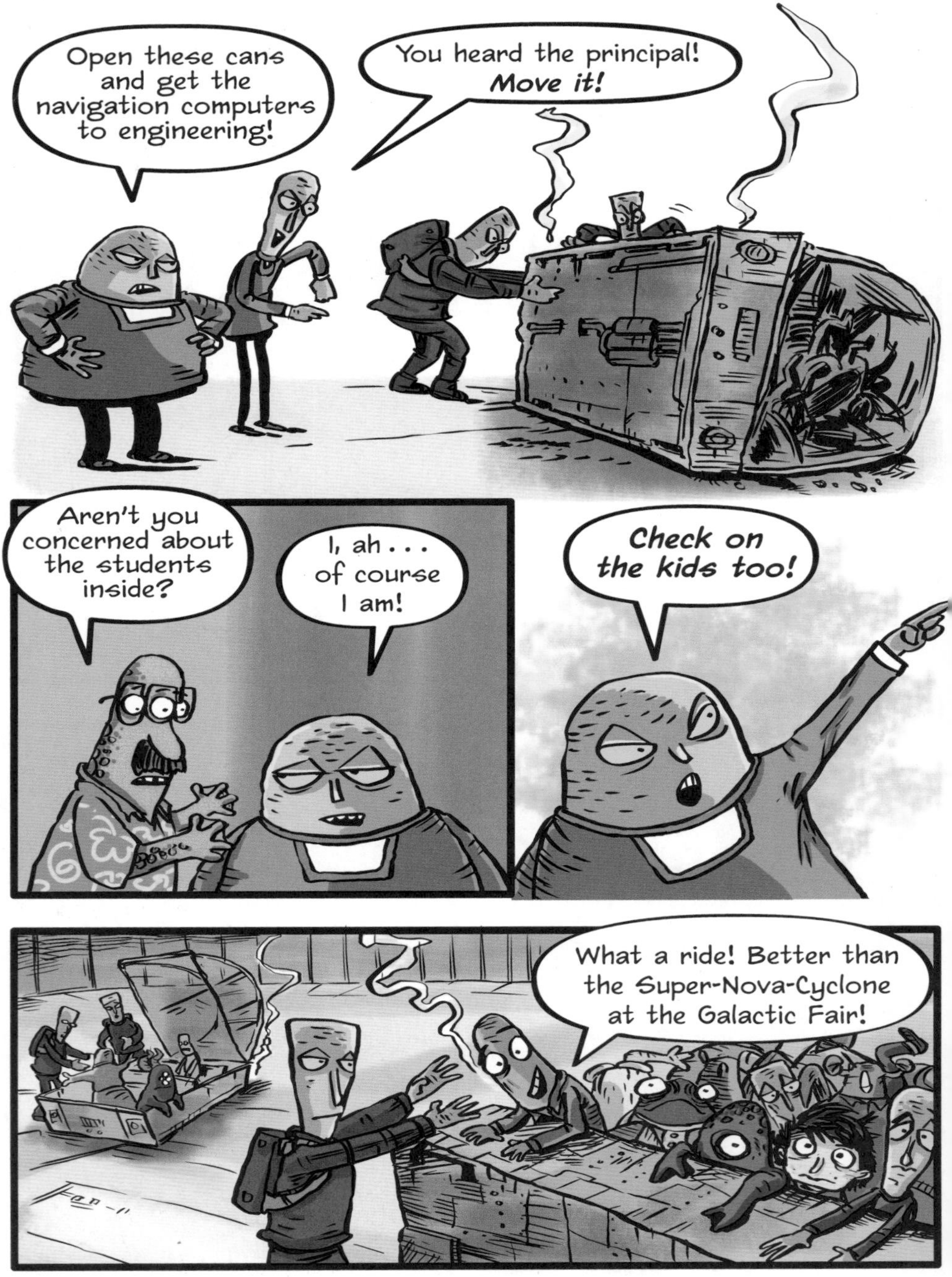
Open these cans and get the navigation computers to engineering!
You heard the principal! *Move it!*
Aren't you concerned about the students inside?
I, ah . . . of course I am!
Check on the kids too!
What a ride! Better than the Super-Nova-Cyclone at the Galactic Fair!

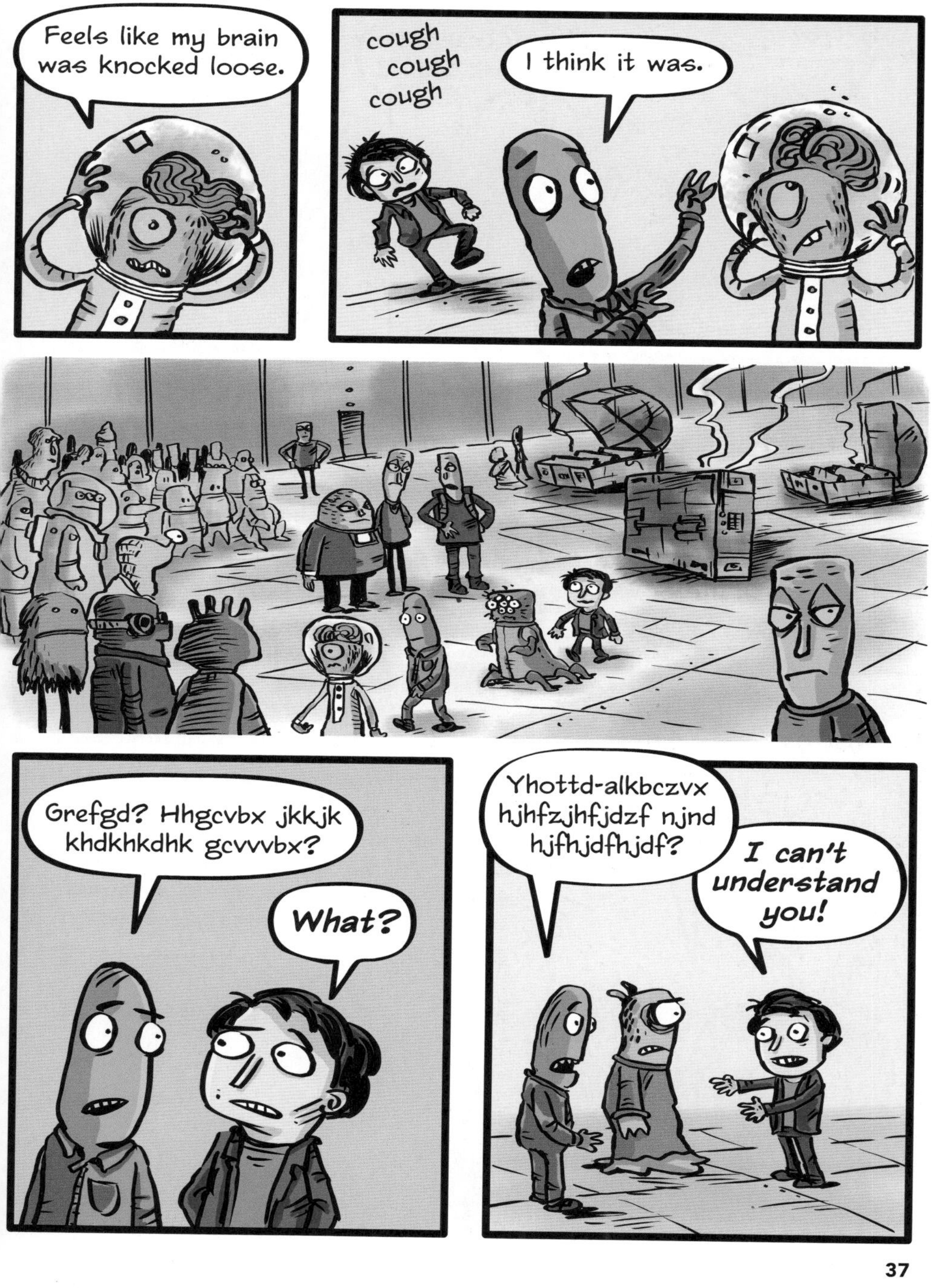
Feels like my brain was knocked loose.
cough cough cough
I think it was.
Grefgd? Hhgcvbx jkkjk khdkhkdhk gcvvvbx?
What?
Yhottd-alkbczvx hjhfzjhfjdzf njnd hjfhjdfhjdf?
I can't understand you!

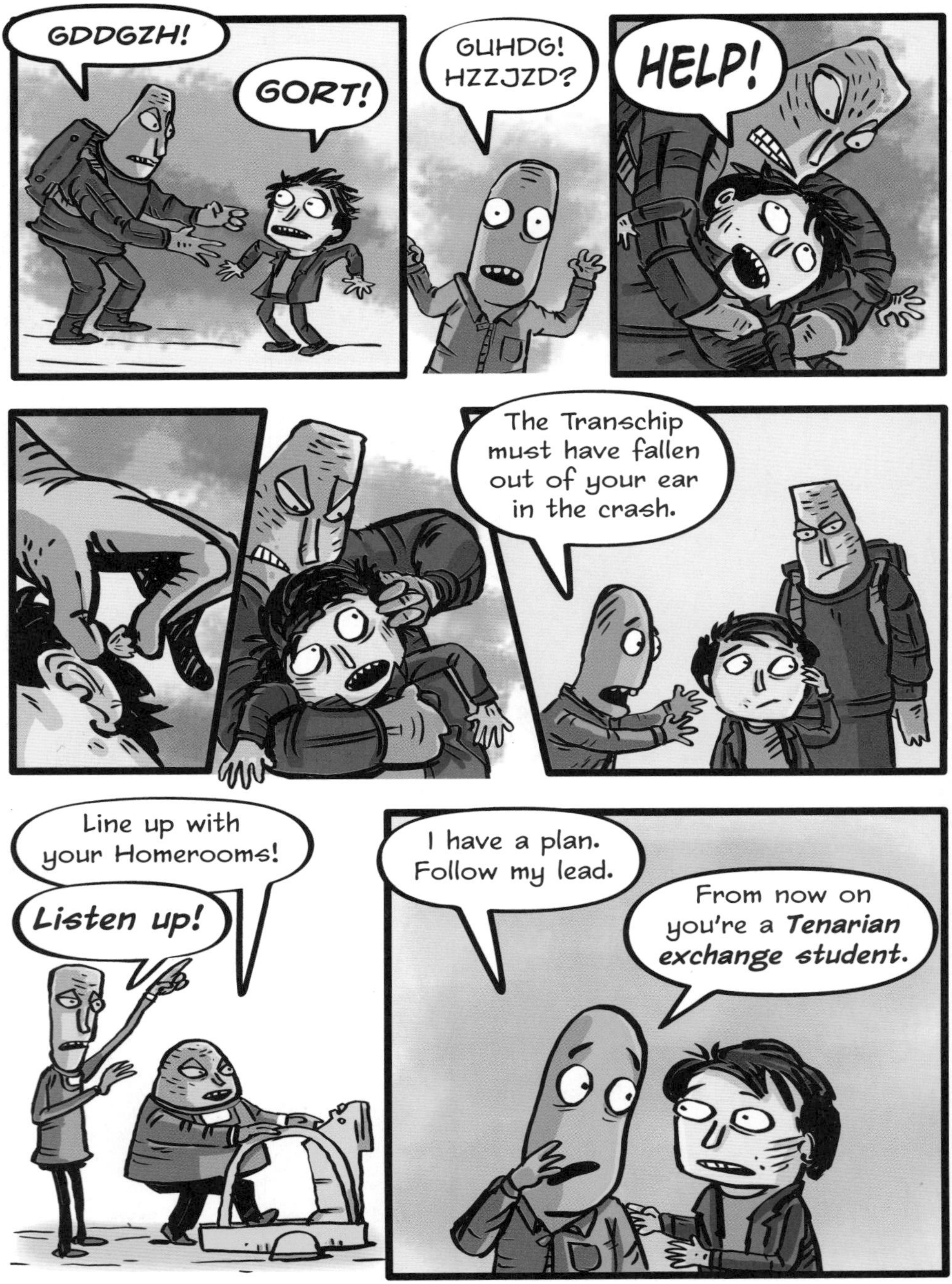
GDDGZH!
GORT!
GUHDG! HZZJZD?
HELP!
The Transchip must have fallen out of your ear in the crash.
Line up with your Homerooms!
Listen up!
I have a plan. Follow my lead.
From now on you're a Tenarian exchange student.

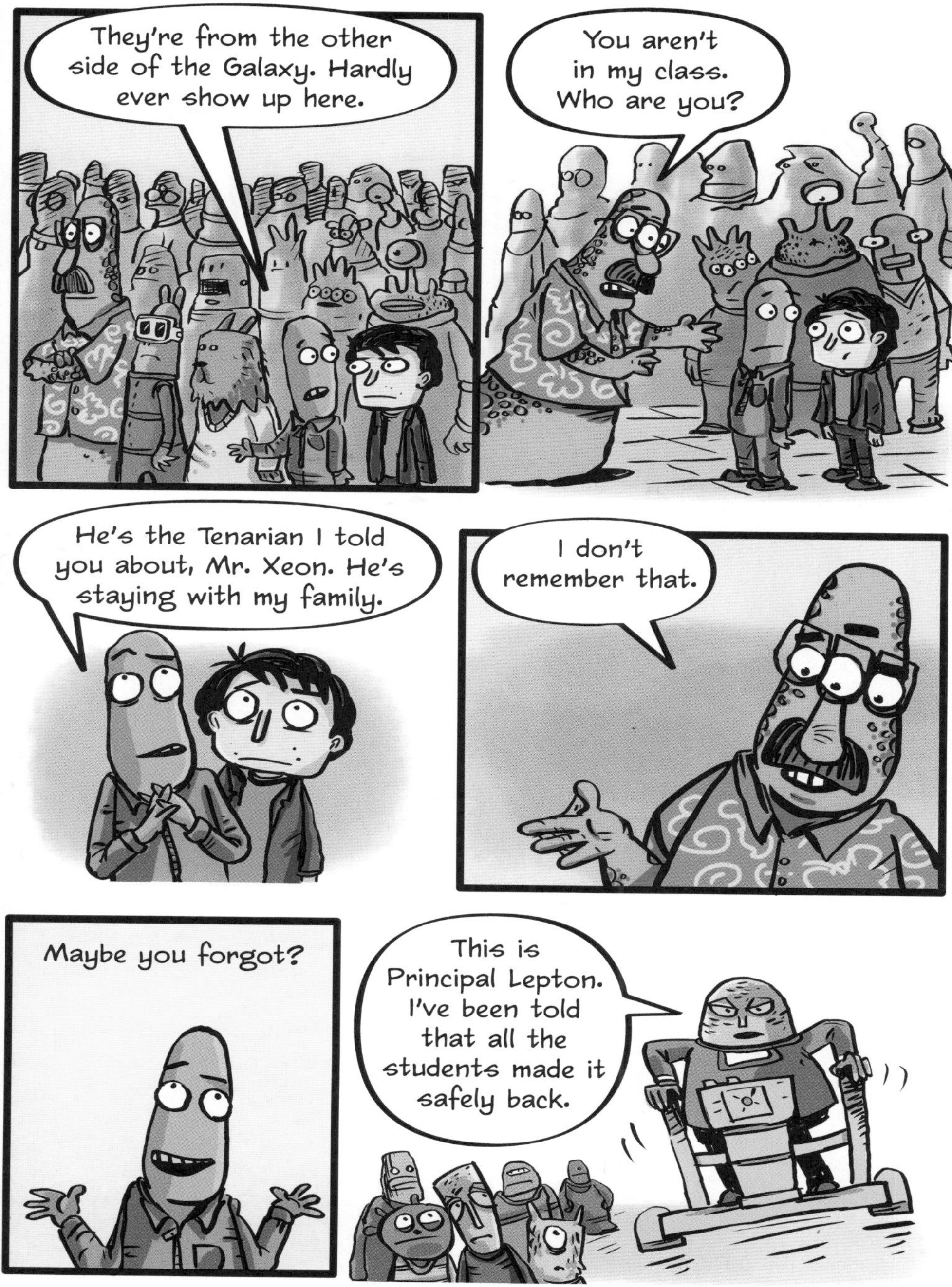
They're from the other side of the Galaxy. Hardly ever show up here.
You aren't in my class. Who are you?
He's the Tenarian I told you about, Mr. Xeon. He's staying with my family.
I don't remember that.
Maybe you forgot?
This is Principal Lepton. I've been told that all the students made it safely back.

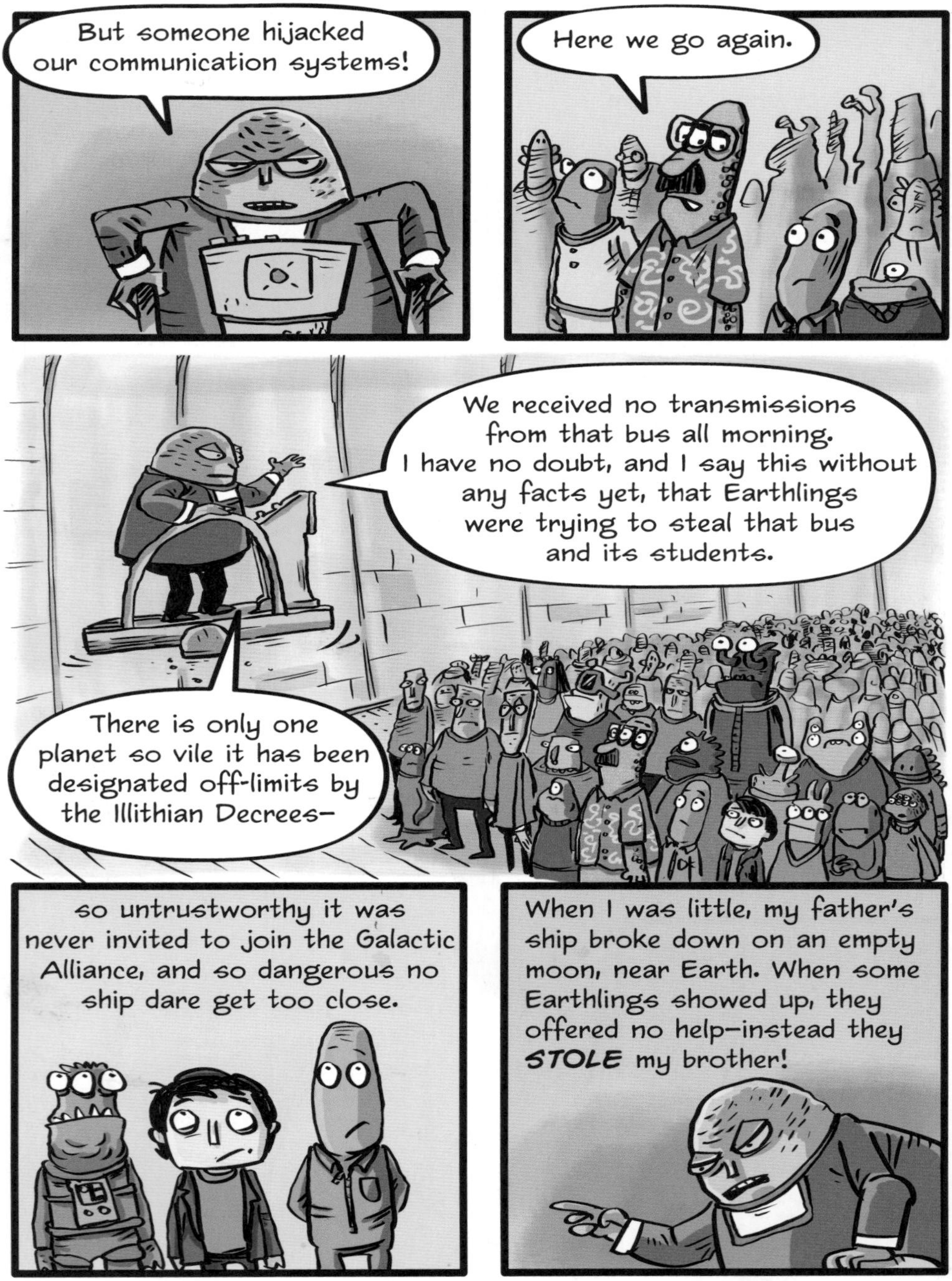

But someone hijacked our communication systems!
Here we go again.
We received no transmissions from that bus all morning. I have no doubt, and I say this without any facts yet, that Earthlings were trying to steal that bus and its students.
There is only one planet so vile it has been designated off-limits by the Illithian Decrees–
so untrustworthy it was never invited to join the Galactic Alliance, and so dangerous no ship dare get too close.
When I was little, my father's ship broke down on an empty moon, near Earth. When some Earthlings showed up, they offered no help–instead they ***STOLE*** my brother!

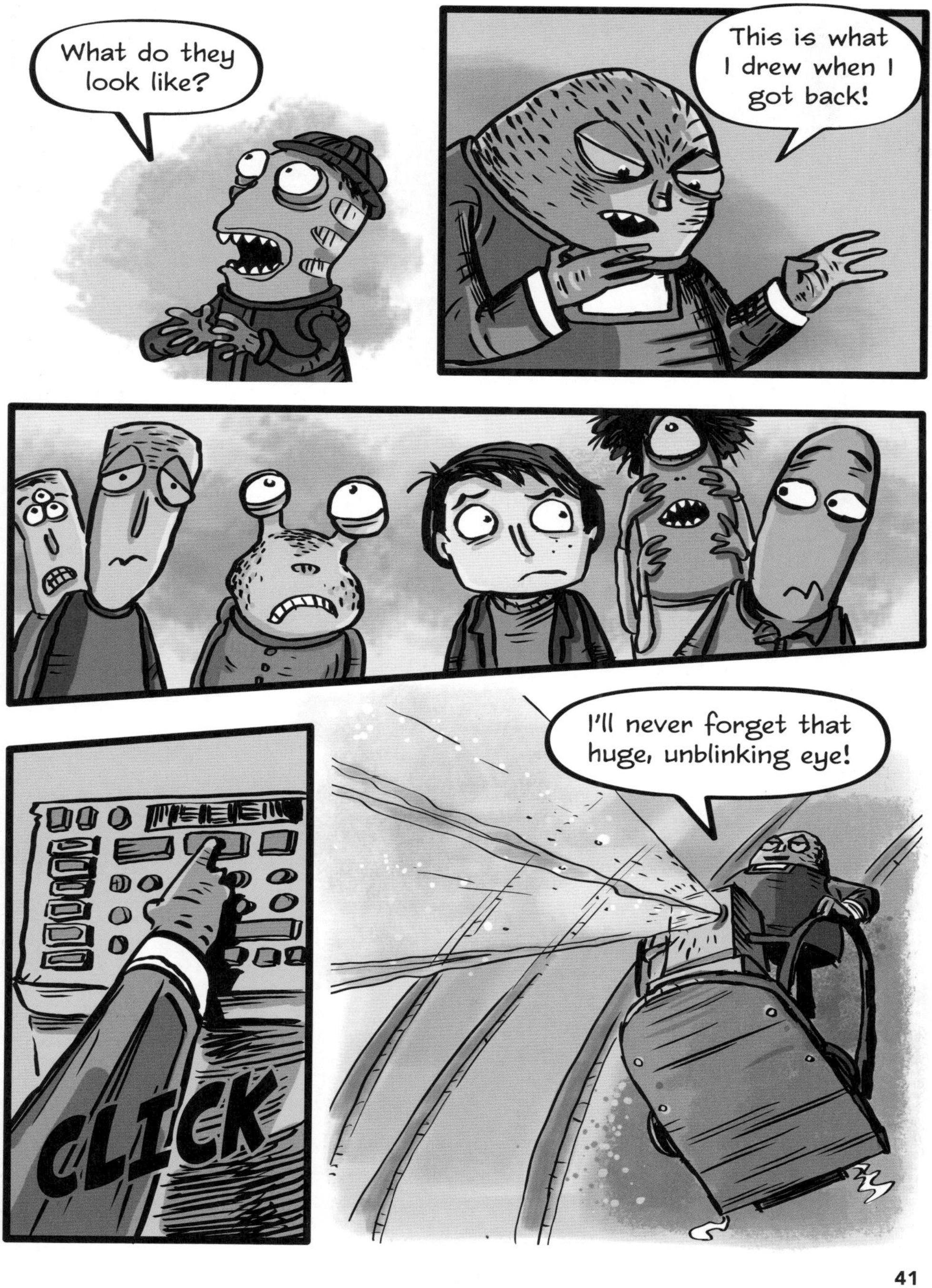
What do they look like?
This is what I drew when I got back!
CLICK
I'll never forget that huge, unblinking eye!

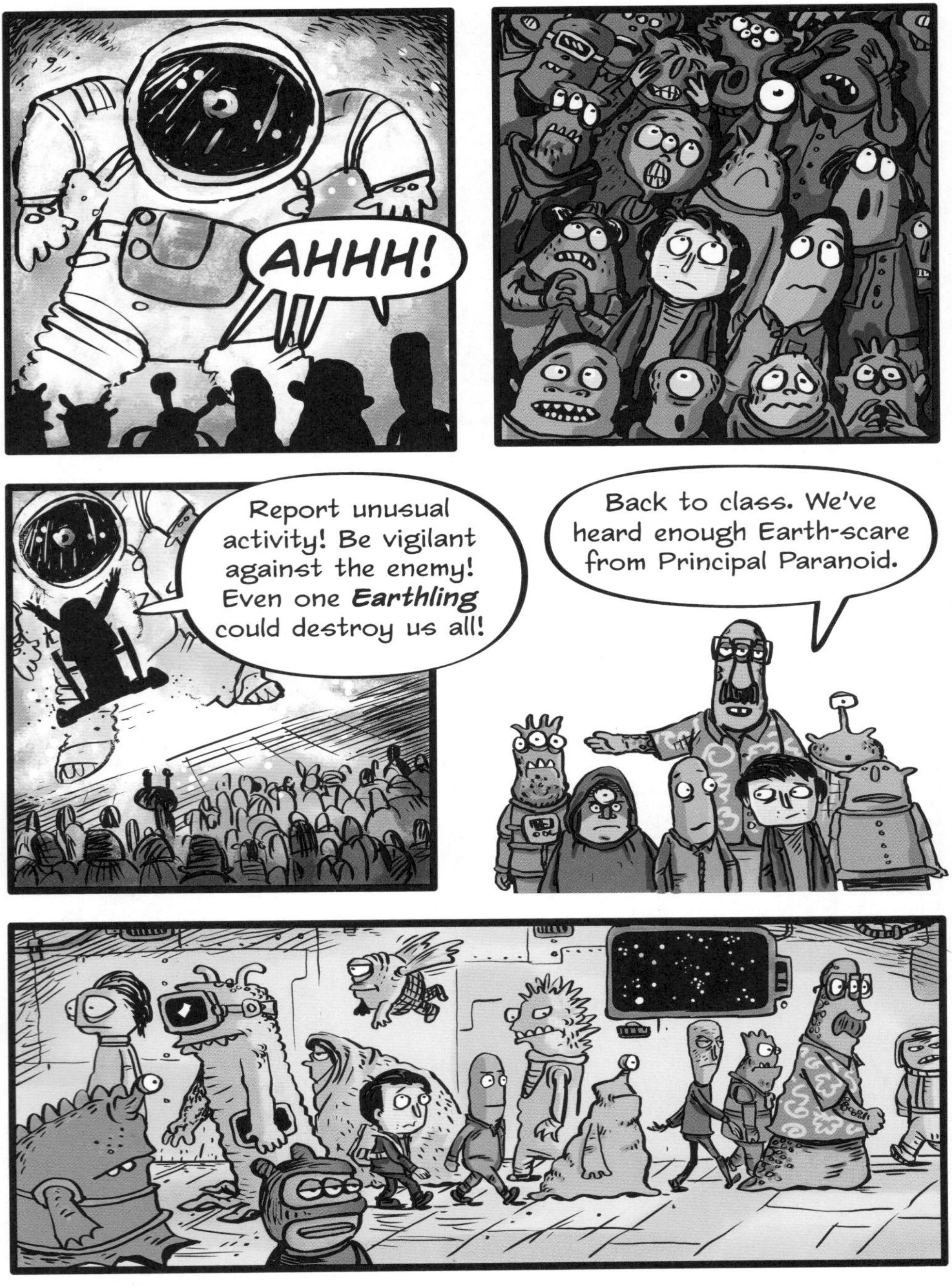
AHHH!
Report unusual activity! Be vigilant against the enemy! Even one ***Earthling*** could destroy us all!
Back to class. We've heard enough Earth-scare from Principal Paranoid.

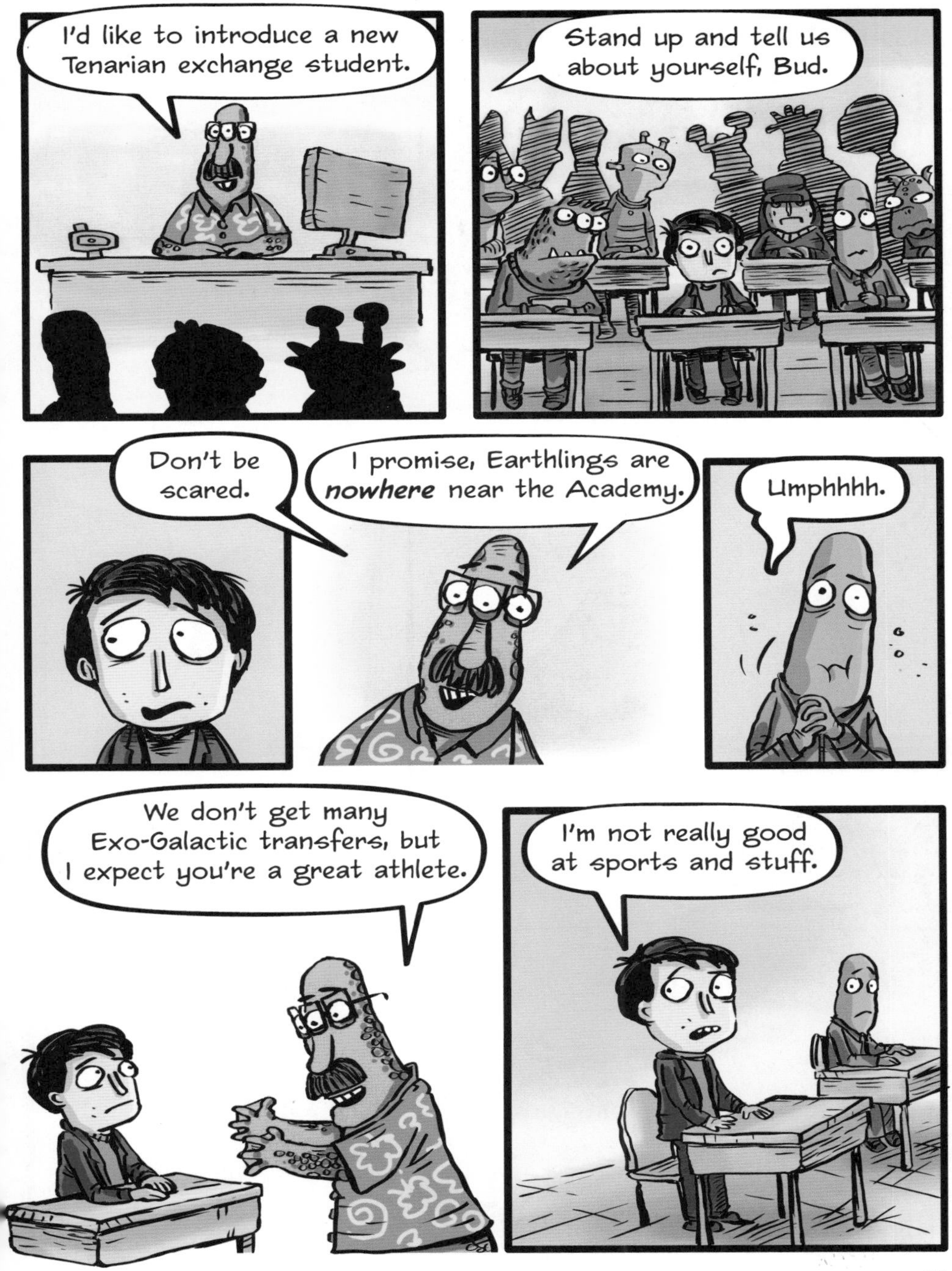
I'd like to introduce a new Tenarian exchange student.
Stand up and tell us about yourself, Bud.
Don't be scared.
I promise, Earthlings are *nowhere* near the Academy.
Umphhhh.
We don't get many Exo-Galactic transfers, but I expect you're a great athlete.
I'm not really good at sports and stuff.

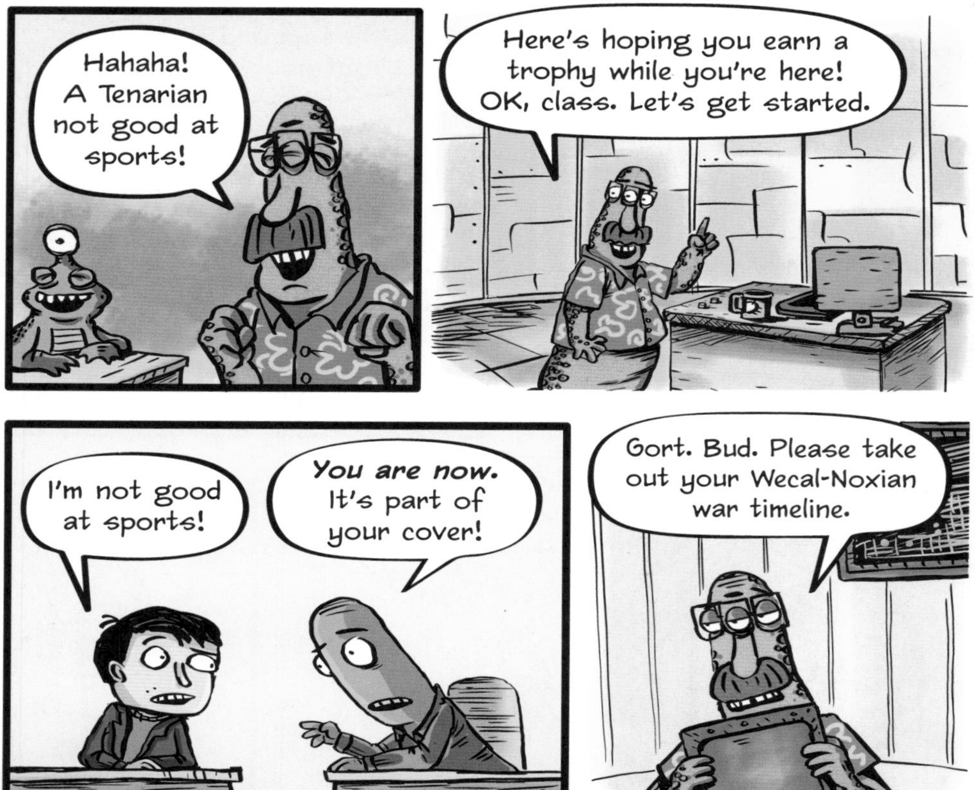
Hahaha! A Tenarian not good at sports!
Here's hoping you earn a trophy while you're here! OK, class. Let's get started.
I'm not good at sports!
You are now. It's part of your cover!
Gort. Bud. Please take out your Wecal-Noxian war timeline.
You will remember from yesterday that the Noxian rebels had . . .
Cool.

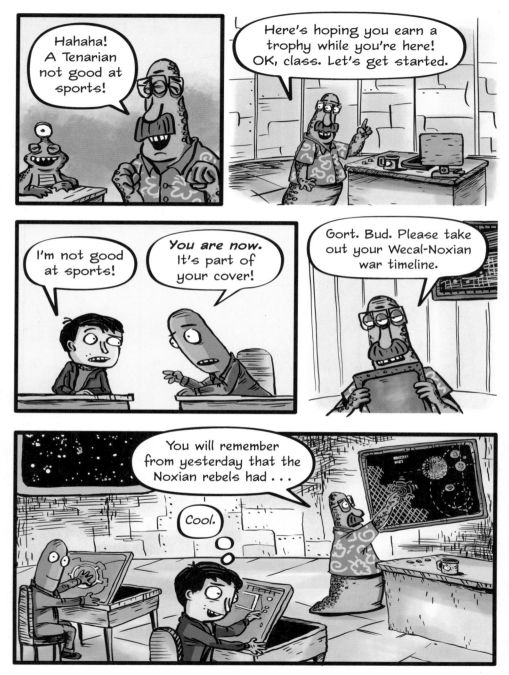

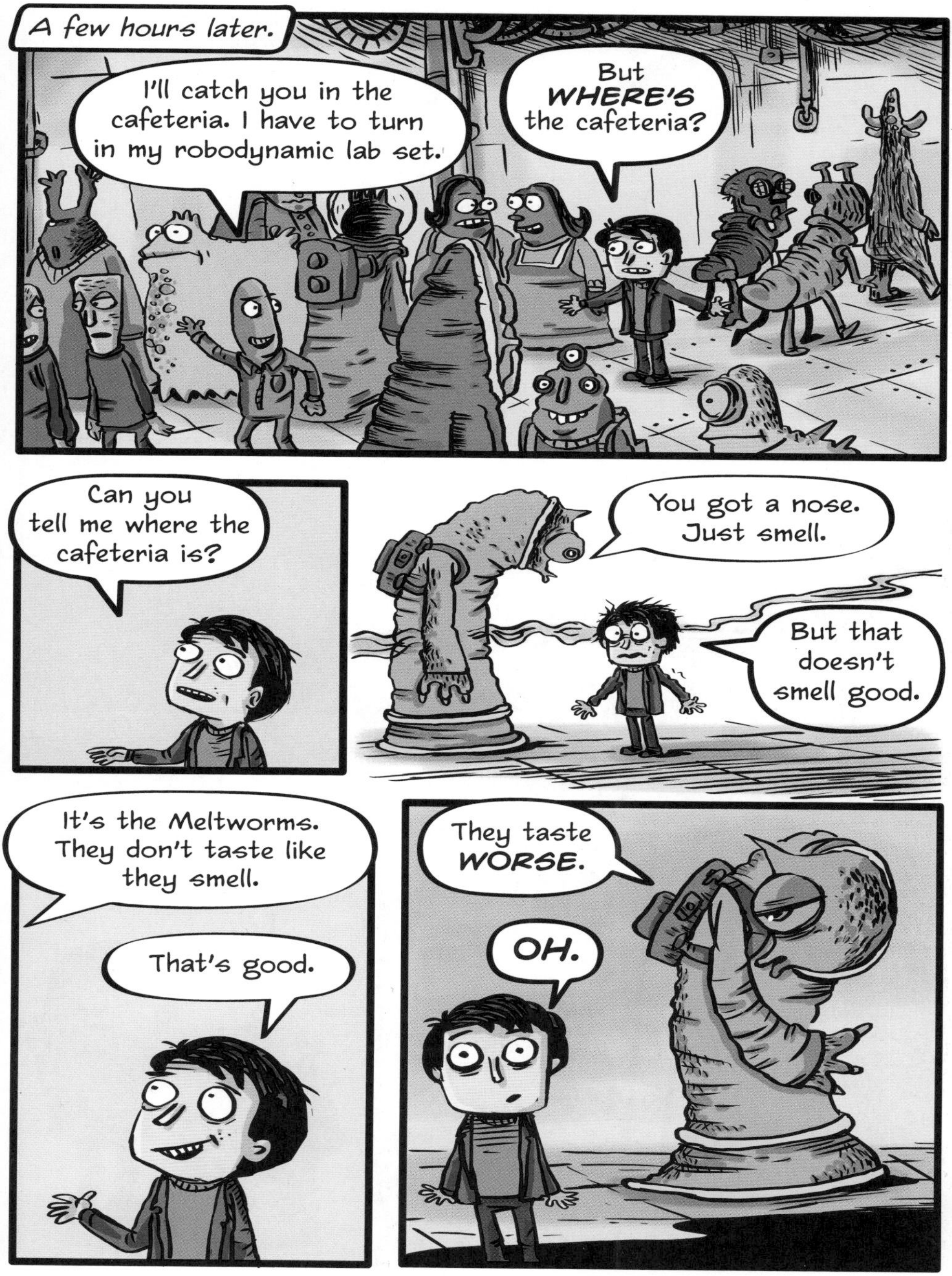
A few hours later.
I'll catch you in the cafeteria. I have to turn in my robodynamic lab set.
But WHERE'S the cafeteria?
Can you tell me where the cafeteria is?
You got a nose. Just smell.
But that doesn't smell good.
It's the Meltworms. They don't taste like they smell.
That's good.
They taste WORSE.
OH.

AH!

HURRY UP!

Grab your eats!

STAB!

HEY! GET THAT FORK OUTTA ME!

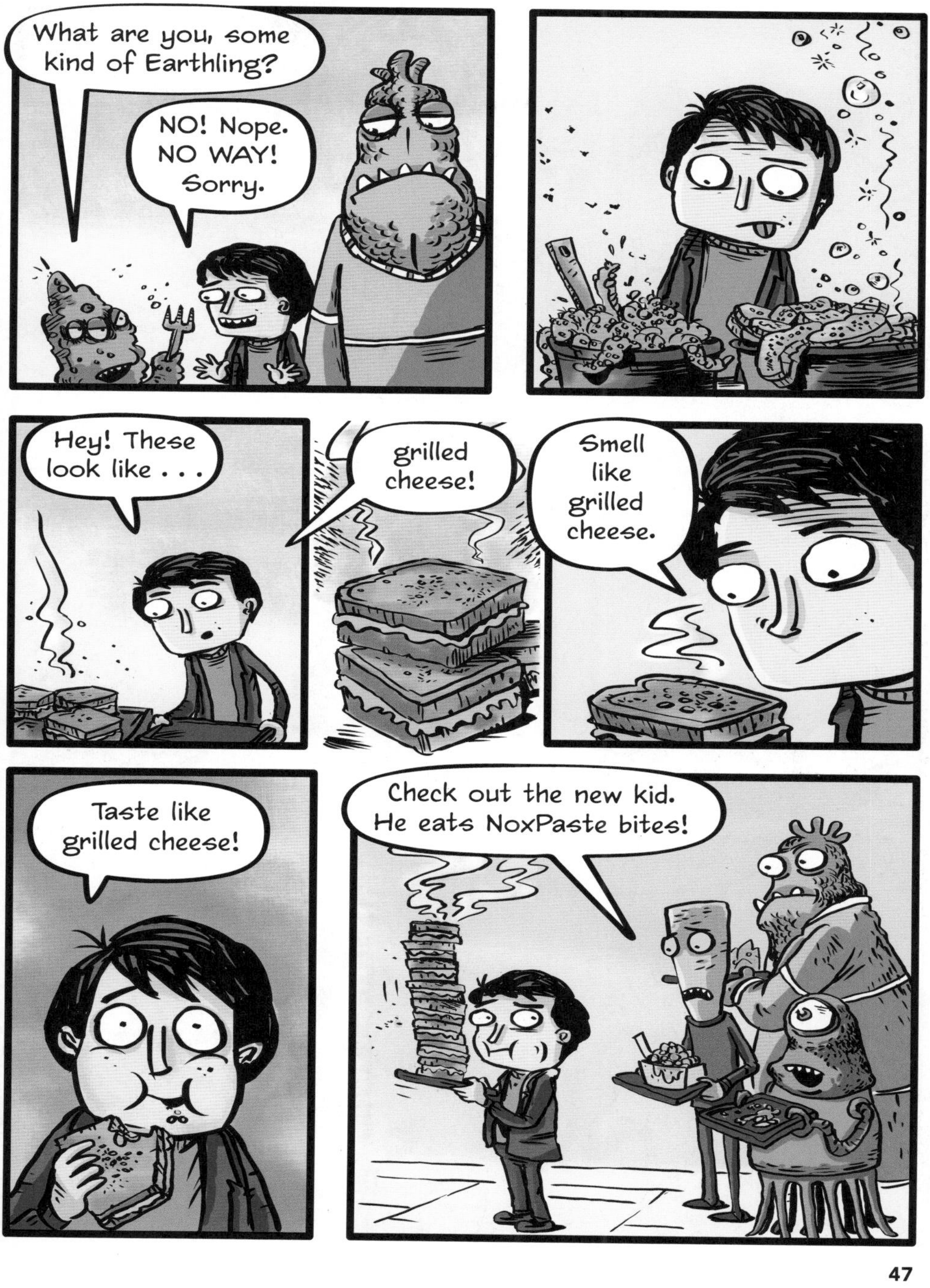
What are you, some kind of Earthling?
NO! Nope. NO WAY! Sorry.
Hey! These look like . . .
grilled cheese!
Smell like grilled cheese.
Taste like grilled cheese!
Check out the new kid. He eats NoxPaste bites!

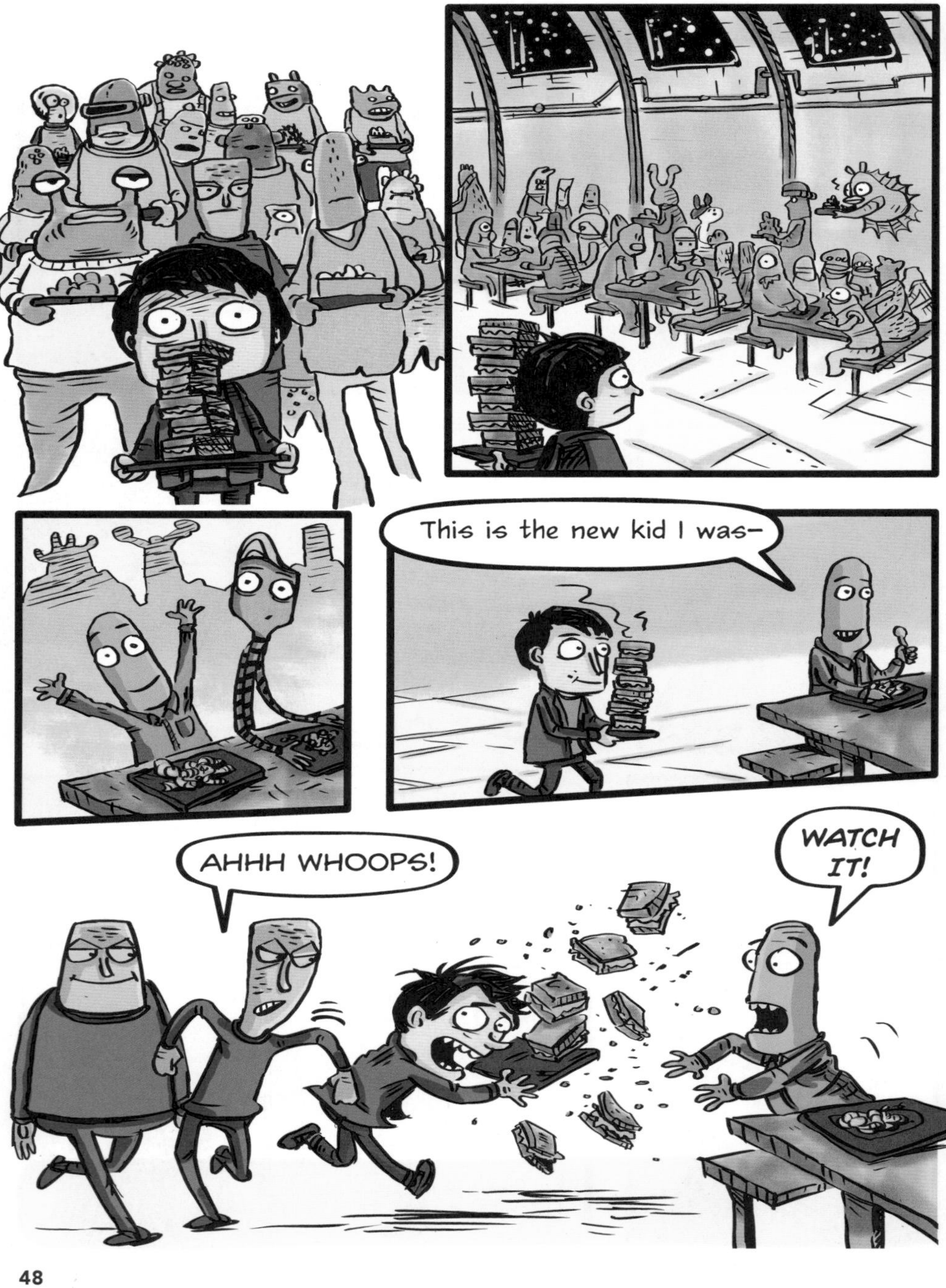
This is the new kid I was–
AHHH WHOOPS!
WATCH IT!

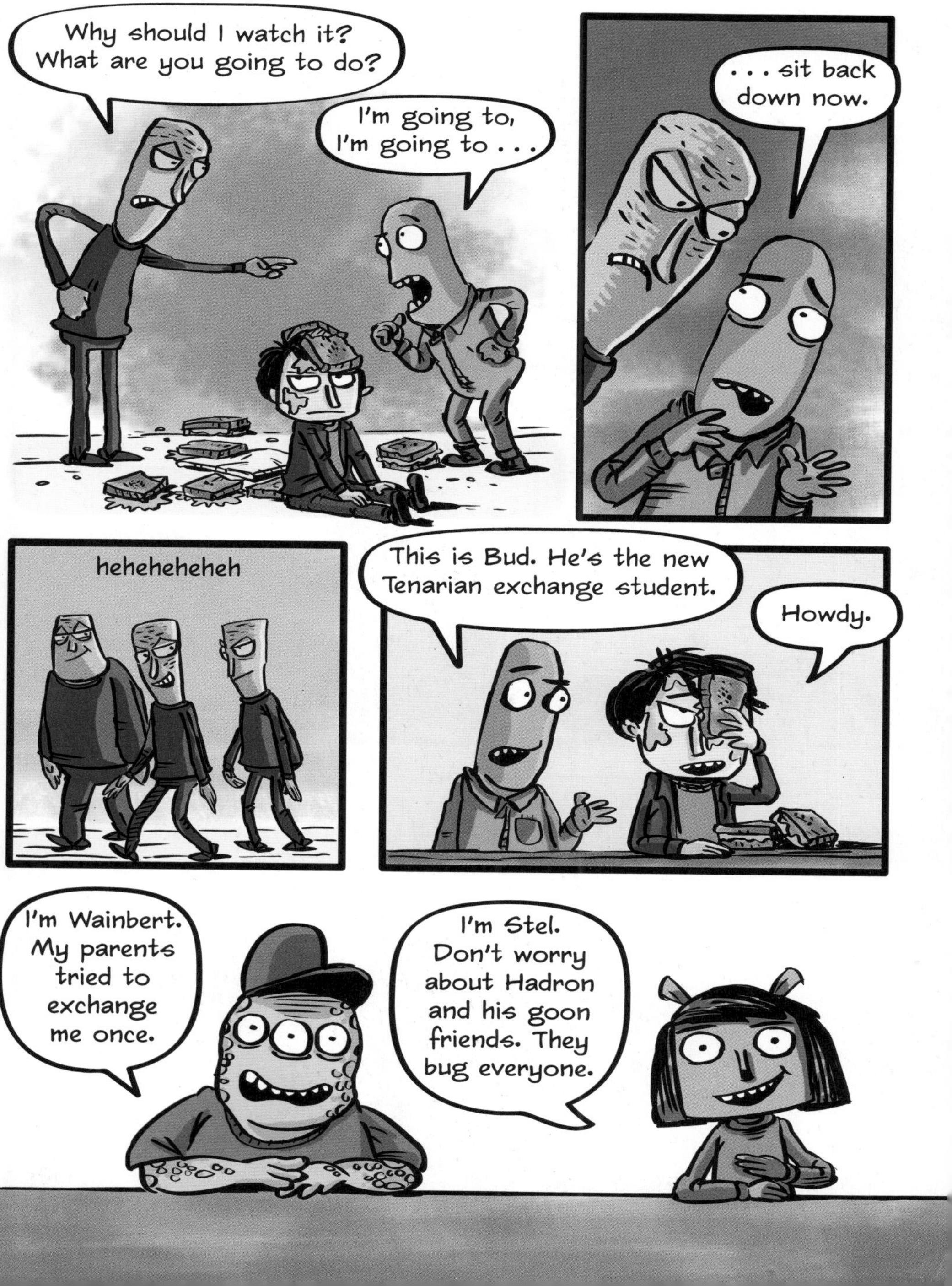
Why should I watch it? What are you going to do?
I'm going to, I'm going to . . .
. . . sit back down now.
heheheheheh
This is Bud. He's the new Tenarian exchange student.
Howdy.
I'm Wainbert. My parents tried to exchange me once.
I'm Stel. Don't worry about Hadron and his goon friends. They bug everyone.

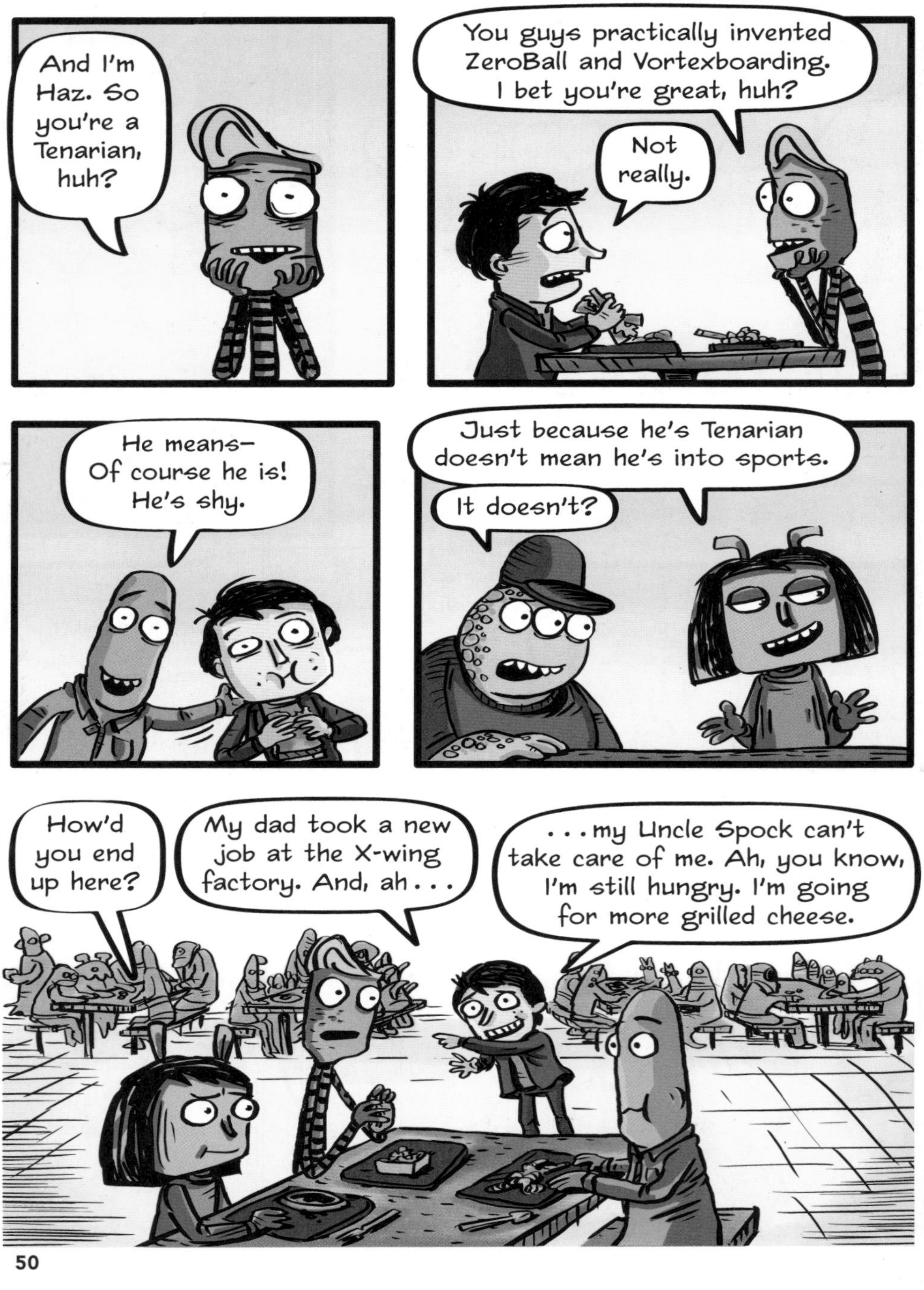
And I'm Haz. So you're a Tenarian, huh?
You guys practically invented ZeroBall and Vortexboarding. I bet you're great, huh?
Not really.
He means– Of course he is! He's shy.
Just because he's Tenarian doesn't mean he's into sports.
It doesn't?
How'd you end up here?
My dad took a new job at the X-wing factory. And, ah . . .
. . . my Uncle Spock can't take care of me. Ah, you know, I'm still hungry. I'm going for more grilled cheese.

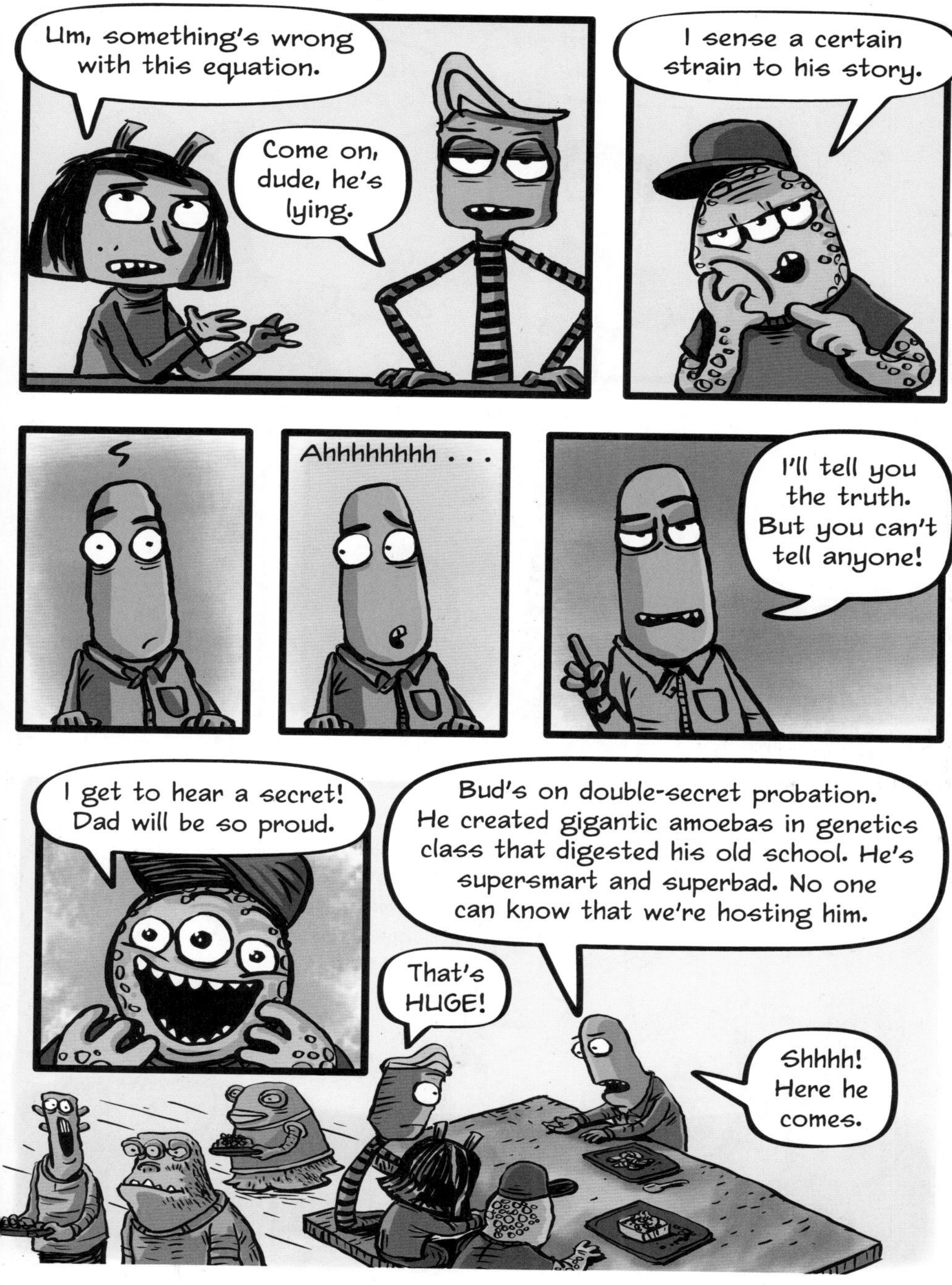
Um, something's wrong with this equation.
Come on, dude, he's lying.
I sense a certain strain to his story.
Ahhhhhhhh . . .
I'll tell you the truth. But you can't tell anyone!
I get to hear a secret! Dad will be so proud.
Bud's on double-secret probation. He created gigantic amoebas in genetics class that digested his old school. He's supersmart and superbad. No one can know that we're hosting him.
That's HUGE!
Shhhh! Here he comes.

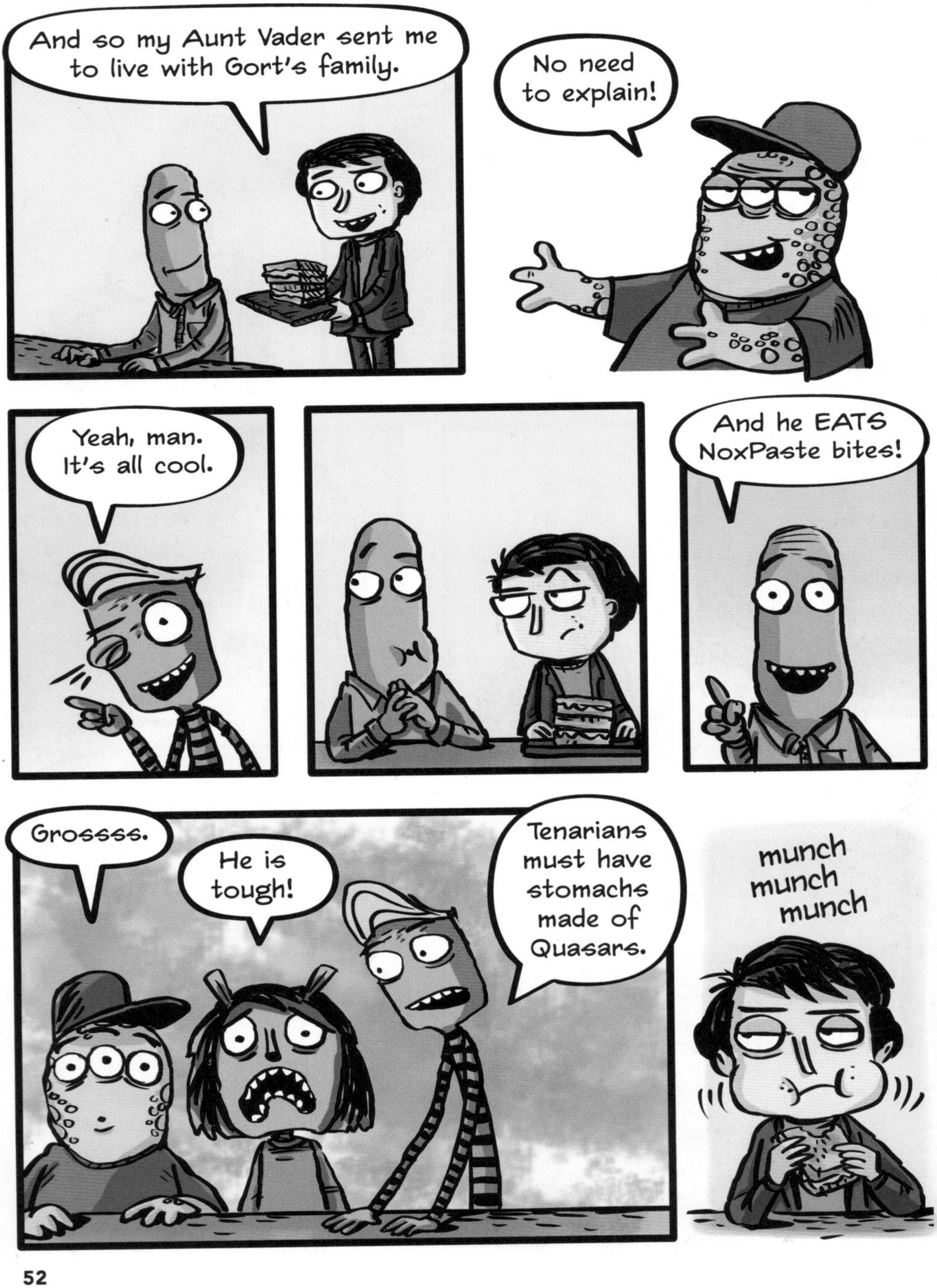
And so my Aunt Vader sent me to live with Gort's family.
No need to explain!
Yeah, man. It's all cool.
And he EATS NoxPaste bites!
Grossss.
He is tough!
Tenarians must have stomachs made of Quasars.
munch munch munch

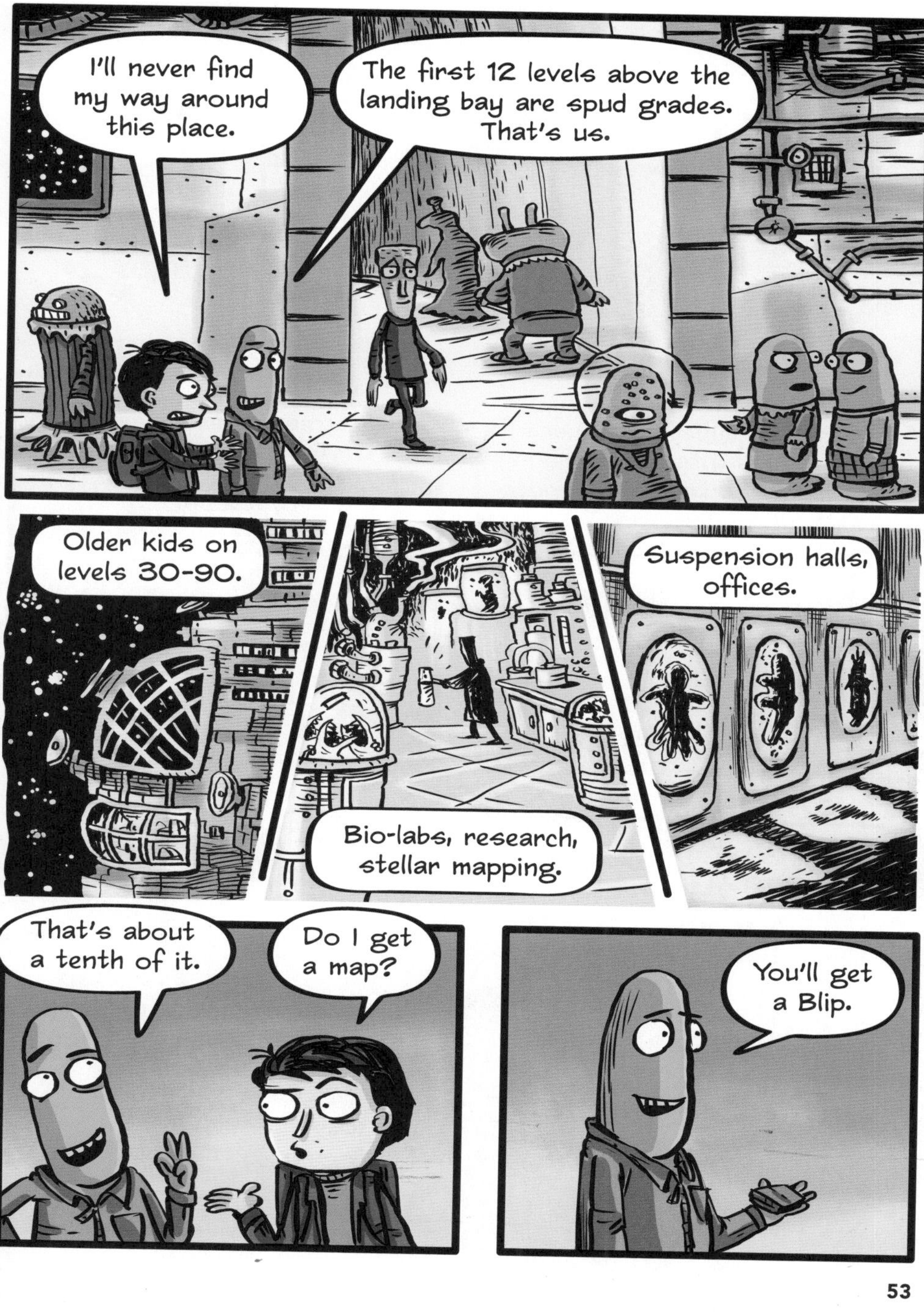
I'll never find my way around this place.
The first 12 levels above the landing bay are spud grades. That's us.
Older kids on levels 30-90.
Bio-labs, research, stellar mapping.
Suspension halls, offices.
That's about a tenth of it.
Do I get a map?
You'll get a Blip.

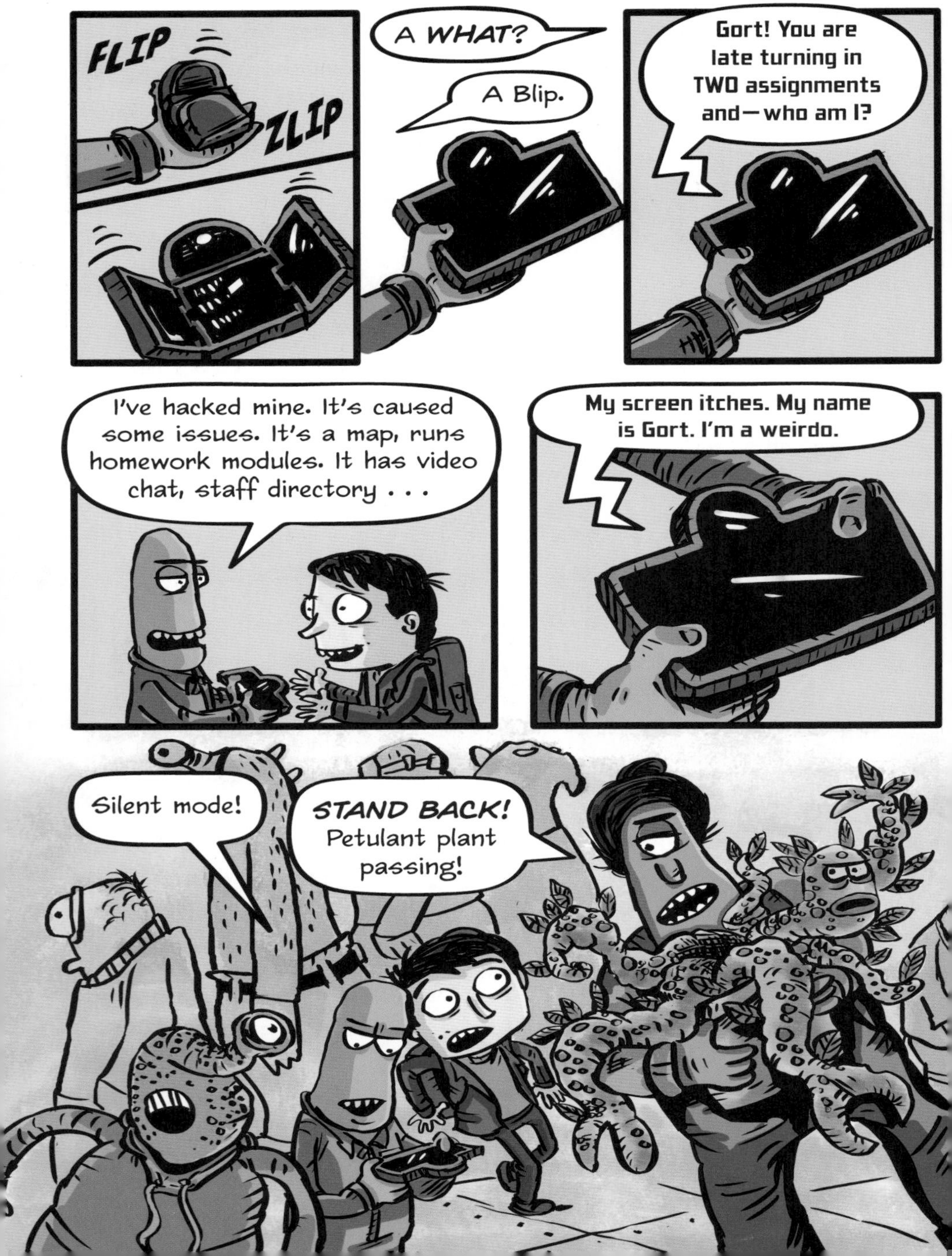
FLIP
ZLIP
A WHAT?
A Blip.
Gort! You are late turning in TWO assignments and—who am I?
I've hacked mine. It's caused some issues. It's a map, runs homework modules. It has video chat, staff directory . . .
My screen itches. My name is Gort. I'm a weirdo.
Silent mode!
STAND BACK! Petulant plant passing!

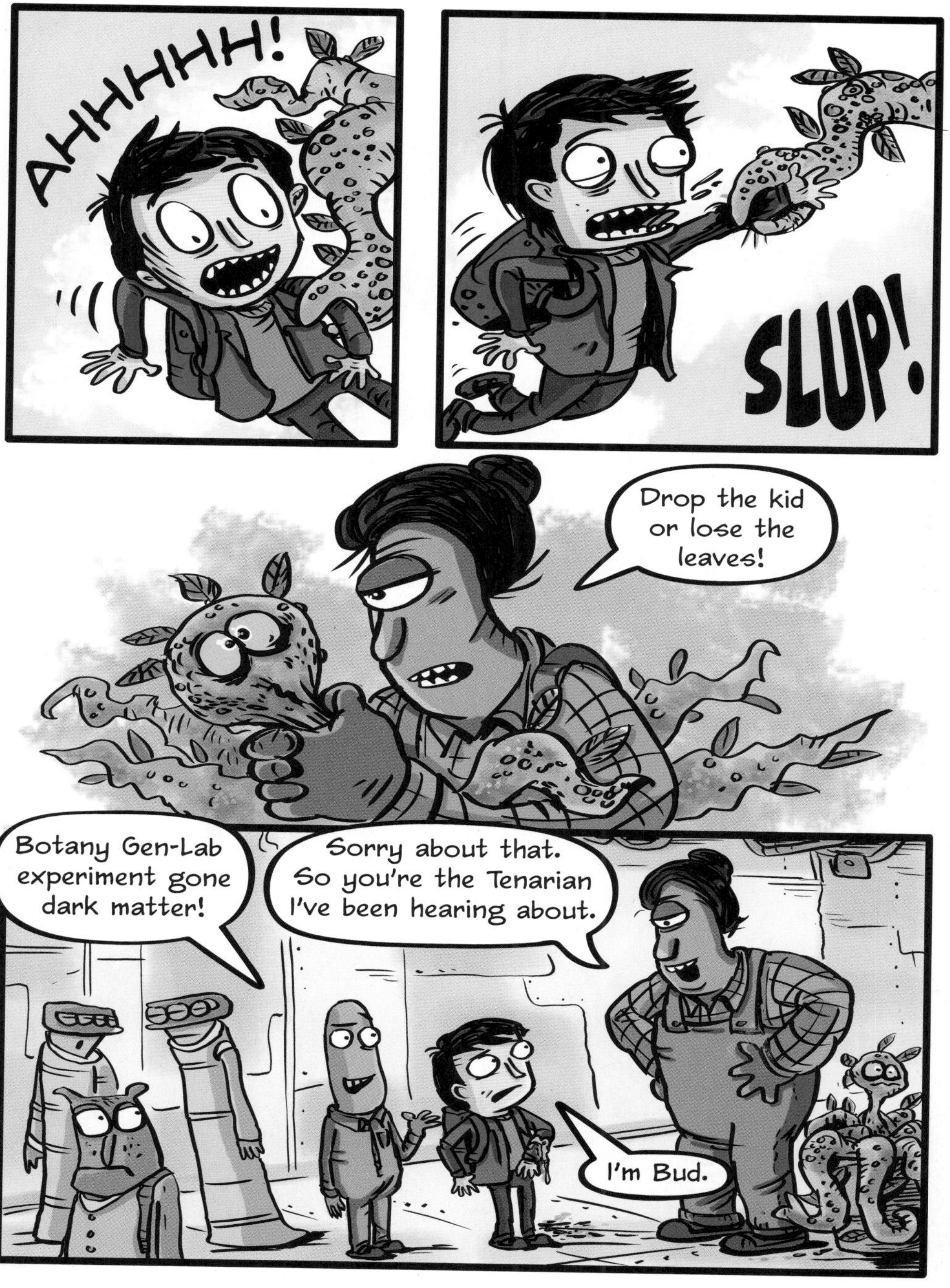
AHHHHH!
SLUP!
Drop the kid or lose the leaves!
Botany Gen-Lab experiment gone dark matter!
Sorry about that. So you're the Tenarian I've been hearing about.
I'm Bud.

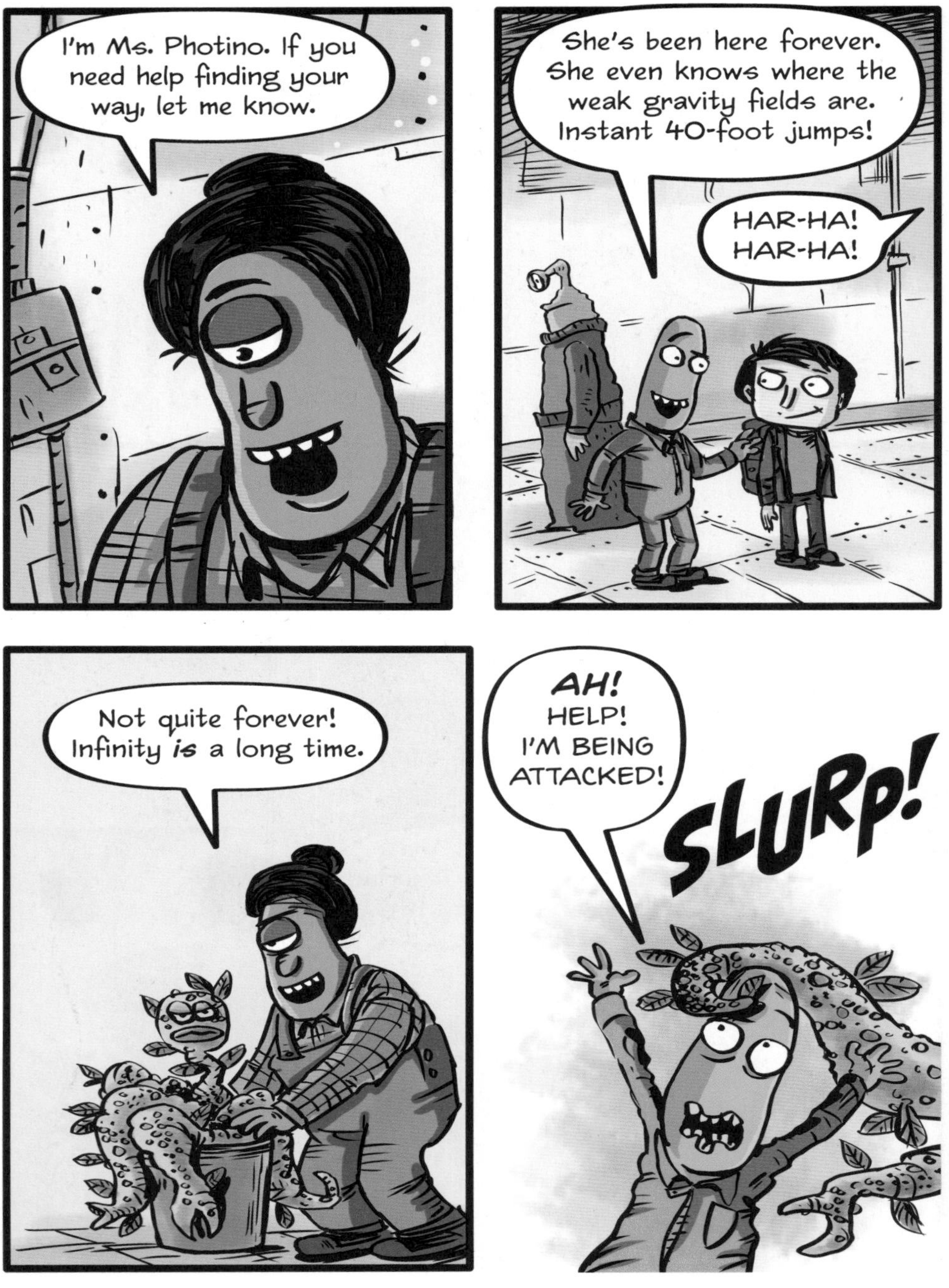
I'm Ms. Photino. If you need help finding your way, let me know.
She's been here forever. She even knows where the weak gravity fields are. Instant 40-foot jumps!
HAR-HA! HAR-HA!
Not quite forever! Infinity *is* a long time.
AH! HELP! I'M BEING ATTACKED!
SLURP!

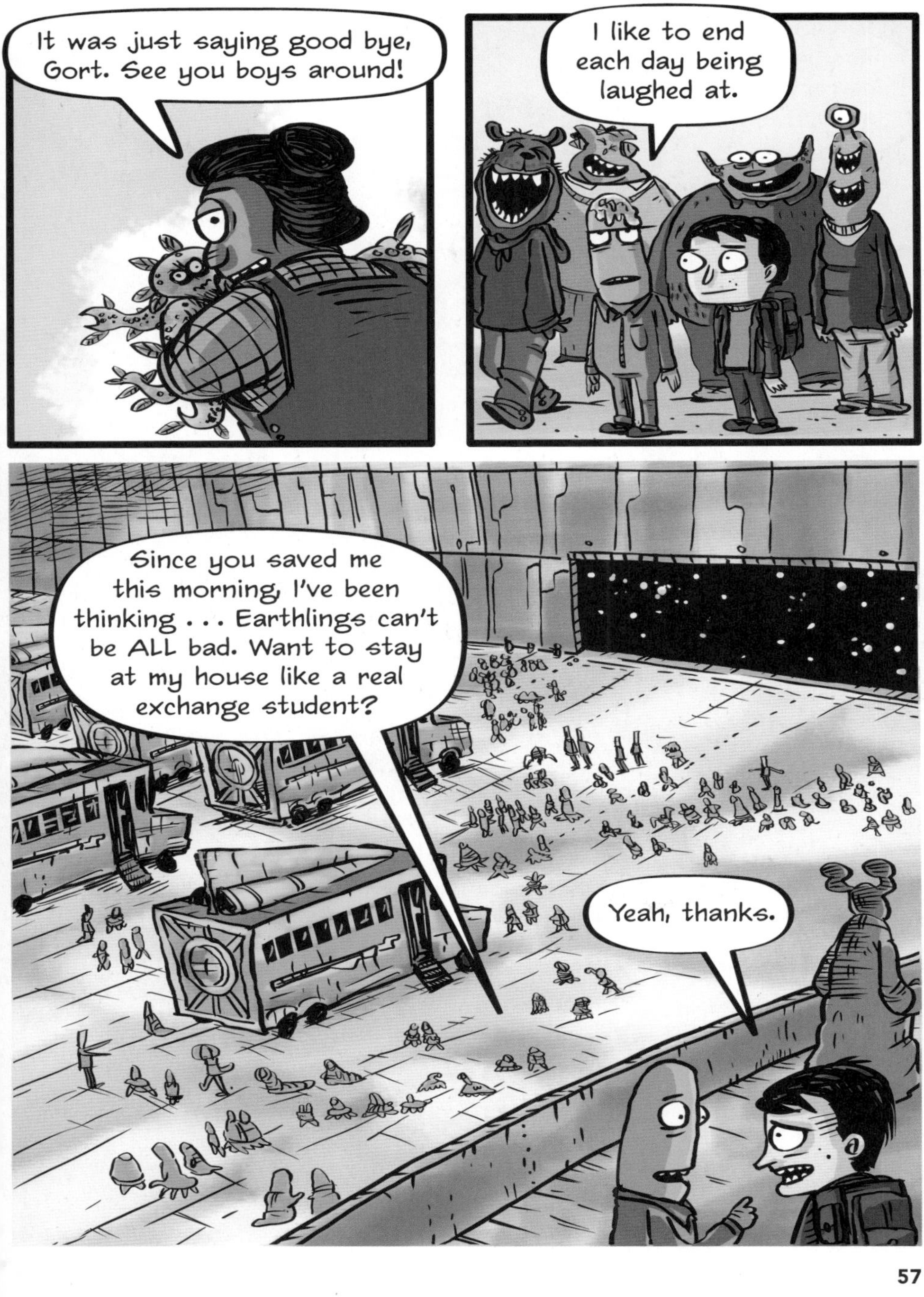
It was just saying good bye, Gort. See you boys around!
I like to end each day being laughed at.
Since you saved me this morning, I've been thinking . . . Earthlings can't be ALL bad. Want to stay at my house like a real exchange student?
Yeah, thanks.

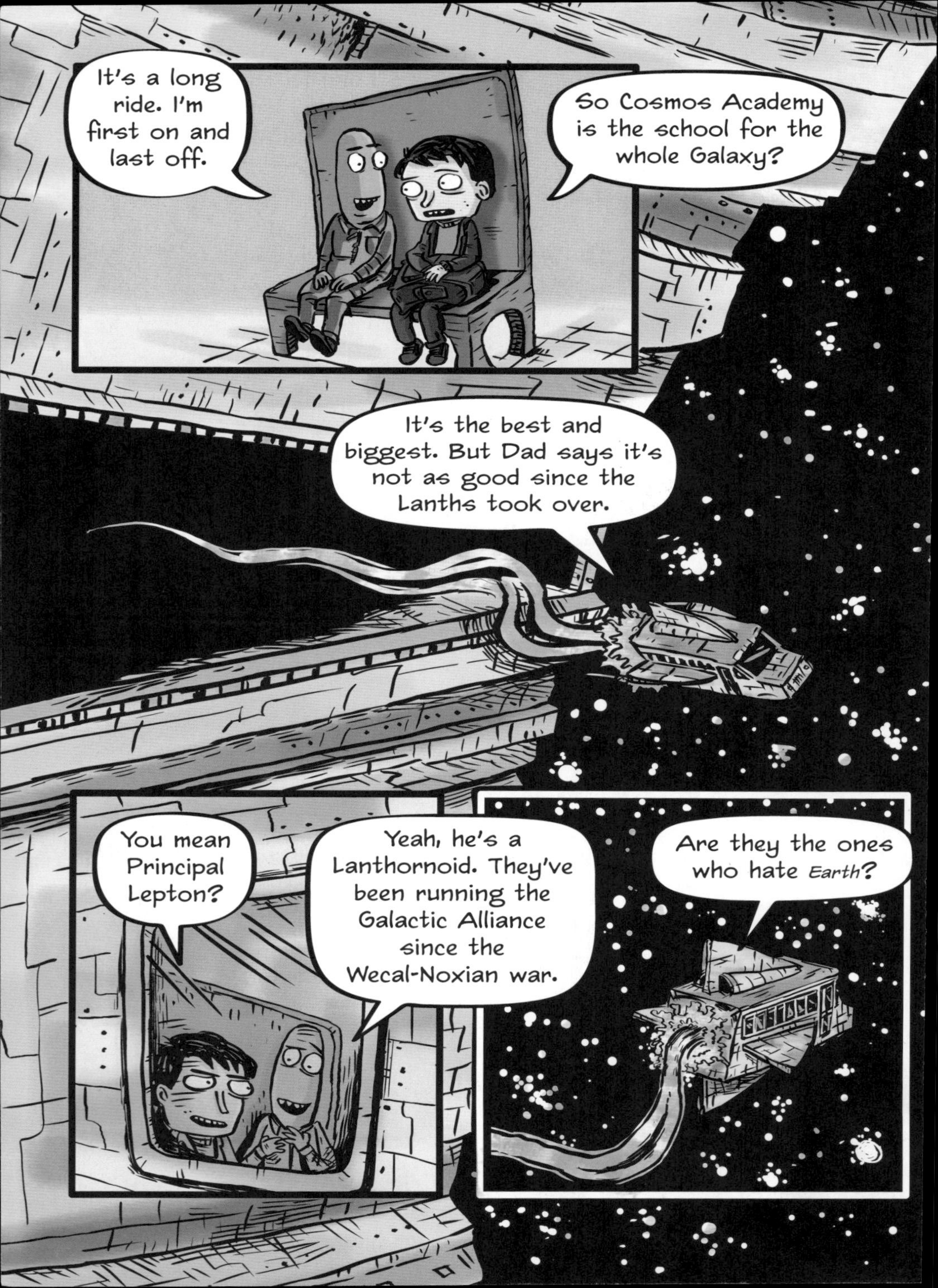
It's a long ride. I'm first on and last off.
So Cosmos Academy is the school for the whole Galaxy?
It's the best and biggest. But Dad says it's not as good since the Lanths took over.
You mean Principal Lepton?
Yeah, he's a Lanthornoid. They've been running the Galactic Alliance since the Wecal-Noxian war.
Are they the ones who hate *Earth*?

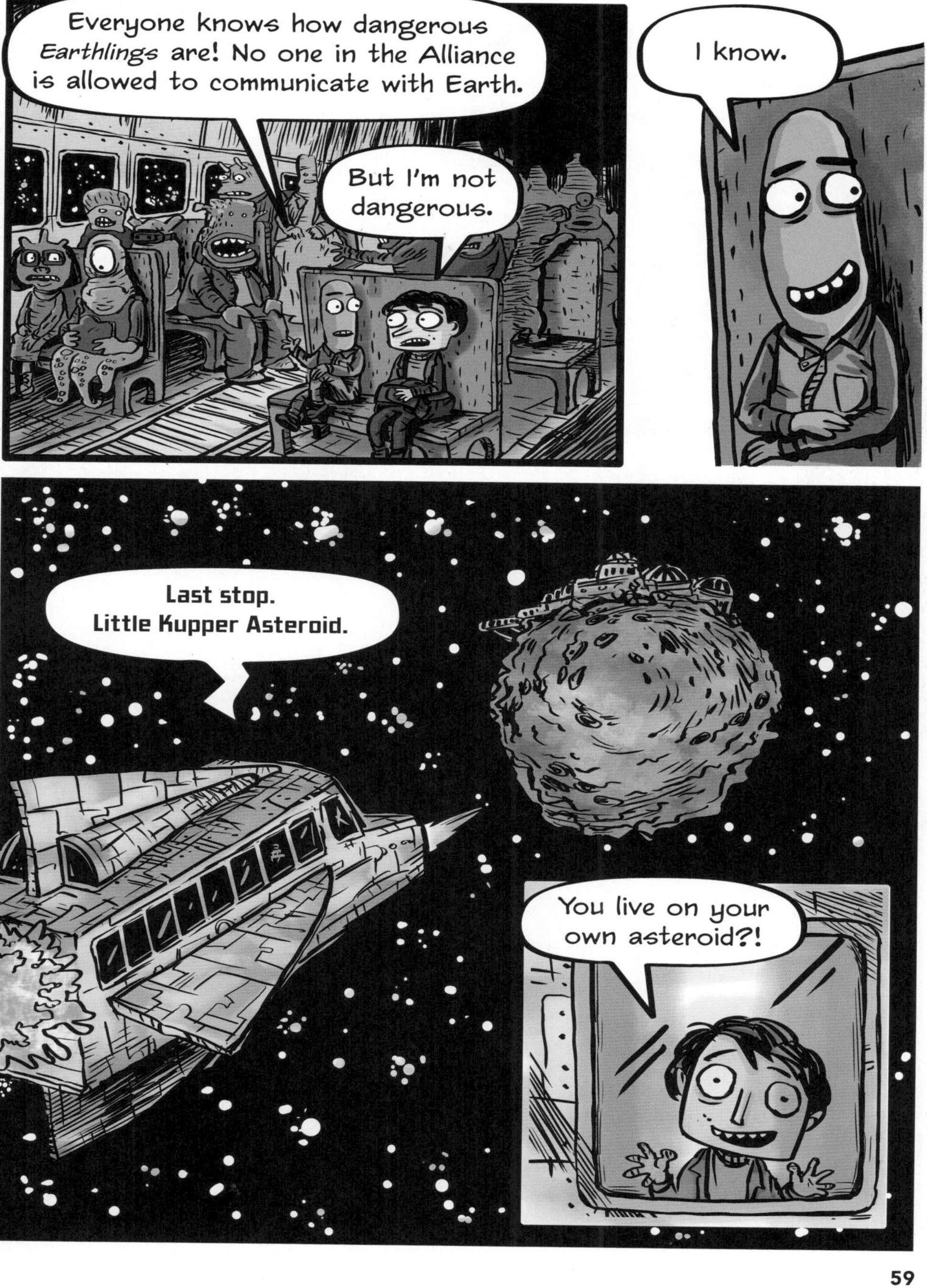
Everyone knows how dangerous *Earthlings* are! No one in the Alliance is allowed to communicate with Earth.
But I'm not dangerous.
I know.
Last stop. Little Kupper Asteroid.
You live on your own asteroid?!

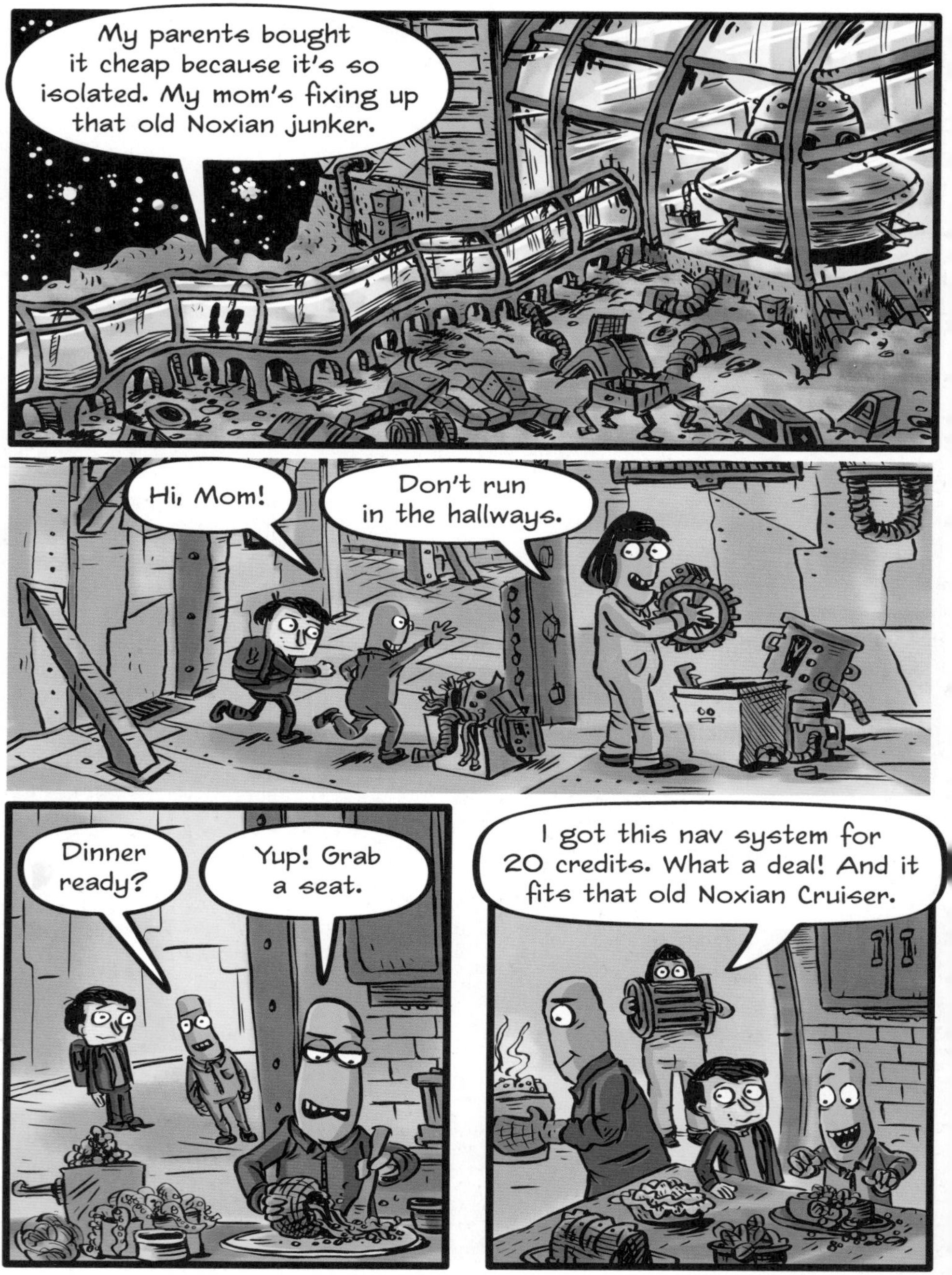
My parents bought it cheap because it's so isolated. My mom's fixing up that old Noxian junker.
Hi, Mom!
Don't run in the hallways.
Dinner ready?
Yup! Grab a seat.
I got this nav system for 20 credits. What a deal! And it fits that old Noxian Cruiser.

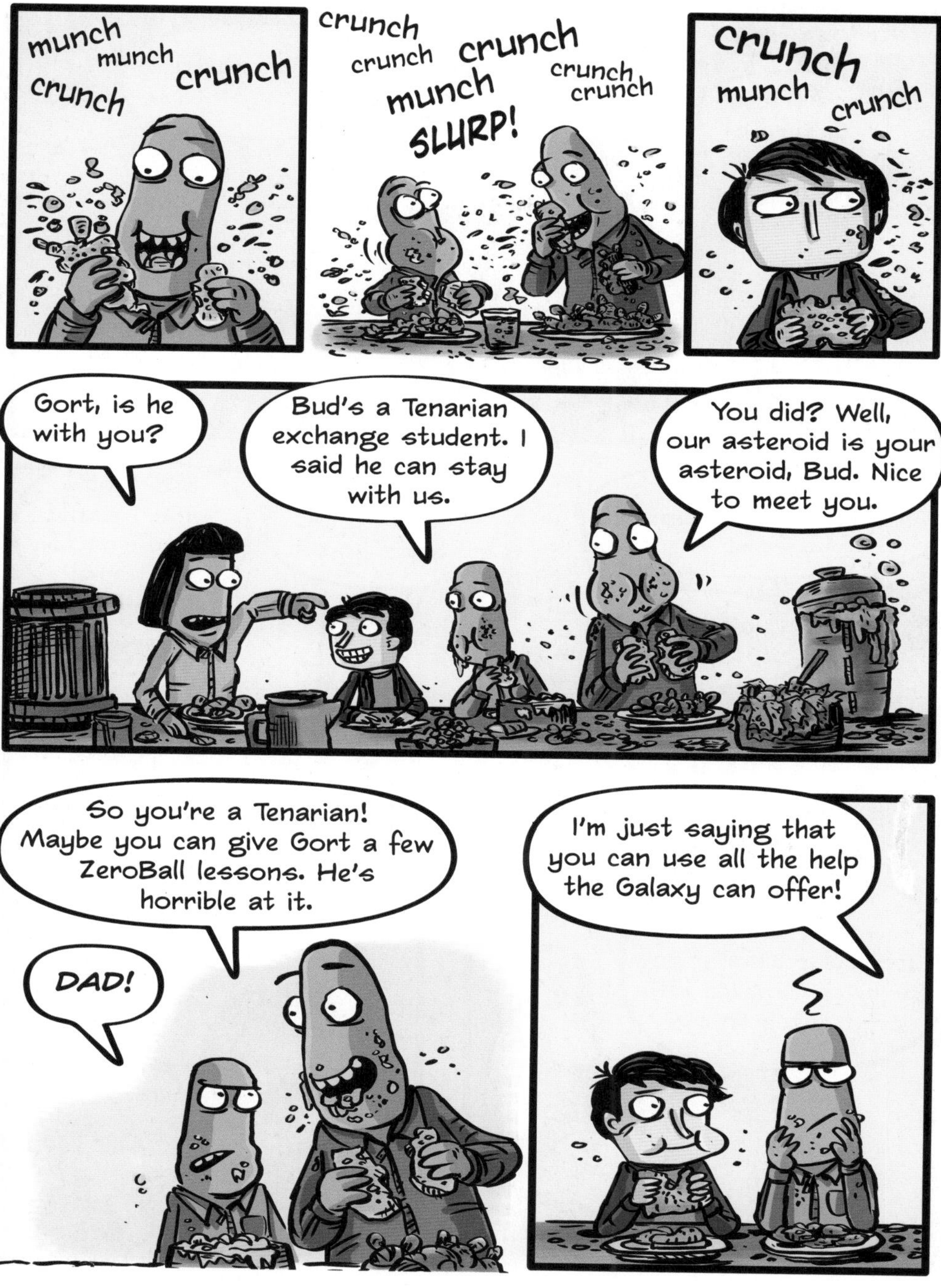
munch
munch
crunch
crunch
crunch
crunch
crunch
munch
SLURP!
crunch
crunch
crunch
munch
crunch
Gort, is he with you?
Bud's a Tenarian exchange student. I said he can stay with us.
You did? Well, our asteroid is your asteroid, Bud. Nice to meet you.
So you're a Tenarian! Maybe you can give Gort a few ZeroBall lessons. He's horrible at it.
DAD!
I'm just saying that you can use all the help the Galaxy can offer!

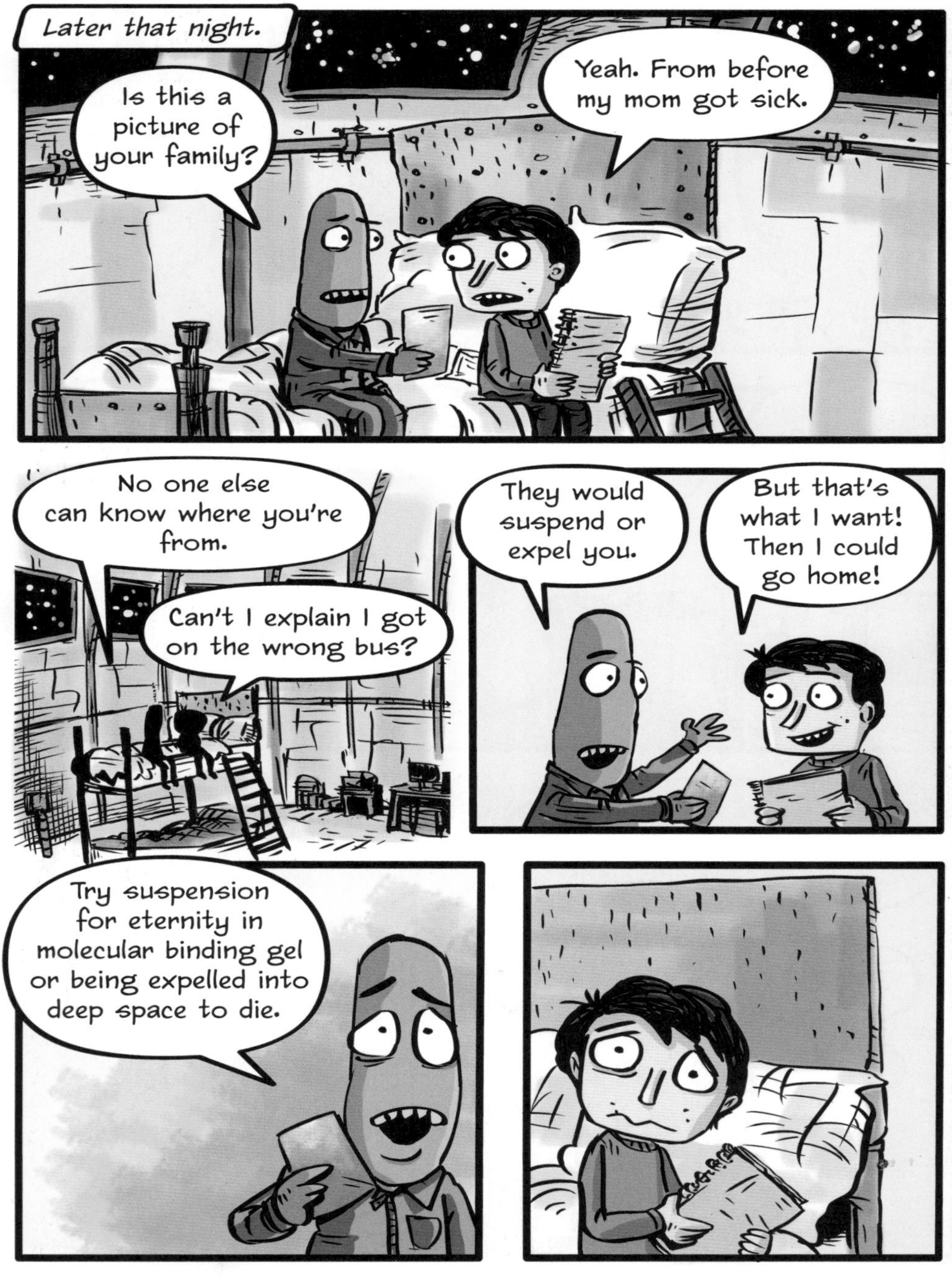
Later that night.
Is this a picture of your family?
Yeah. From before my mom got sick.
No one else can know where you're from.
Can't I explain I got on the wrong bus?
They would suspend or expel you.
But that's what I want! Then I could go home!
Try suspension for eternity in molecular binding gel or being expelled into deep space to die.

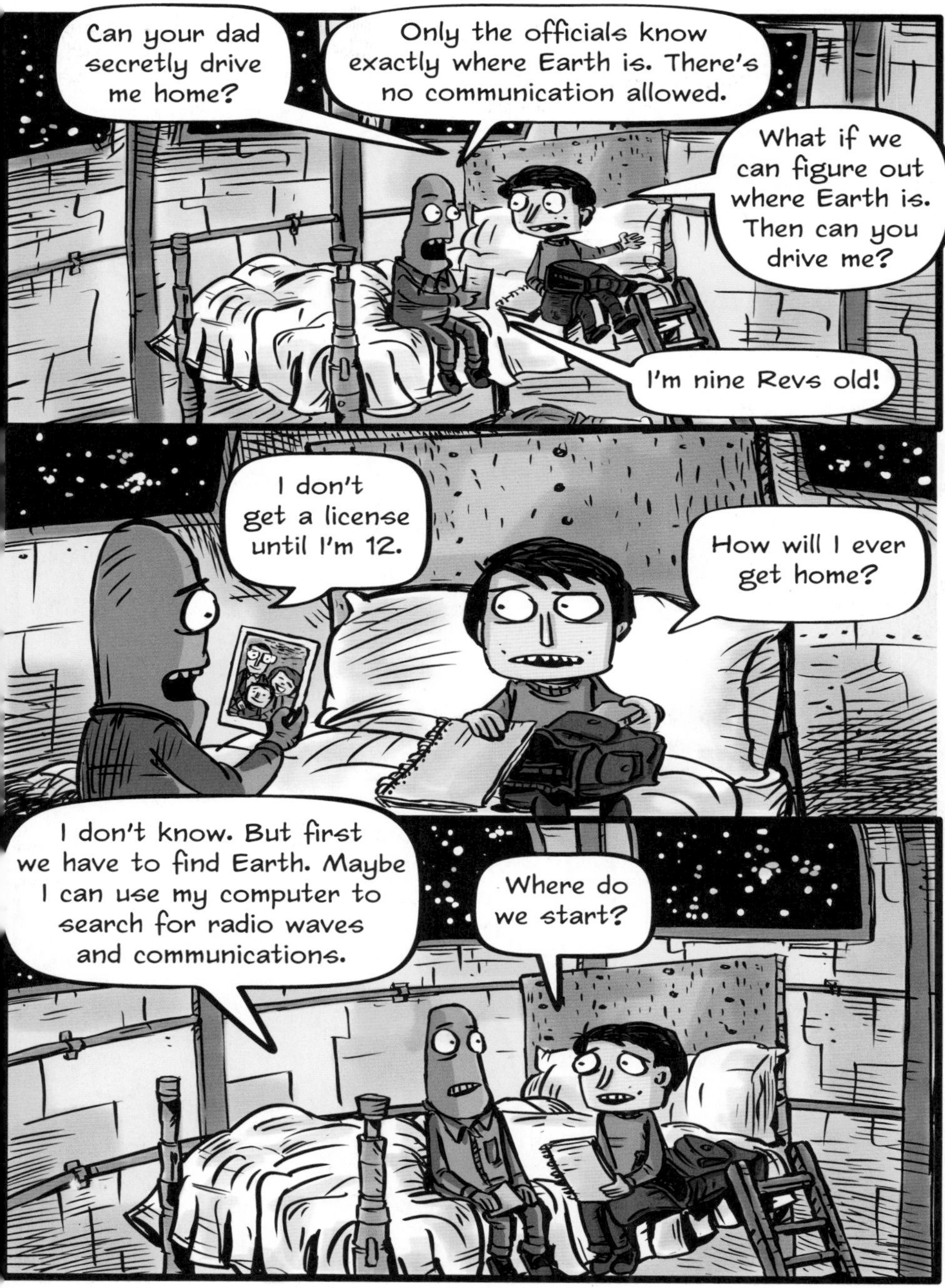
Can your dad secretly drive me home?
Only the officials know exactly where Earth is. There's no communication allowed.
What if we can figure out where Earth is. Then can you drive me?
I'm nine Revs old!
I don't get a license until I'm 12.
How will I ever get home?
I don't know. But first we have to find Earth. Maybe I can use my computer to search for radio waves and communications.
Where do we start?

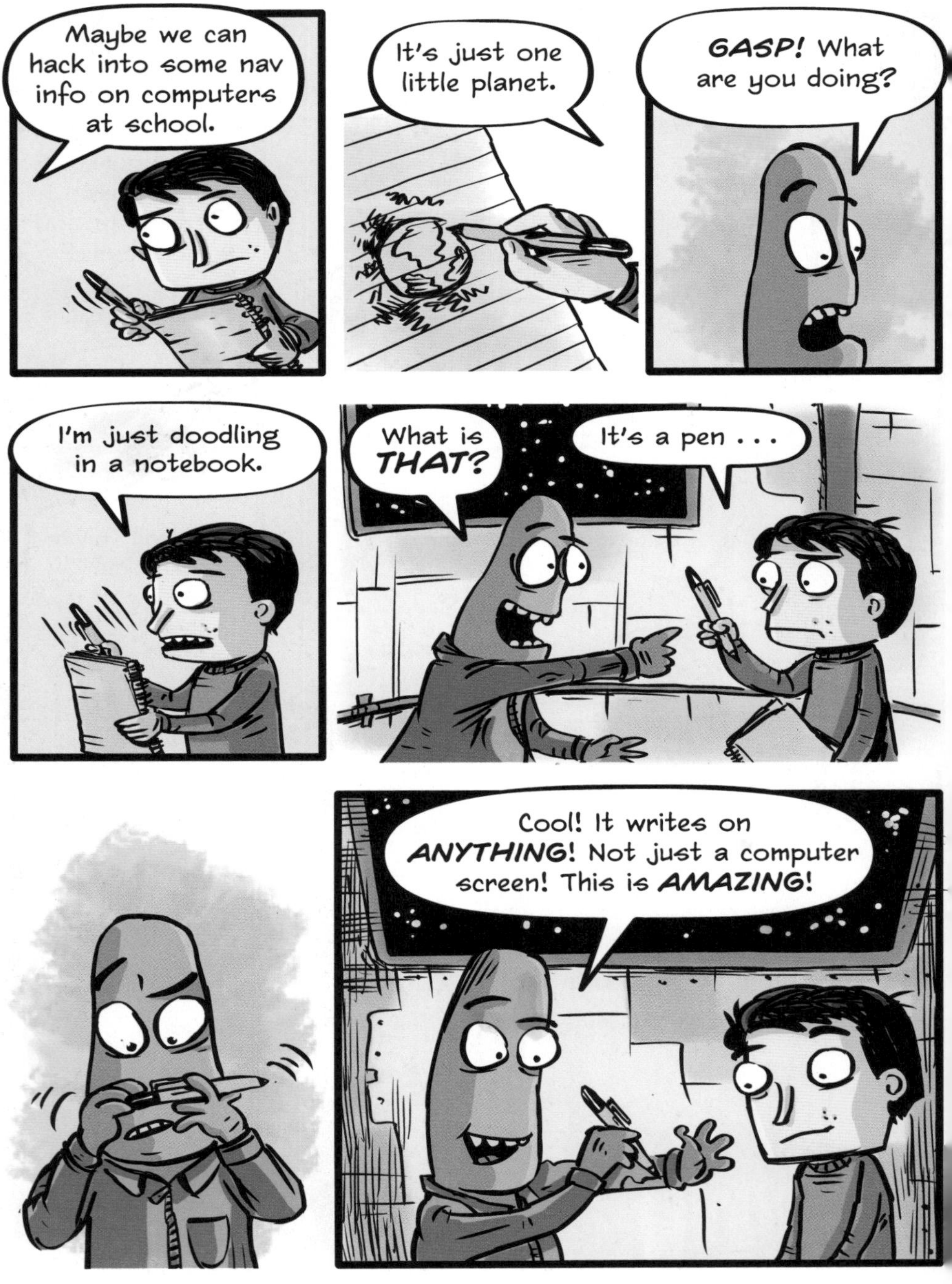
Maybe we can hack into some nav info on computers at school.
It's just one little planet.
GASP! What are you doing?
I'm just doodling in a notebook.
What is THAT?
It's a pen . . .
Cool! It writes on ANYTHING! Not just a computer screen! This is AMAZING!

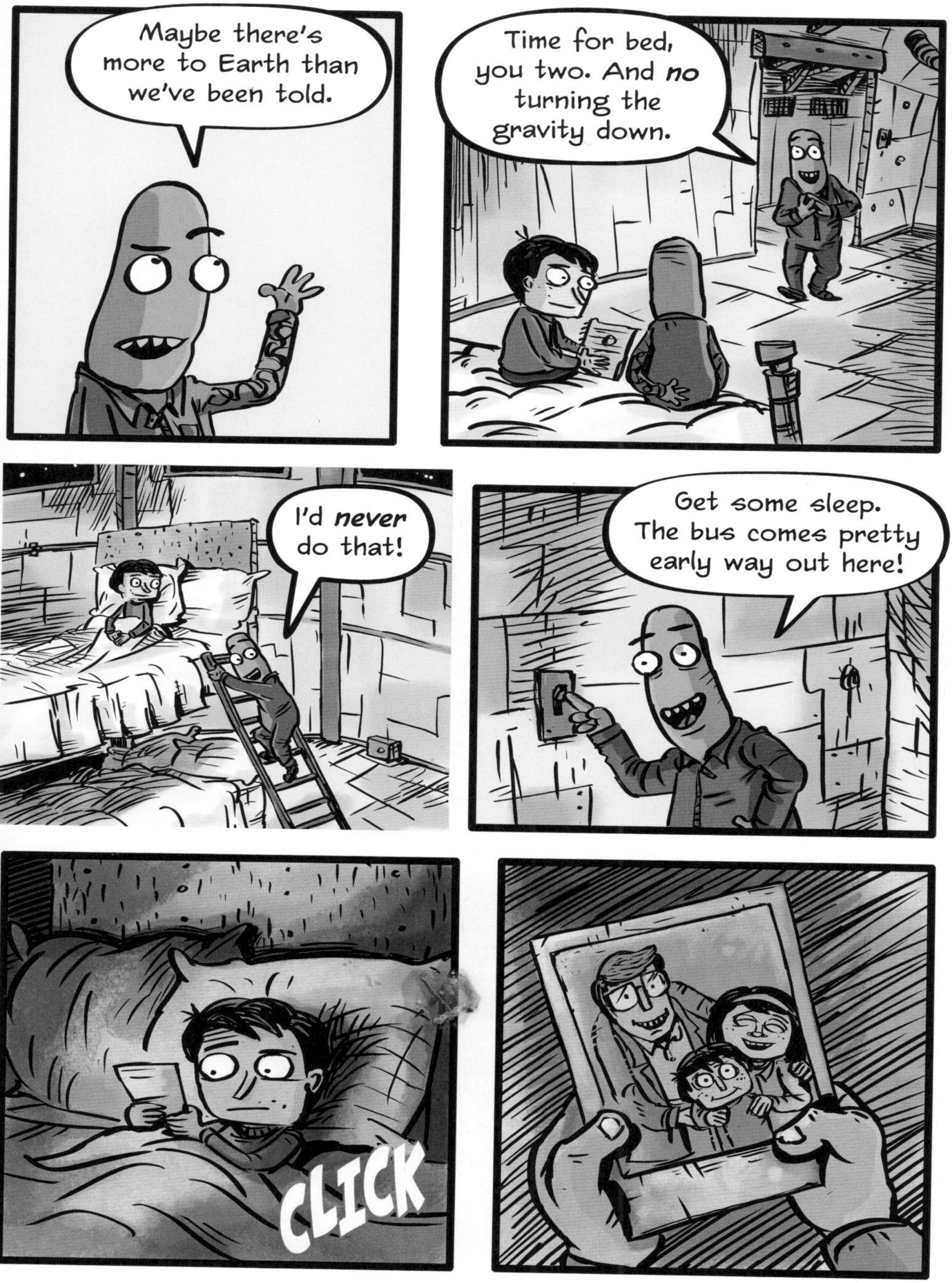
Maybe there's more to Earth than we've been told.
Time for bed, you two. And **no** turning the gravity down.
I'd **never** do that!
Get some sleep. The bus comes pretty early way out here!
CLICK

CHAPTER 3

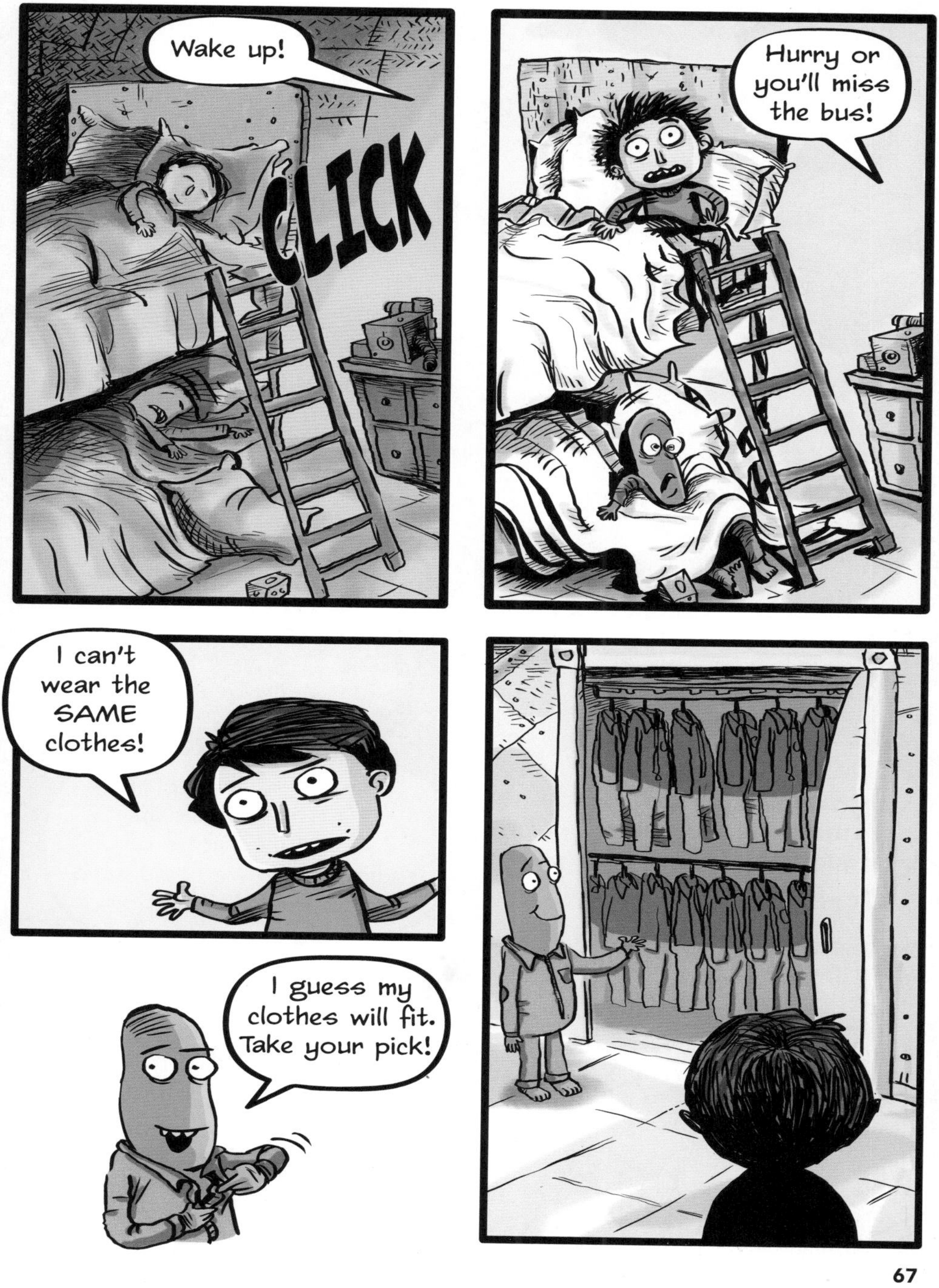
Wake up!
CLICK
Hurry or you'll miss the bus!
I can't wear the SAME clothes!
I guess my clothes will fit. Take your pick!

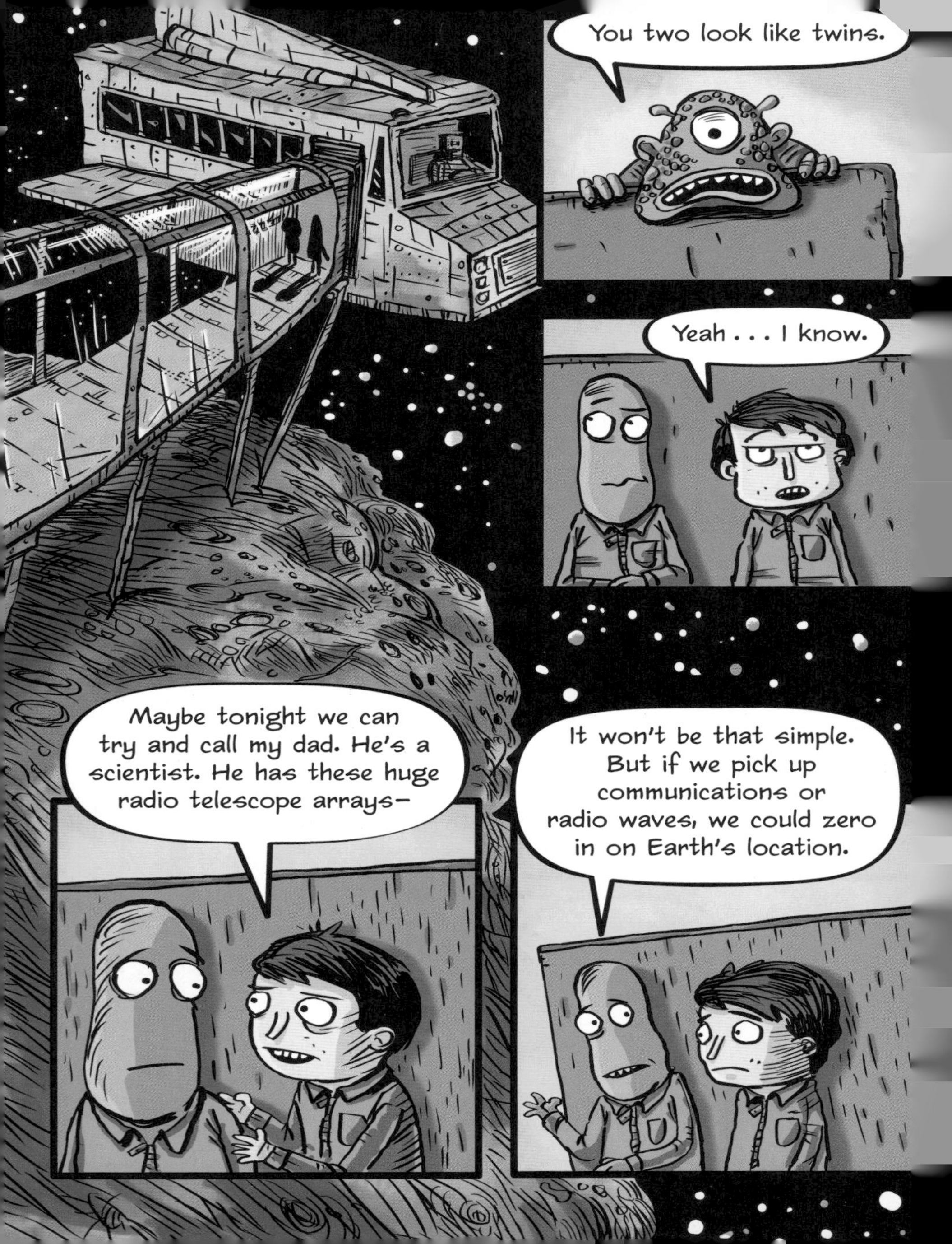
You two look like twins.
Yeah . . . I know.
Maybe tonight we can try and call my dad. He's a scientist. He has these huge radio telescope arrays—
It won't be that simple. But if we pick up communications or radio waves, we could zero in on Earth's location.

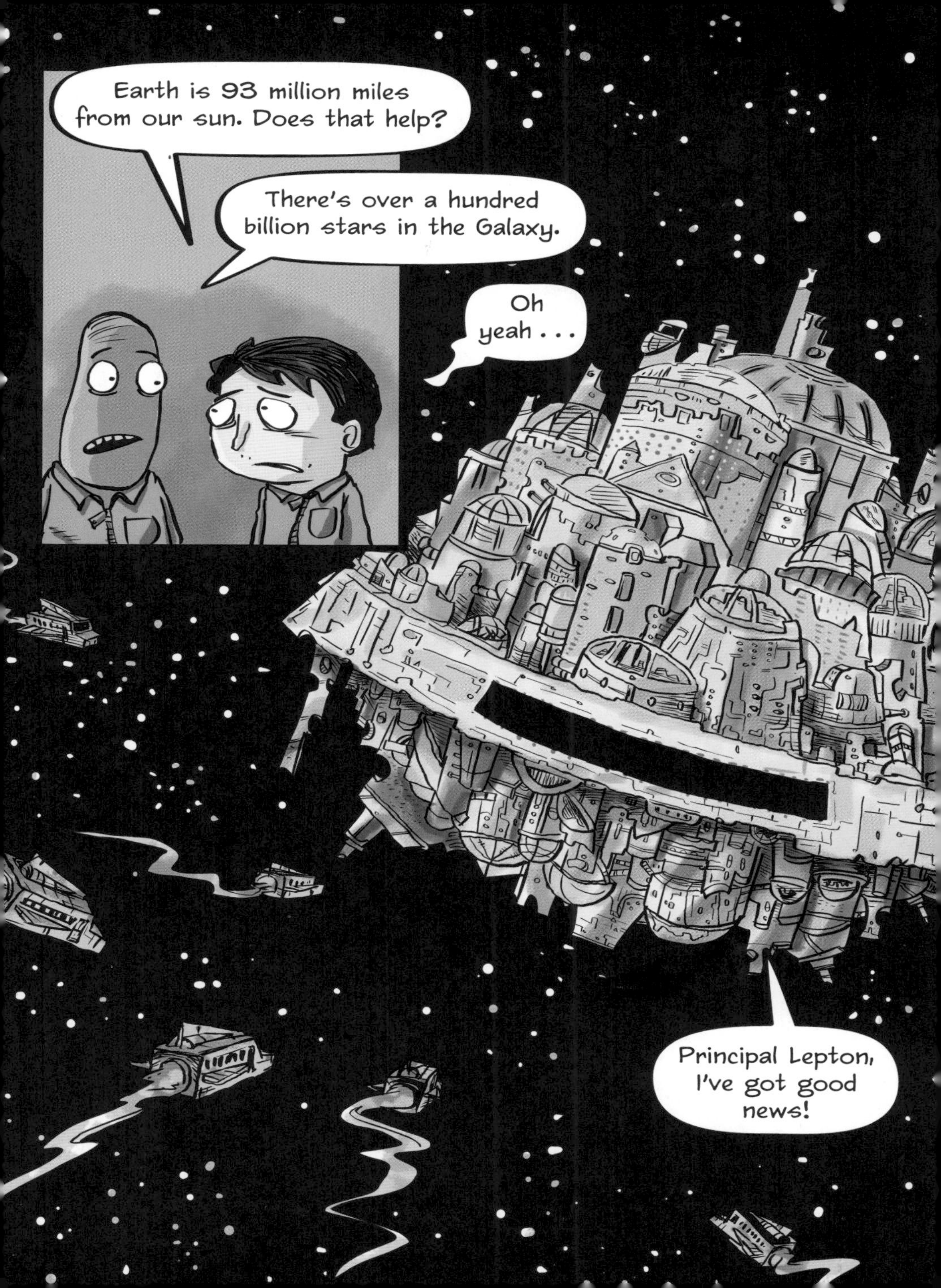

Earth is 93 million miles from our sun. Does that help?
There's over a hundred billion stars in the Galaxy.
Oh yeah . . .
Principal Lepton, I've got good news!

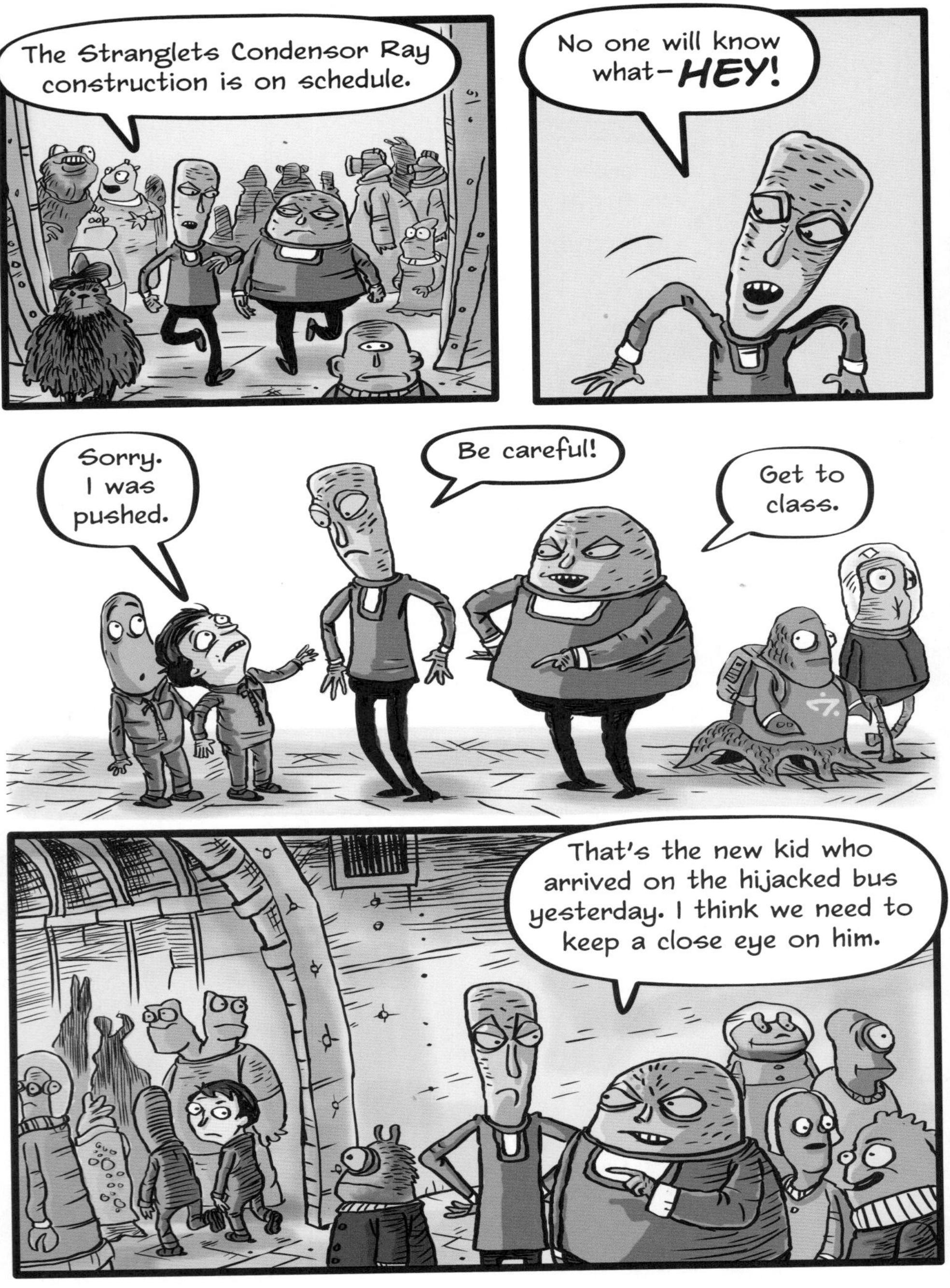
The Stranglets Condensor Ray construction is on schedule.
No one will know what–HEY!
Sorry. I was pushed.
Be careful!
Get to class.
That's the new kid who arrived on the hijacked bus yesterday. I think we need to keep a close eye on him.

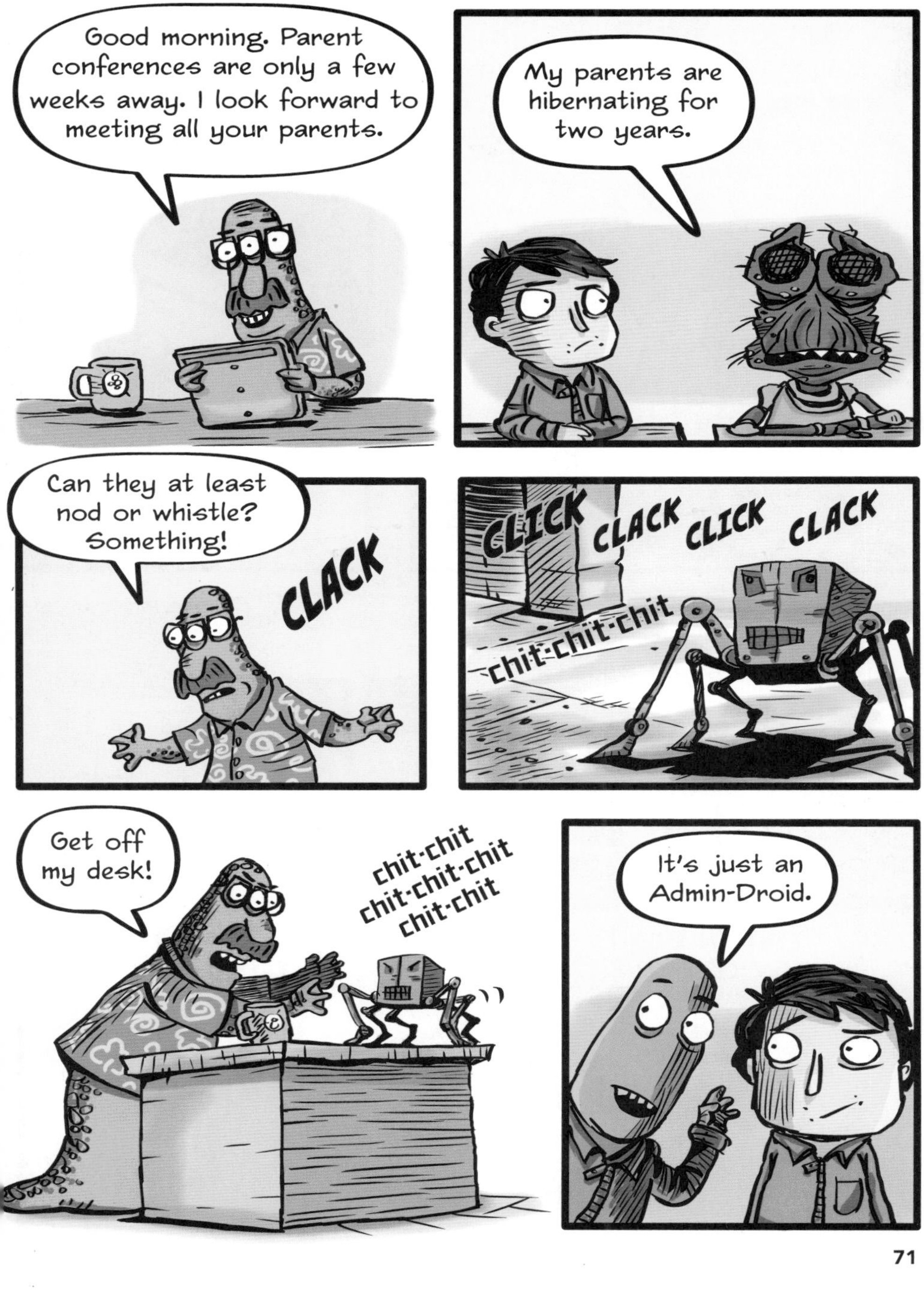
Good morning. Parent conferences are only a few weeks away. I look forward to meeting all your parents.
My parents are hibernating for two years.
Can they at least nod or whistle? Something!
CLACK
CLICK
CLACK
CLICK
CLACK
chit·chit·chit·chit
Get off my desk!
chit·chit
chit·chit·chit
chit·chit·chit
chit·chit
It's just an Admin-Droid.

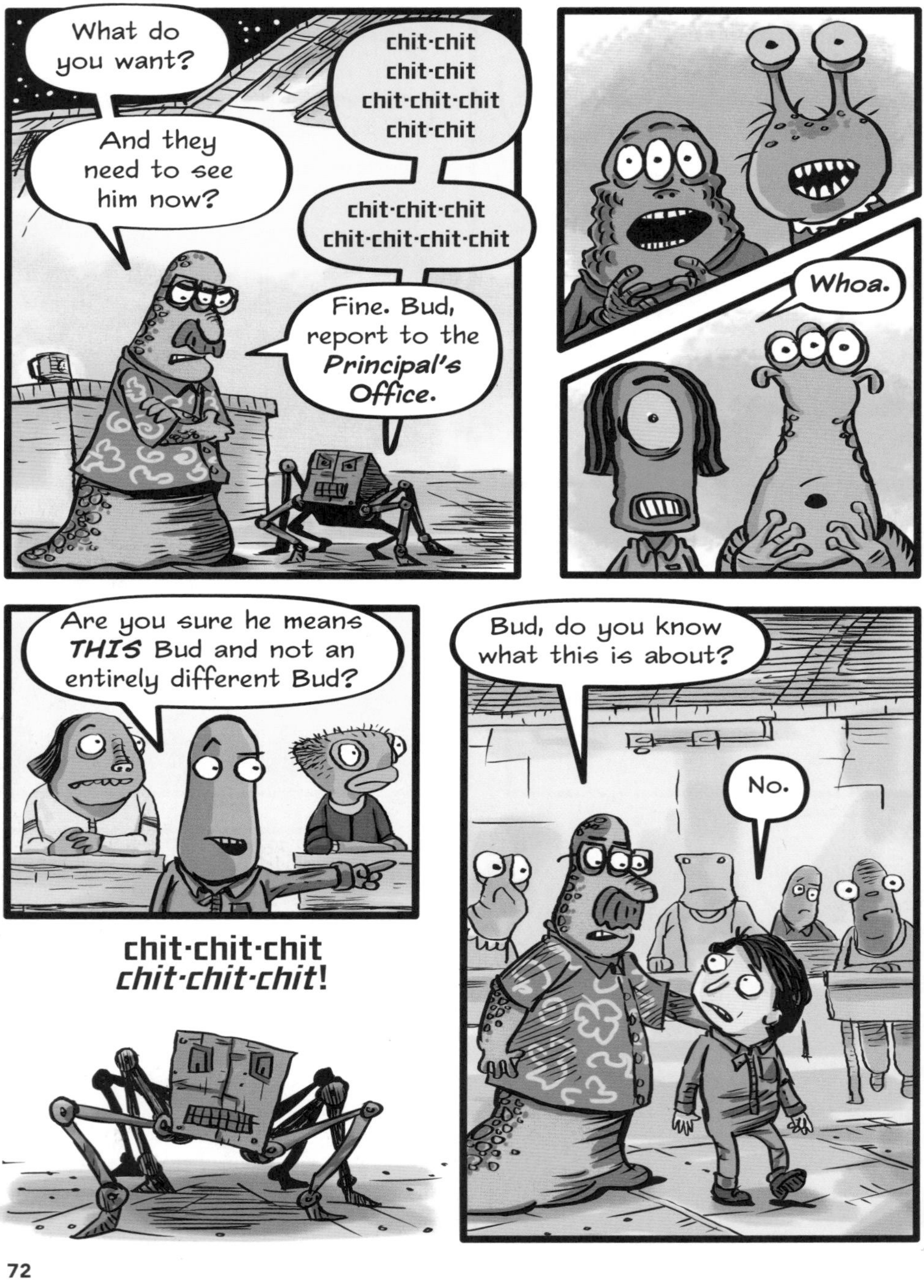
What do you want?
chit·chit chit·chit chit·chit·chit chit·chit
And they need to see him now?
chit·chit·chit chit·chit·chit·chit
Fine. Bud, report to the *Principal's Office.*
Whoa.
Are you sure he means *THIS* Bud and not an entirely different Bud?
chit·chit·chit *chit·chit·chit*!
Bud, do you know what this is about?
No.

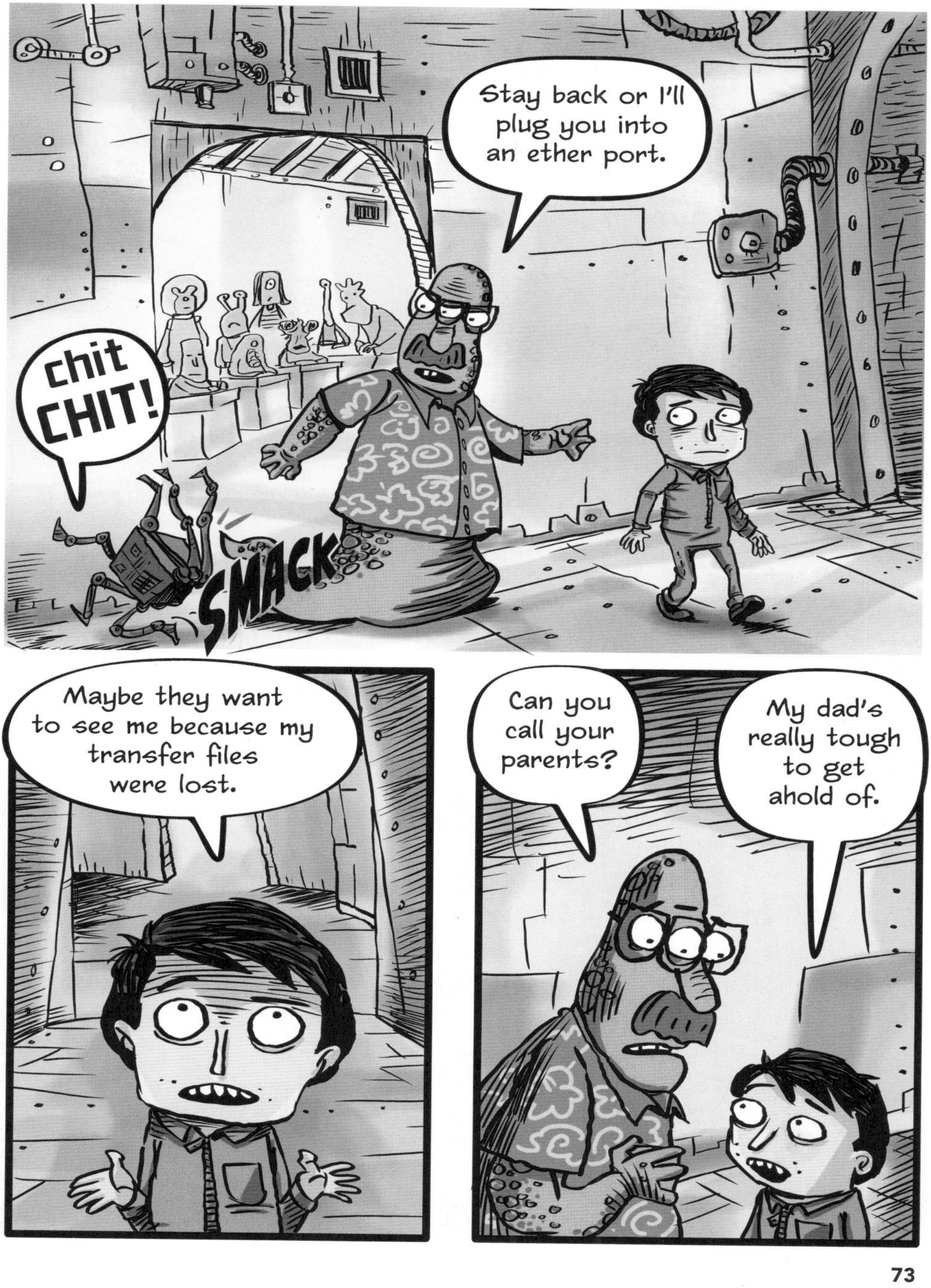
Stay back or I'll plug you into an ether port.
chit CHIT!
SMACK
Maybe they want to see me because my transfer files were lost.
Can you call your parents?
My dad's really tough to get ahold of.

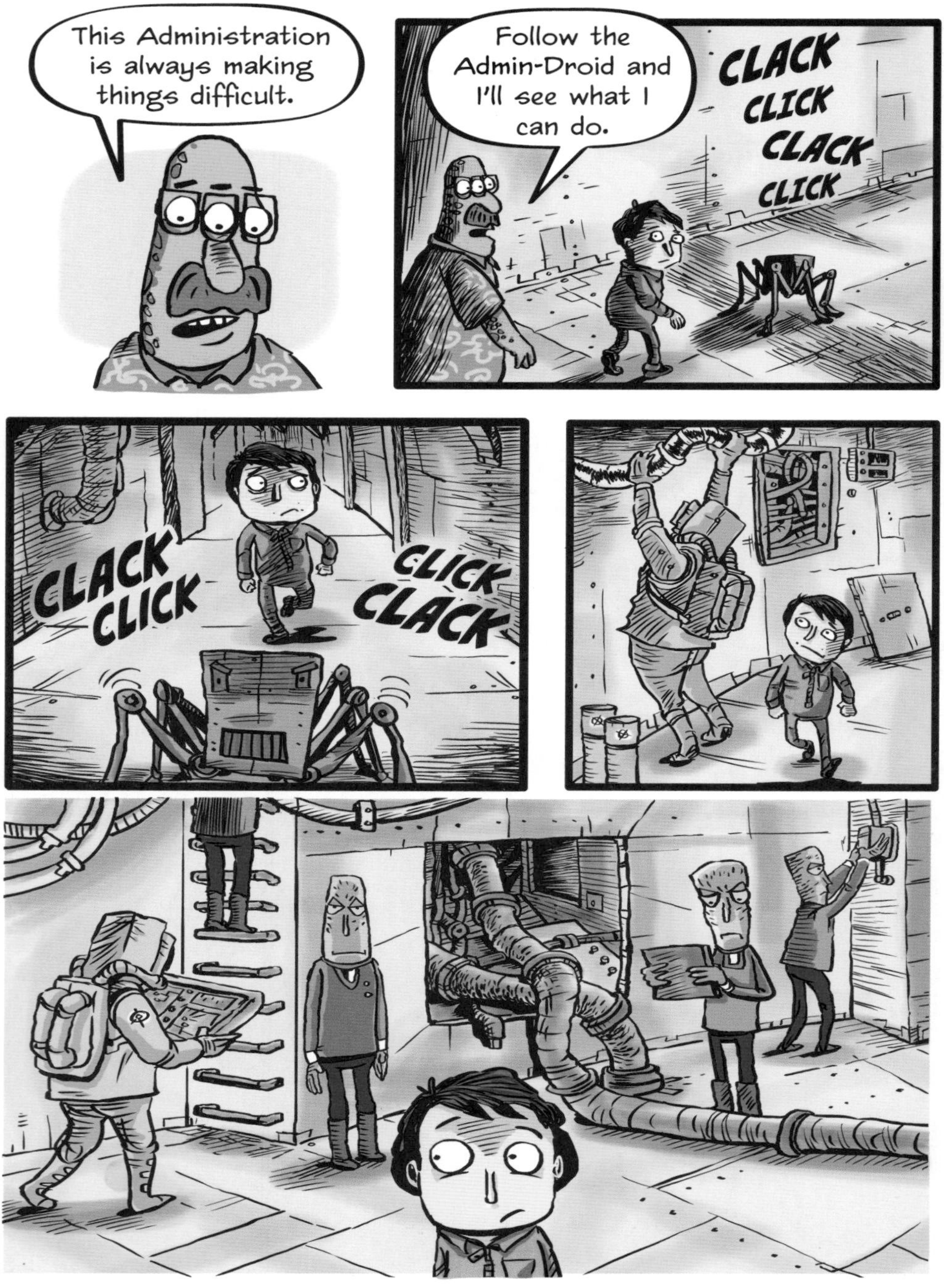

This Administration is always making things difficult.
Follow the Admin-Droid and I'll see what I can do.
CLACK CLICK CLACK CLICK
CLACK CLICK
CLICK CLACK

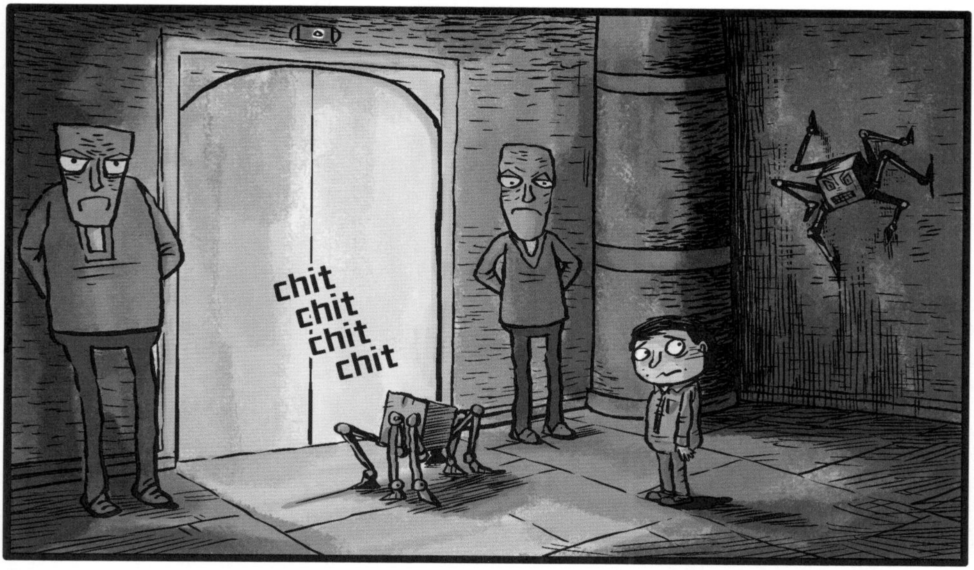
chit
chit
chit
chit

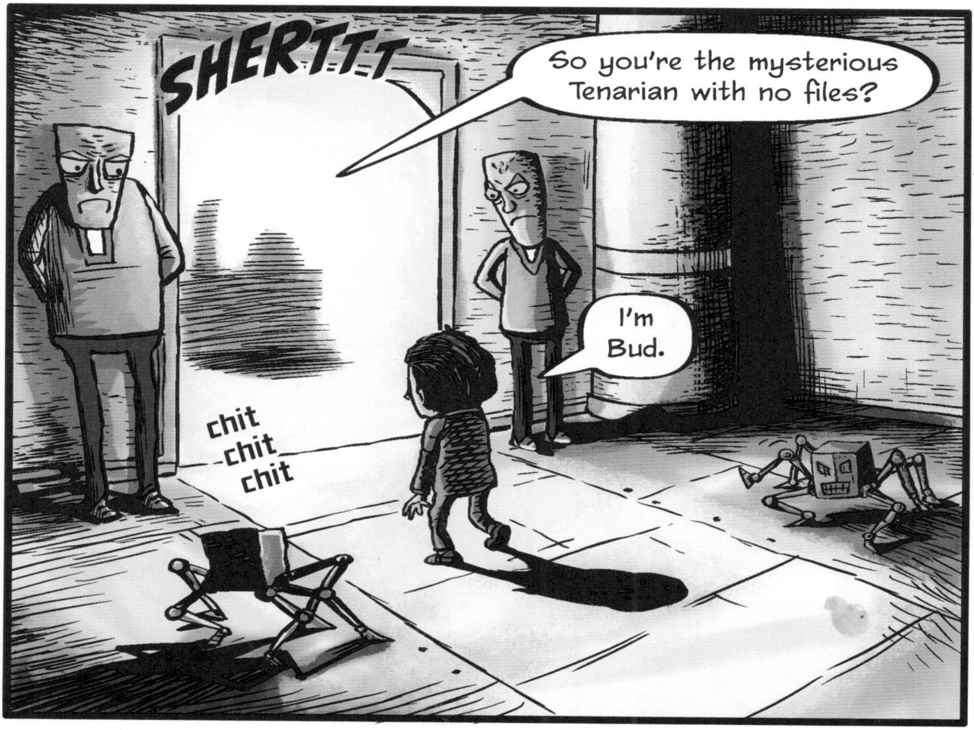
SHERTTT
So you're the mysterious Tenarian with no files?
I'm Bud.
chit
chit
chit

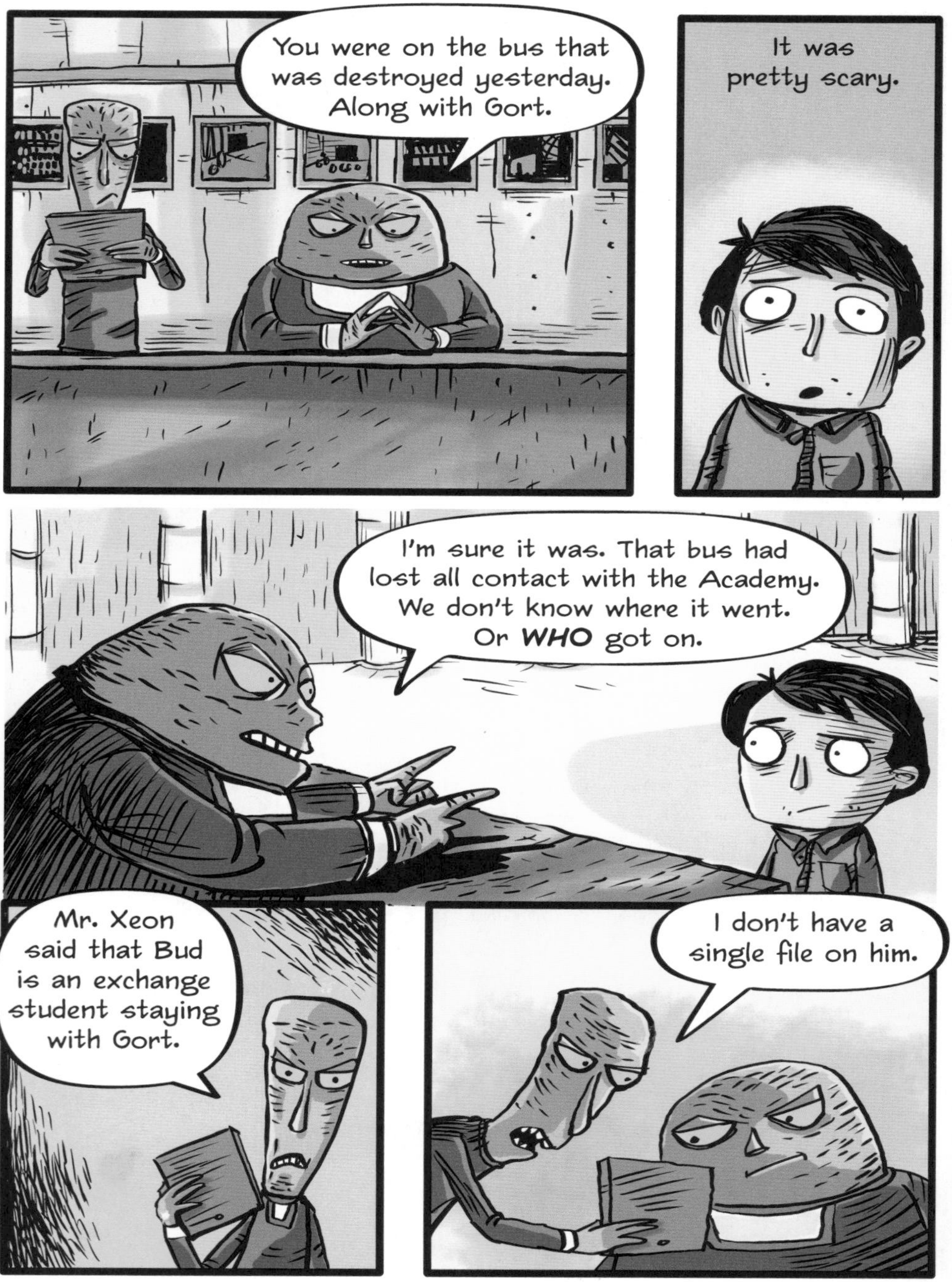
You were on the bus that was destroyed yesterday. Along with Gort.
It was pretty scary.
I'm sure it was. That bus had lost all contact with the Academy. We don't know where it went. Or **WHO** got on.
Mr. Xeon said that Bud is an exchange student staying with Gort.
I don't have a single file on him.

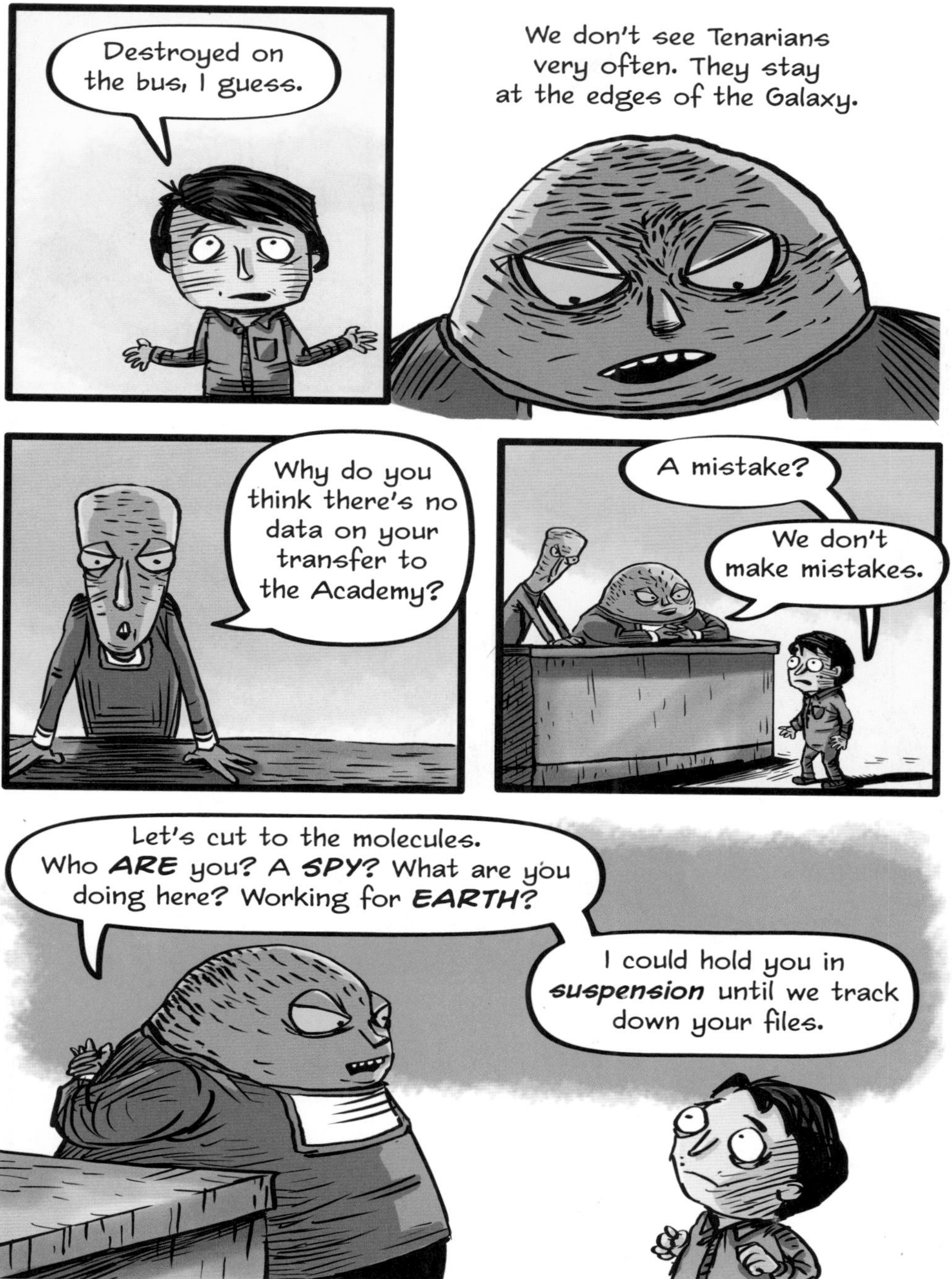
Destroyed on the bus, I guess.
We don't see Tenarians very often. They stay at the edges of the Galaxy.
Why do you think there's no data on your transfer to the Academy?
A mistake?
We don't make mistakes.
Let's cut to the molecules. Who ARE you? A SPY? What are you doing here? Working for EARTH?
I could hold you in suspension until we track down your files.

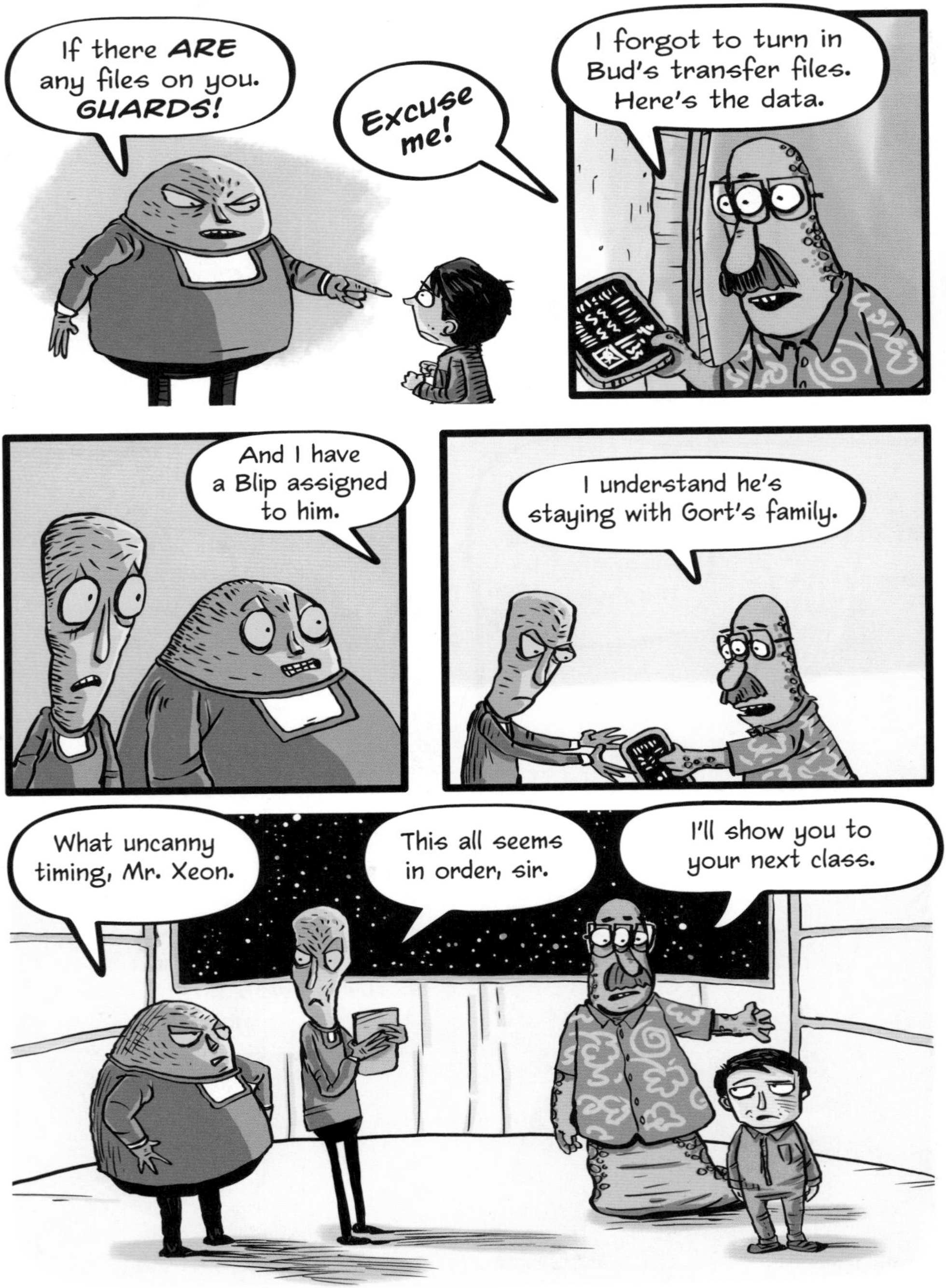
If there ARE any files on you. GUARDS!
Excuse me!
I forgot to turn in Bud's transfer files. Here's the data.
And I have a Blip assigned to him.
I understand he's staying with Gort's family.
What uncanny timing, Mr. Xeon.
This all seems in order, sir.
I'll show you to your next class.

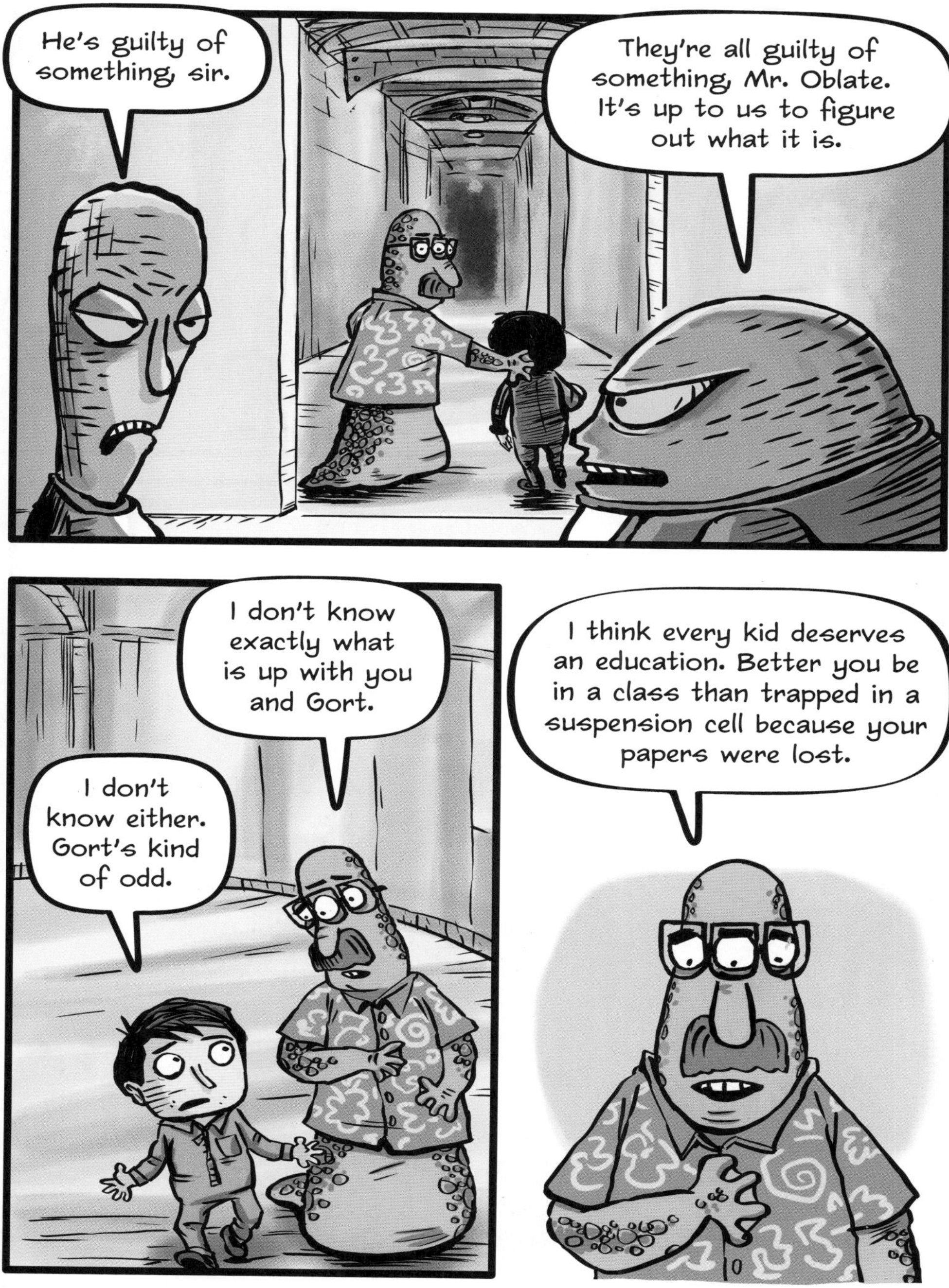
He's guilty of something, sir.
They're all guilty of something, Mr. Oblate. It's up to us to figure out what it is.
I don't know exactly what is up with you and Gort.
I don't know either. Gort's kind of odd.
I think every kid deserves an education. Better you be in a class than trapped in a suspension cell because your papers were lost.

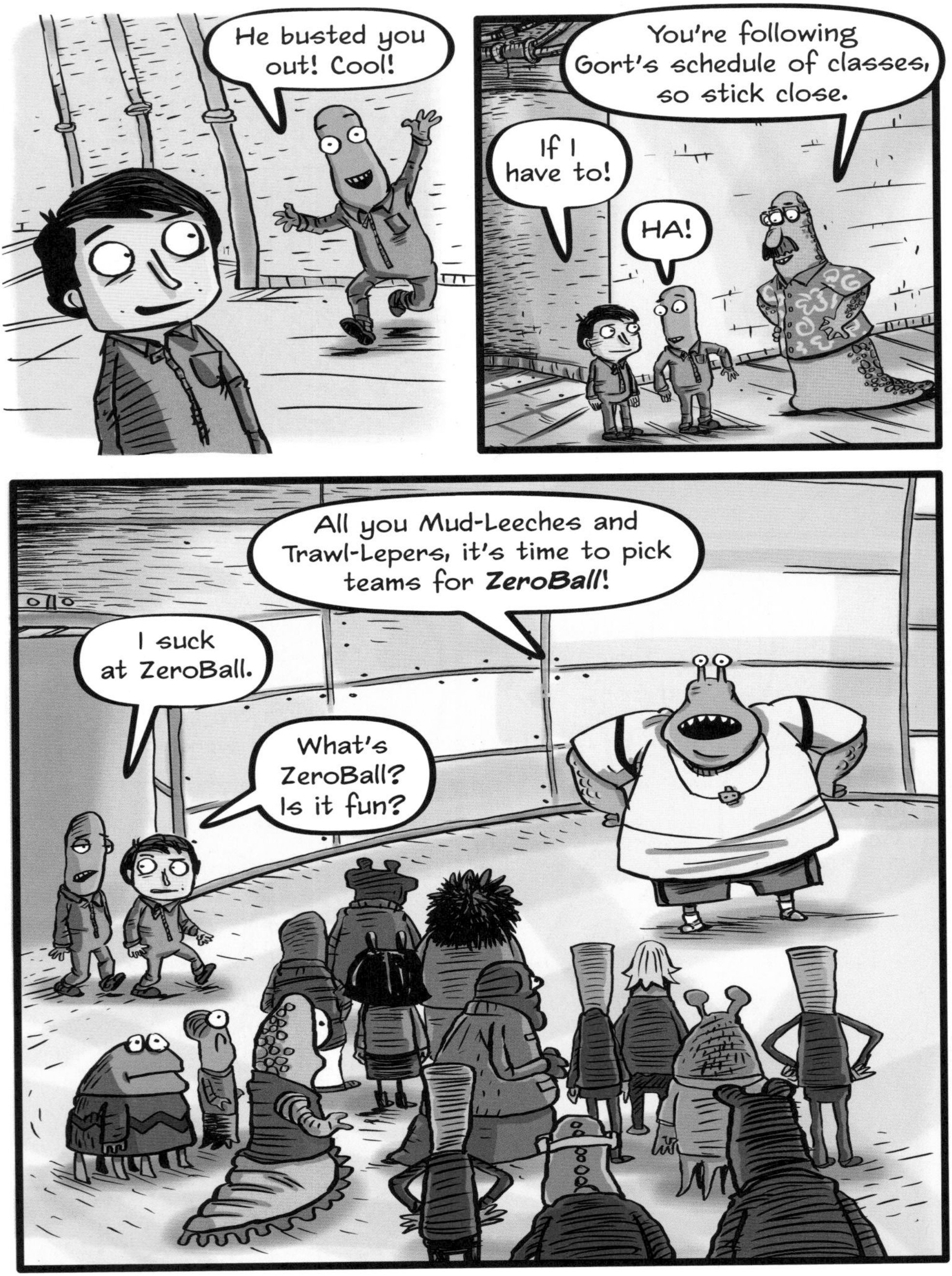
He busted you out! Cool!
You're following Gort's schedule of classes, so stick close.
If I have to!
HA!
All you Mud-Leeches and Trawl-Lepers, it's time to pick teams for **ZeroBall**!
I suck at ZeroBall.
What's ZeroBall? Is it fun?

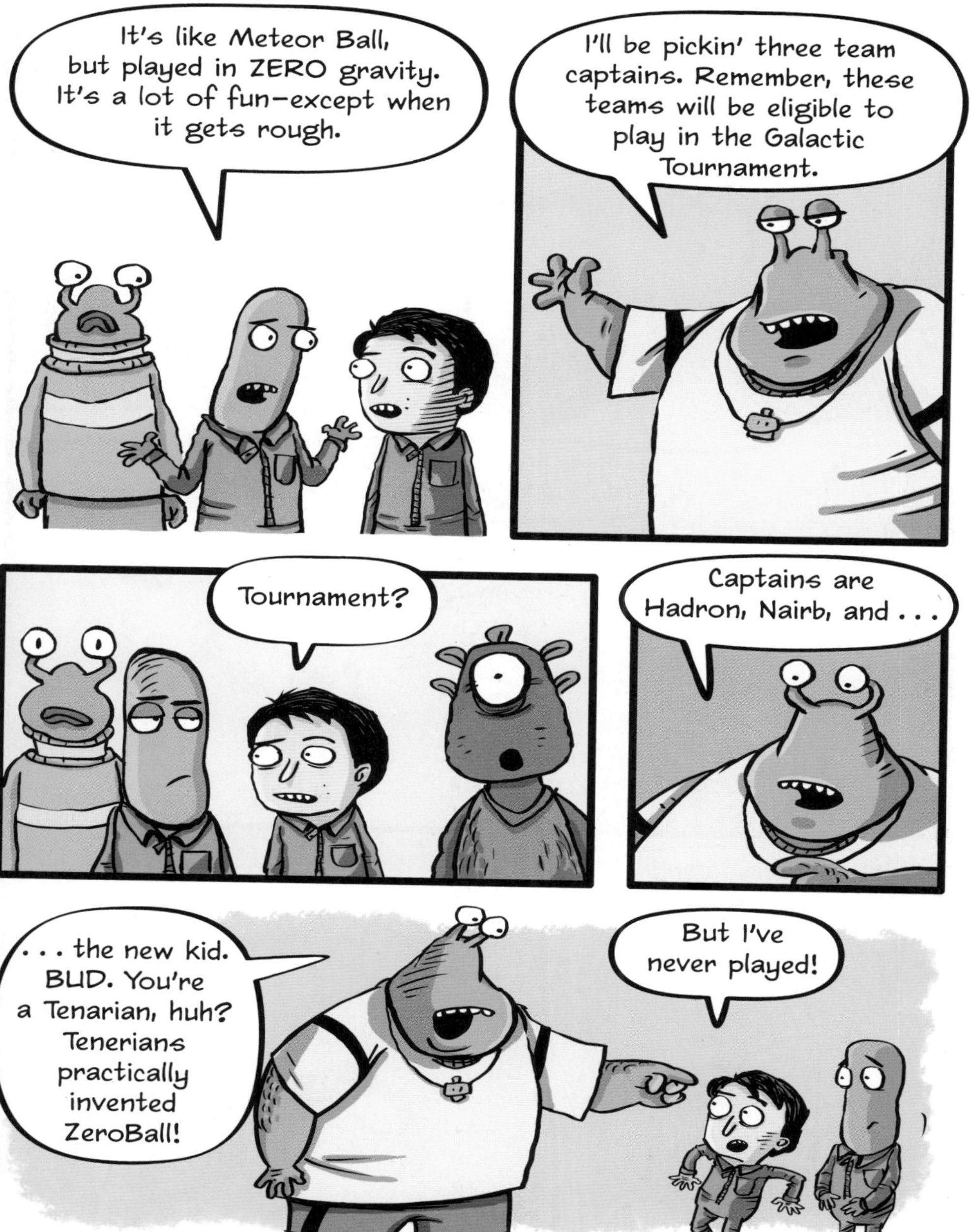
It's like Meteor Ball, but played in ZERO gravity. It's a lot of fun—except when it gets rough.
I'll be pickin' three team captains. Remember, these teams will be eligible to play in the Galactic Tournament.
Tournament?
Captains are Hadron, Nairb, and . . .
. . . the new kid. BUD. You're a Tenarian, huh? Tenerians practically invented ZeroBall!
But I've never played!

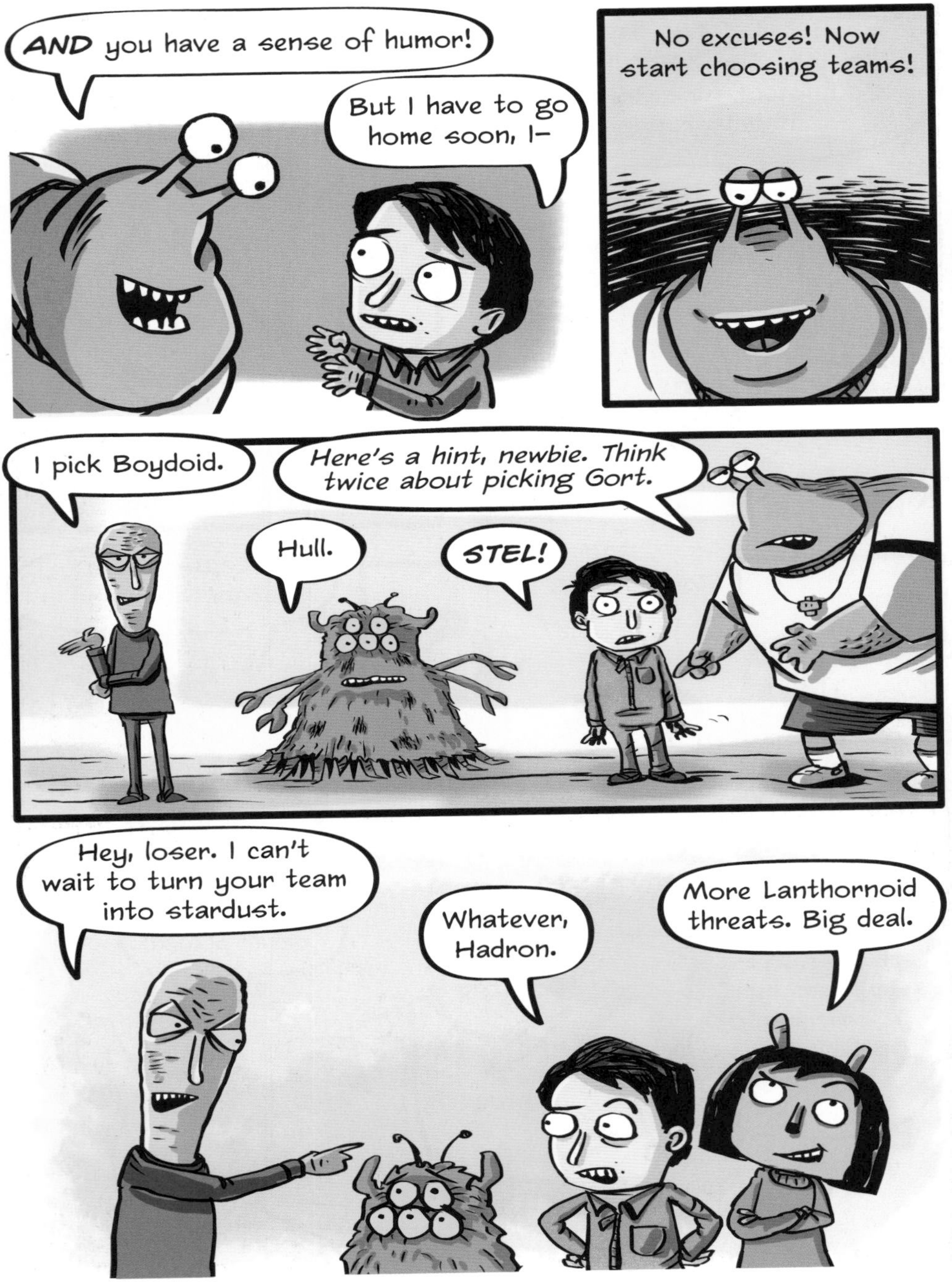

AND you have a sense of humor!
But I have to go home soon, I–
No excuses! Now start choosing teams!
I pick Boydoid.
Here's a hint, newbie. Think twice about picking Gort.
Hull.
STEL!
Hey, loser. I can't wait to turn your team into stardust.
Whatever, Hadron.
More Lanthornoid threats. Big deal.

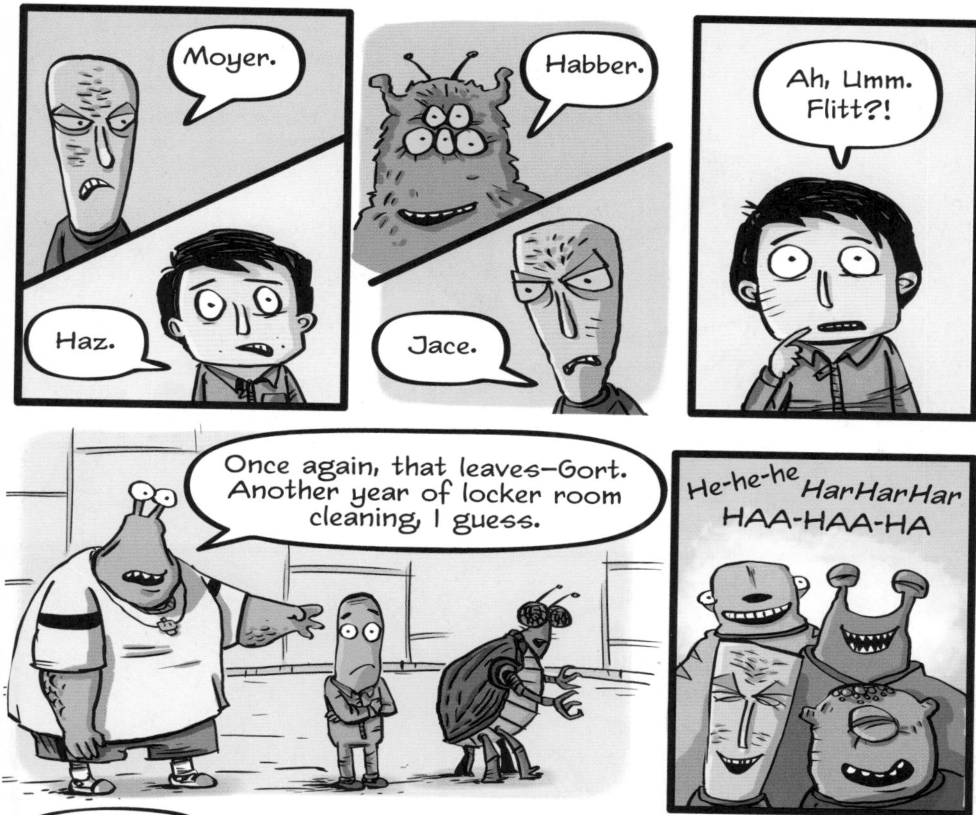
Moyer.
Haz.
Habber.
Jace.
Ah, Umm. Flitt?!
Once again, that leaves—Gort. Another year of locker room cleaning, I guess.
He-he-he HarHarHar HAA-HAA-HA
Thanks for picking me!
You said you *sucked* at ZeroBall.
Well, I do! But I thought we were *friends.*
Mr. Trusk, I think Flitt's pupating!

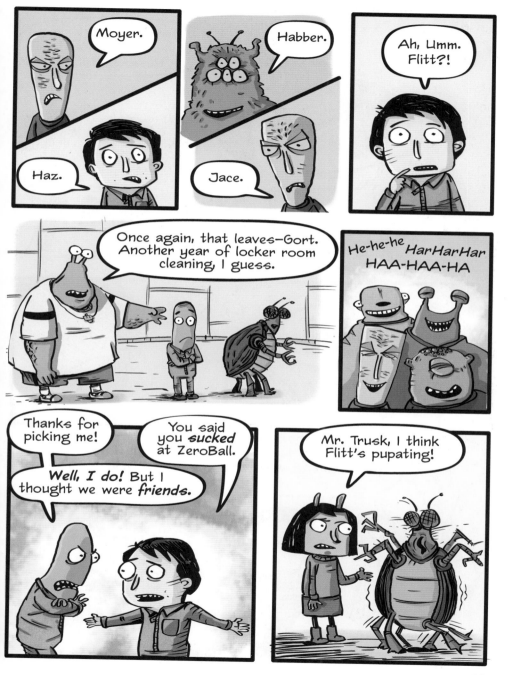

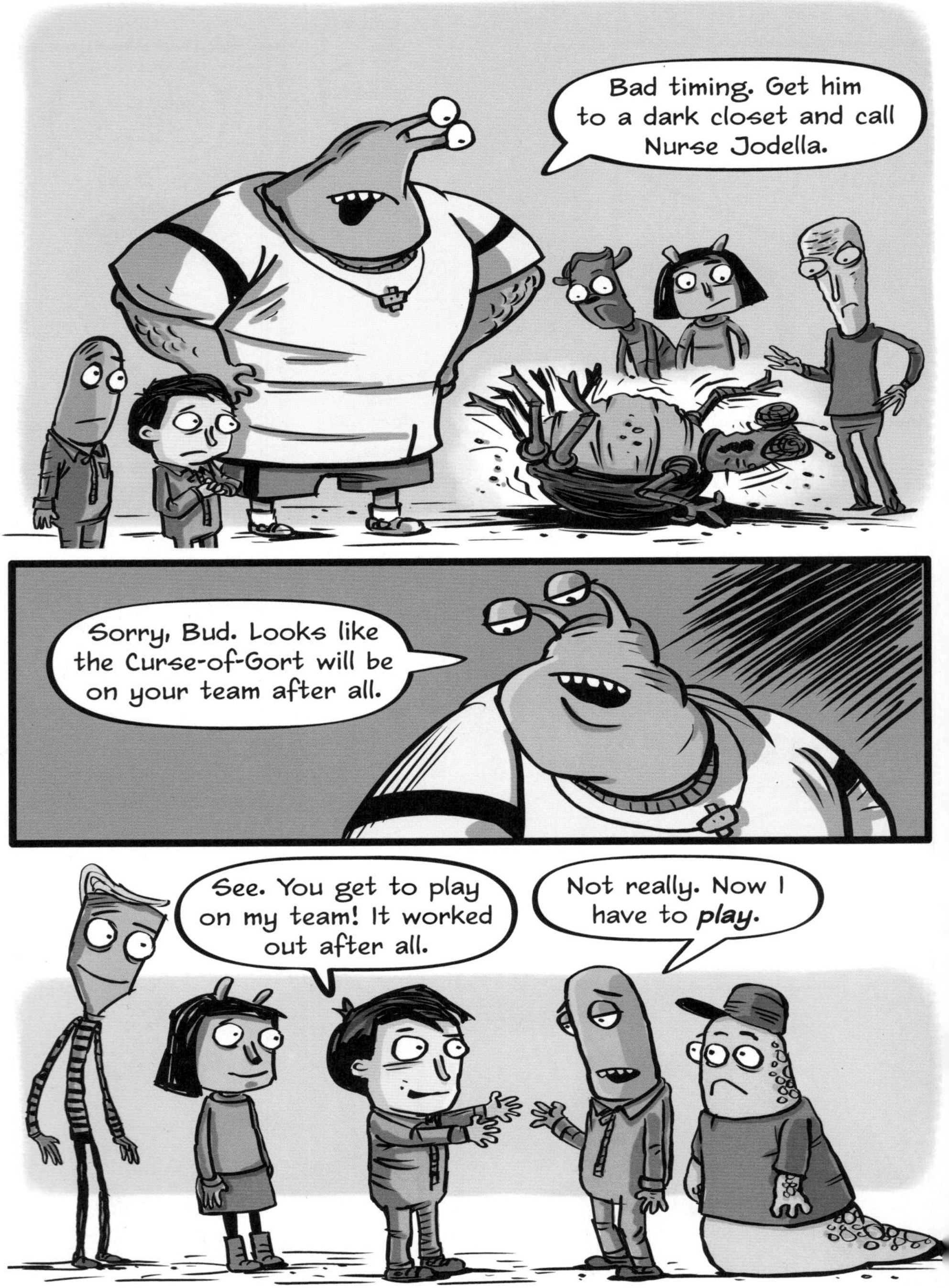
Bad timing. Get him to a dark closet and call Nurse Jodella.
Sorry, Bud. Looks like the Curse-of-Gort will be on your team after all.
See. You get to play on my team! It worked out after all.
Not really. Now I have to *play*.

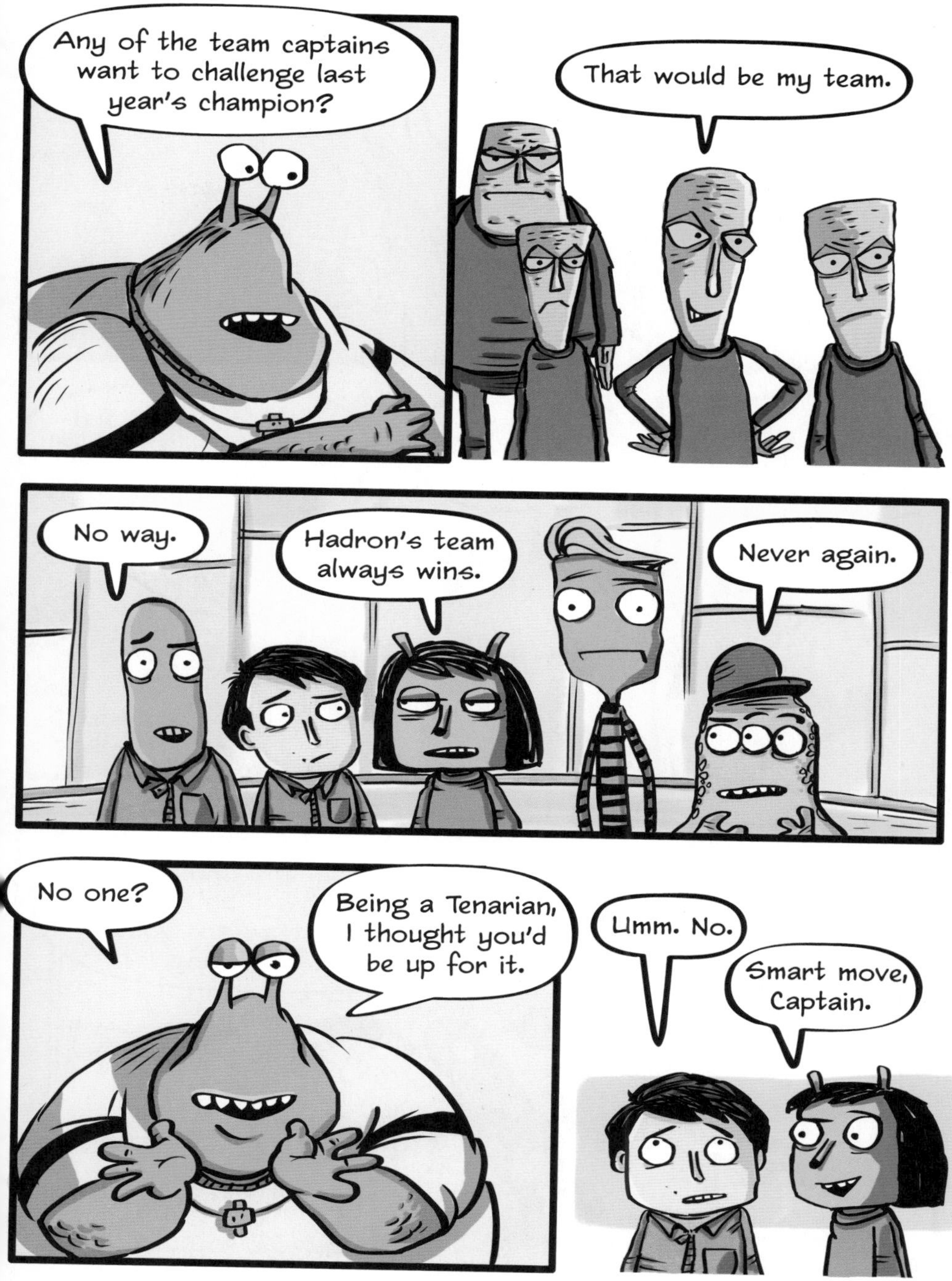
Any of the team captains want to challenge last year's champion?
That would be my team.
No way.
Hadron's team always wins.
Never again.
No one?
Being a Tenarian, I thought you'd be up for it.
Umm. No.
Smart move, Captain.

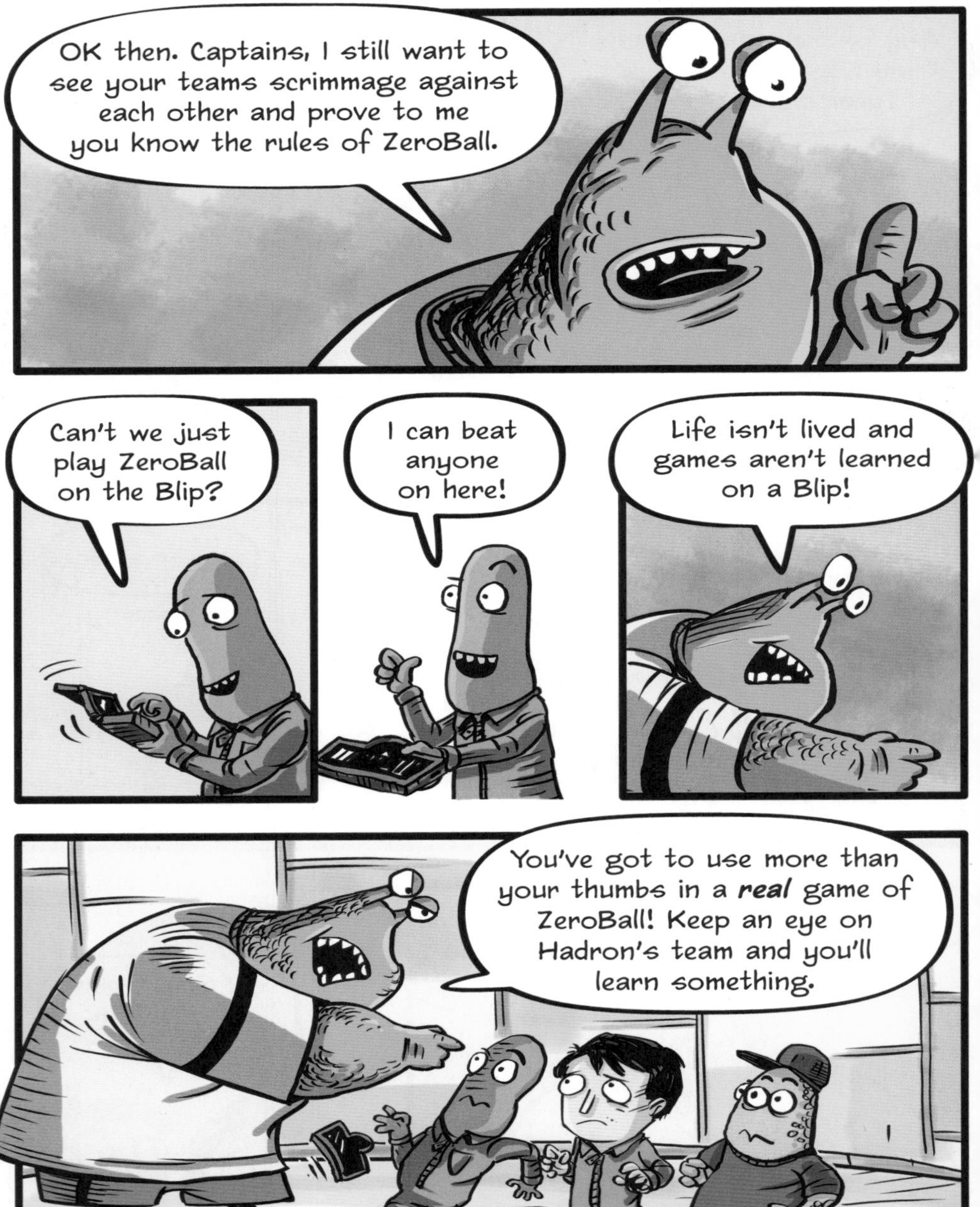
OK then. Captains, I still want to see your teams scrimmage against each other and prove to me you know the rules of ZeroBall.
Can't we just play ZeroBall on the Blip?
I can beat anyone on here!
Life isn't lived and games aren't learned on a Blip!
You've got to use more than your thumbs in a *real* game of ZeroBall! Keep an eye on Hadron's team and you'll learn something.

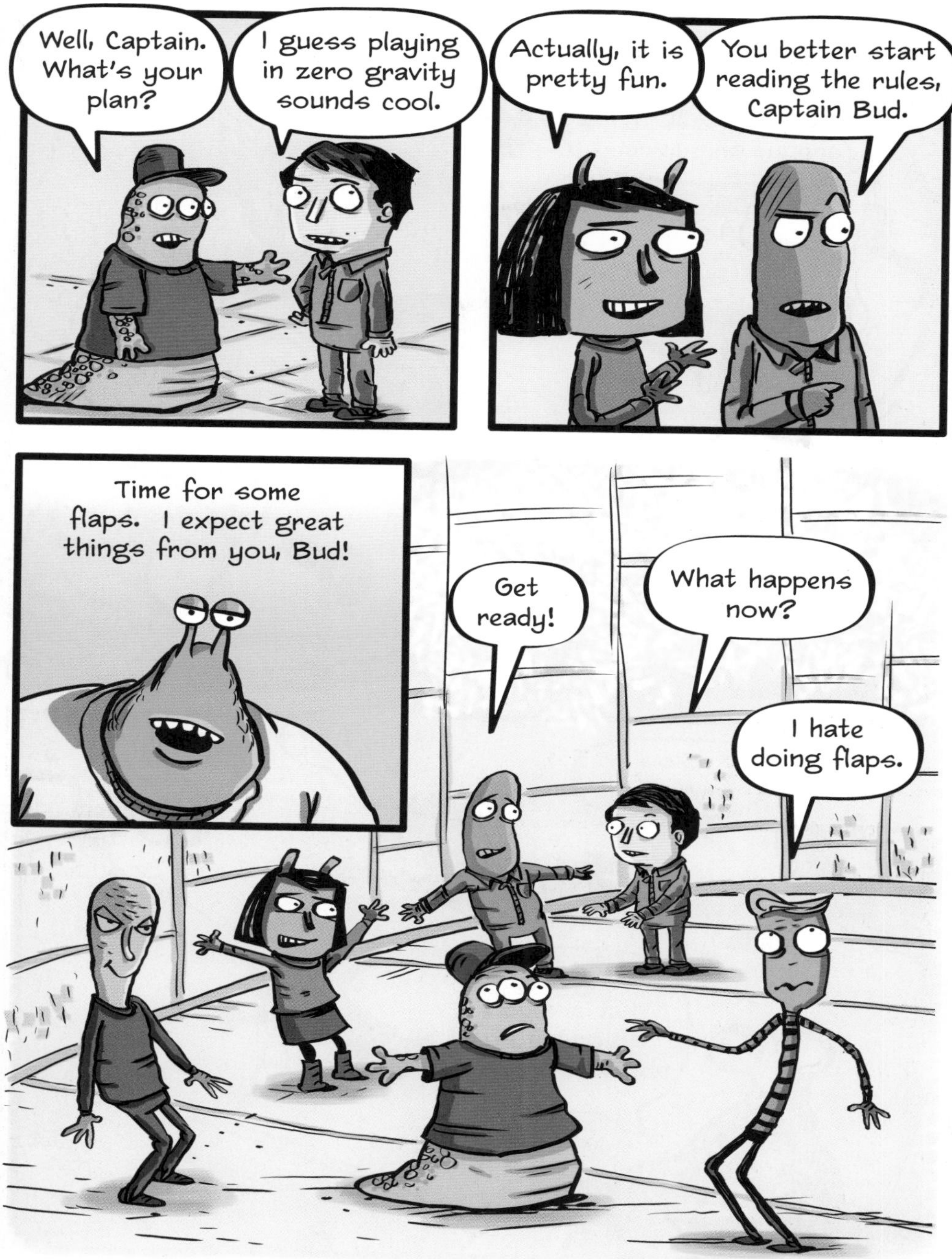
Well, Captain. What's your plan?
I guess playing in zero gravity sounds cool.
Actually, it is pretty fun.
You better start reading the rules, Captain Bud.
Time for some flaps. I expect great things from you, Bud!
Get ready!
What happens now?
I hate doing flaps.

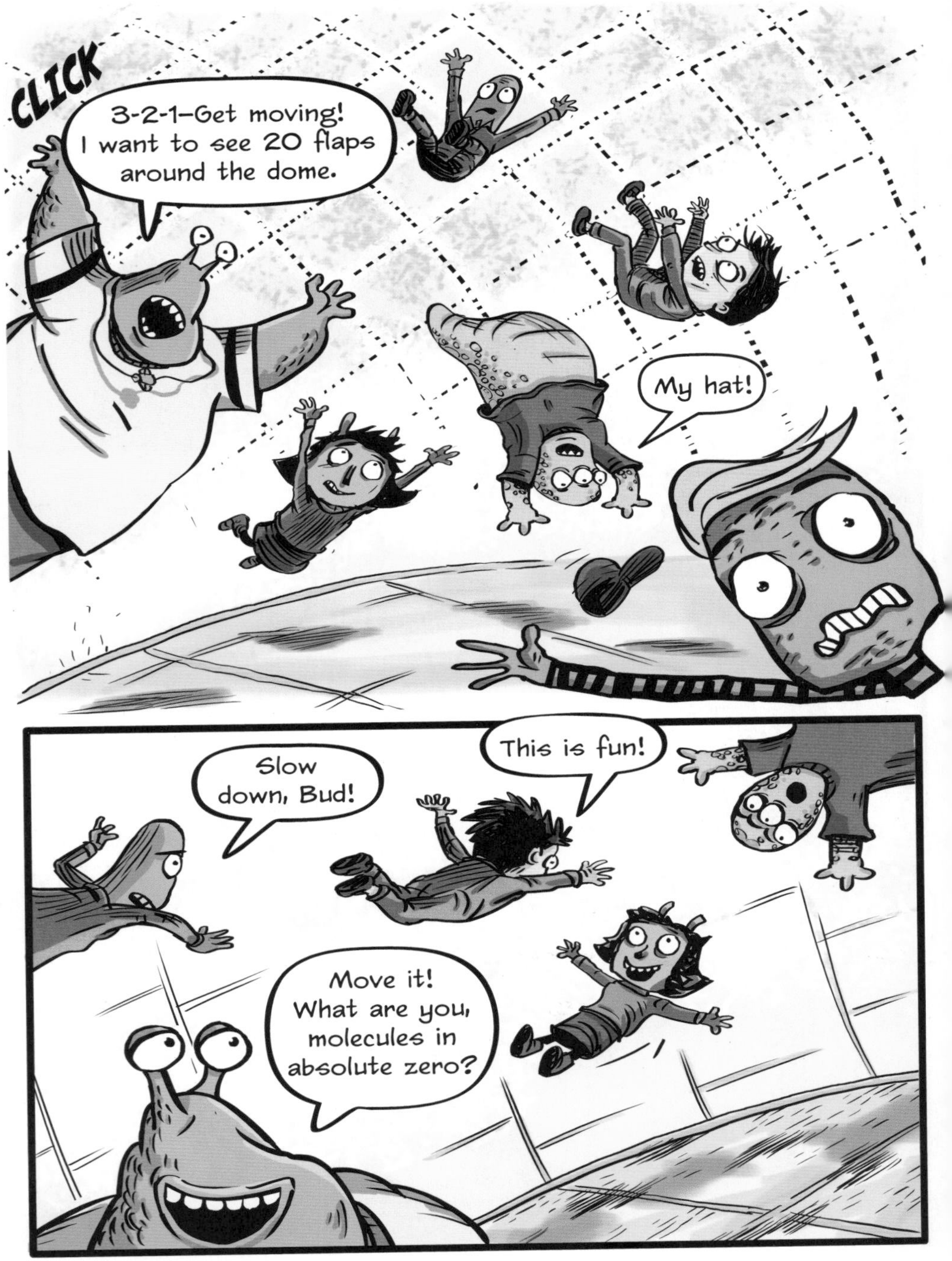
CLICK
3-2-1–Get moving! I want to see 20 flaps around the dome.
My hat!
Slow down, Bud!
This is fun!
Move it! What are you, molecules in absolute zero?

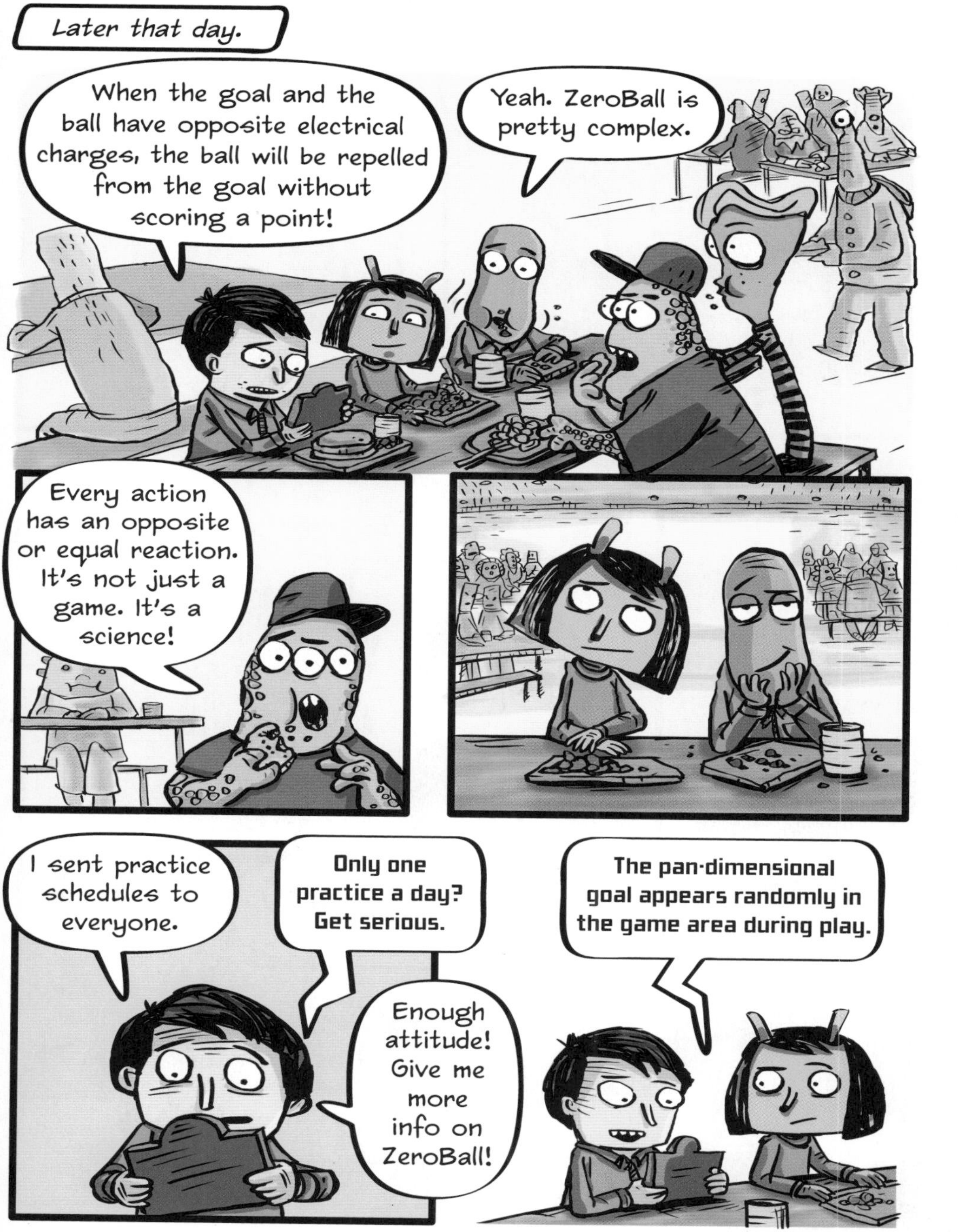
Later that day.
When the goal and the ball have opposite electrical charges, the ball will be repelled from the goal without scoring a point!
Yeah. ZeroBall is pretty complex.
Every action has an opposite or equal reaction. It's not just a game. It's a science!
I sent practice schedules to everyone.
Only one practice a day? Get serious.
Enough attitude! Give me more info on ZeroBall!
The pan-dimensional goal appears randomly in the game area during play.

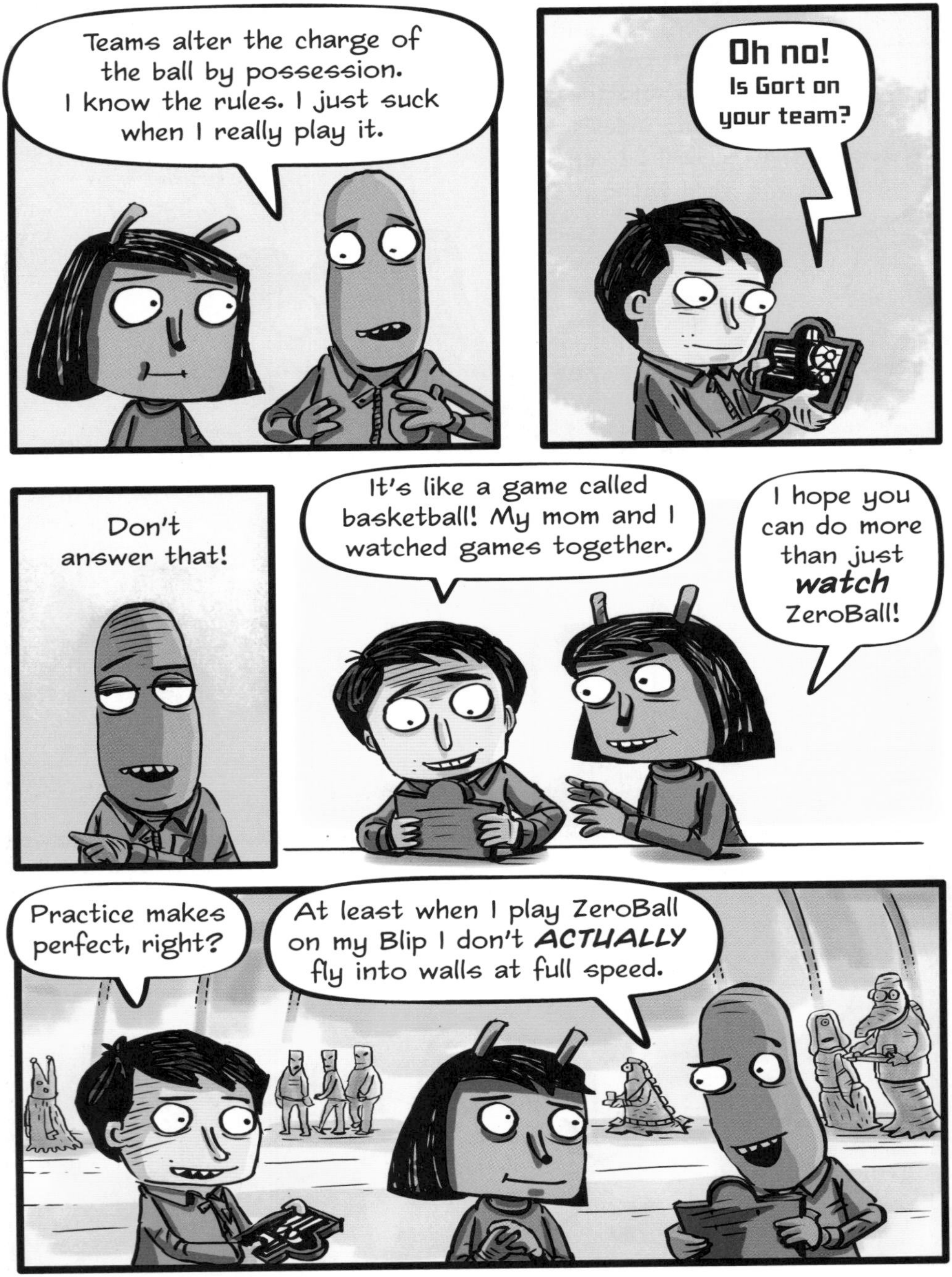

Teams alter the charge of the ball by possession. I know the rules. I just suck when I really play it.
Oh no! Is Gort on your team?
Don't answer that!
It's like a game called basketball! My mom and I watched games together.
I hope you can do more than just *watch* ZeroBall!
Practice makes perfect, right?
At least when I play ZeroBall on my Blip I don't ***ACTUALLY*** fly into walls at full speed.

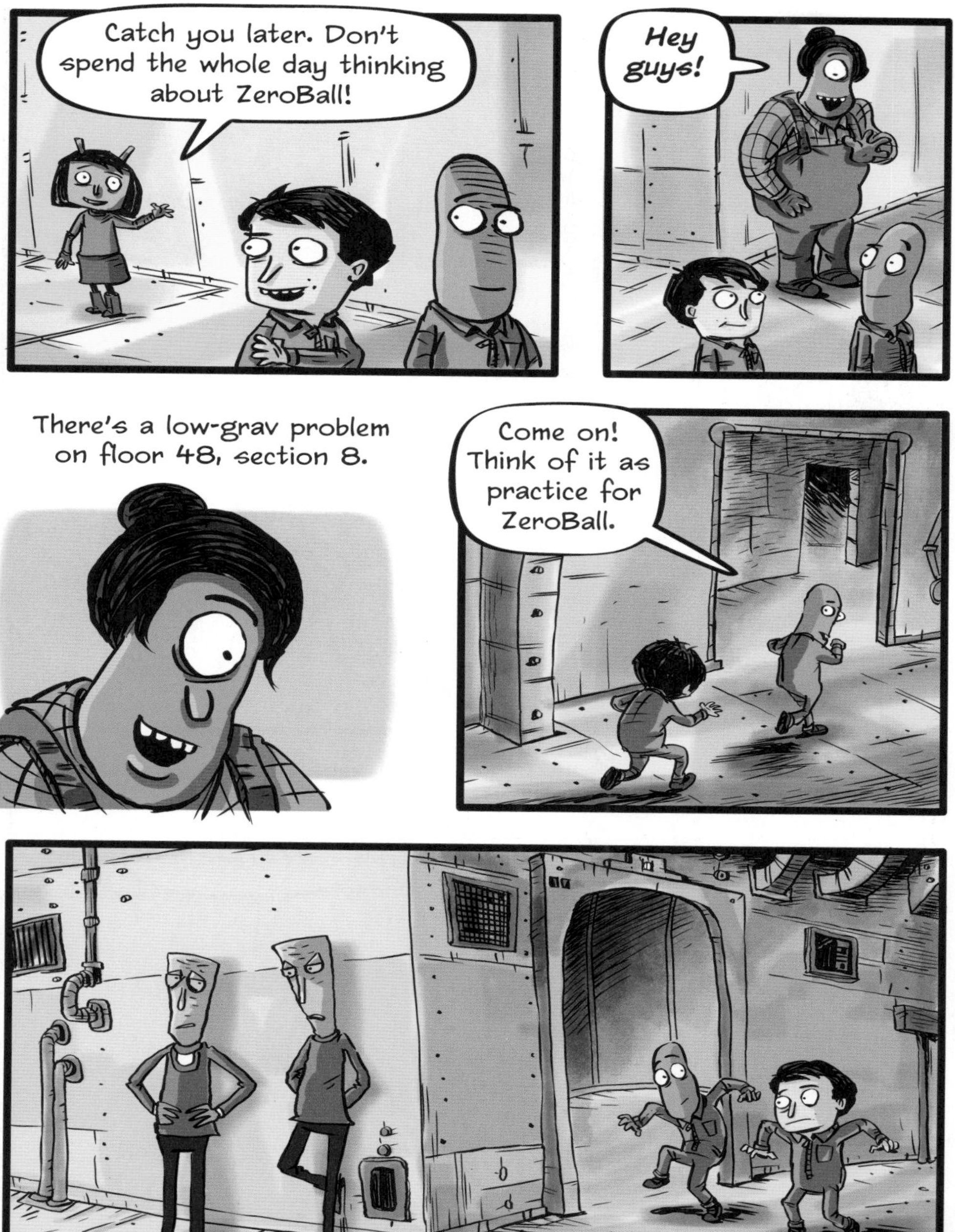
Catch you later. Don't spend the whole day thinking about ZeroBall!
Hey guys!
There's a low-grav problem on floor 48, section 8.
Come on! Think of it as practice for ZeroBall.

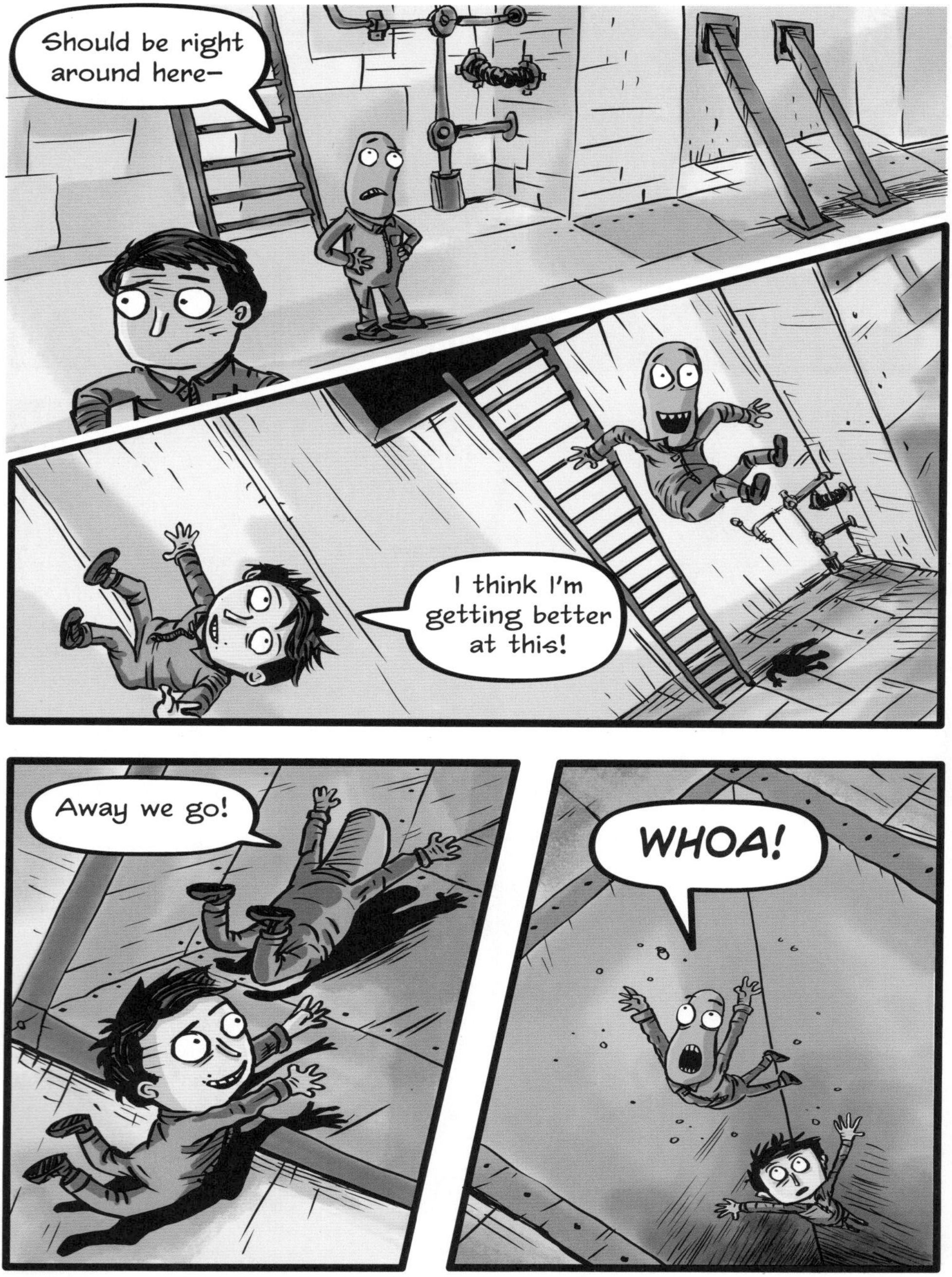

Should be right around here–
I think I'm getting better at this!
Away we go!
WHOA!

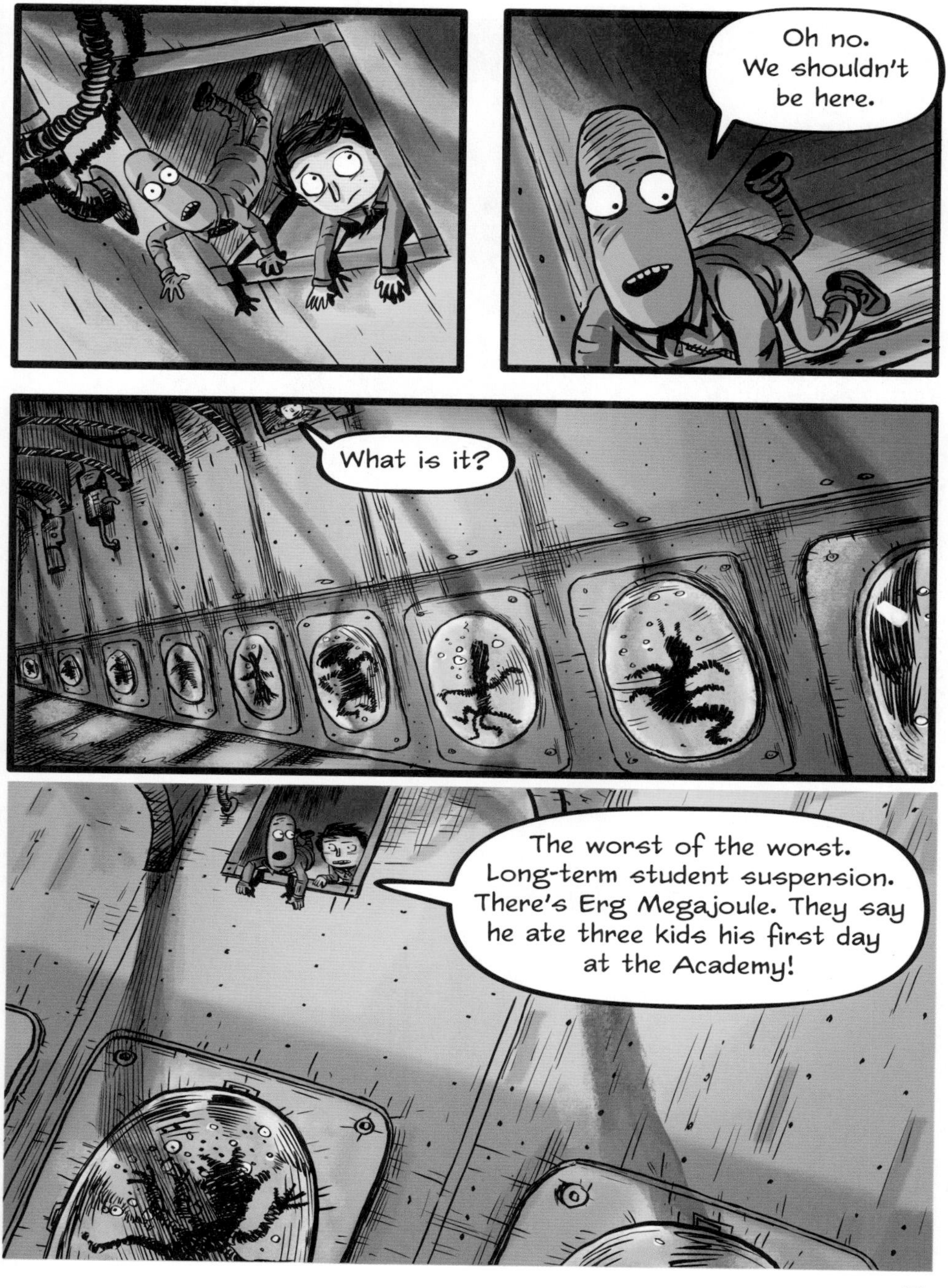
Oh no.
We shouldn't be here.
What is it?
The worst of the worst. Long-term student suspension. There's Erg Megajoule. They say he ate three kids his first day at the Academy!

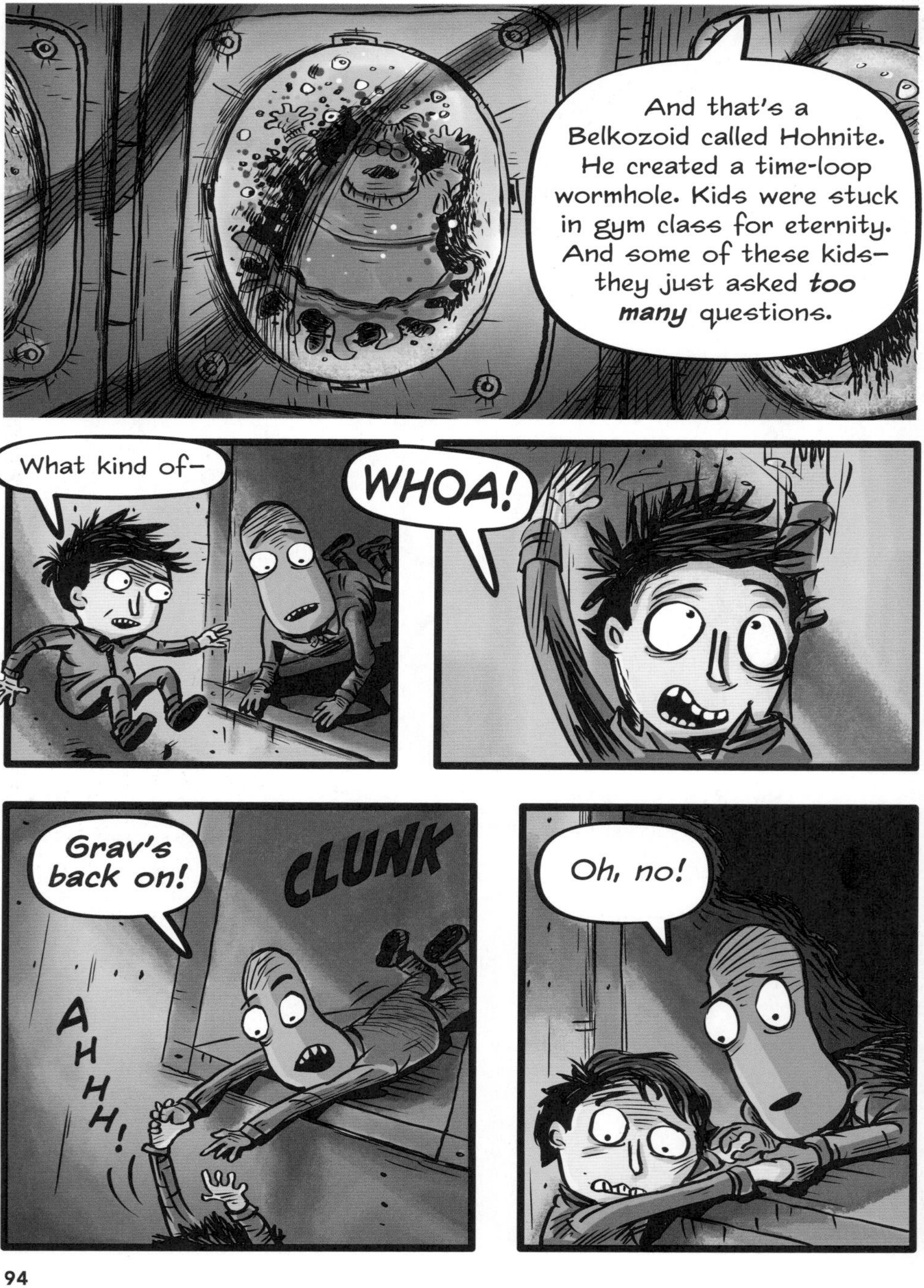
And that's a Belkozoid called Hohnite. He created a time-loop wormhole. Kids were stuck in gym class for eternity. And some of these kids– they just asked ***too many*** questions.
What kind of–
WHOA!
Grav's back on!
CLUNK
AHHH!
Oh, no!

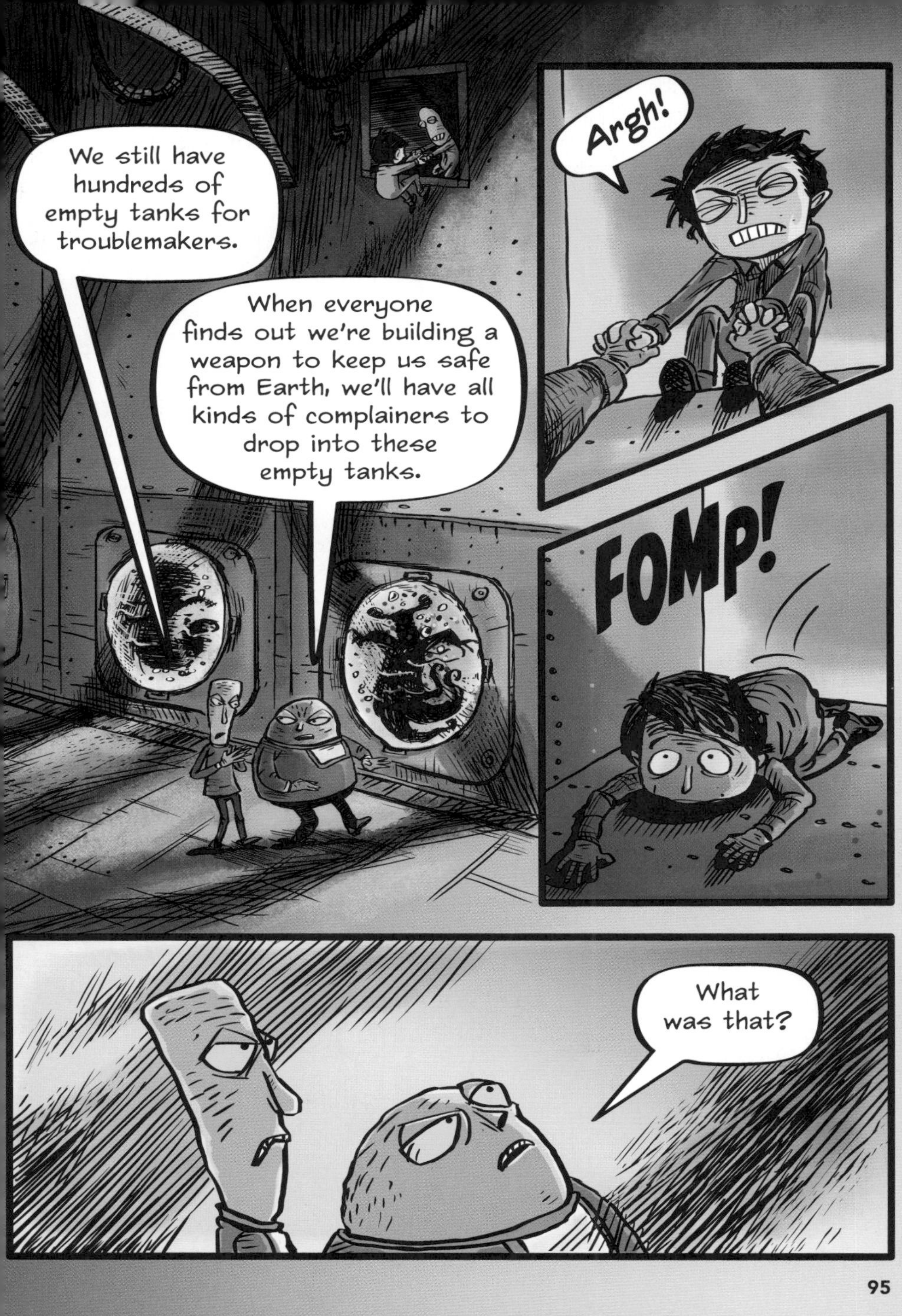
We still have hundreds of empty tanks for troublemakers.
When everyone finds out we're building a weapon to keep us safe from Earth, we'll have all kinds of complainers to drop into these empty tanks.
Argh!
FOMP!
What was that?

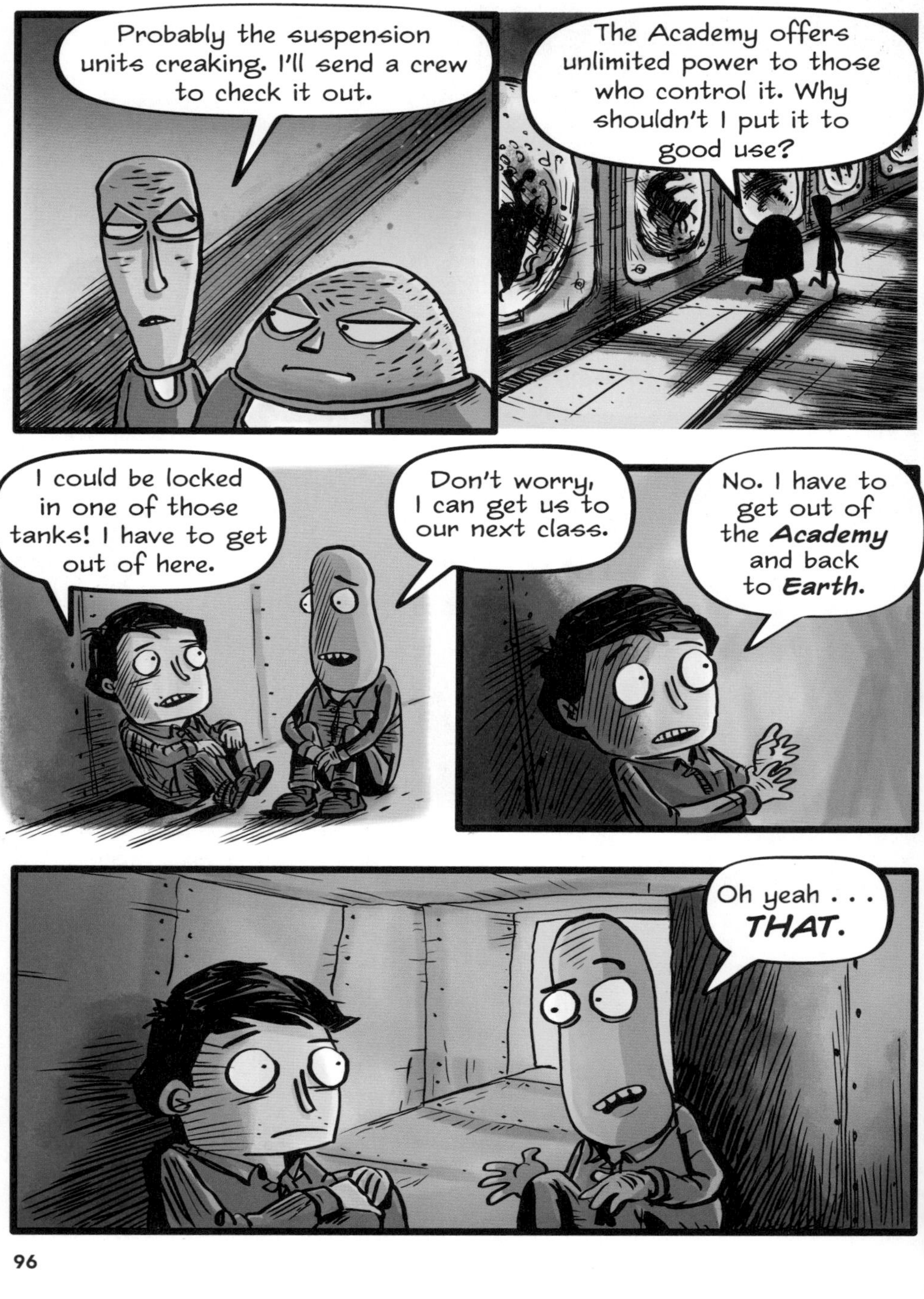
Probably the suspension units creaking. I'll send a crew to check it out.
The Academy offers unlimited power to those who control it. Why shouldn't I put it to good use?
I could be locked in one of those tanks! I have to get out of here.
Don't worry, I can get us to our next class.
No. I have to get out of the *Academy* and back to *Earth*.
Oh yeah . . . *THAT*.

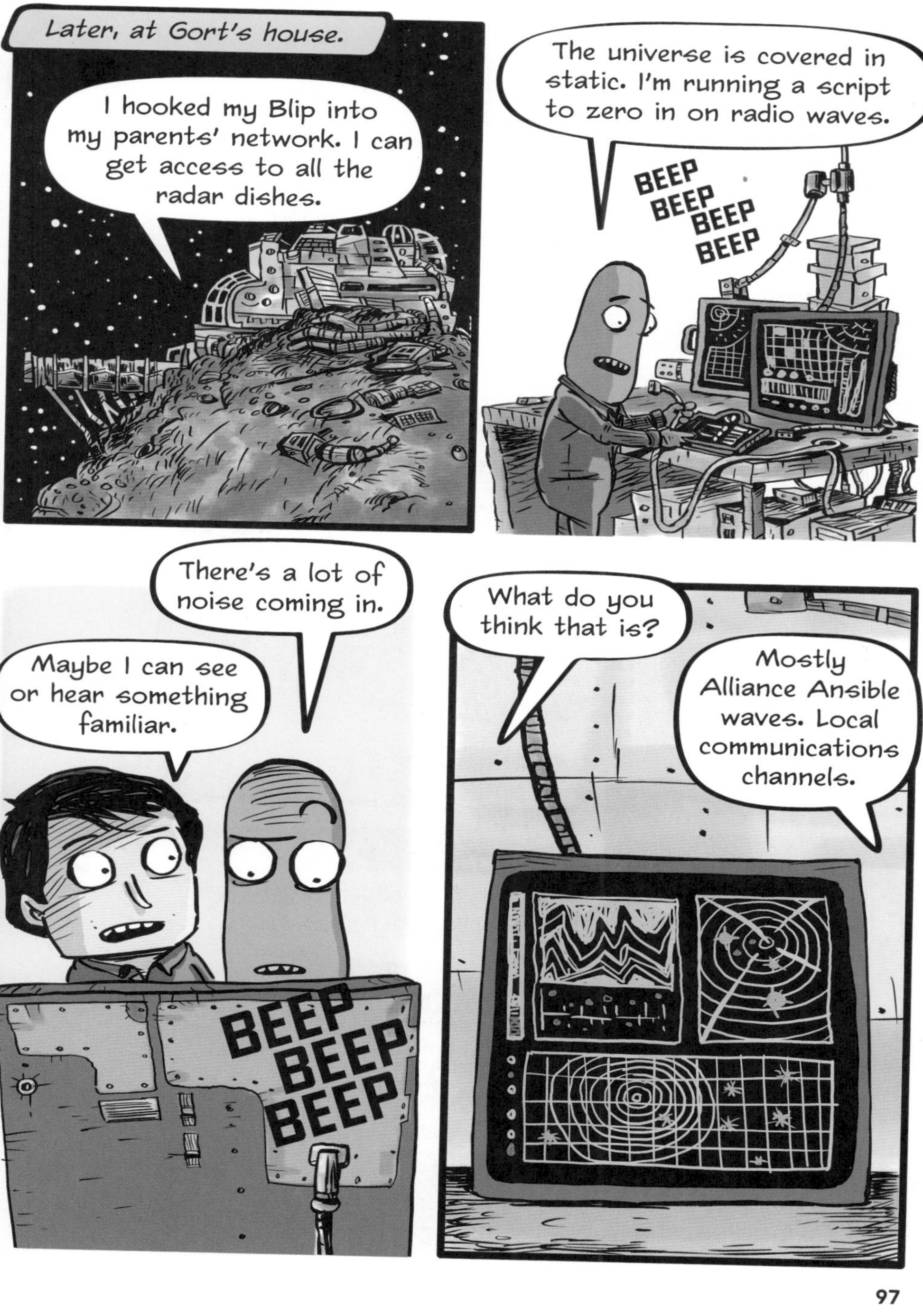
Later, at Gort's house.
I hooked my Blip into my parents' network. I can get access to all the radar dishes.
The universe is covered in static. I'm running a script to zero in on radio waves.
BEEP BEEP BEEP BEEP
There's a lot of noise coming in.
Maybe I can see or hear something familiar.
BEEP BEEP BEEP
What do you think that is?
Mostly Alliance Ansible waves. Local communications channels.

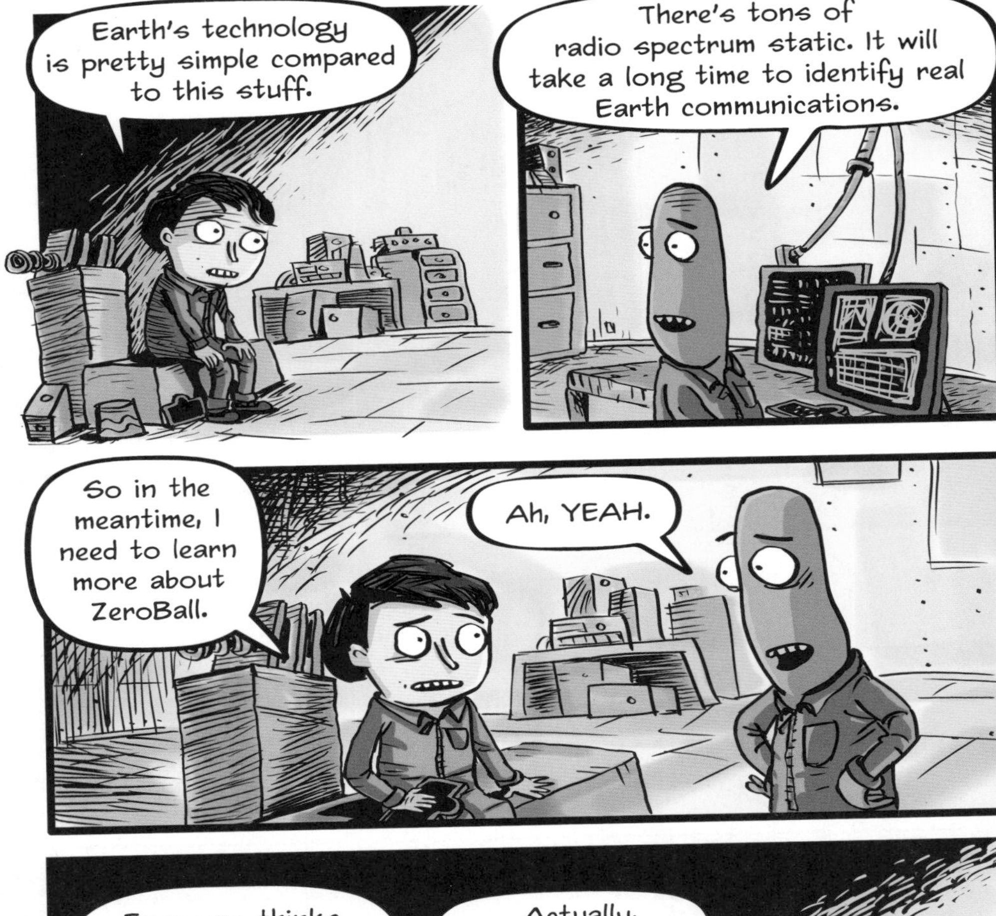
Earth's technology is pretty simple compared to this stuff.
There's tons of radio spectrum static. It will take a long time to identify real Earth communications.
So in the meantime, I need to learn more about ZeroBall.
Ah, YEAH.
Everyone thinks I'm amazing at sports *just* because I kind of look like a Tenarian, some other alien?
Actually, ***YOU'RE*** the alien.

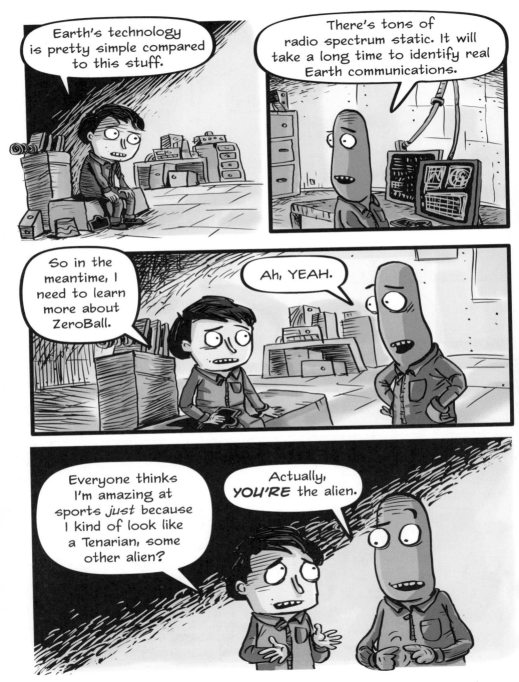

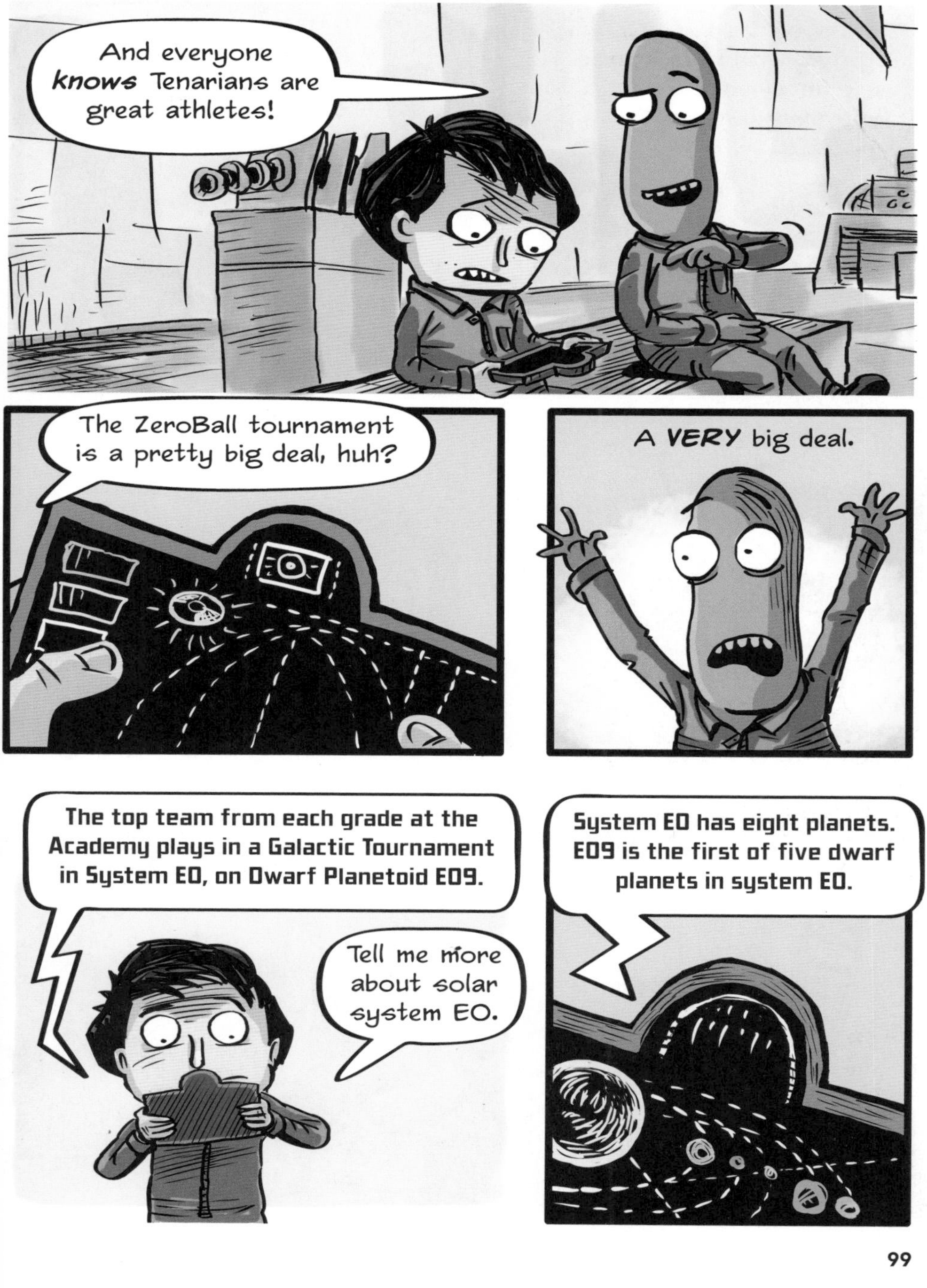
And everyone knows Tenarians are great athletes!
The ZeroBall tournament is a pretty big deal, huh?
A VERY big deal.
The top team from each grade at the Academy plays in a Galactic Tournament in System EO, on Dwarf Planetoid EO9.
Tell me more about solar system EO.
System EO has eight planets. EO9 is the first of five dwarf planets in system EO.

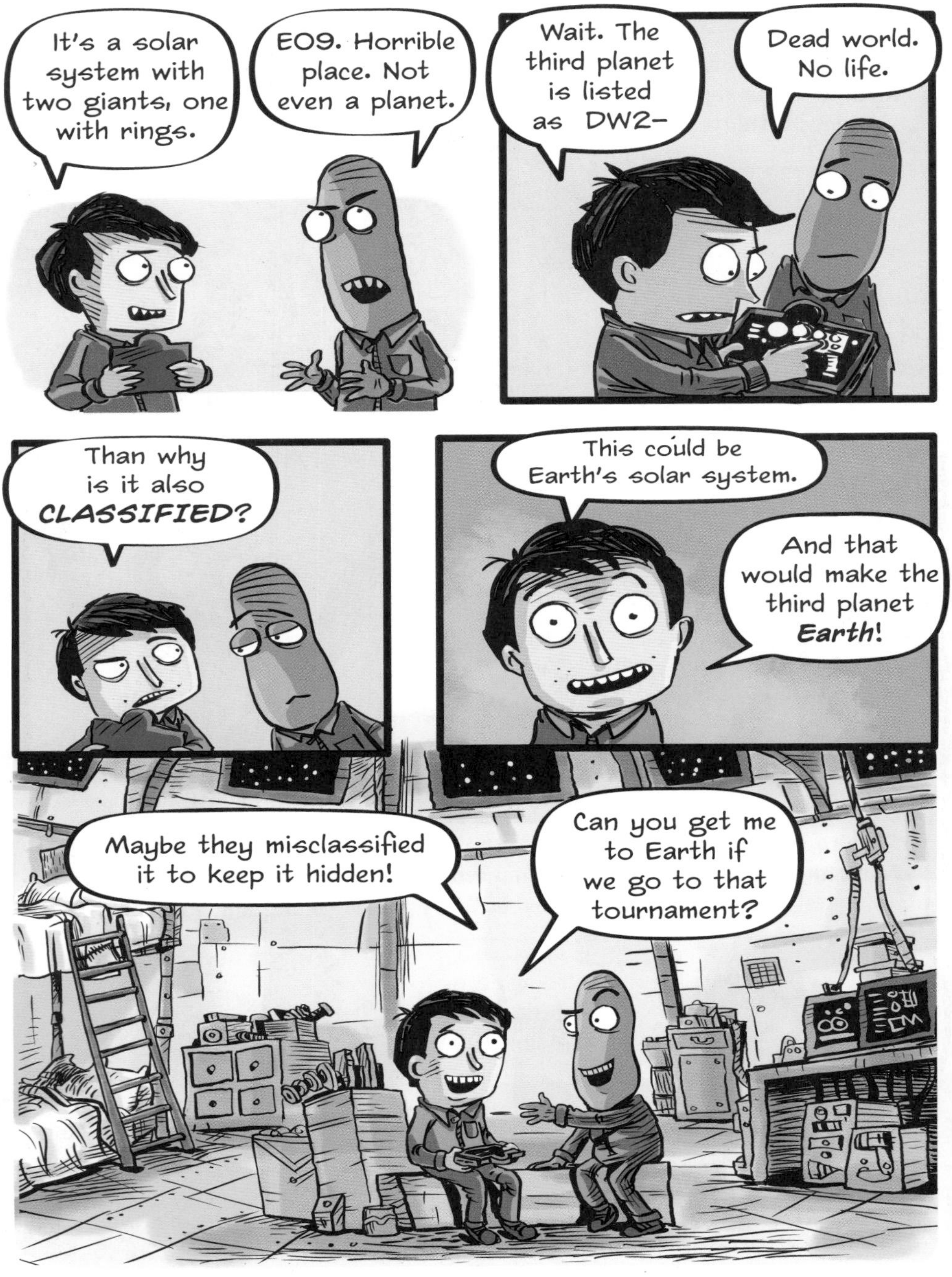

It's a solar system with two giants, one with rings.
E09. Horrible place. Not even a planet.
Wait. The third planet is listed as DW2–
Dead world. No life.
Than why is it also *CLASSIFIED*?
This could be Earth's solar system.
And that would make the third planet *Earth*!
Maybe they misclassified it to keep it hidden!
Can you get me to Earth if we go to that tournament?

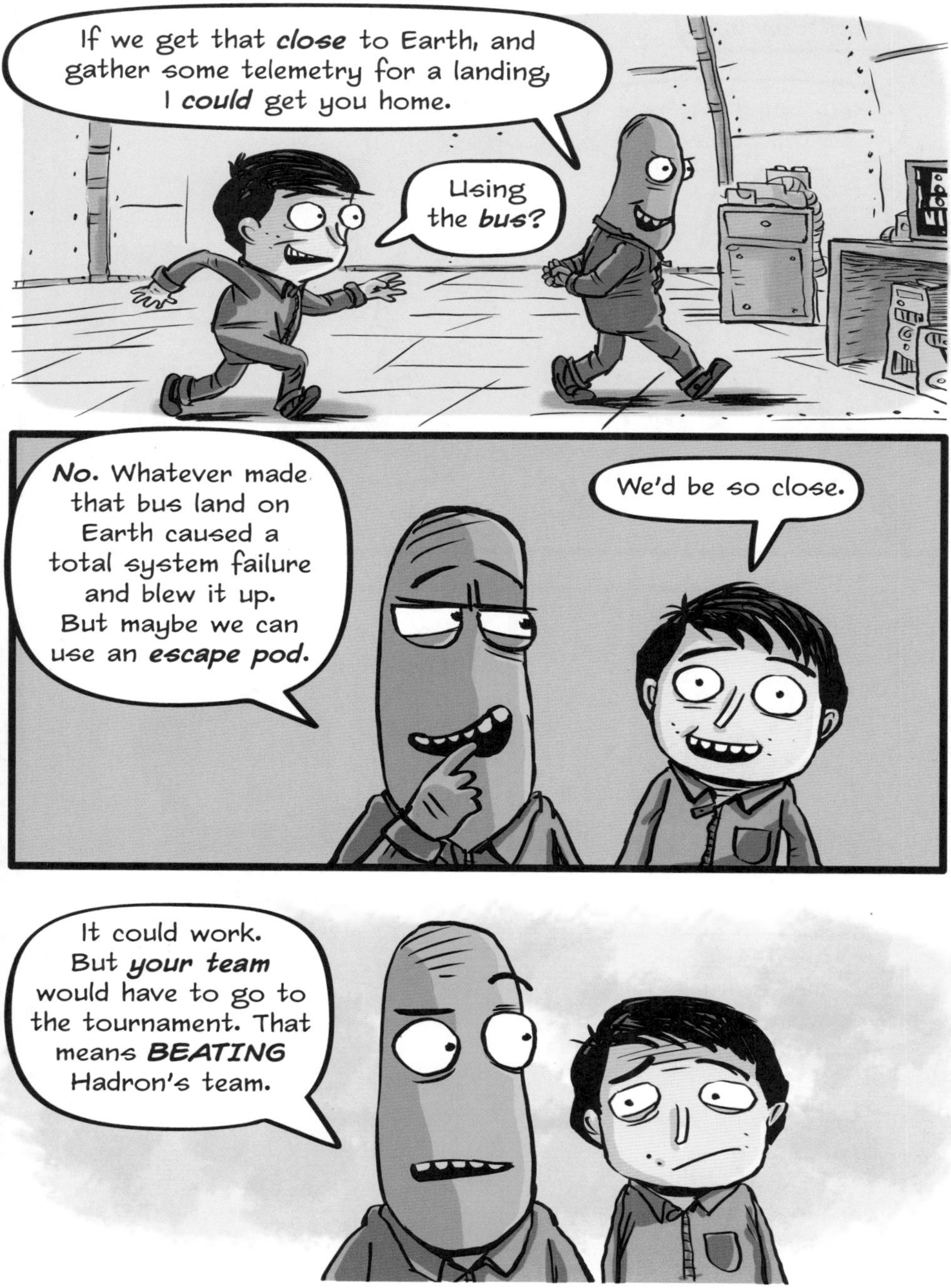
If we get that *close* to Earth, and gather some telemetry for a landing, I *could* get you home.
Using the *bus?*
No. Whatever made that bus land on Earth caused a total system failure and blew it up. But maybe we can use an ***escape pod.***
We'd be so close.
It could work. But ***your team*** would have to go to the tournament. That means ***BEATING*** Hadron's team.

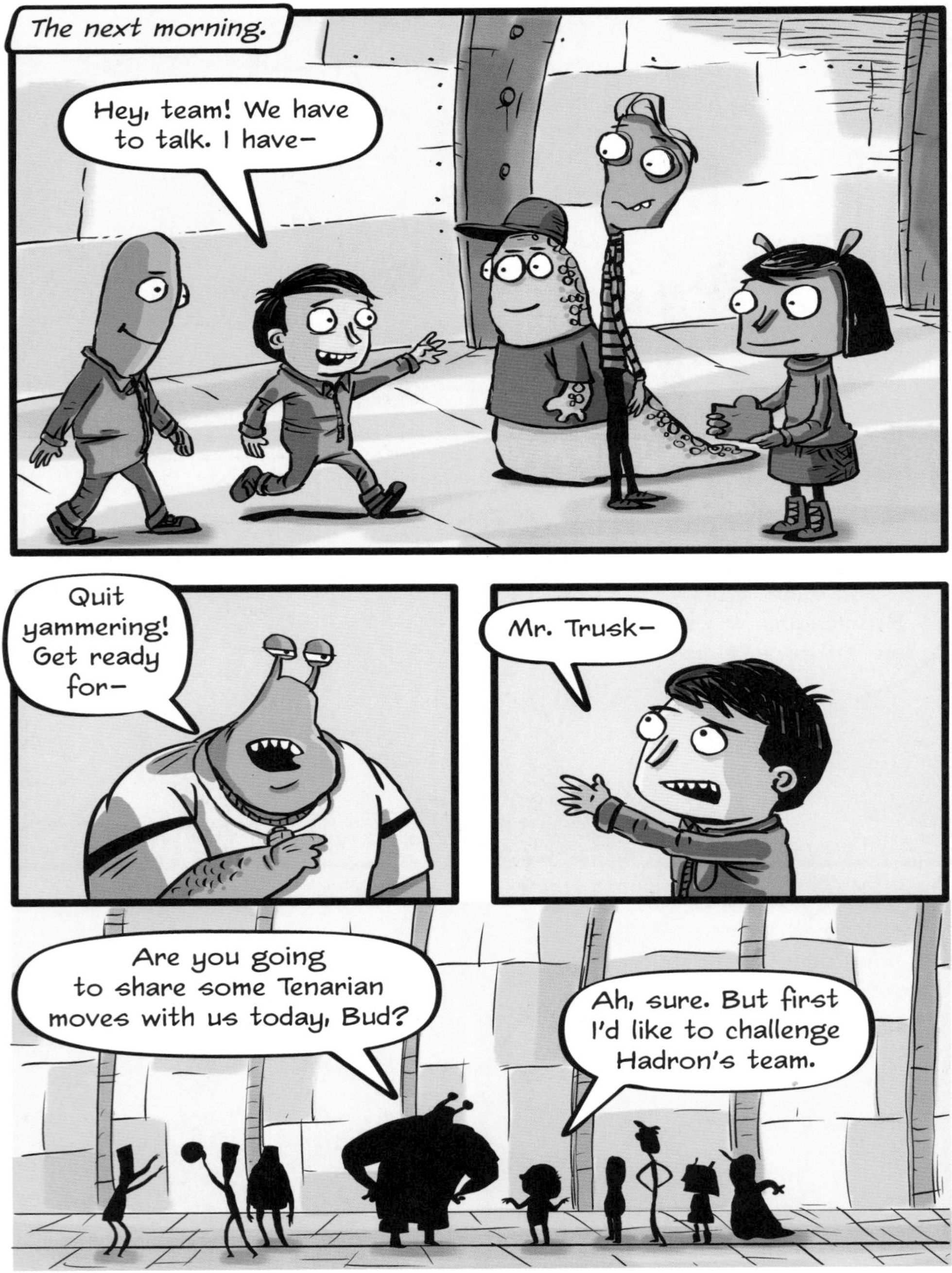
The next morning.
Hey, team! We have to talk. I have–
Quit yammering! Get ready for–
Mr. Trusk–
Are you going to share some Tenarian moves with us today, Bud?
Ah, sure. But first I'd like to challenge Hadron's team.

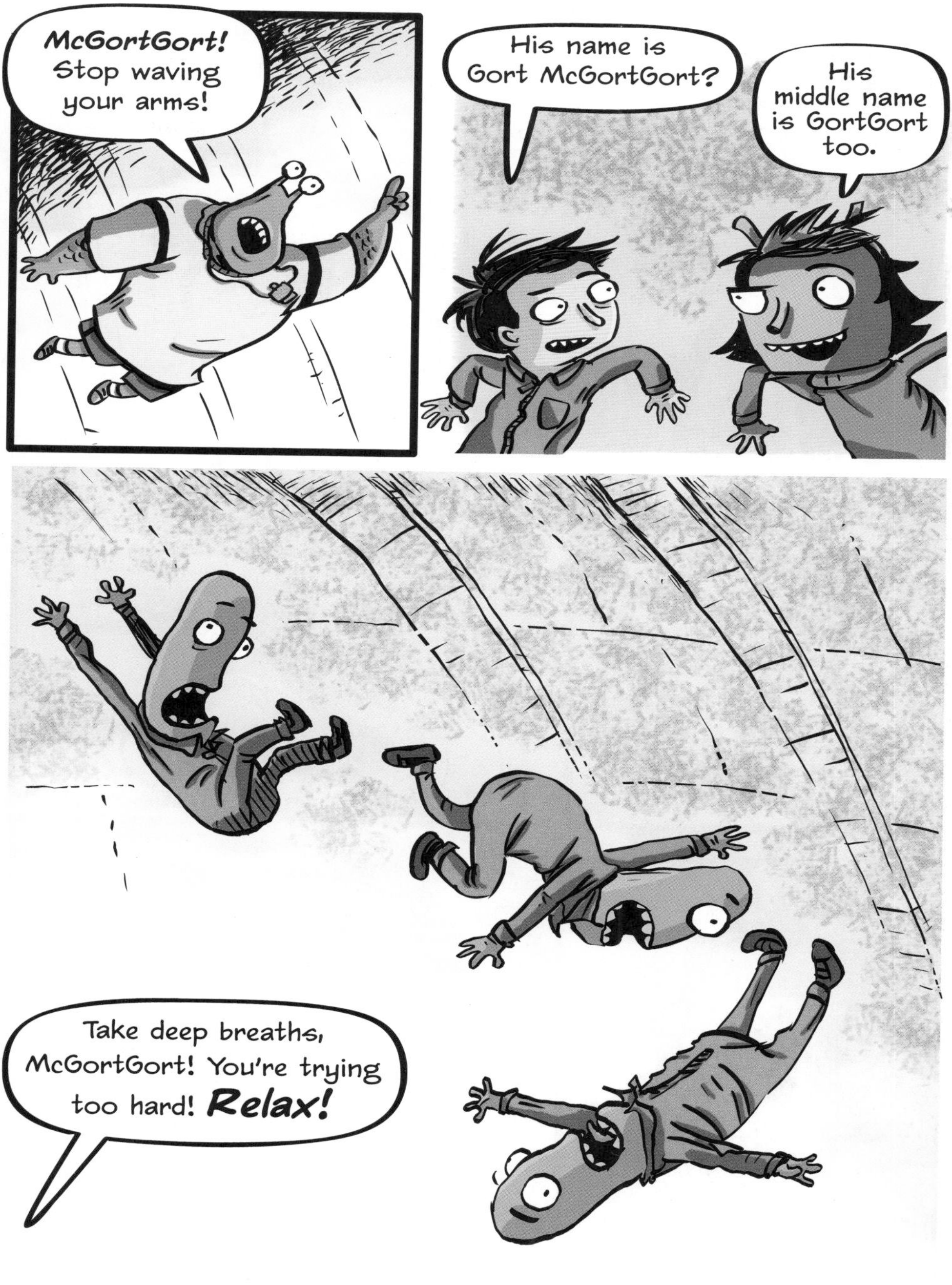
McGortGort! Stop waving your arms!
His name is Gort McGortGort?
His middle name is GortGort too.
Take deep breaths, McGortGort! You're trying too hard! Relax!

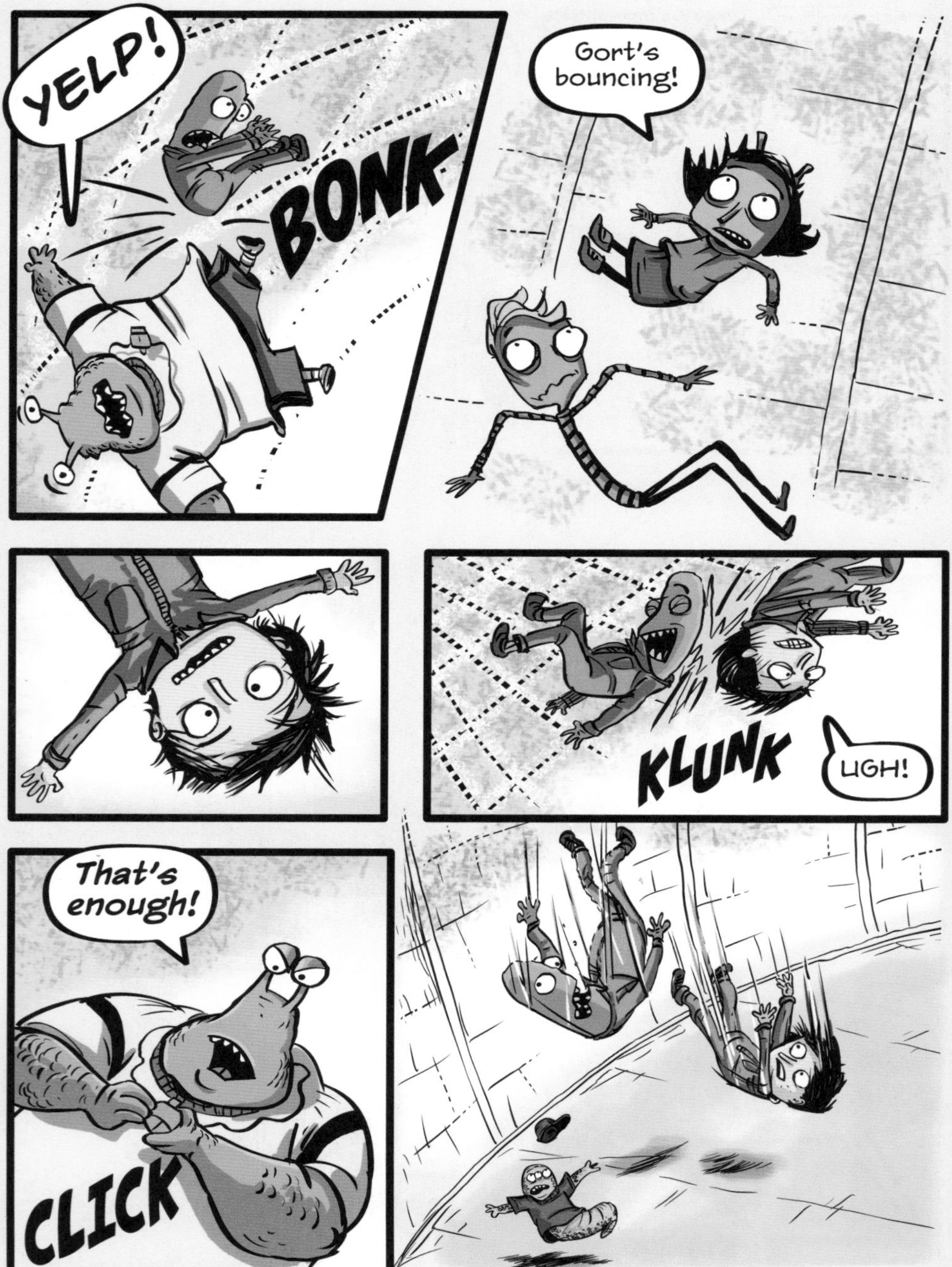
YELP!
BONK
Gort's bouncing!
KLUNK
UGH!
That's enough!
CLICK

107

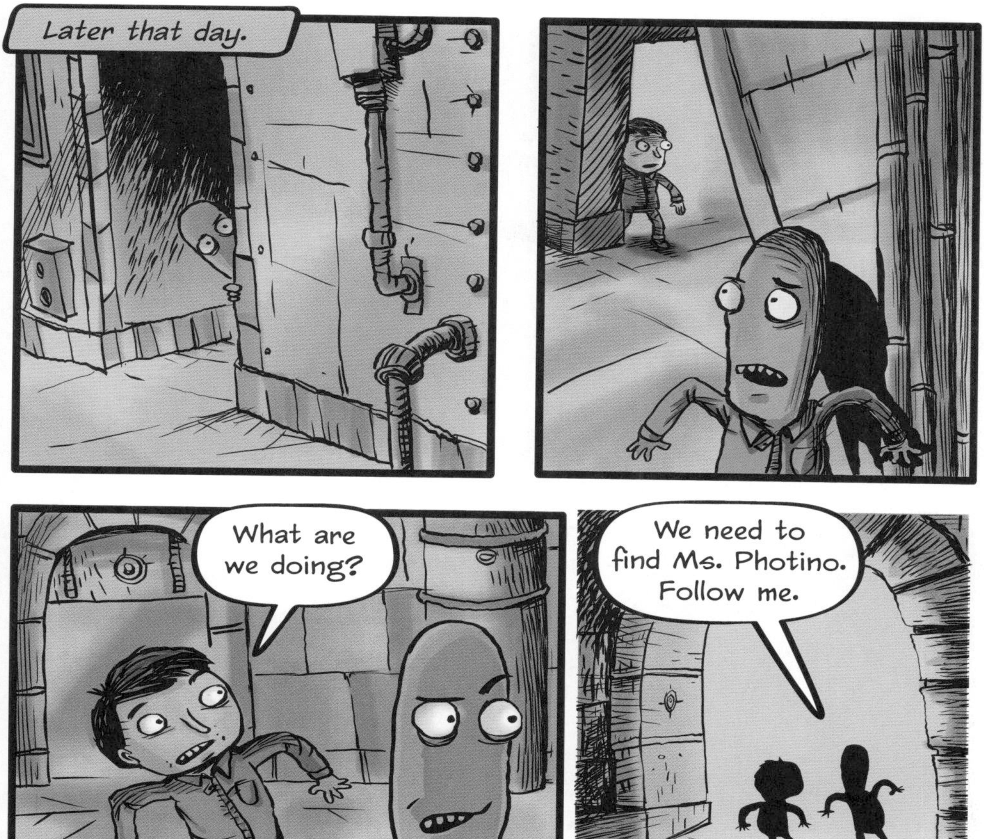
Later that day.
What are we doing?
We need to find Ms. Photino. Follow me.

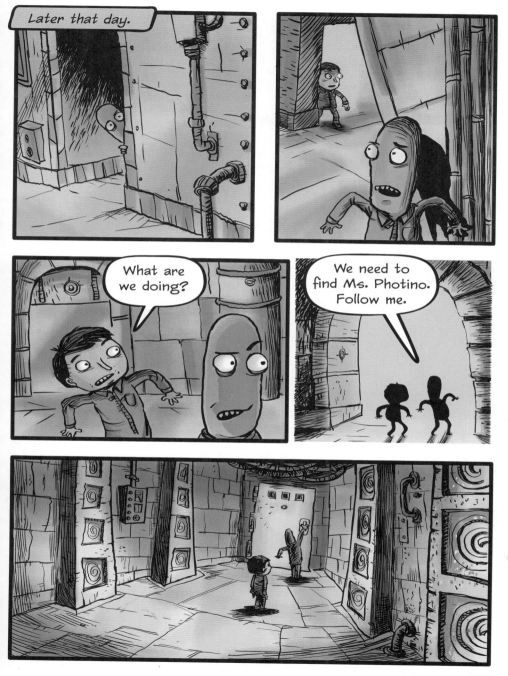

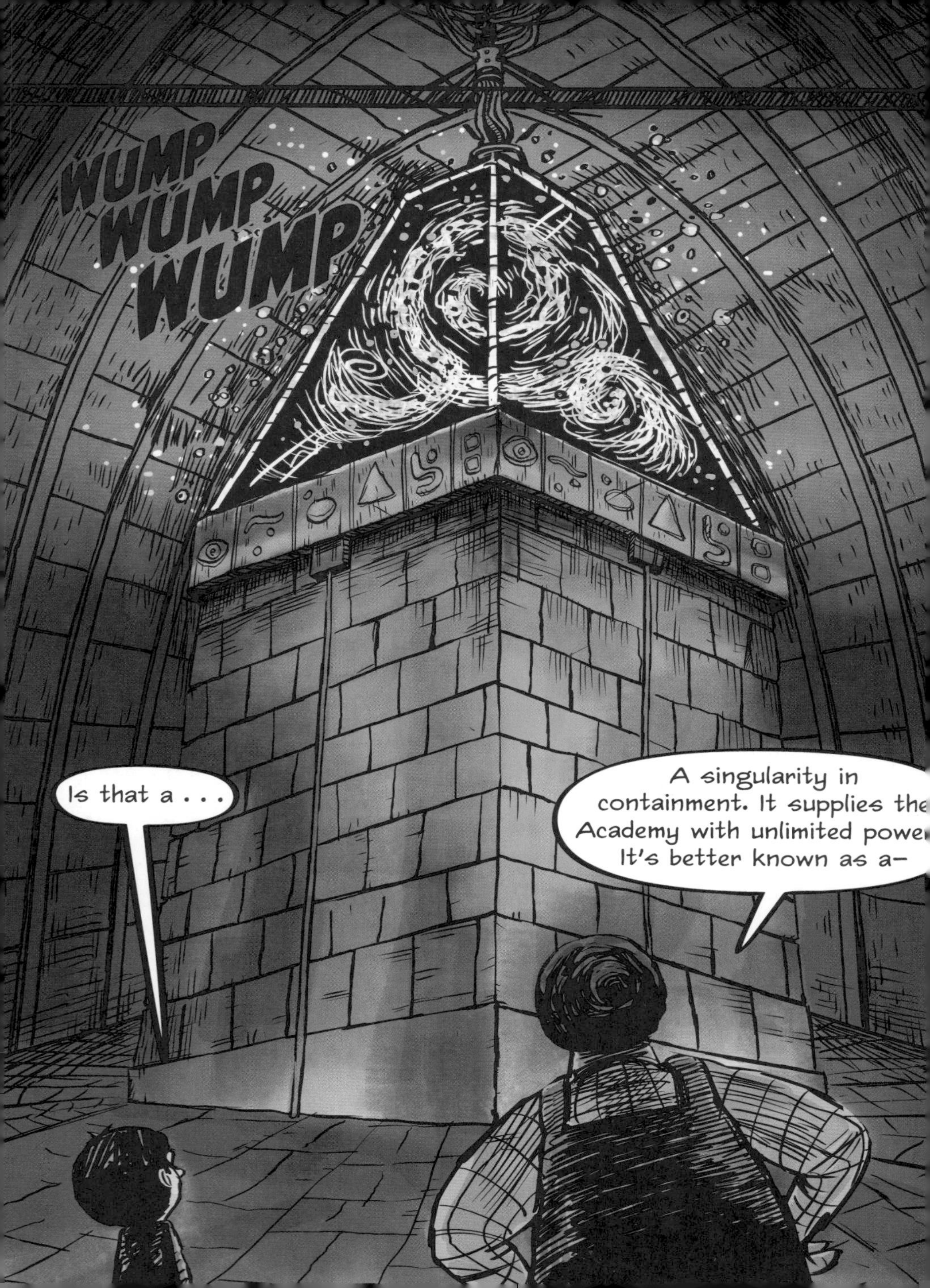
WUMP WUMP WUMP
Is that a . . .
A singularity in containment. It supplies the Academy with unlimited powe
It's better known as a–

117

CHAPTER 4

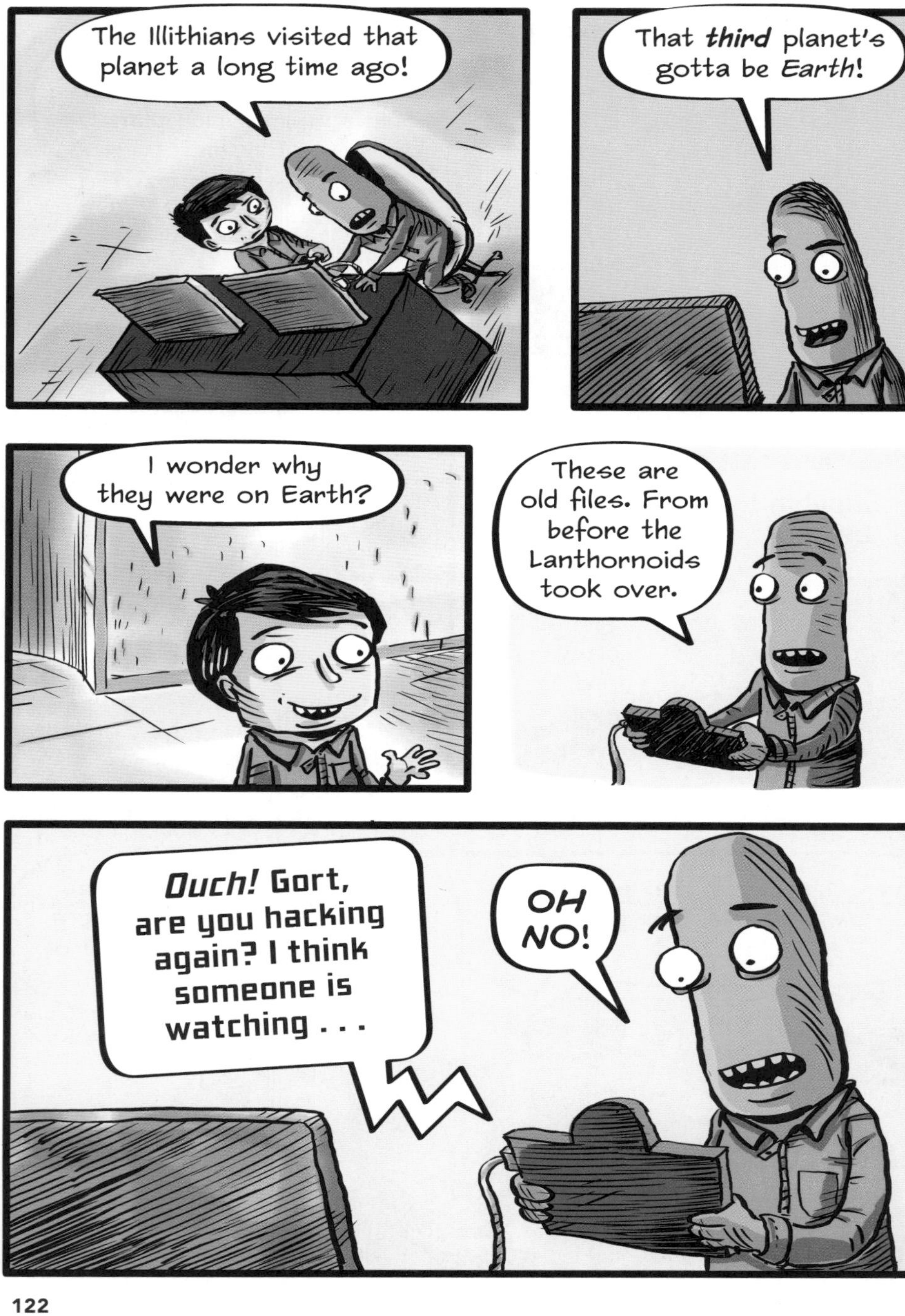
The Illithians visited that planet a long time ago!
That *third* planet's gotta be *Earth*!
I wonder why they were on Earth?
These are old files. From before the Lanthornoids took over.
Ouch! Gort, are you hacking again? I think someone is watching . . .
OH NO!

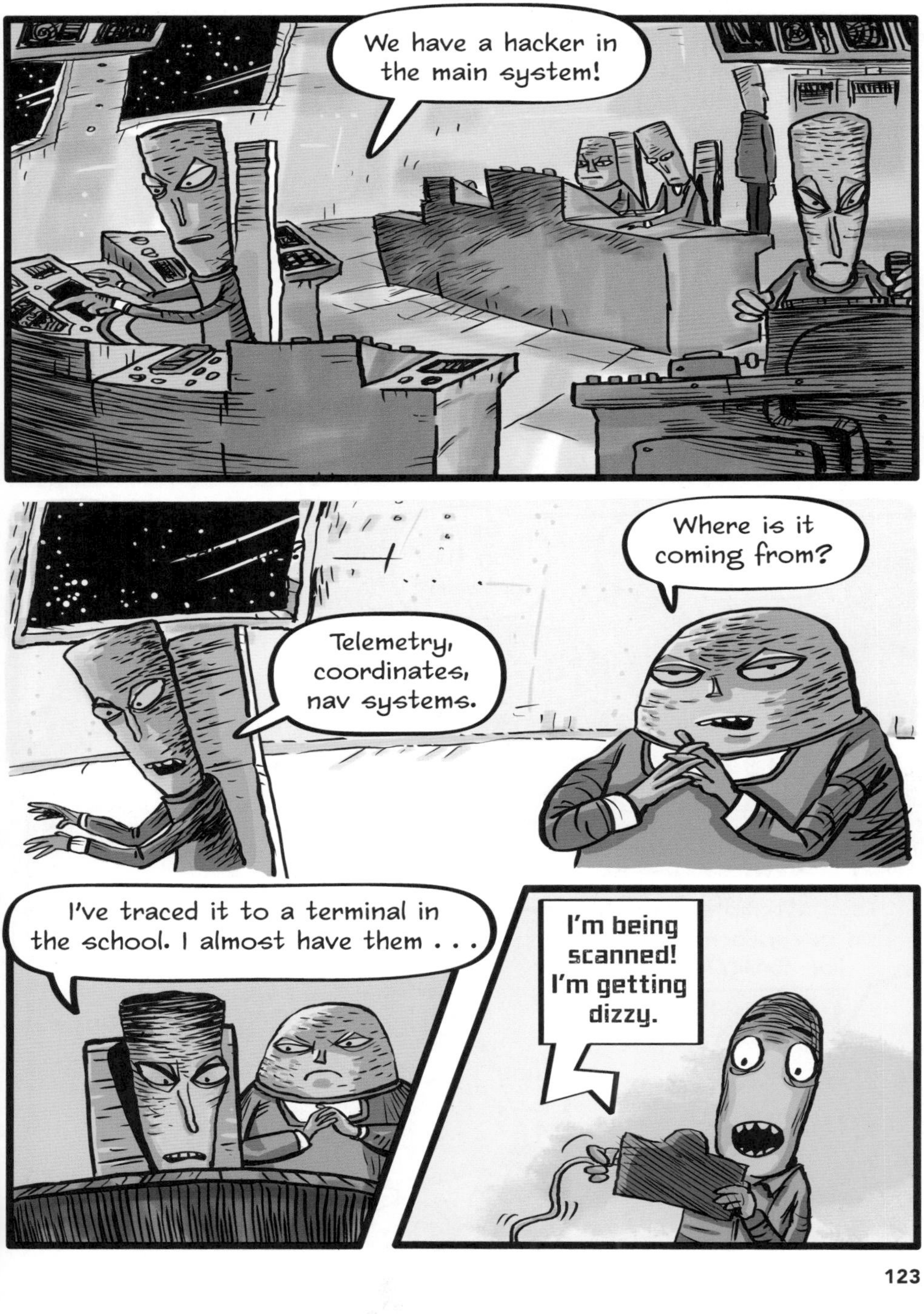
We have a hacker in the main system!
Where is it coming from?
Telemetry, coordinates, nav systems.
I've traced it to a terminal in the school. I almost have them . . .
I'm being scanned! I'm getting dizzy.

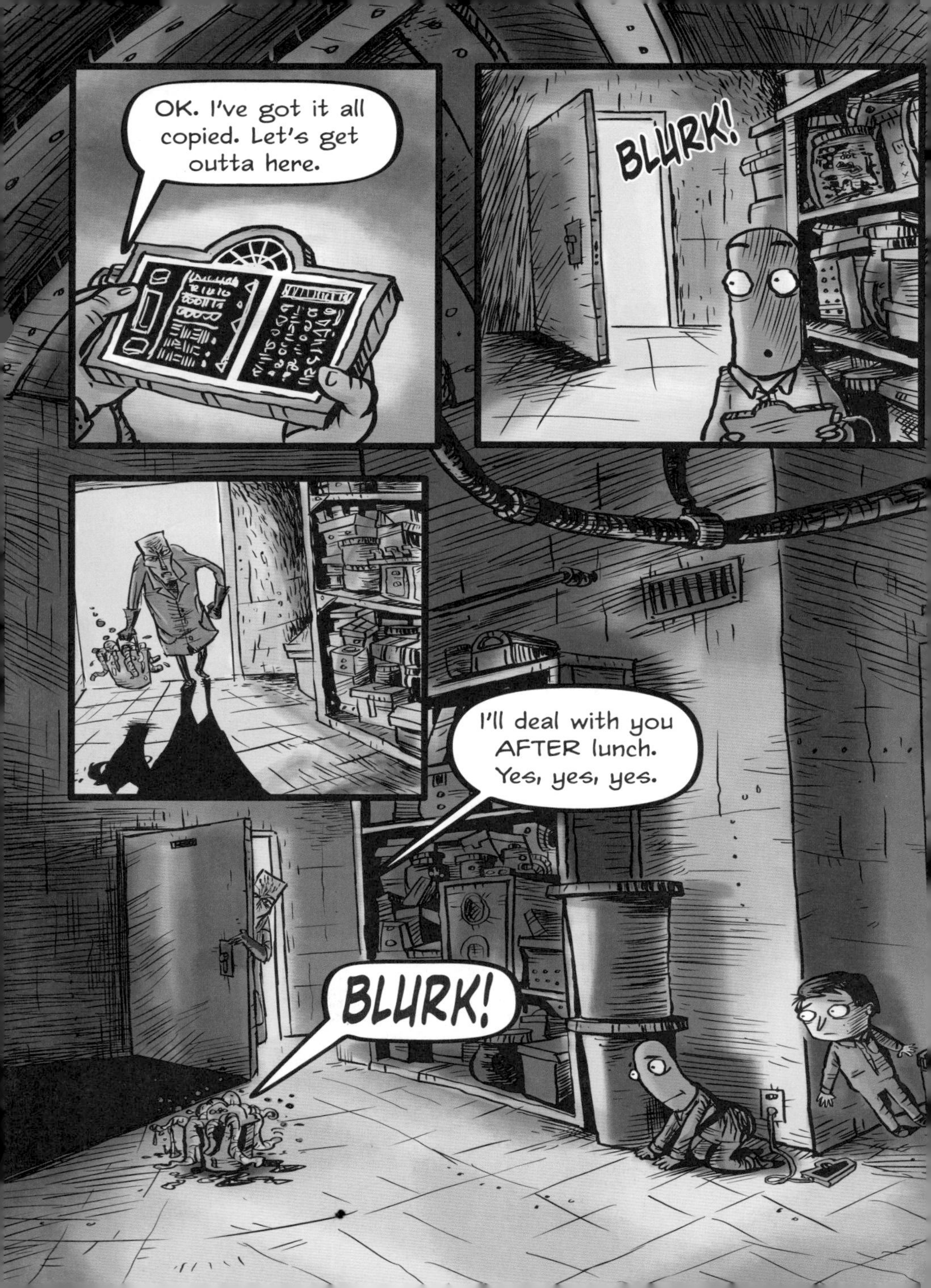
OK. I've got it all copied. Let's get outta here.
BLURK!
I'll deal with you AFTER lunch. Yes, yes, yes.
BLURK!

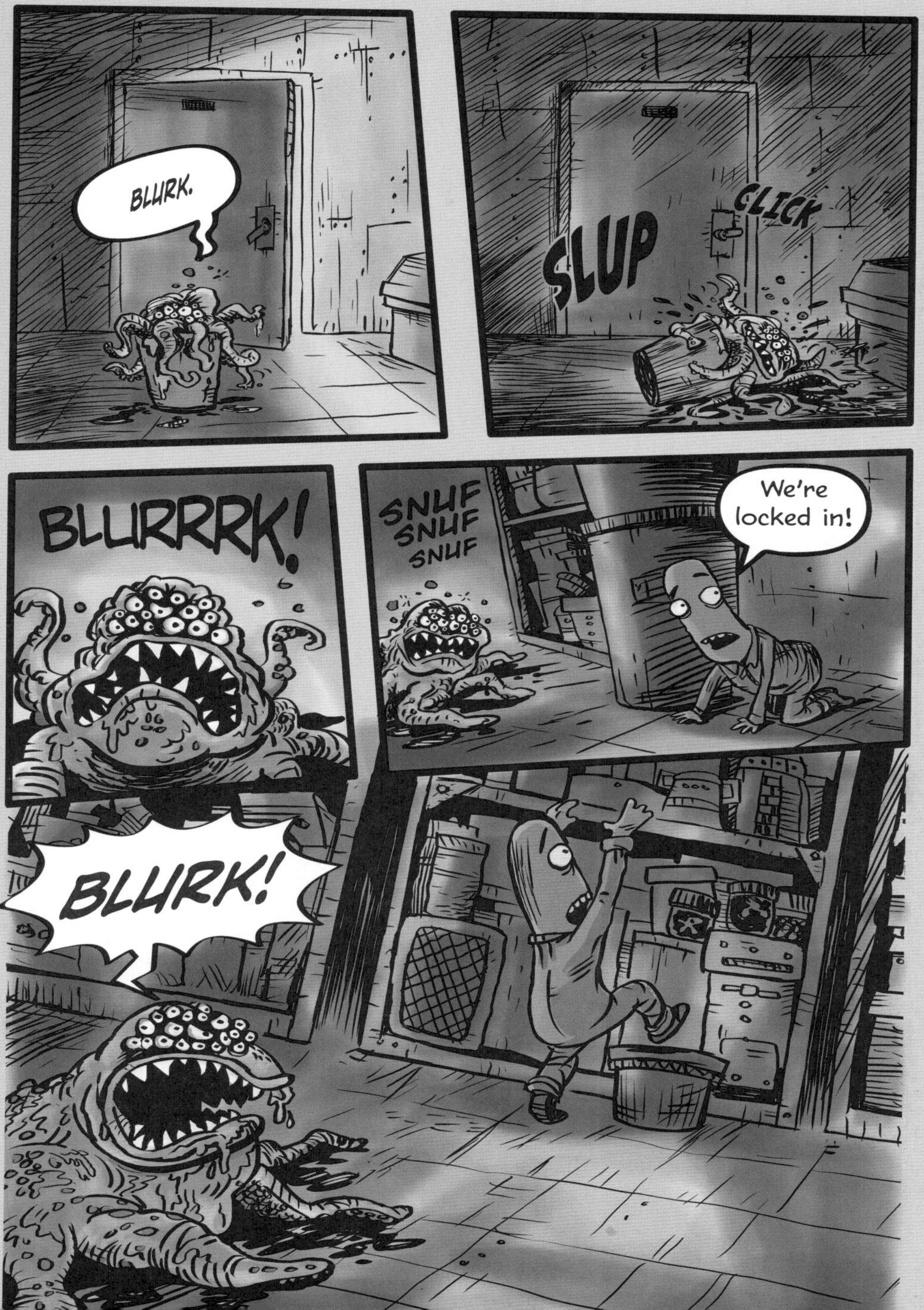
BLURK.
SLUP
CLICK
BLURRRK!
SNUF
SNUF
SNUF
We're locked in!
BLURK!

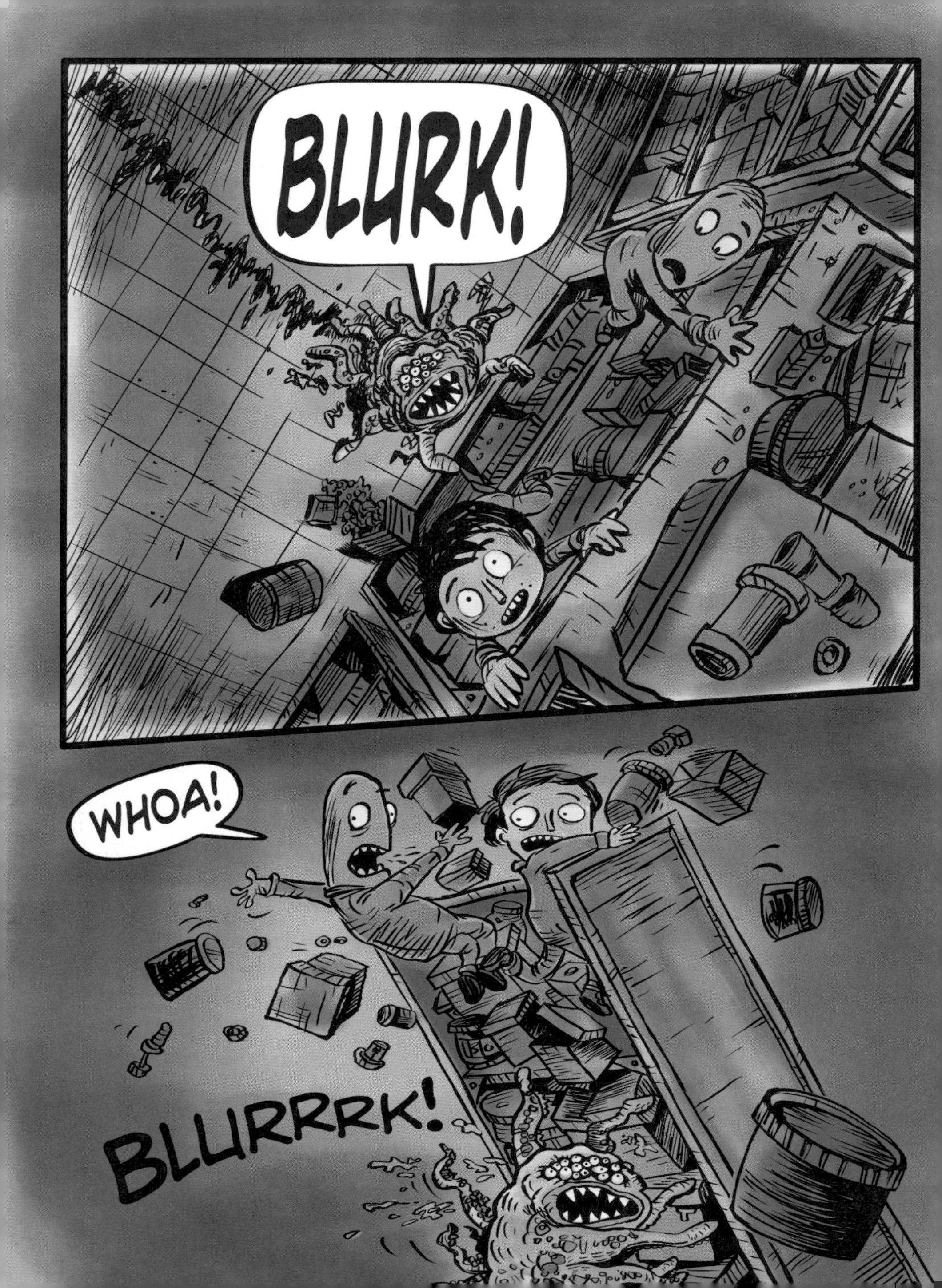
BLURK!
WHOA!
BLURRRK!

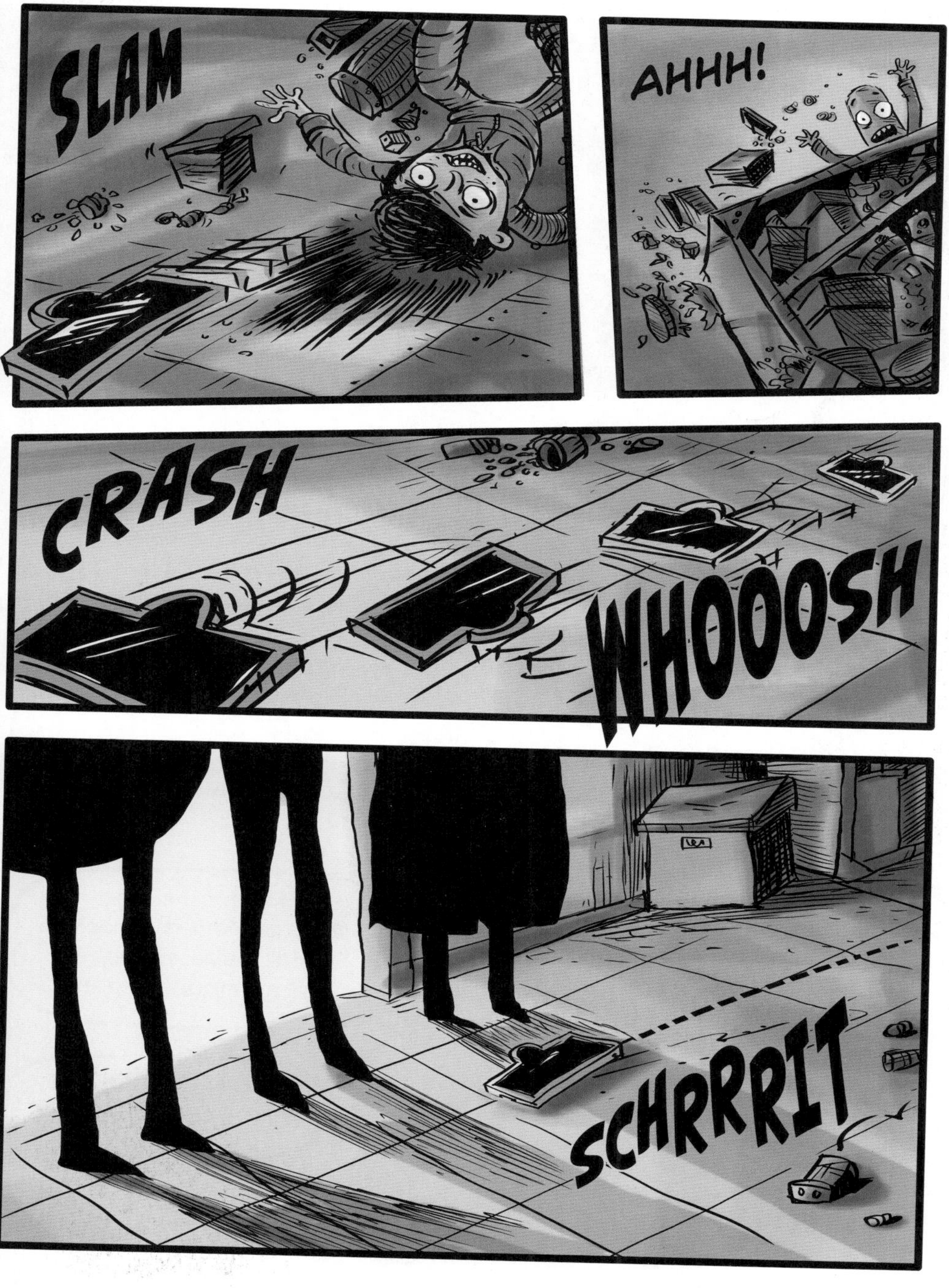
SLAM
AHHH!
CRASH
WHOOOSH
SCHRRRIT

134

CHAPTER 5

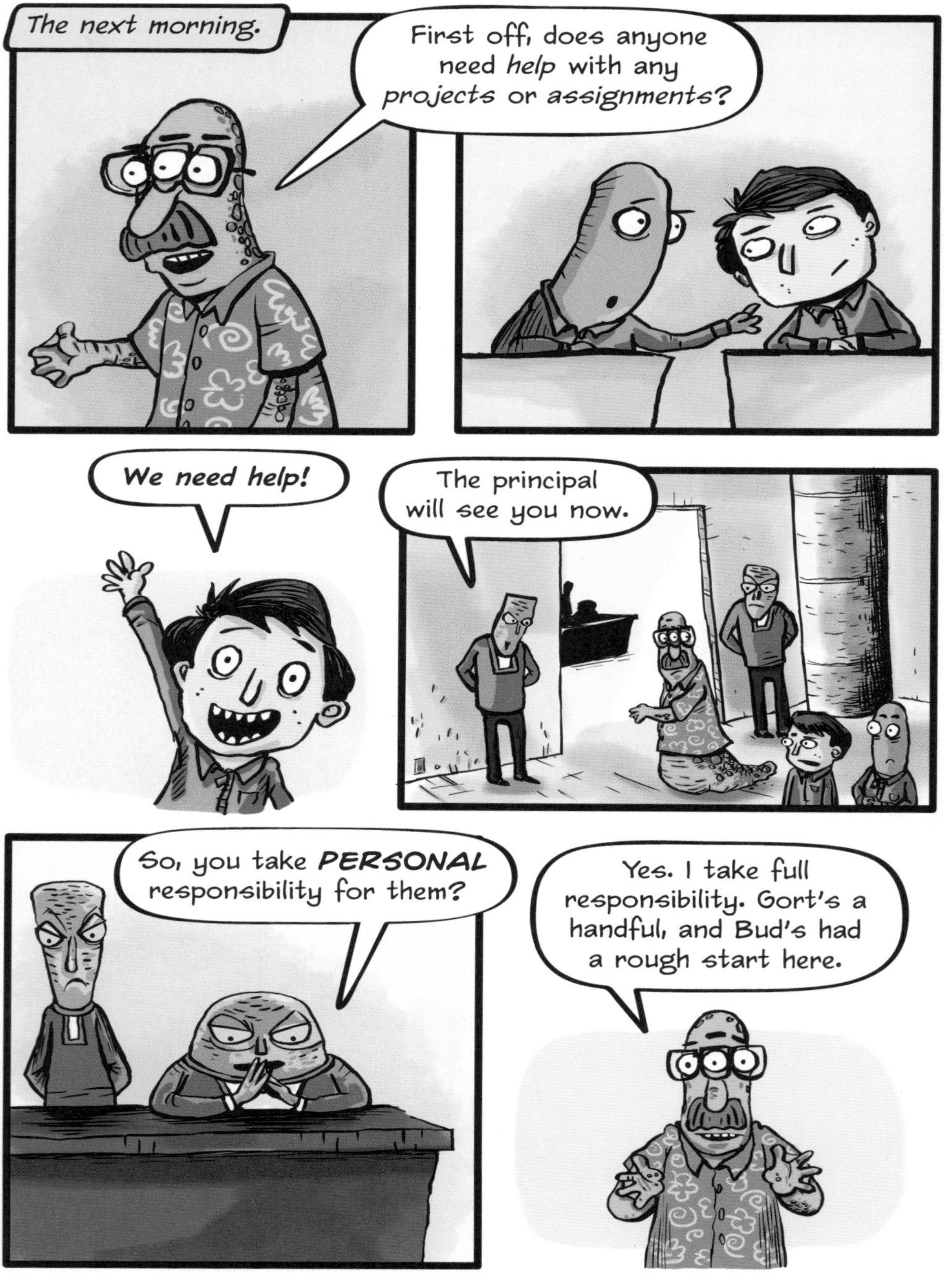
The next morning.
First off, does anyone need *help* with any *projects* or *assignments*?
We need help!
The principal will see you now.
So, you take ***PERSONAL*** responsibility for them?
Yes. I take full responsibility. Gort's a handful, and Bud's had a rough start here.

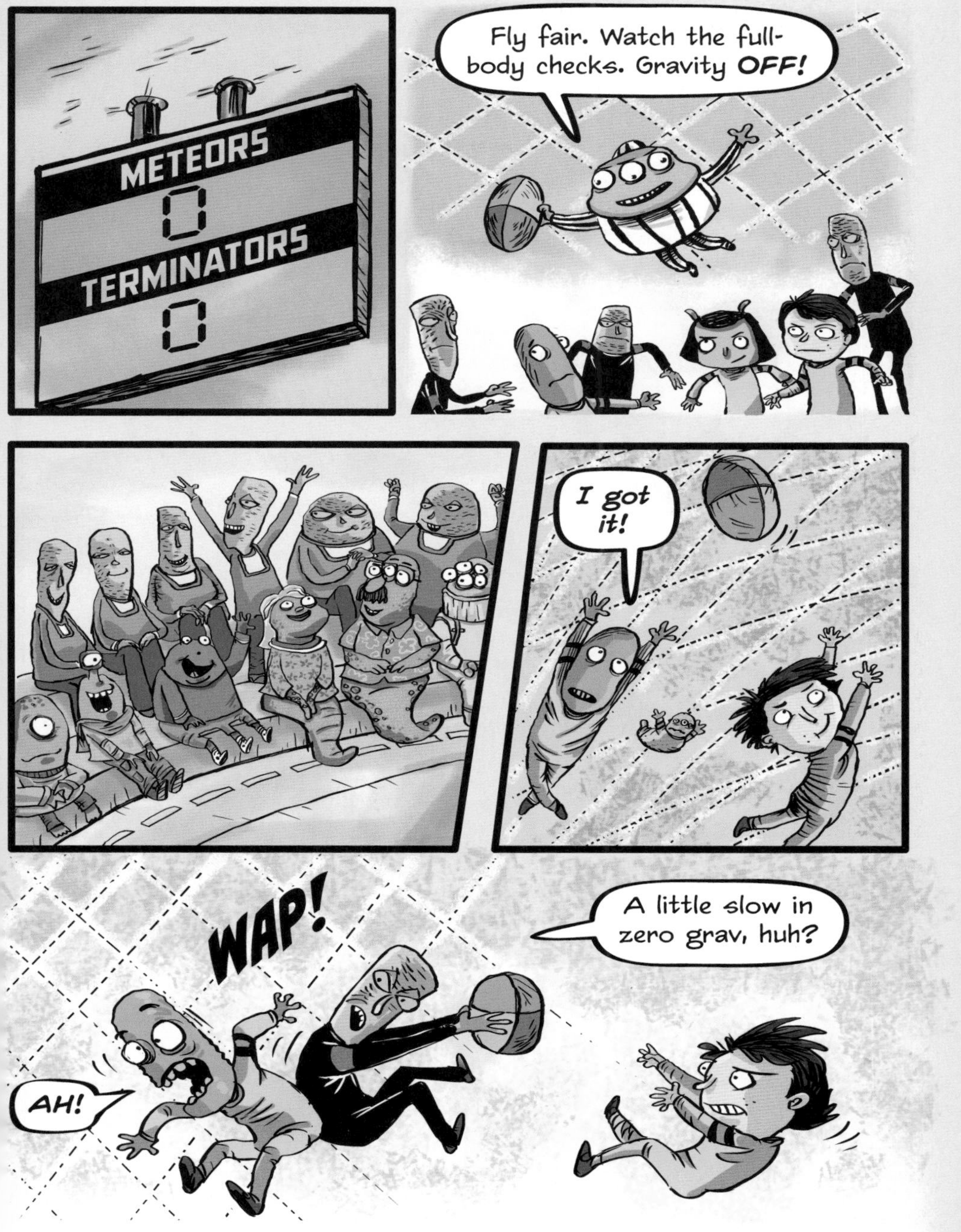
METEORS
0
TERMINATORS
0
Fly fair. Watch the full-body checks. Gravity **OFF!**
I got it!
WAP!
A little slow in zero grav, huh?
AH!

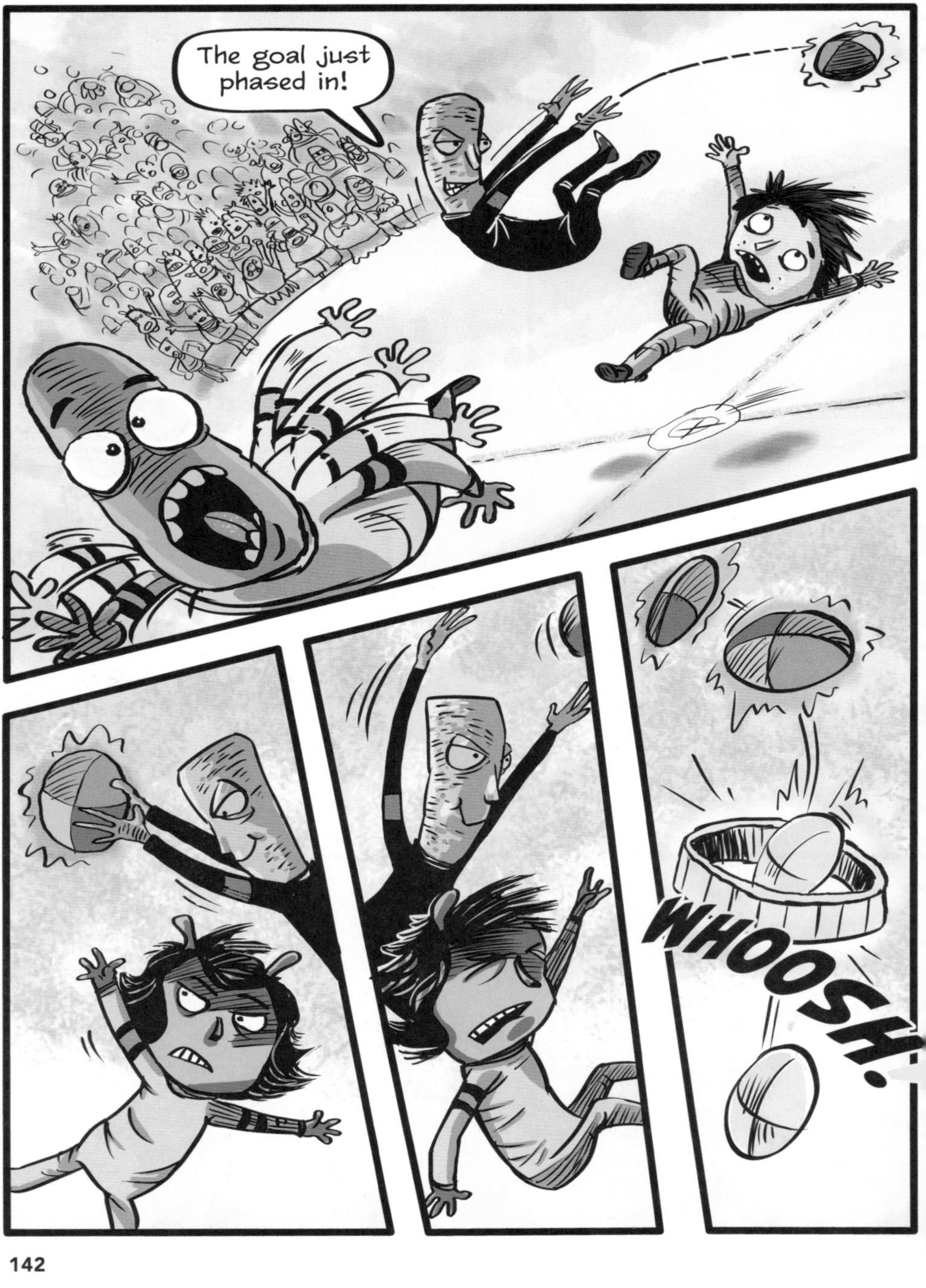

The goal just phased in!
WHOOSH!

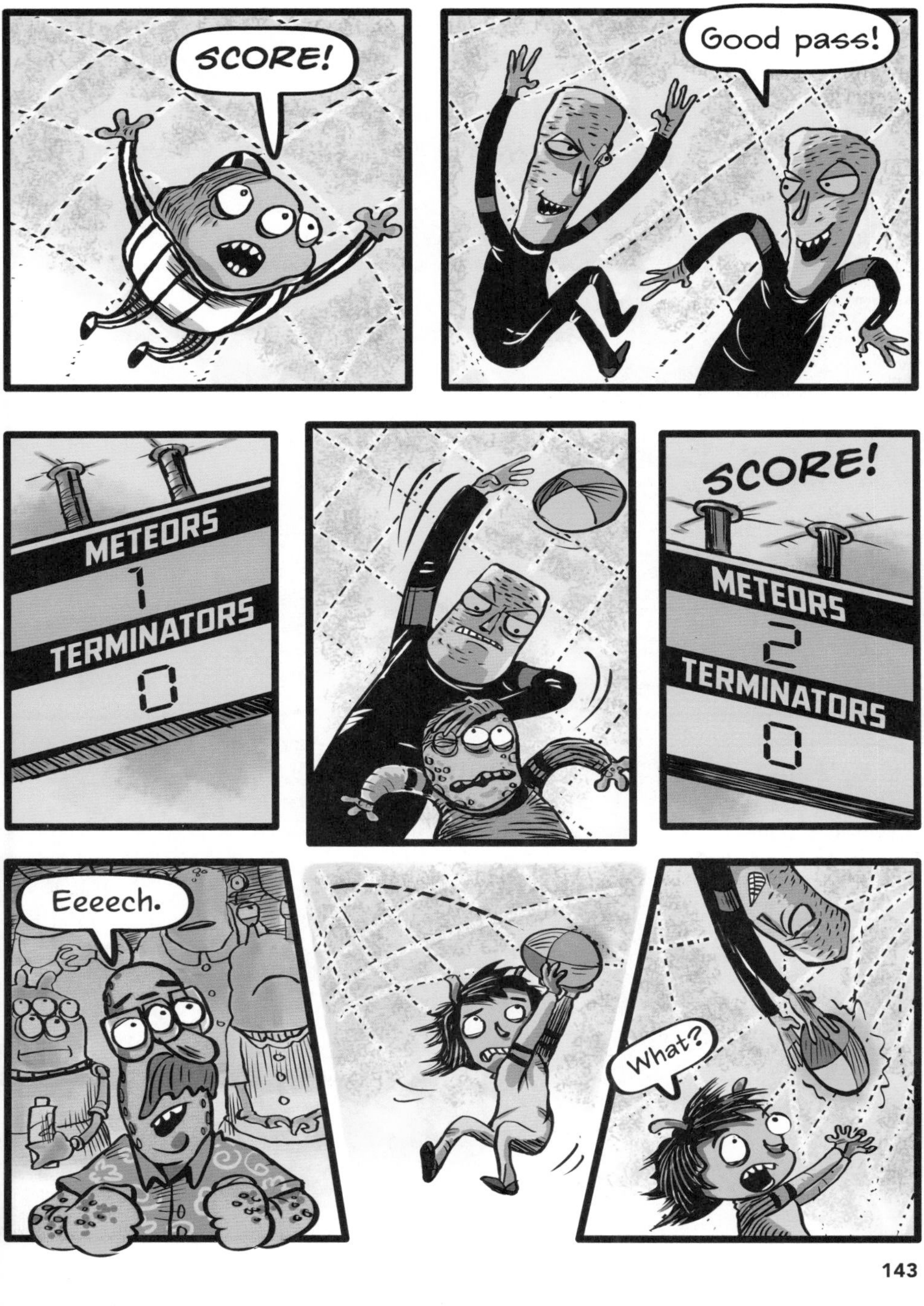

SCORE!
Good pass!
METEORS
1
TERMINATORS
0
SCORE!
METEORS
2
TERMINATORS
0
Eeeech.
What?

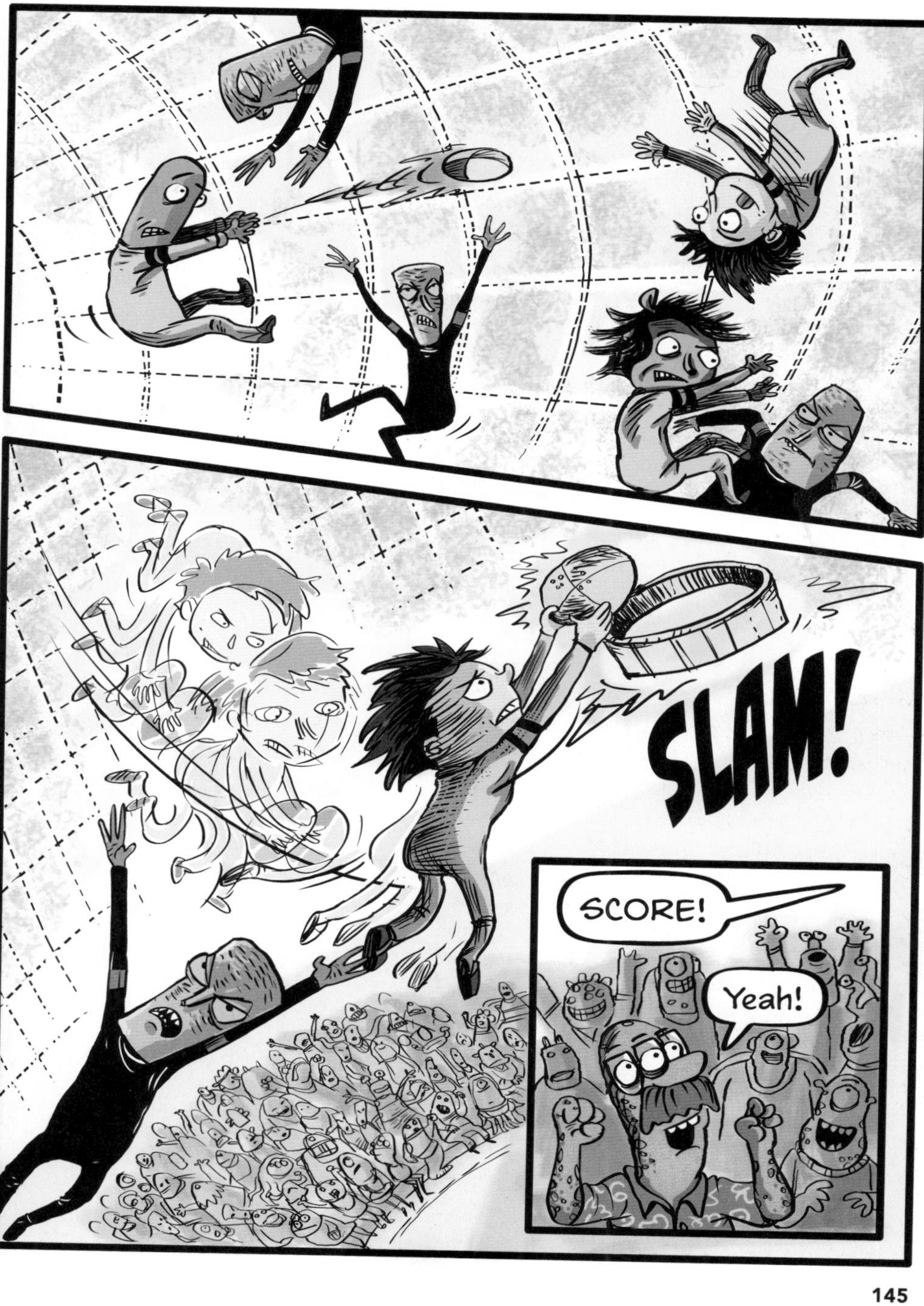

SLAM!
SCORE!
Yeah!

146

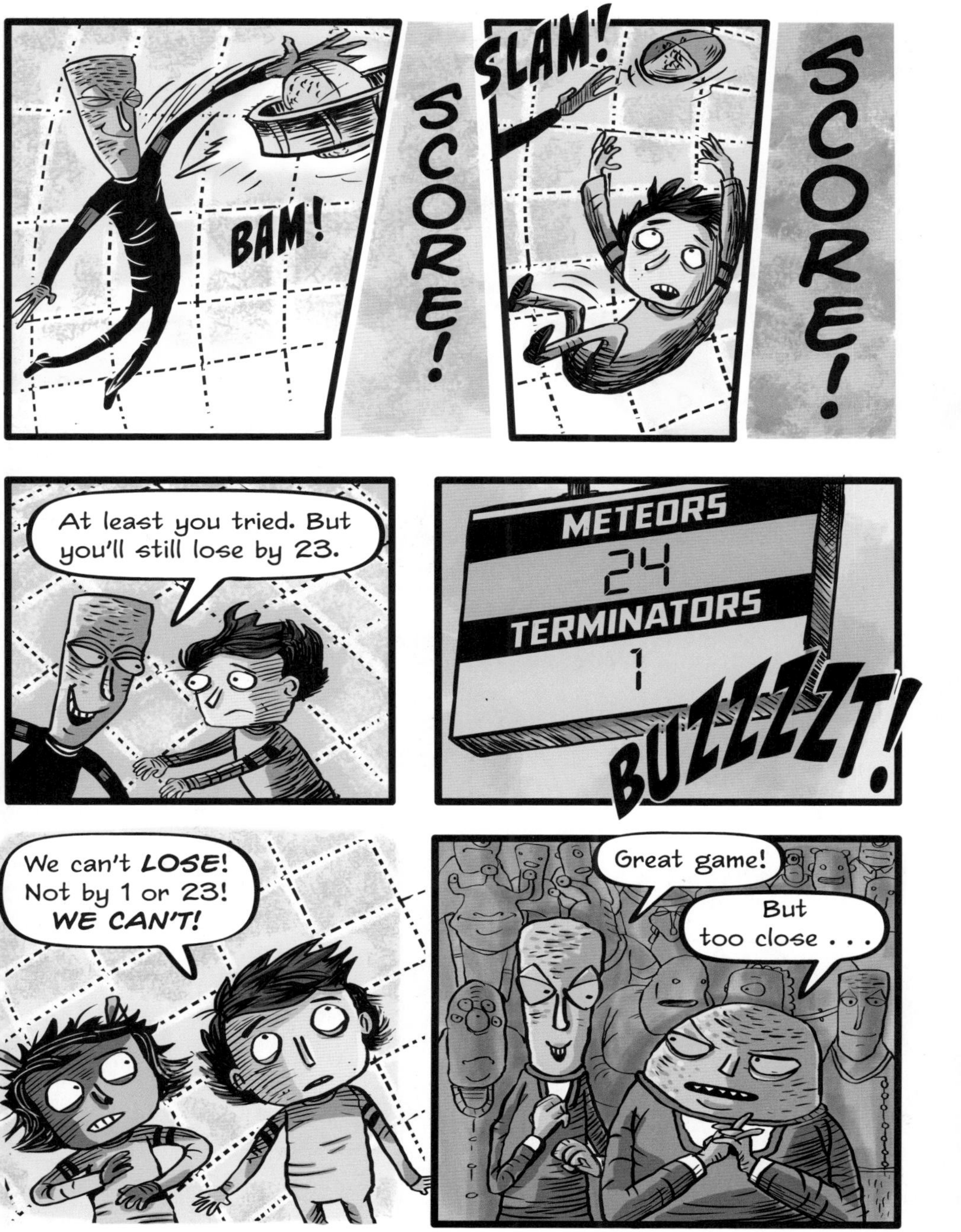
BAM!
SCORE!
SLAM!
SCORE!
At least you tried. But you'll still lose by 23.
METEORS
24
TERMINATORS
1
BUZZZZZT!
We can't LOSE! Not by 1 or 23! WE CAN'T!
Great game!
But too close . . .

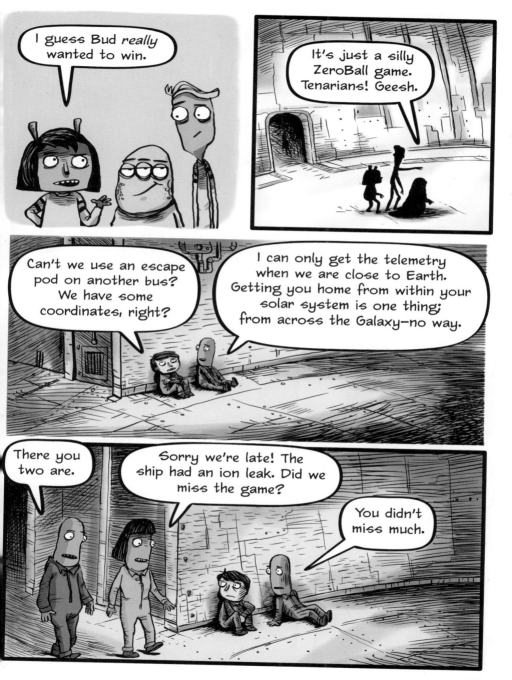

CHAPTER 6

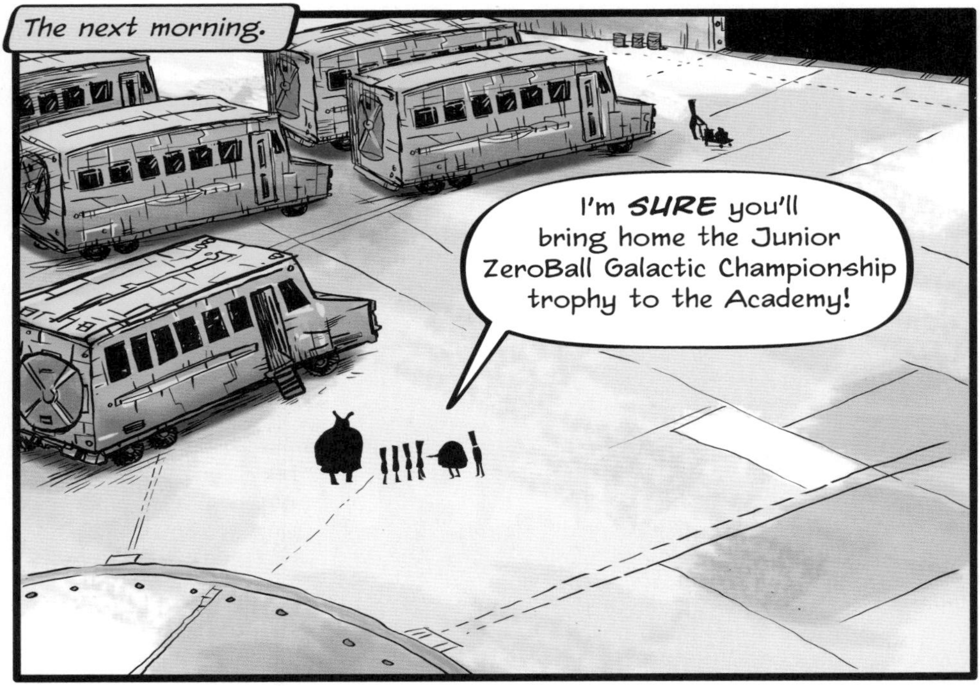
The next morning.
I'm SURE you'll bring home the Junior ZeroBall Galactic Championship trophy to the Academy!

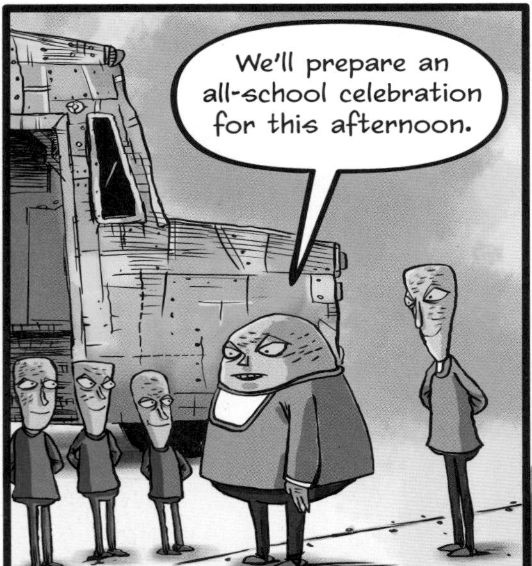
We'll prepare an all-school celebration for this afternoon.

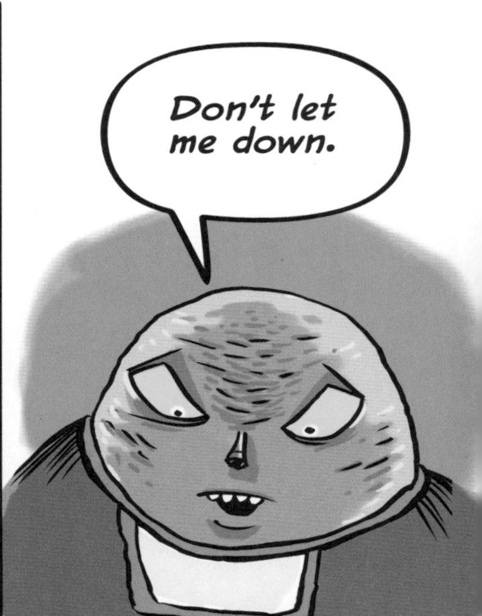
Don't let me down.

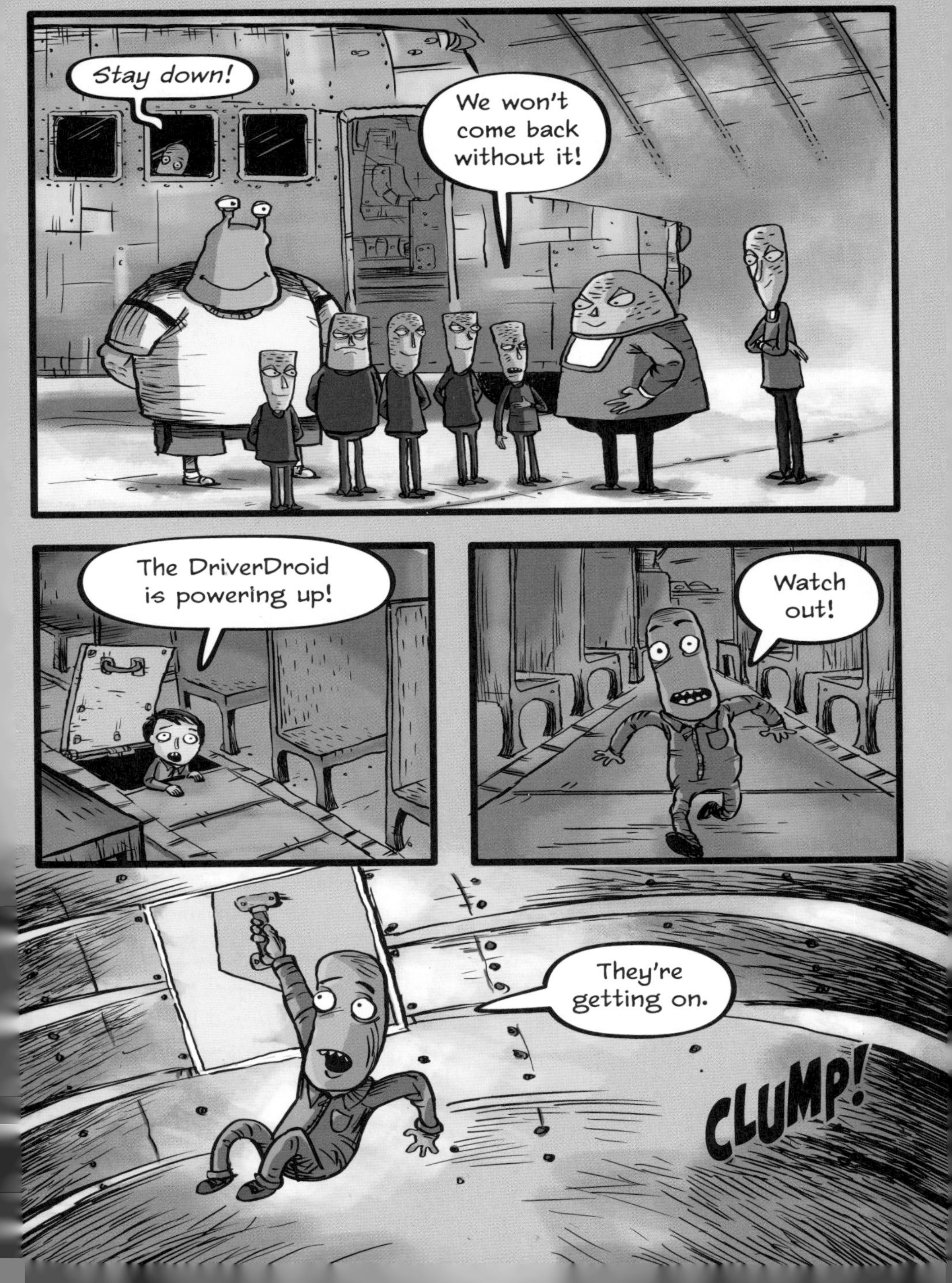
Stay down!
We won't come back without it!
The DriverDroid is powering up!
Watch out!
They're getting on.
CLUMP!

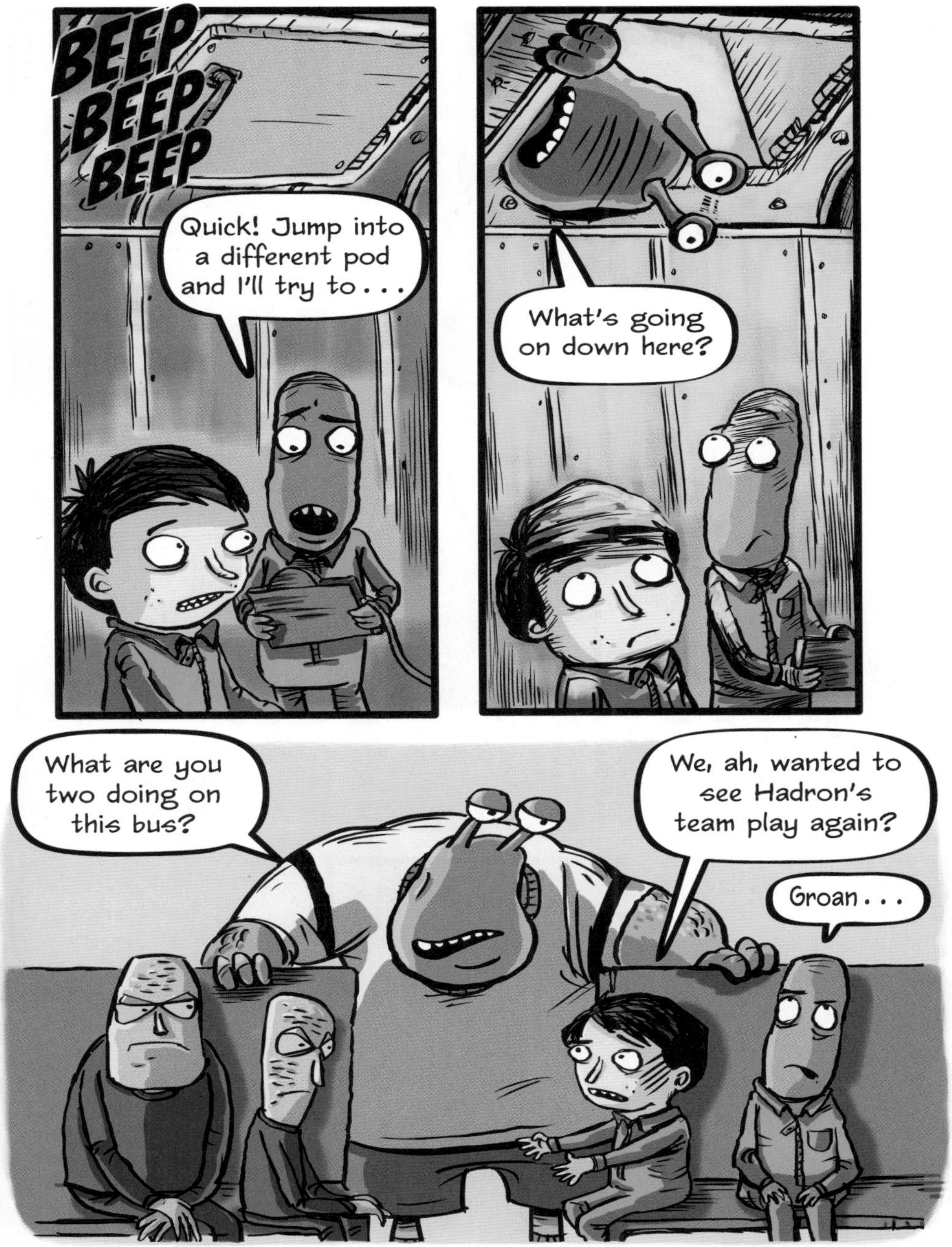
BEEP
BEEP
BEEP
Quick! Jump into a different pod and I'll try to . . .
What's going on down here?
What are you two doing on this bus?
We, ah, wanted to see Hadron's team play again?
Groan . . .

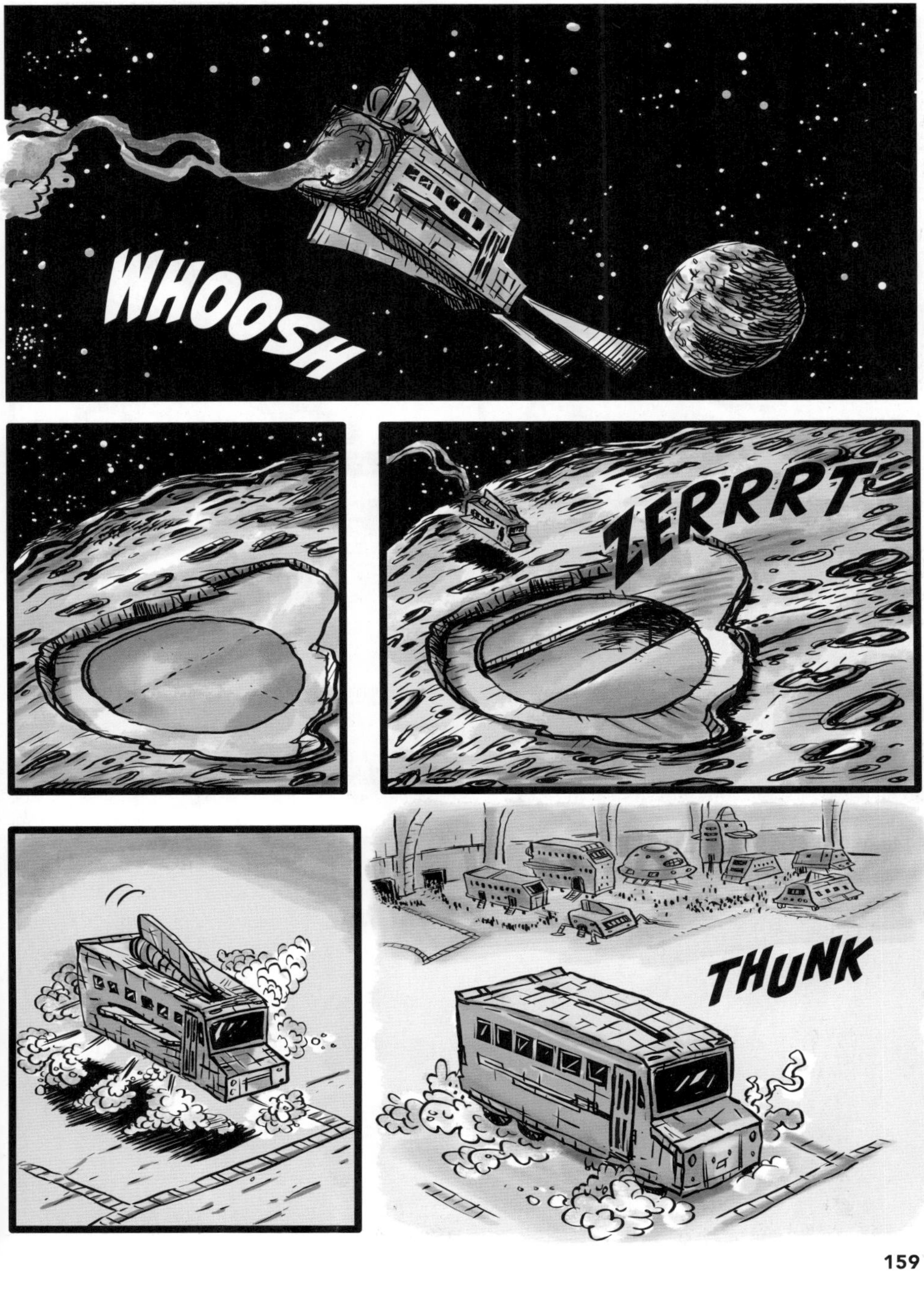
WHOOSH
ZERRRT
THUNK

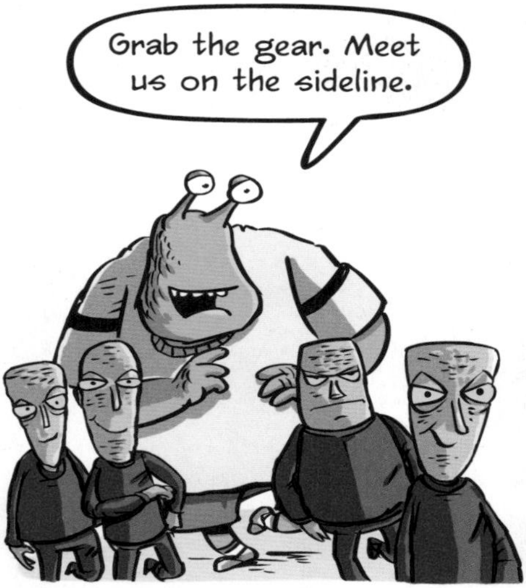
Grab the gear. Meet us on the sideline.

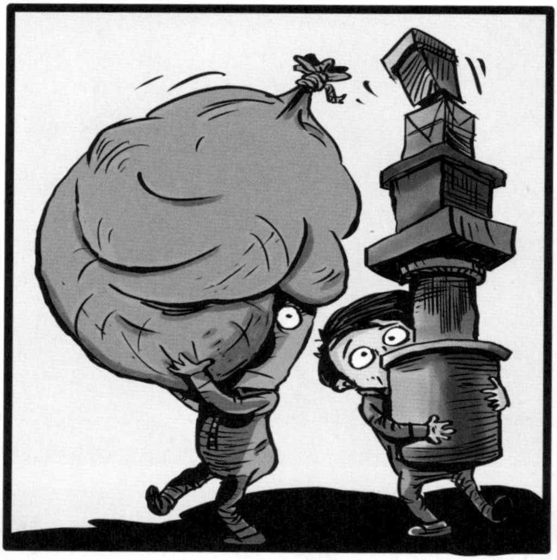

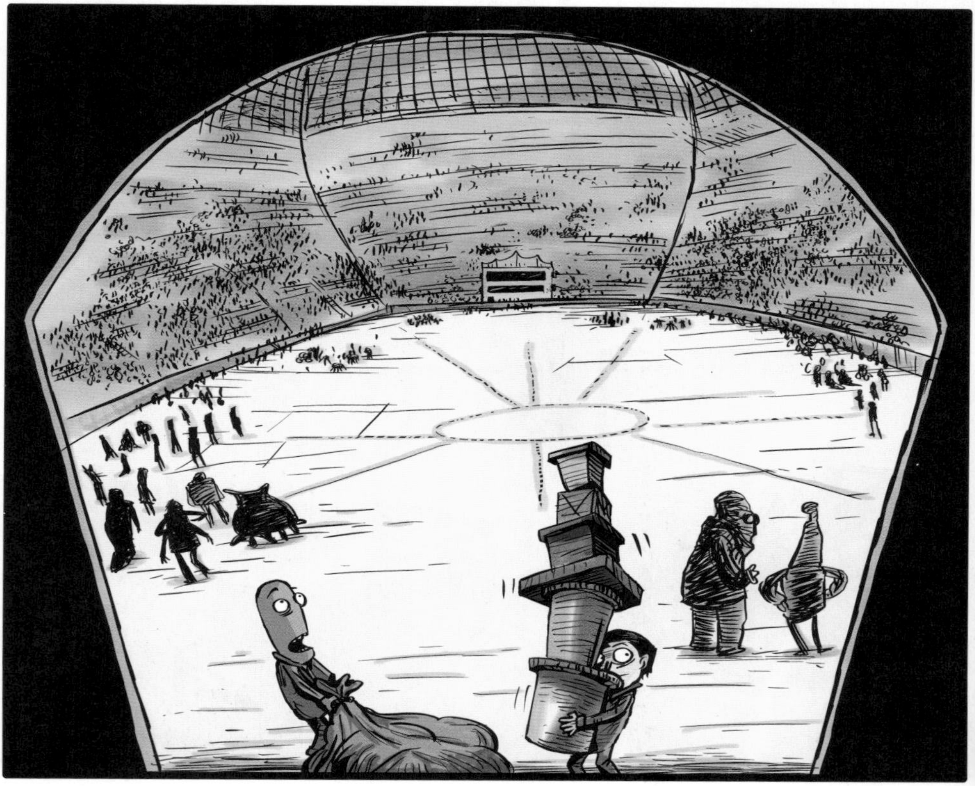

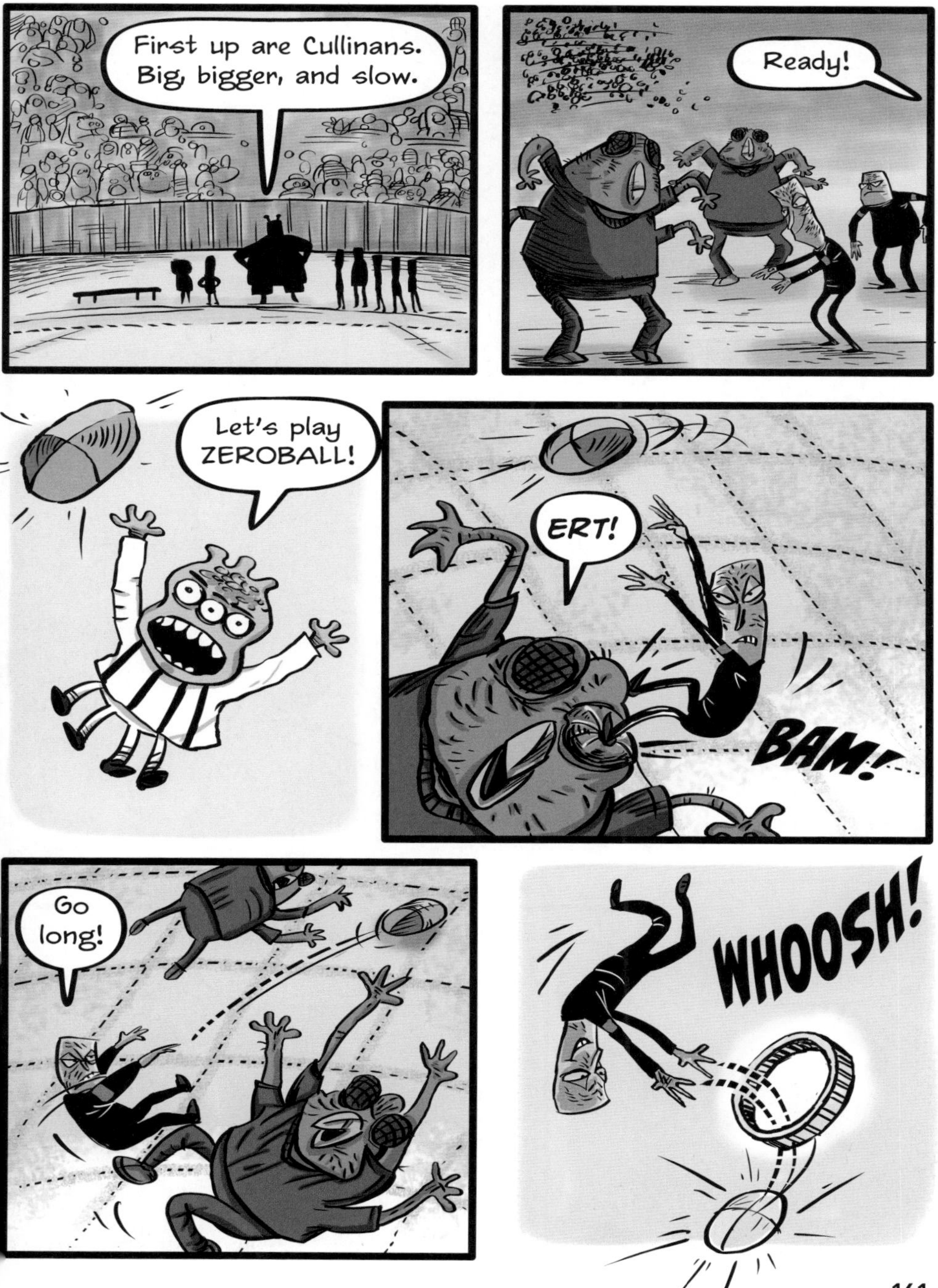
First up are Cullinans. Big, bigger, and slow.
Ready!
Let's play ZEROBALL!
ERT!
BAM!
Go long!
WHOOSH!

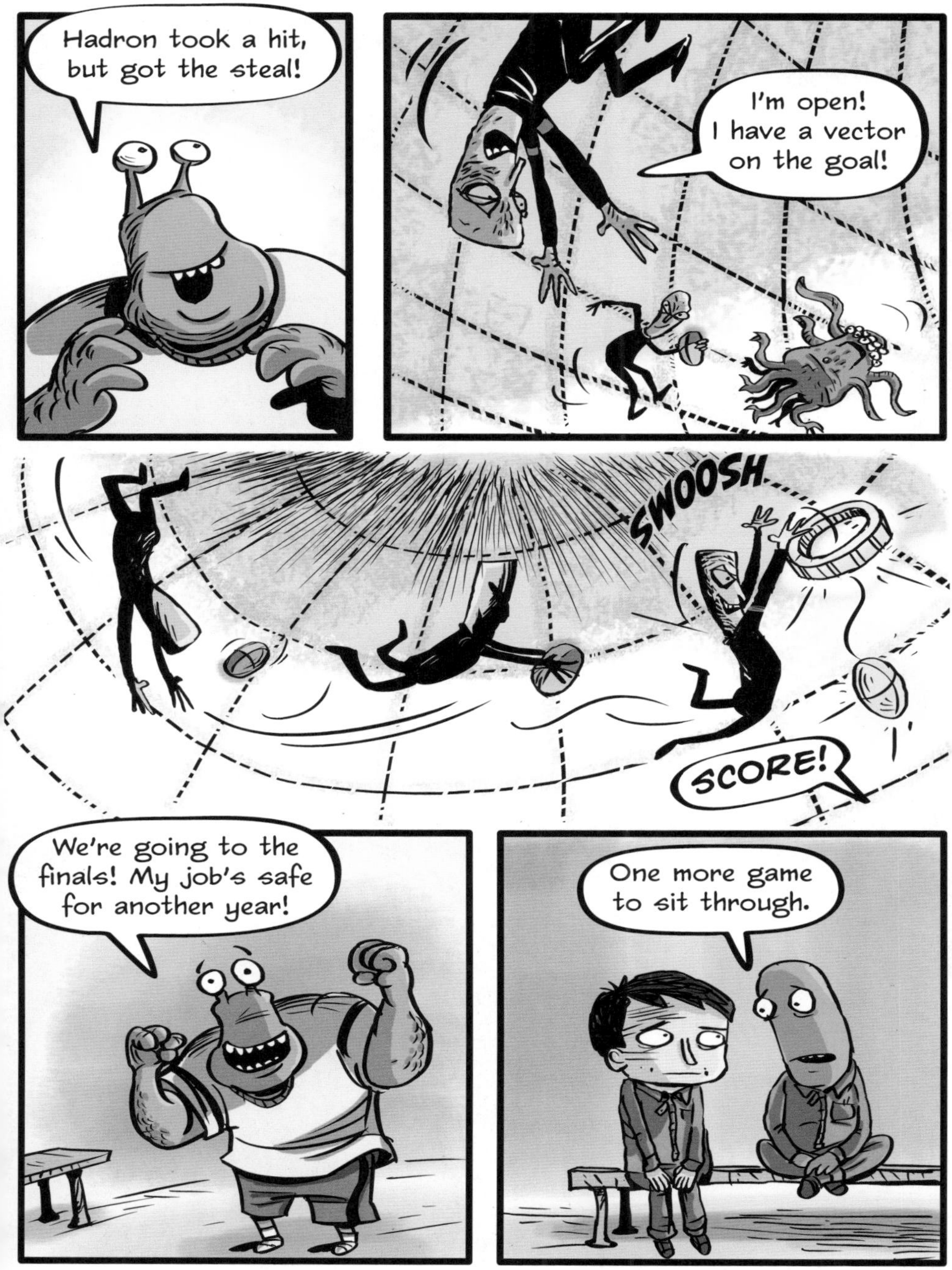
Hadron took a hit, but got the steal!
I'm open! I have a vector on the goal!
SWOOSH
SCORE!
We're going to the finals! My job's safe for another year!
One more game to sit through.

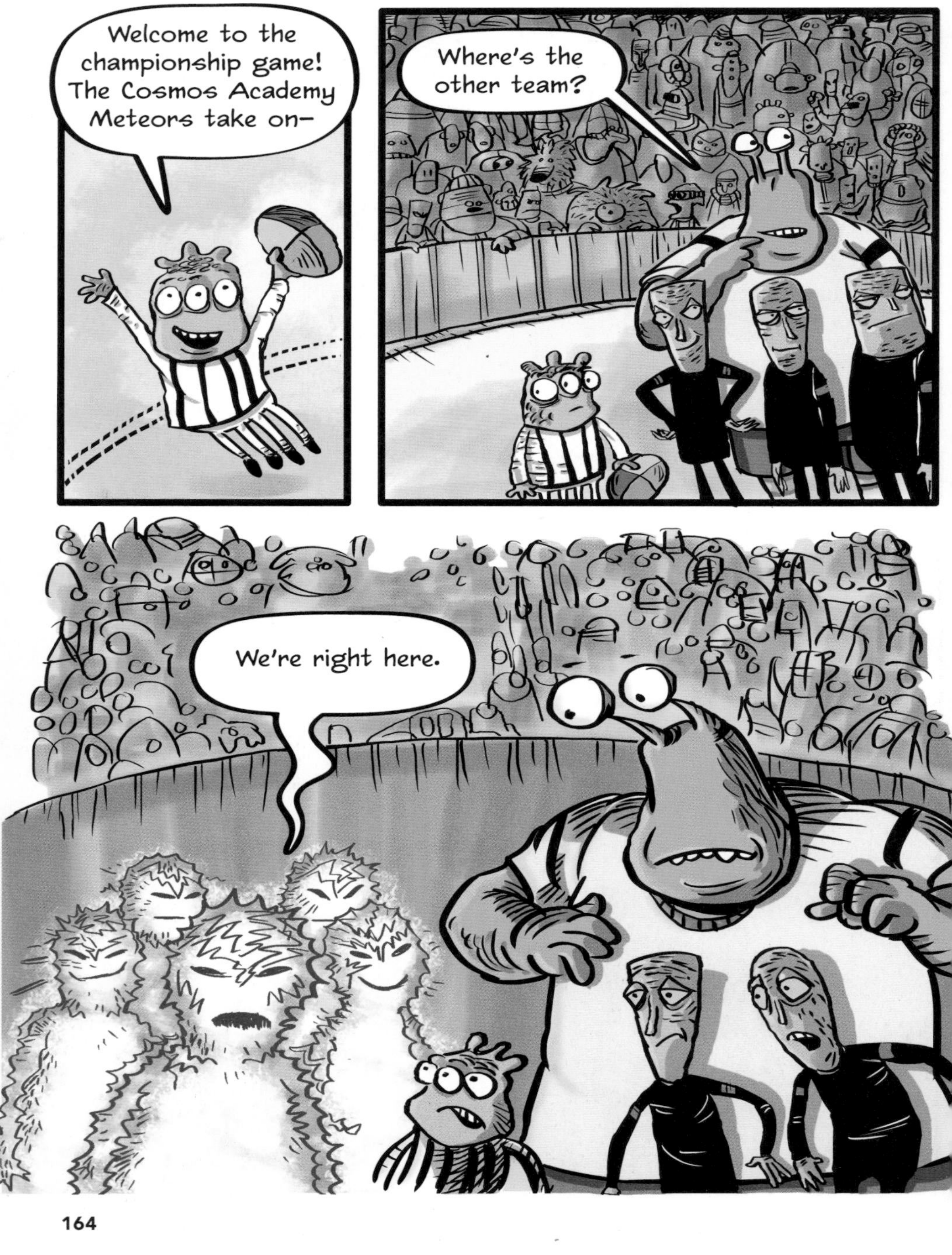
Welcome to the championship game! The Cosmos Academy Meteors take on–
Where's the other team?
We're right here.

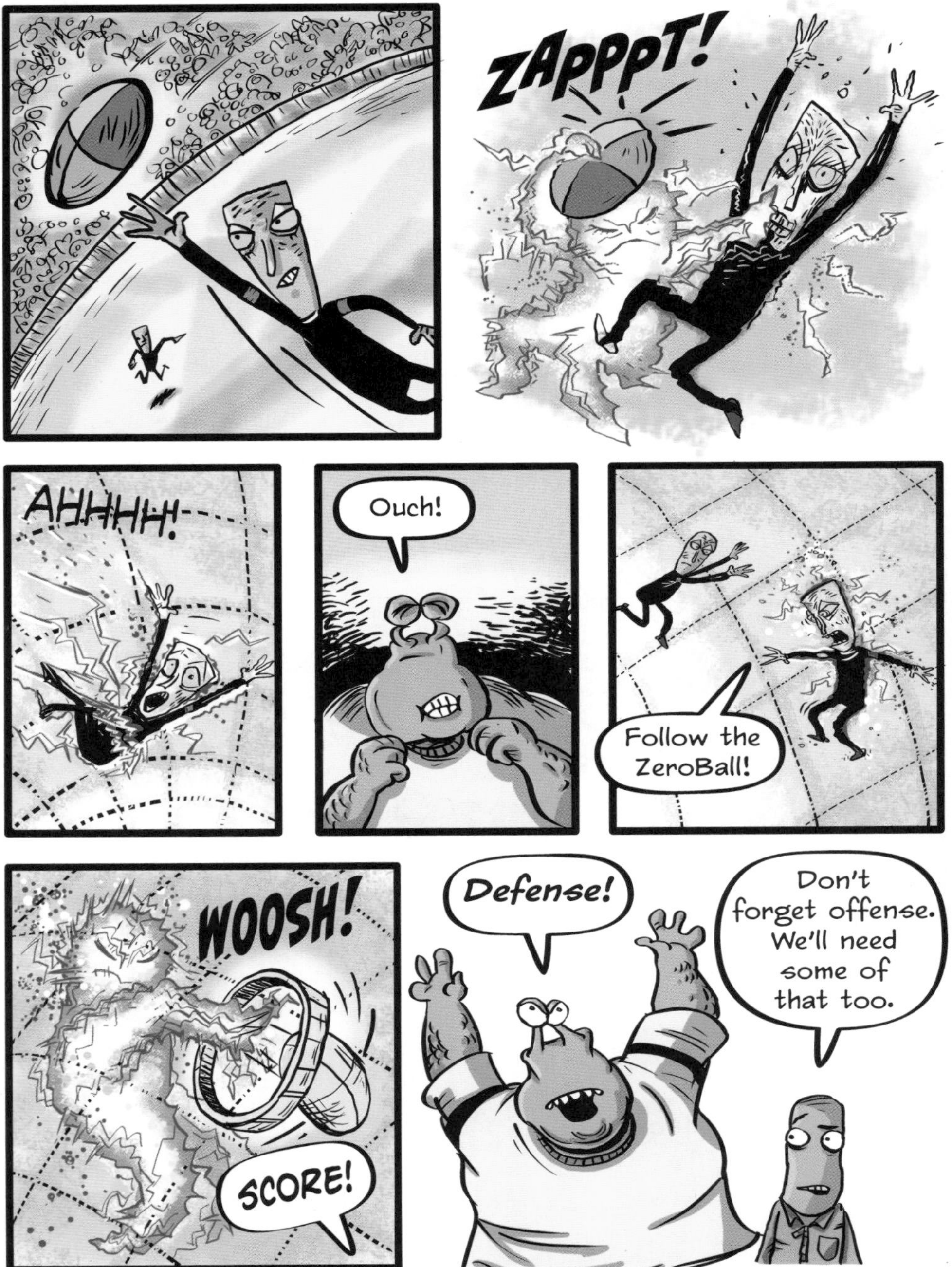
ZAPPPT!
AHHHH!
Ouch!
Follow the ZeroBall!
WOOSH!
SCORE!
Defense!
Don't forget offense. We'll need some of that too.

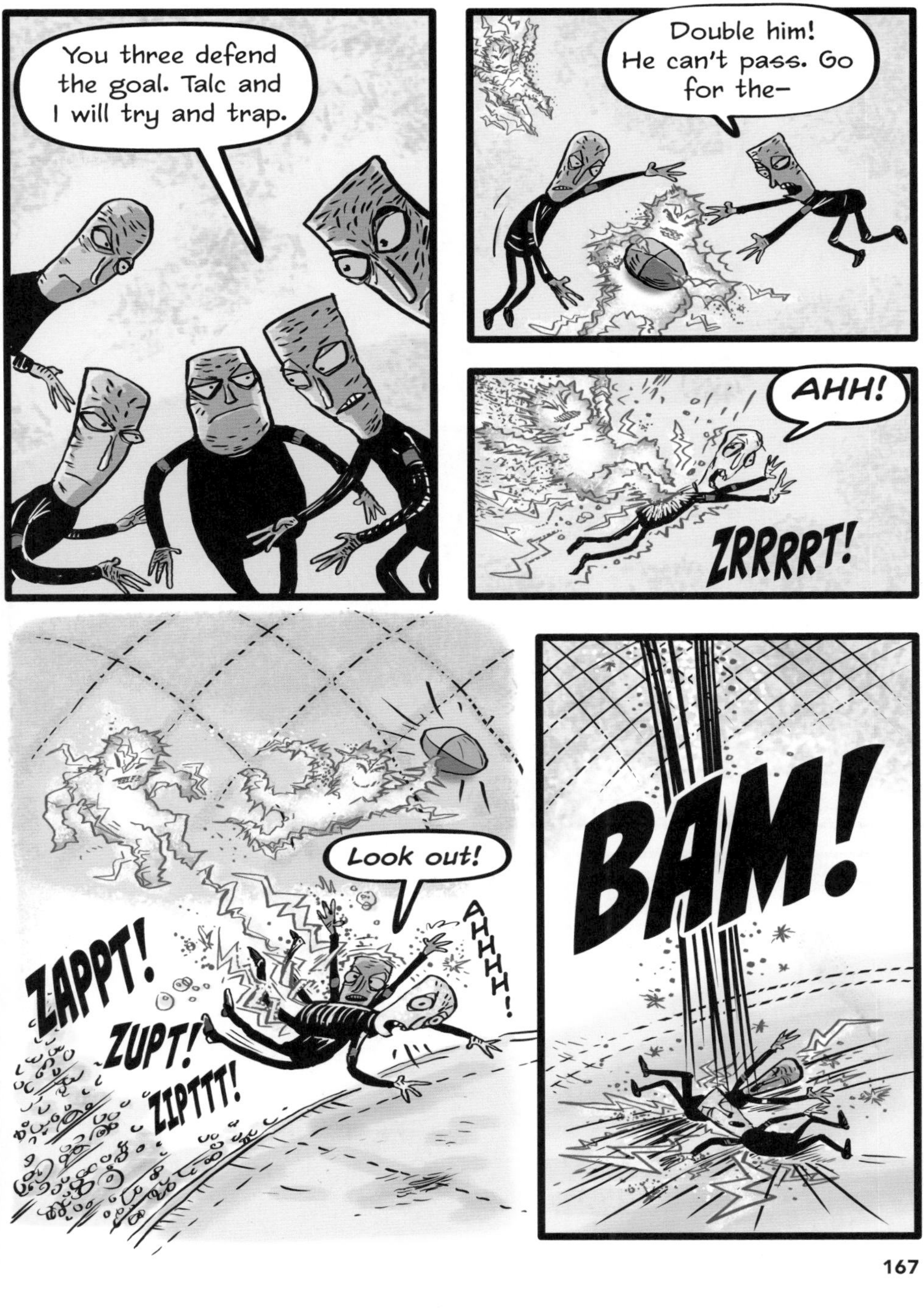
You three defend the goal. Talc and I will try and trap.
Double him! He can't pass. Go for the–
AHH!
ZRRRRT!
Look out!
AHHHH!
ZAPPT!
ZUPT!
ZIPTTT!
BAM!

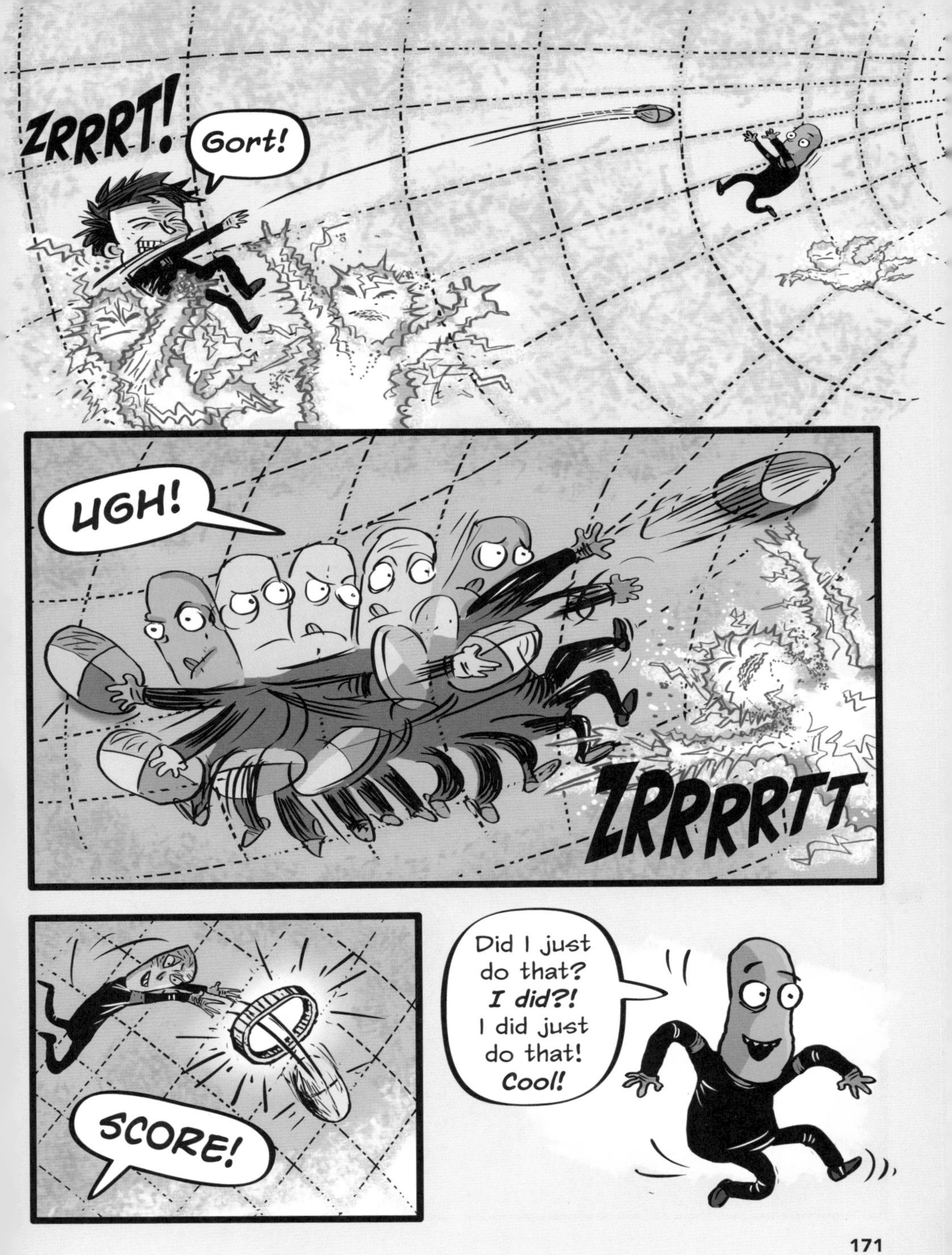
ZRRRT!
Gort!
UGH!
ZRRRRTT
SCORE!
Did I just do that? *I did?!* I did just do that! Cool!

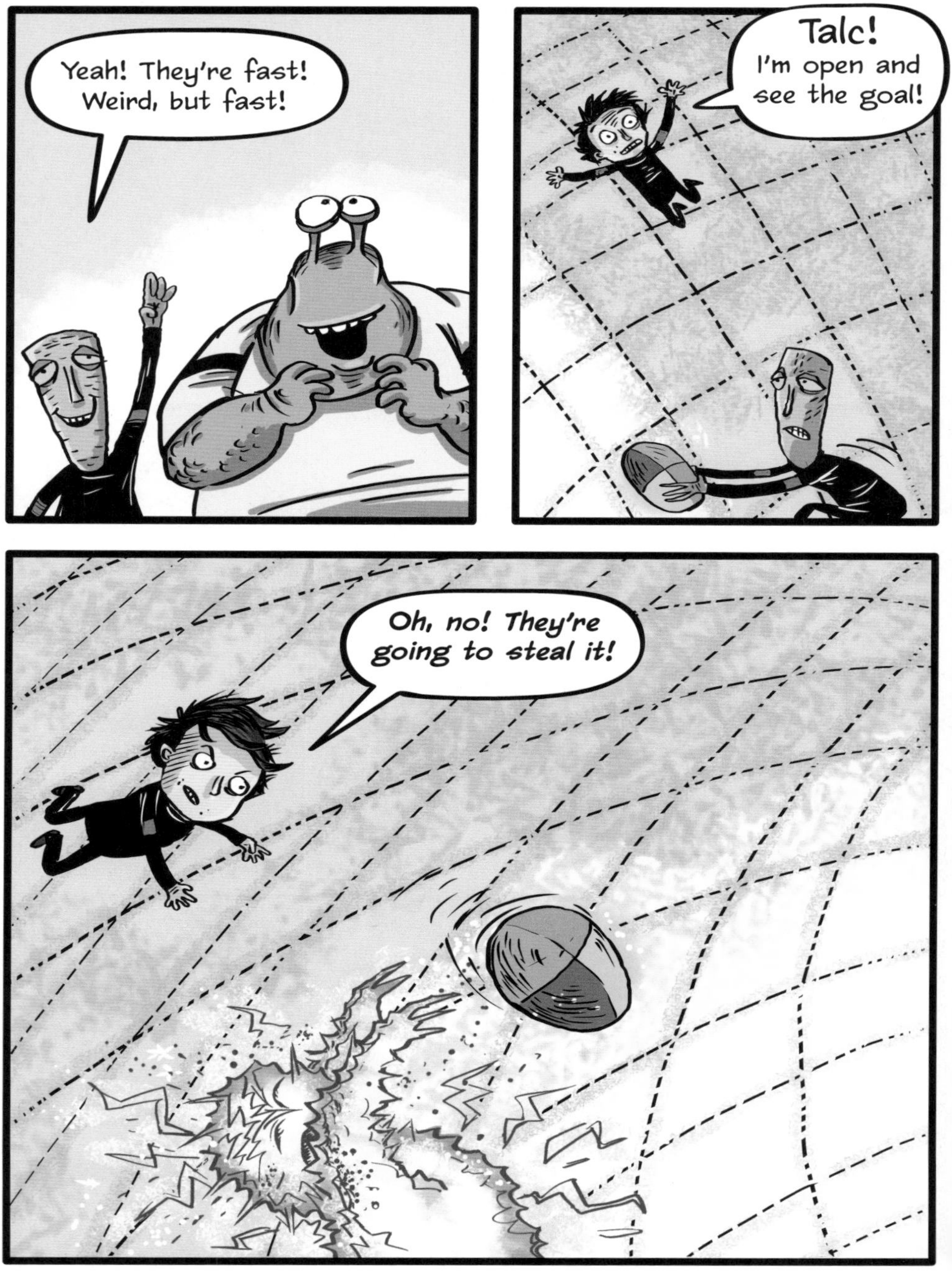
Yeah! They're fast! Weird, but fast!
Talc! I'm open and see the goal!
Oh, no! They're going to steal it!

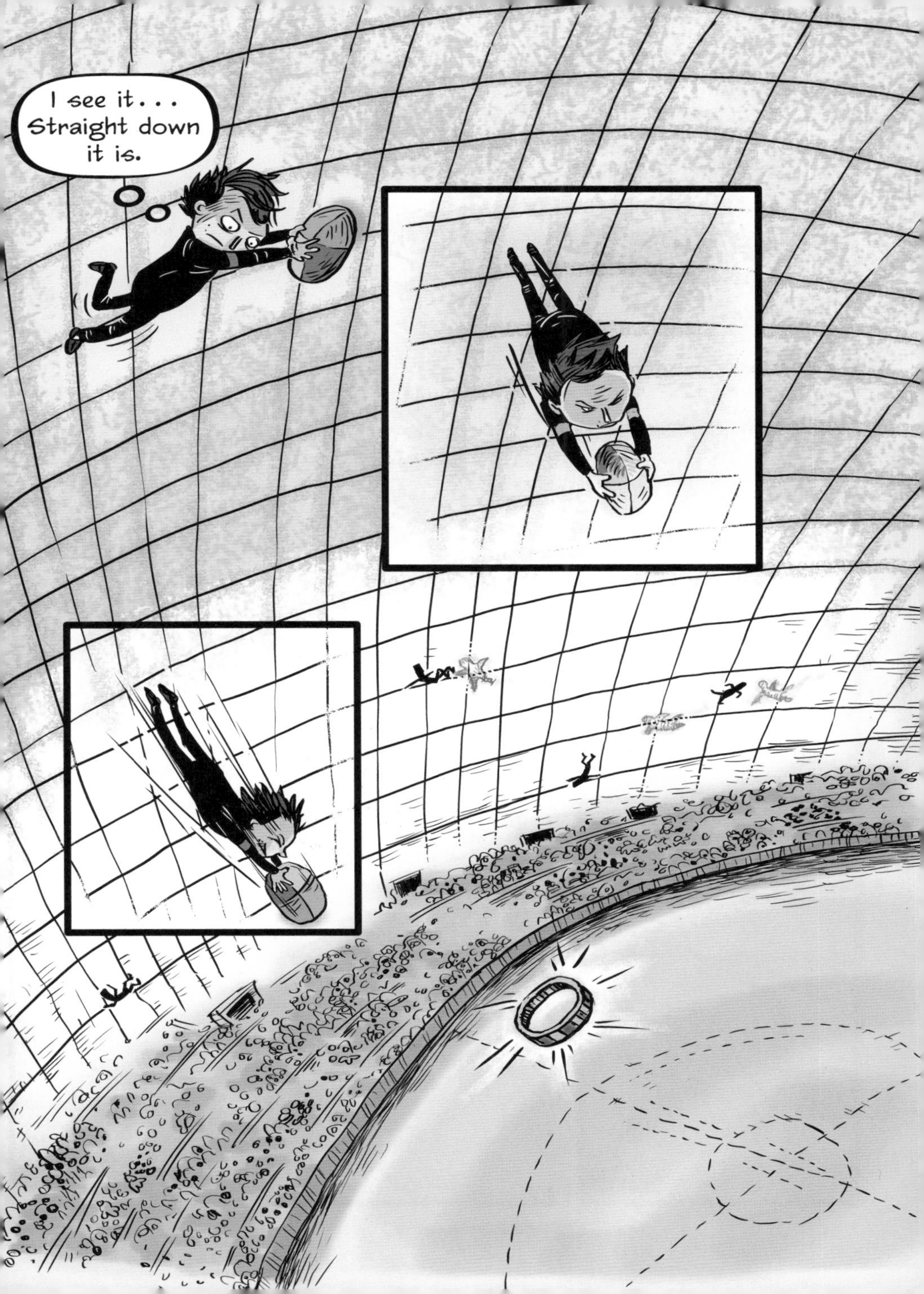
I see it... Straight down it is.

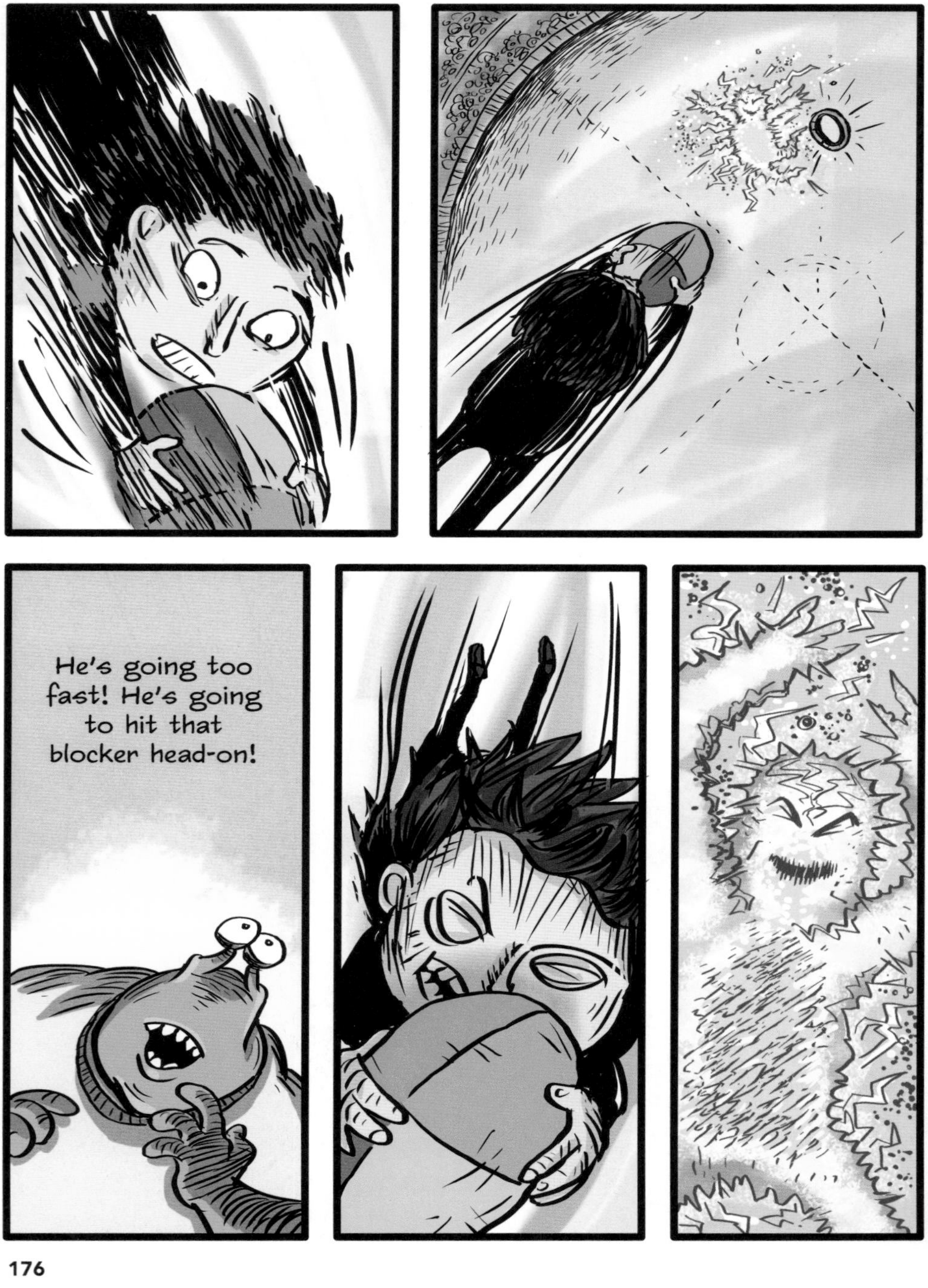
He's going too fast! He's going to hit that blocker head-on!

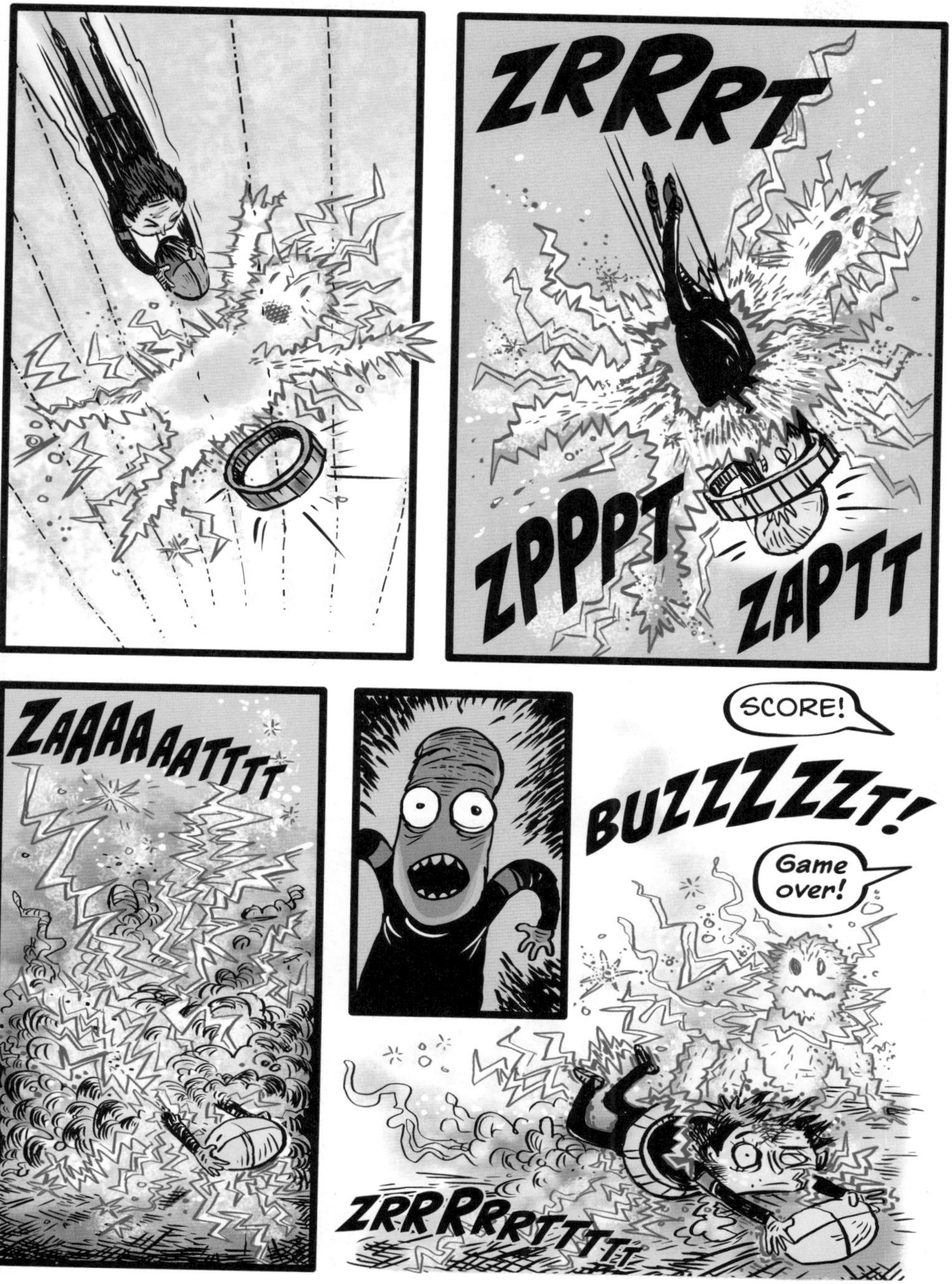
ZRRRT
ZPPPT
ZAPTT
ZAAAAAATTTTT
SCORE!
BUZZZZZT!
Game over!
ZRRRRRTTTTTT

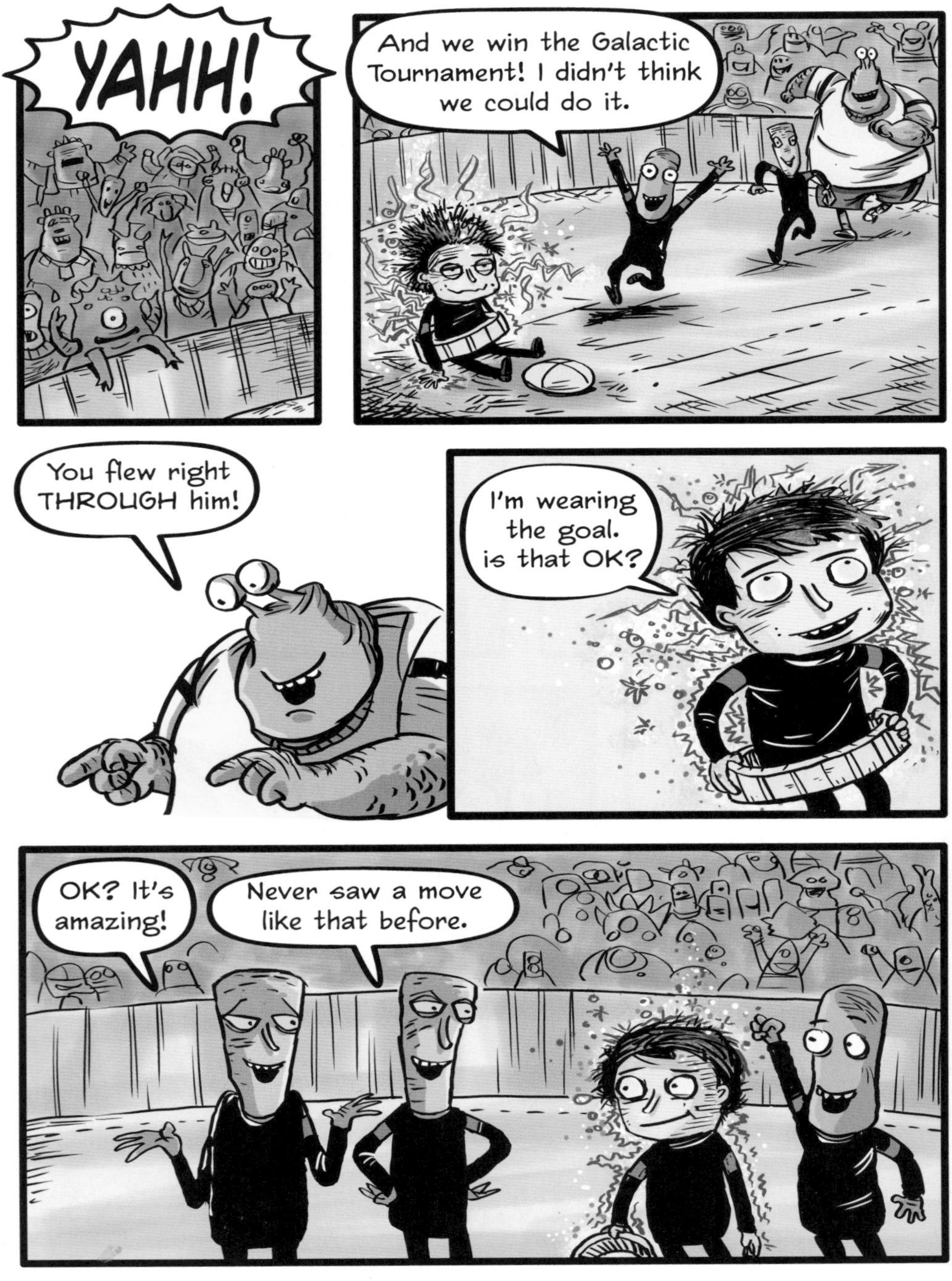
YAHH!
And we win the Galactic Tournament! I didn't think we could do it.
You flew right THROUGH him!
I'm wearing the goal. is that OK?
OK? It's amazing!
Never saw a move like that before.

CHAPTER 7

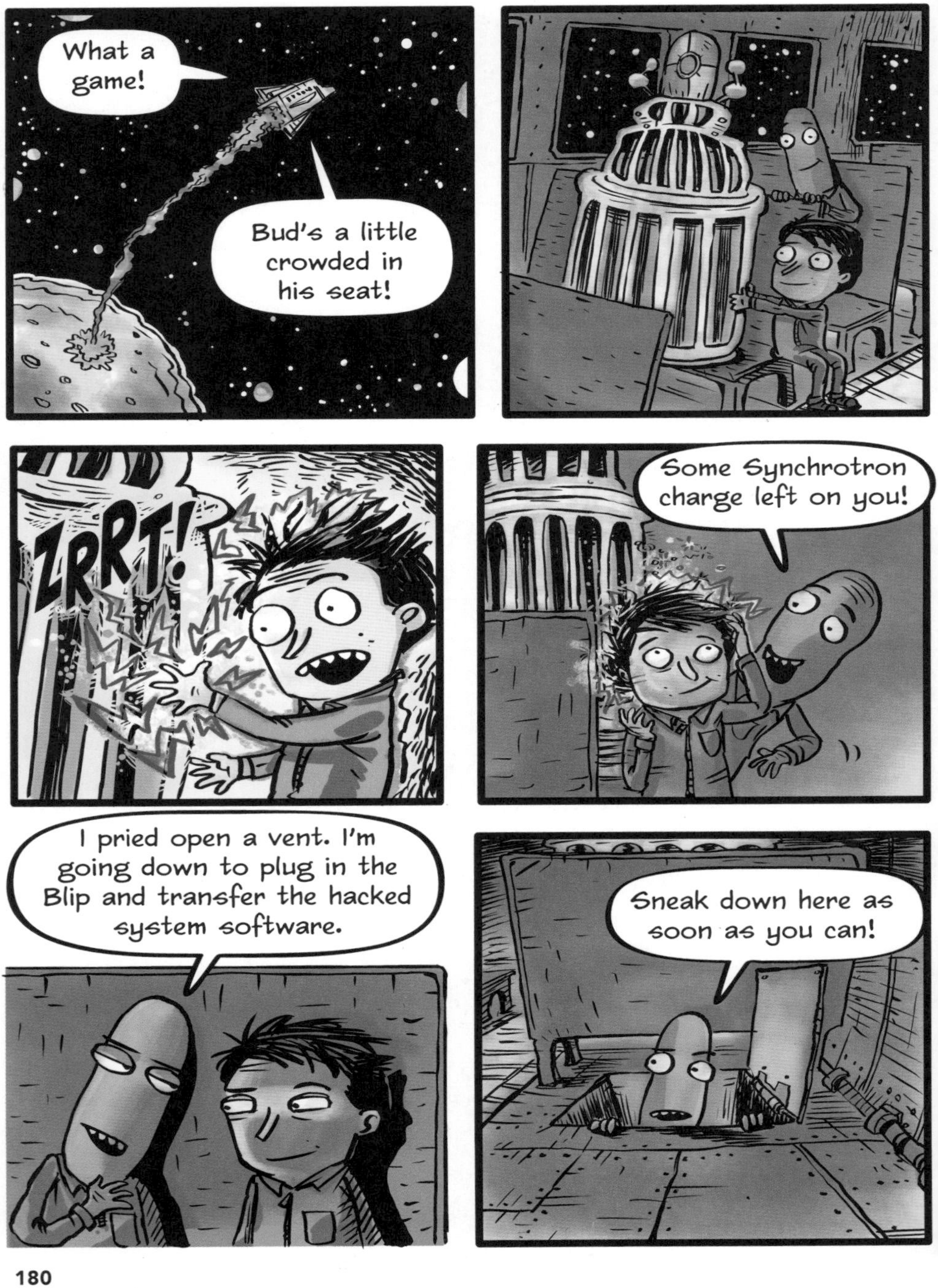
What a game!
Bud's a little crowded in his seat!
ZRRT!
Some Synchrotron charge left on you!
I pried open a vent. I'm going down to plug in the Blip and transfer the hacked system software.
Sneak down here as soon as you can!

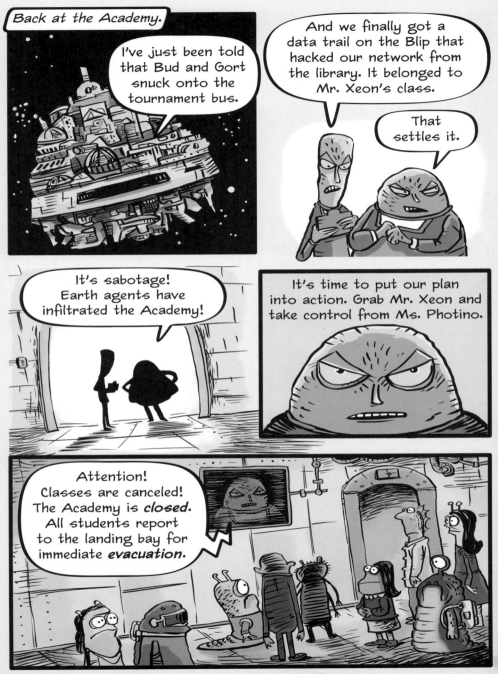

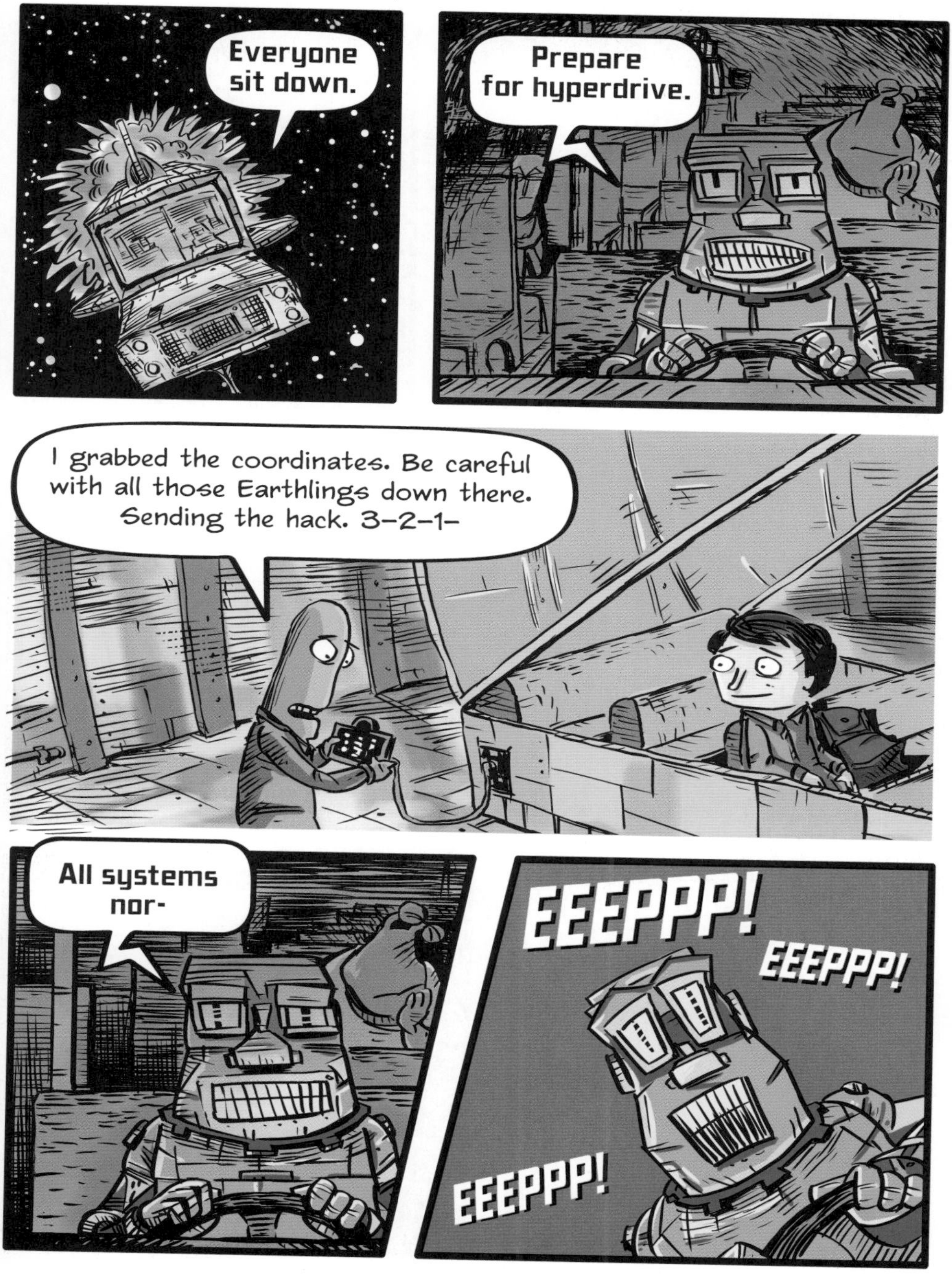
Everyone sit down.
Prepare for hyperdrive.
I grabbed the coordinates. Be careful with all those Earthlings down there. Sending the hack. 3-2-1-
All systems nor-
EEEPPP!
EEEPPP!
EEEPPP!

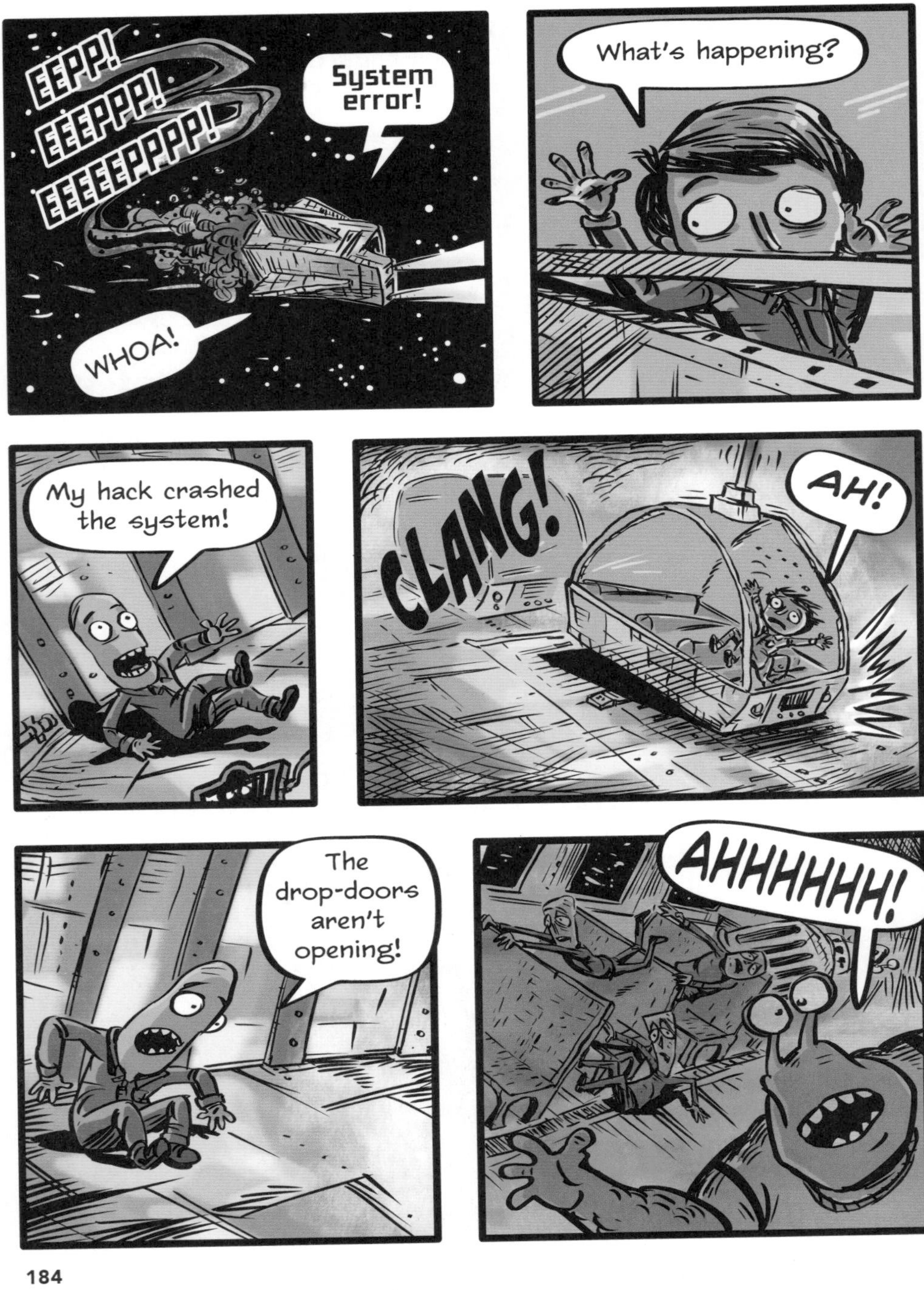
EEPP!
EEEPPP!
EEEEEPPPP!
System error!
WHOA!
What's happening?
My hack crashed the system!
CLANG!
AH!
The drop-doors aren't opening!
AHHHHHH!

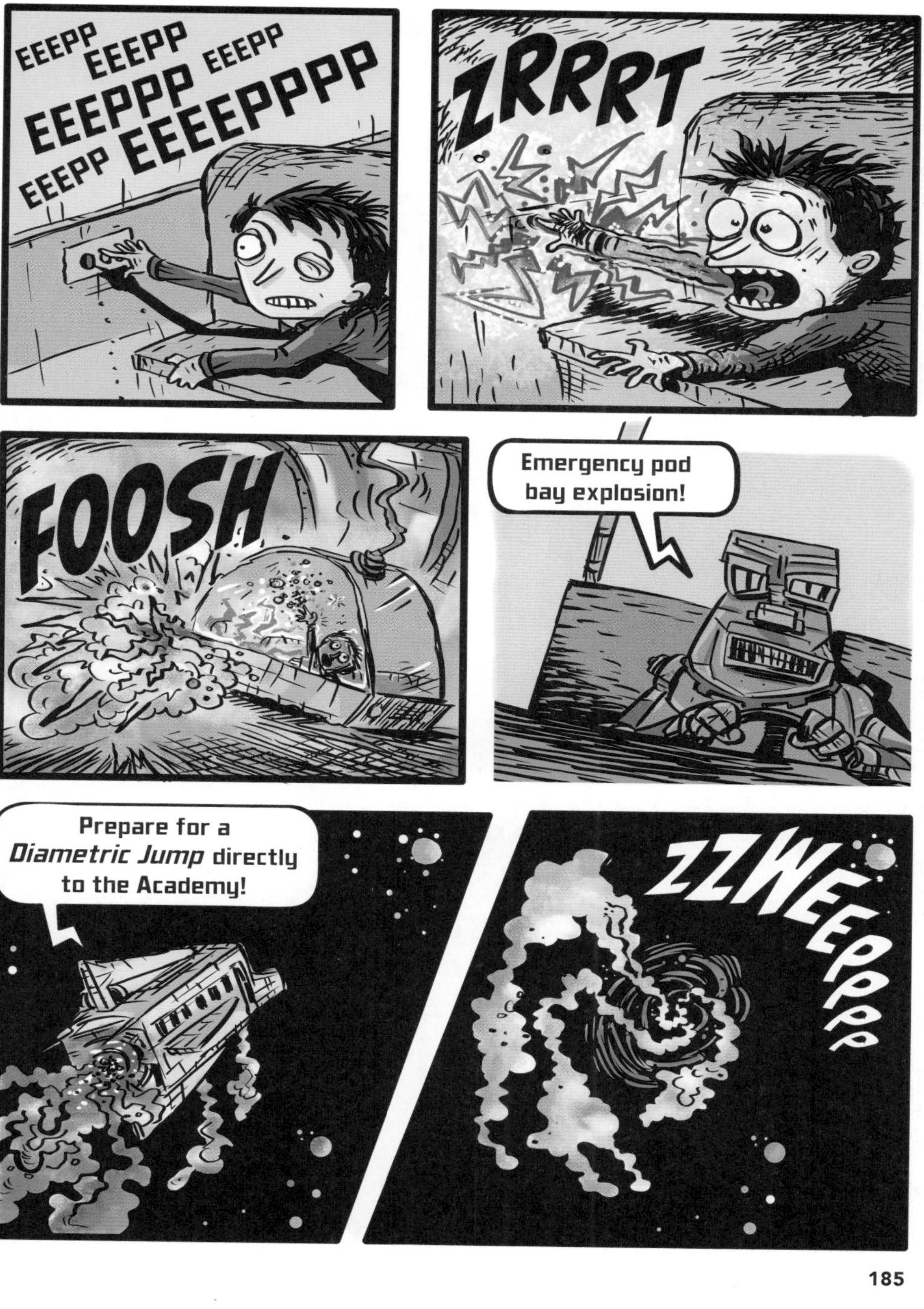
EEEPP EEEPP EEEPP EEEPPP EEEEPPPP EEEPP EEEEPP
ZRRRT
FOOSH
Emergency pod bay explosion!
Prepare for a *Diametric Jump* directly to the Academy!
ZZWEEPPP

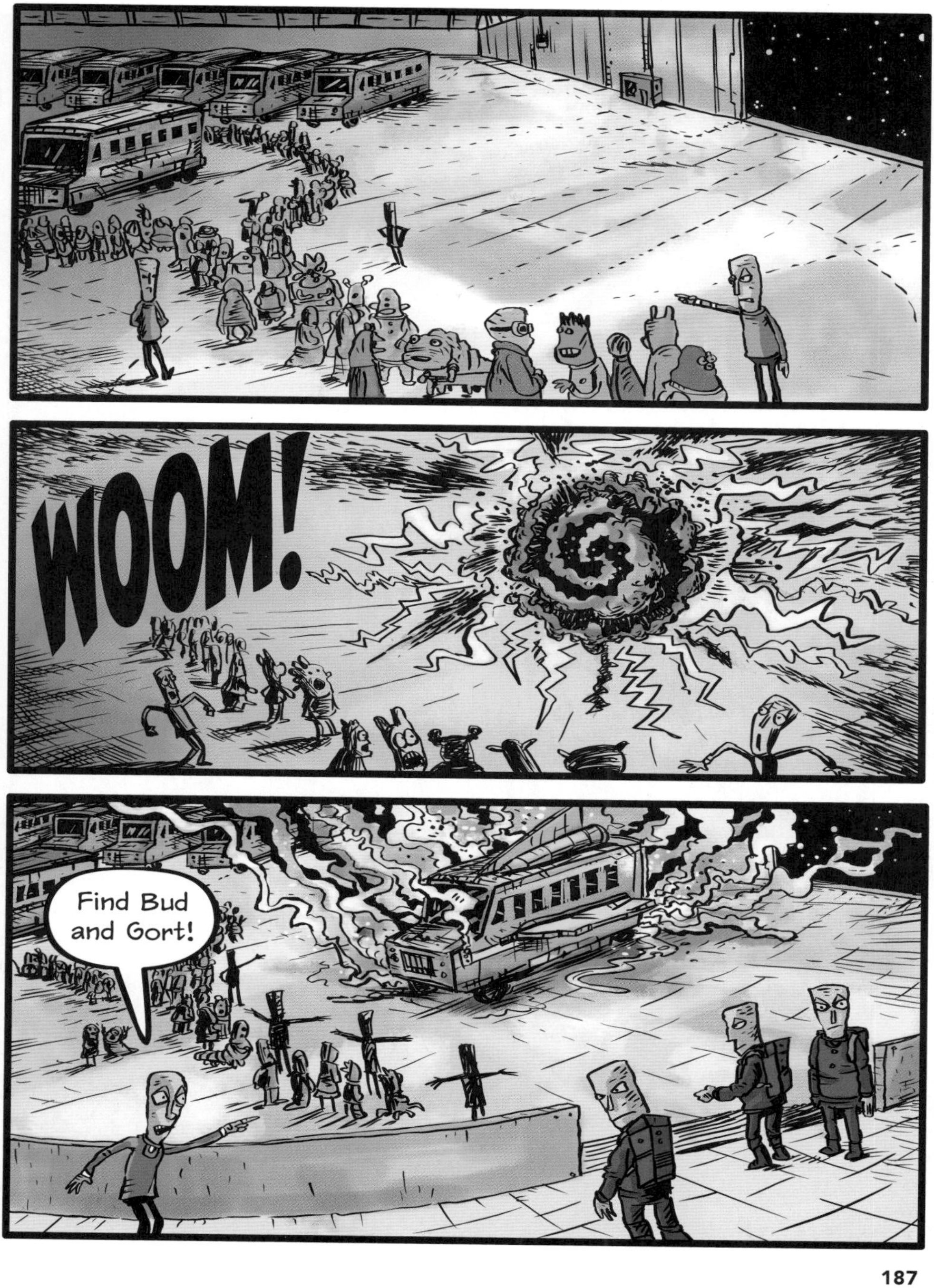
WOOM!
Find Bud and Gort!

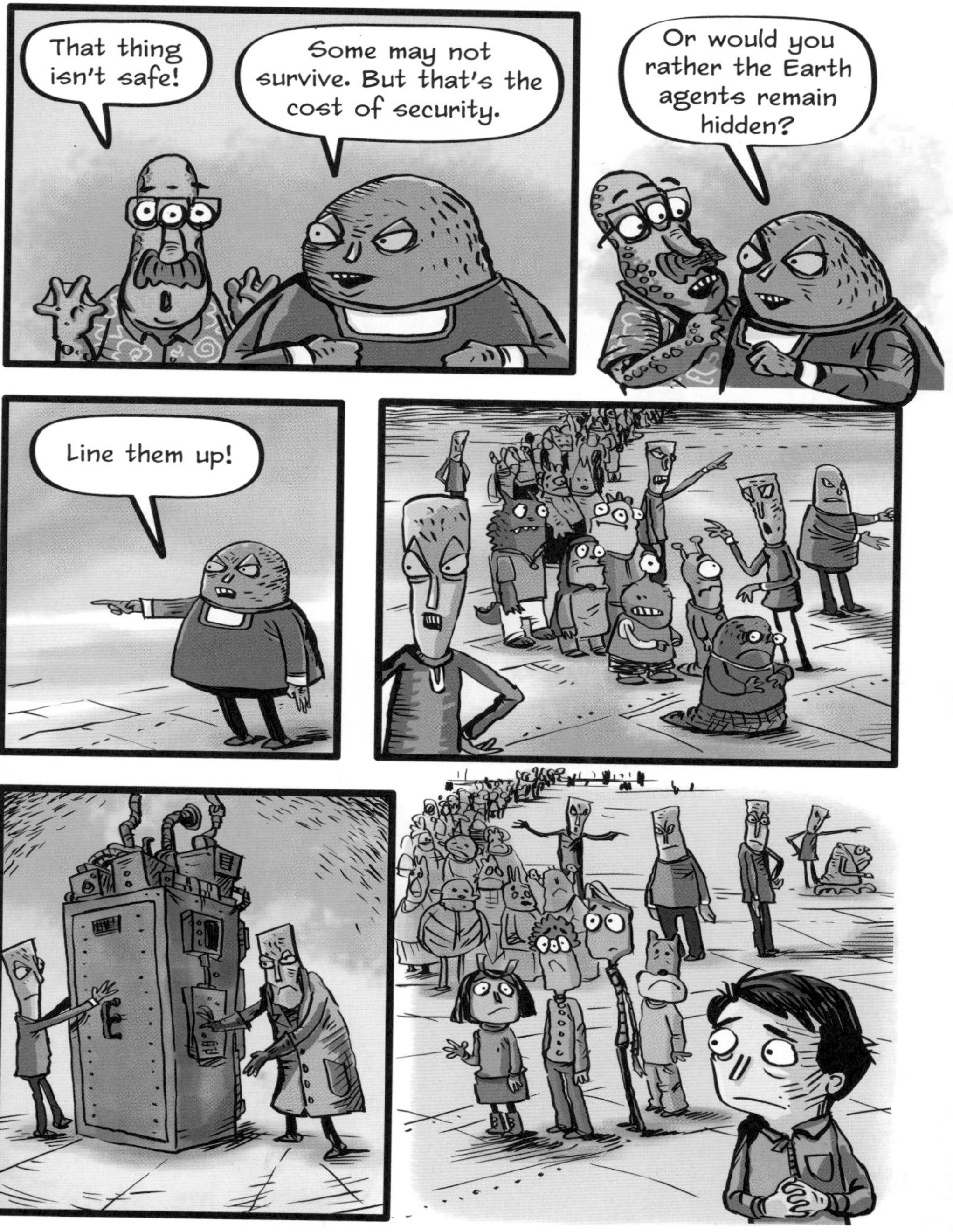
That thing isn't safe!
Some may not survive. But that's the cost of security.
Or would you rather the Earth agents remain hidden?
Line them up!

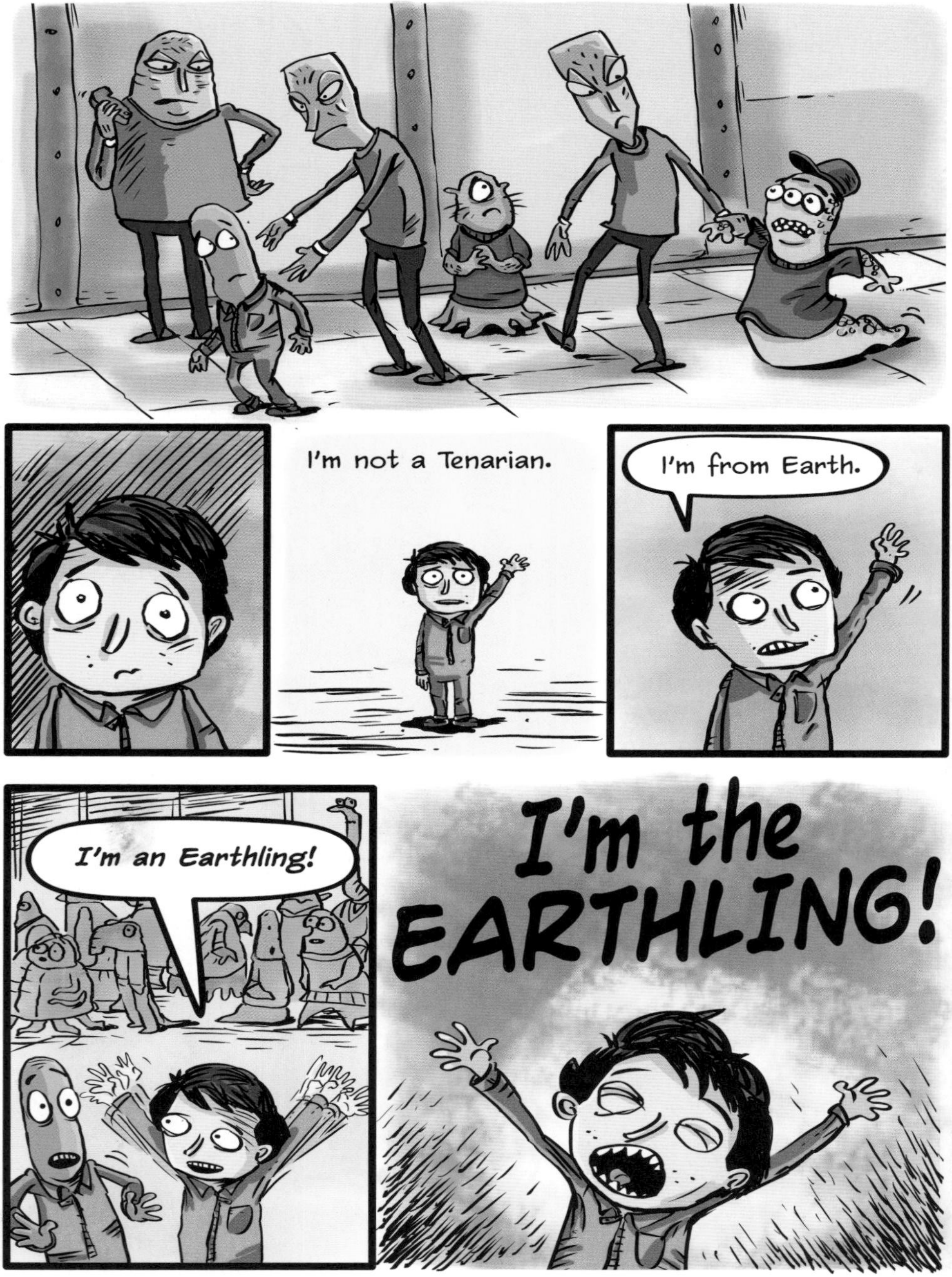

I'm not a Tenarian.
I'm from Earth.
I'm an Earthling!
I'm the EARTHLING!

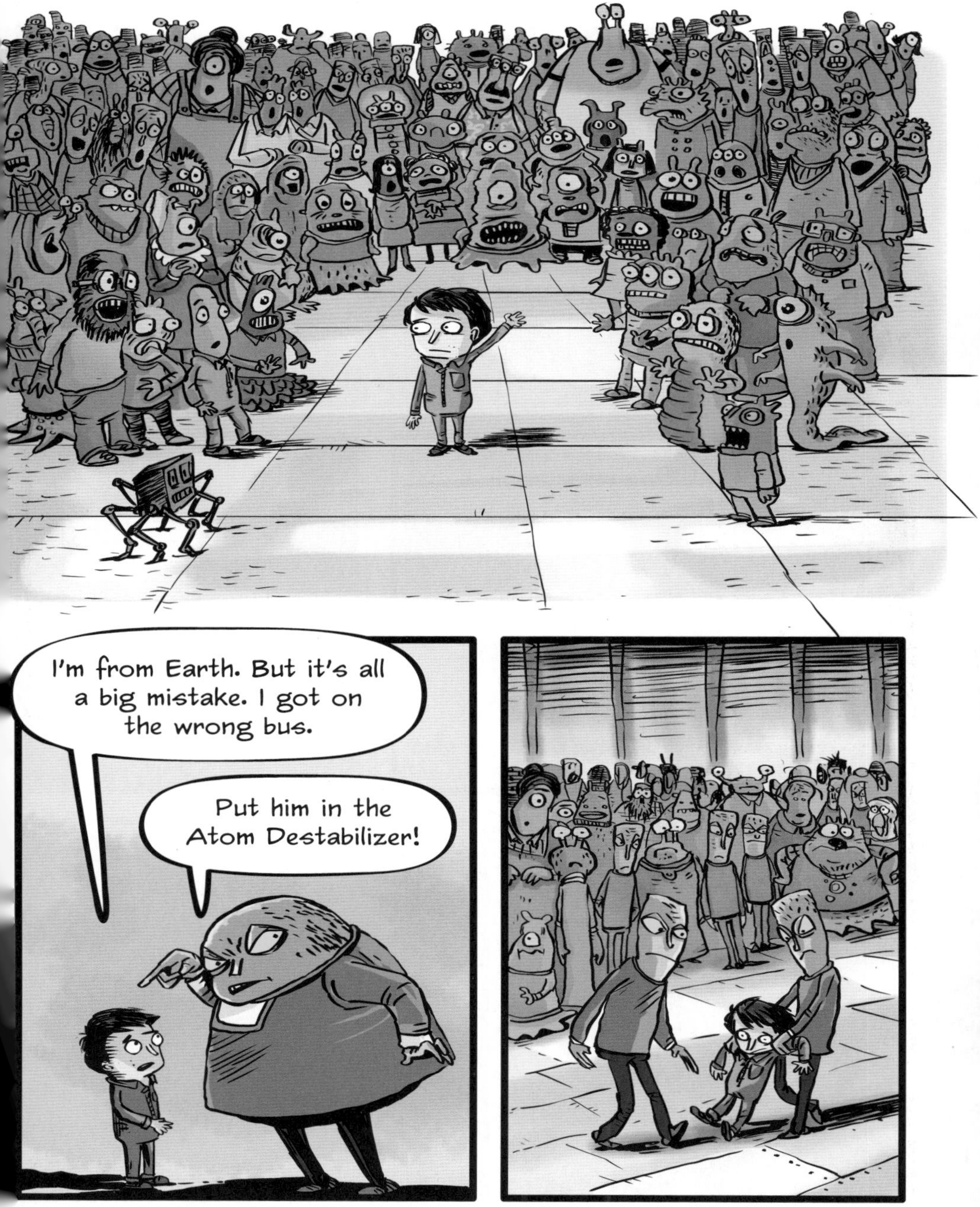
I'm from Earth. But it's all a big mistake. I got on the wrong bus.
Put him in the Atom Destabilizer!

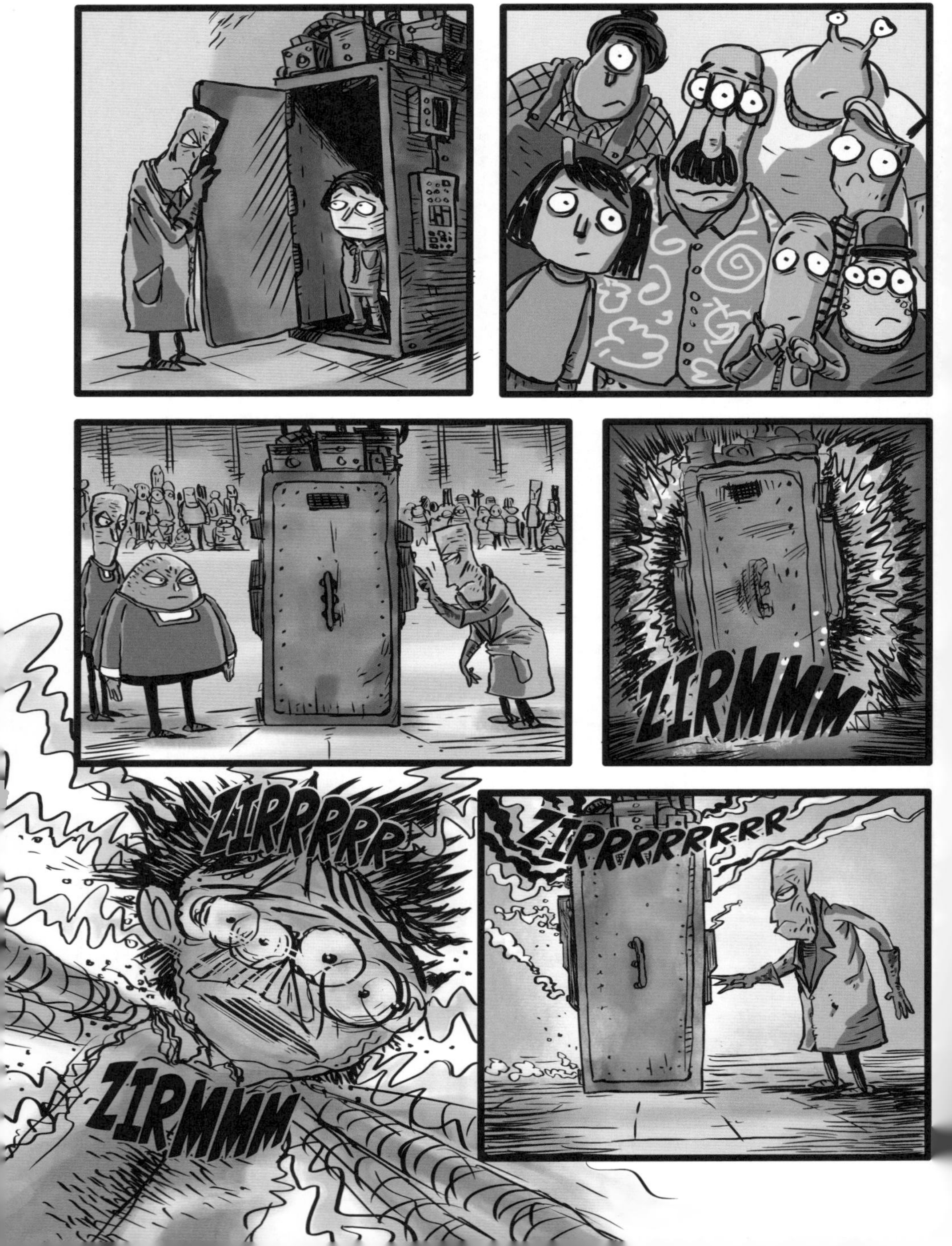
ZIRMMM
ZIRRRRR
ZIRMMM
ZIRRRRRRRR

CHAPTER 8

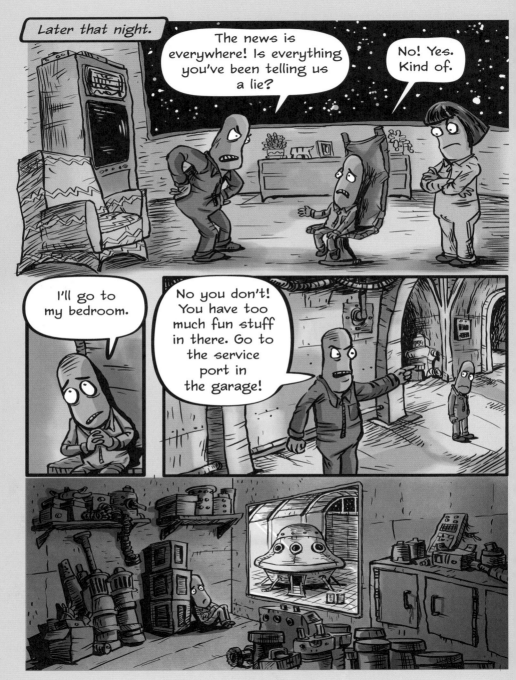

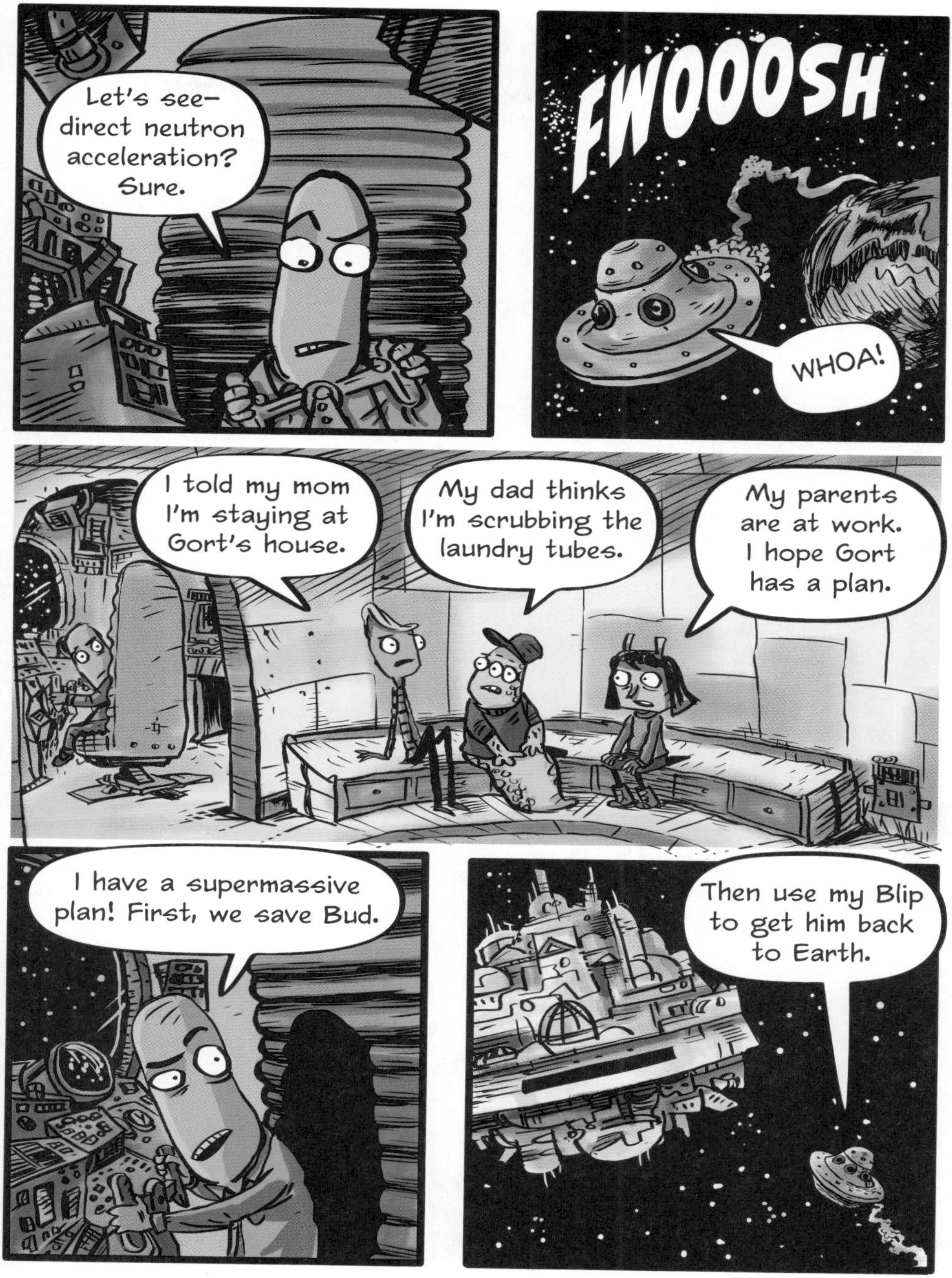
Let's see-
direct neutron
acceleration?
Sure.
FWOOOSH
WHOA!
I told my mom
I'm staying at
Gort's house.
My dad thinks
I'm scrubbing the
laundry tubes.
My parents
are at work.
I hope Gort
has a plan.
I have a supermassive
plan! First, we save Bud.
Then use my Blip
to get him back
to Earth.

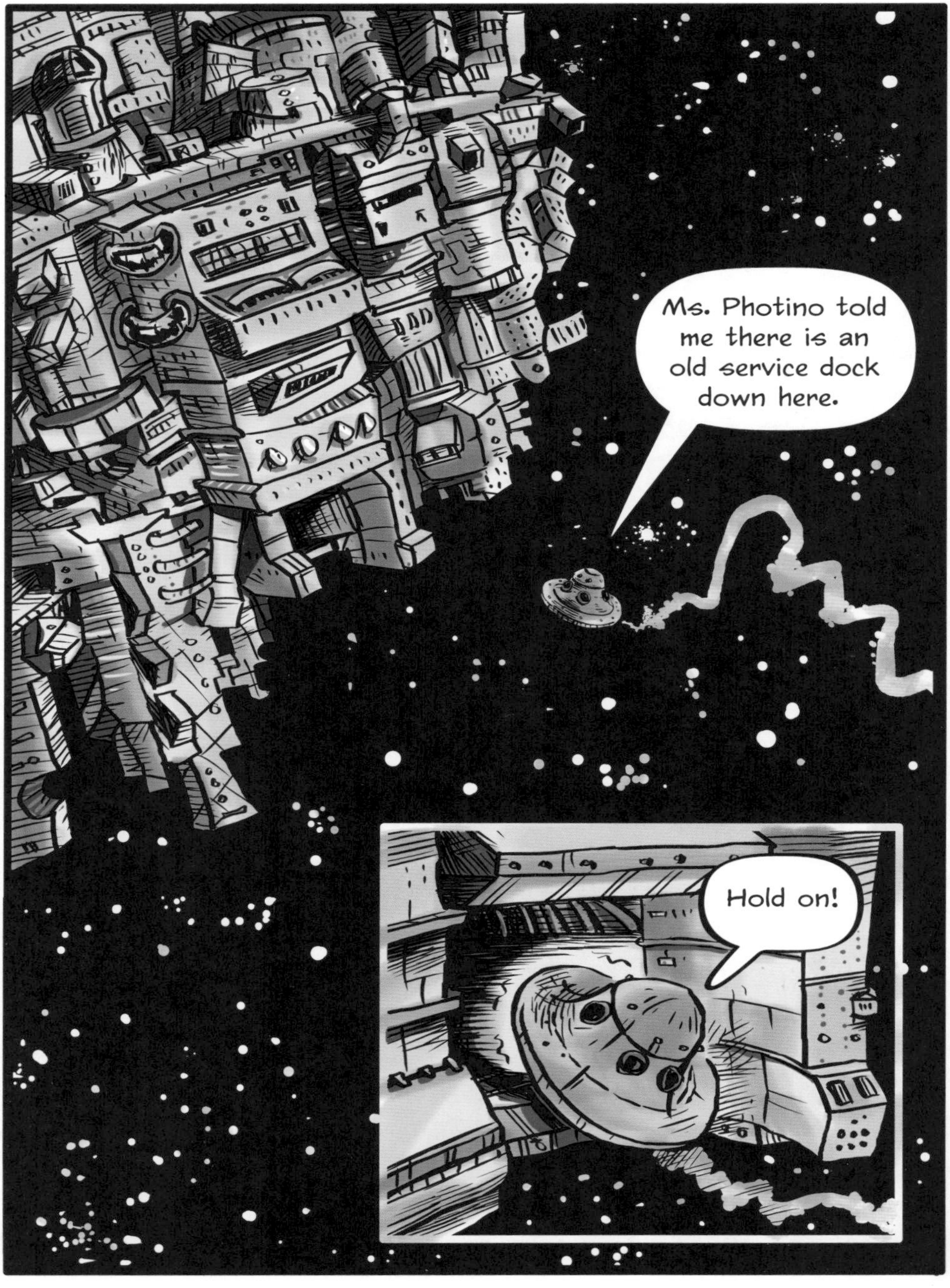
Ms. Photino told me there is an old service dock down here.
Hold on!

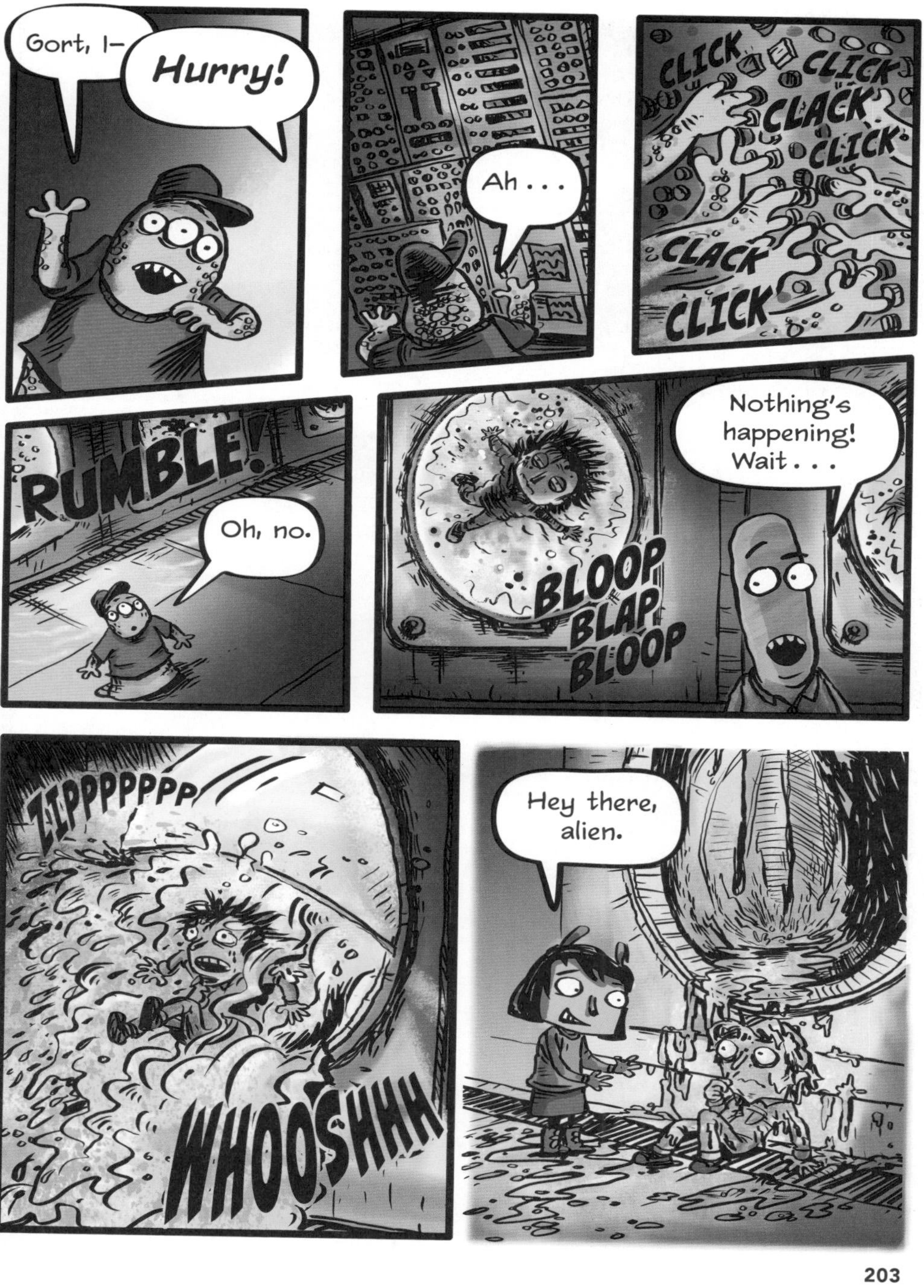
Gort, I—
Hurry!
Ah . . .
CLICK
CLICK
CLACK
CLICK
CLACK
CLICK
RUMBLE!
Oh, no.
Nothing's happening! Wait . . .
BLOOP
BLAP
BLOOP
ZIPPPPPPP
WHOOSHHH
Hey there, alien.

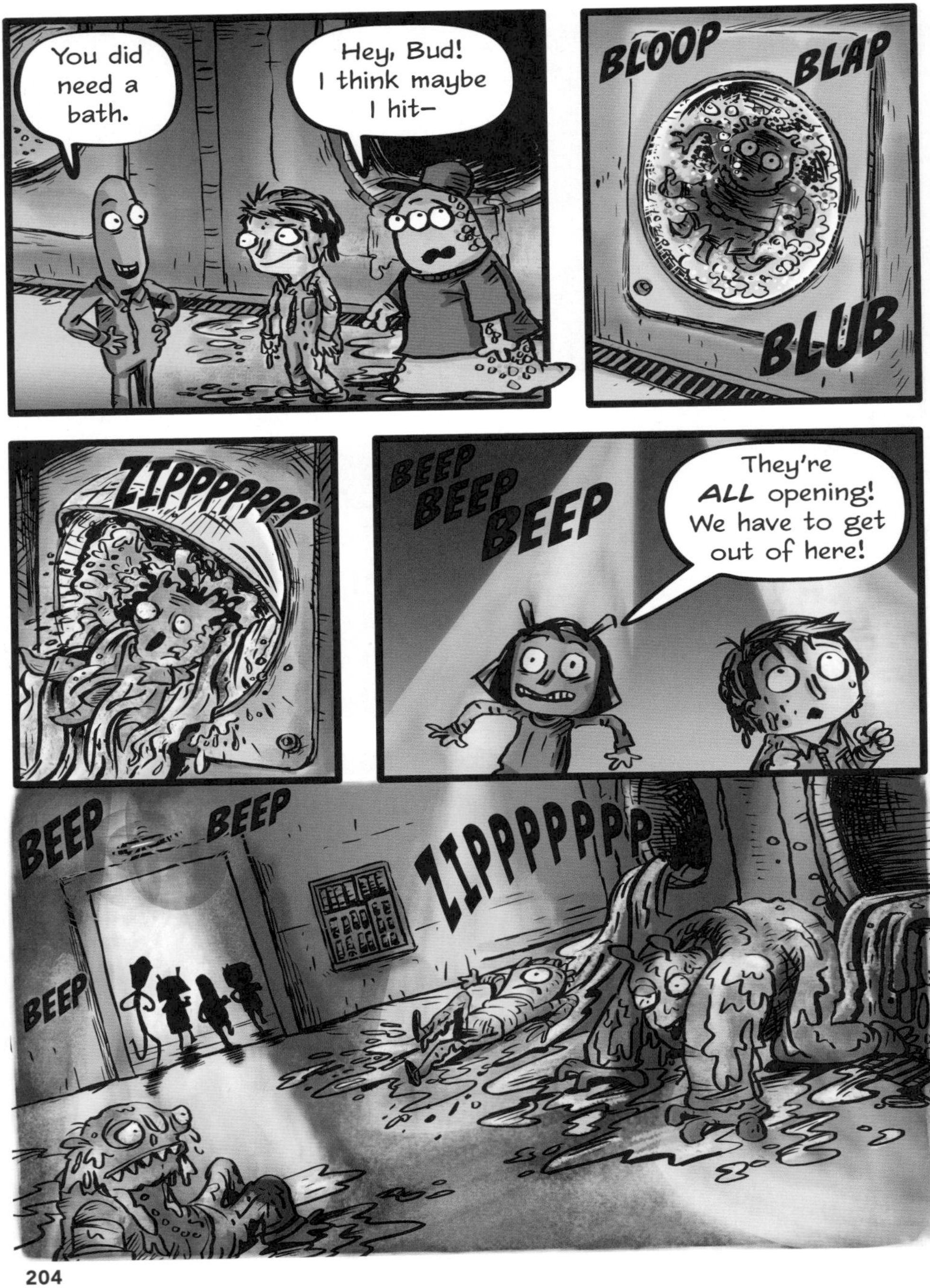
You did need a bath.
Hey, Bud! I think maybe I hit—
BLOOP
BLAP
BLUB
ZIPPPPPPP
BEEP
BEEP
BEEP
They're ALL opening! We have to get out of here!
BEEP
BEEP
ZIPPPPPPP
BEEP

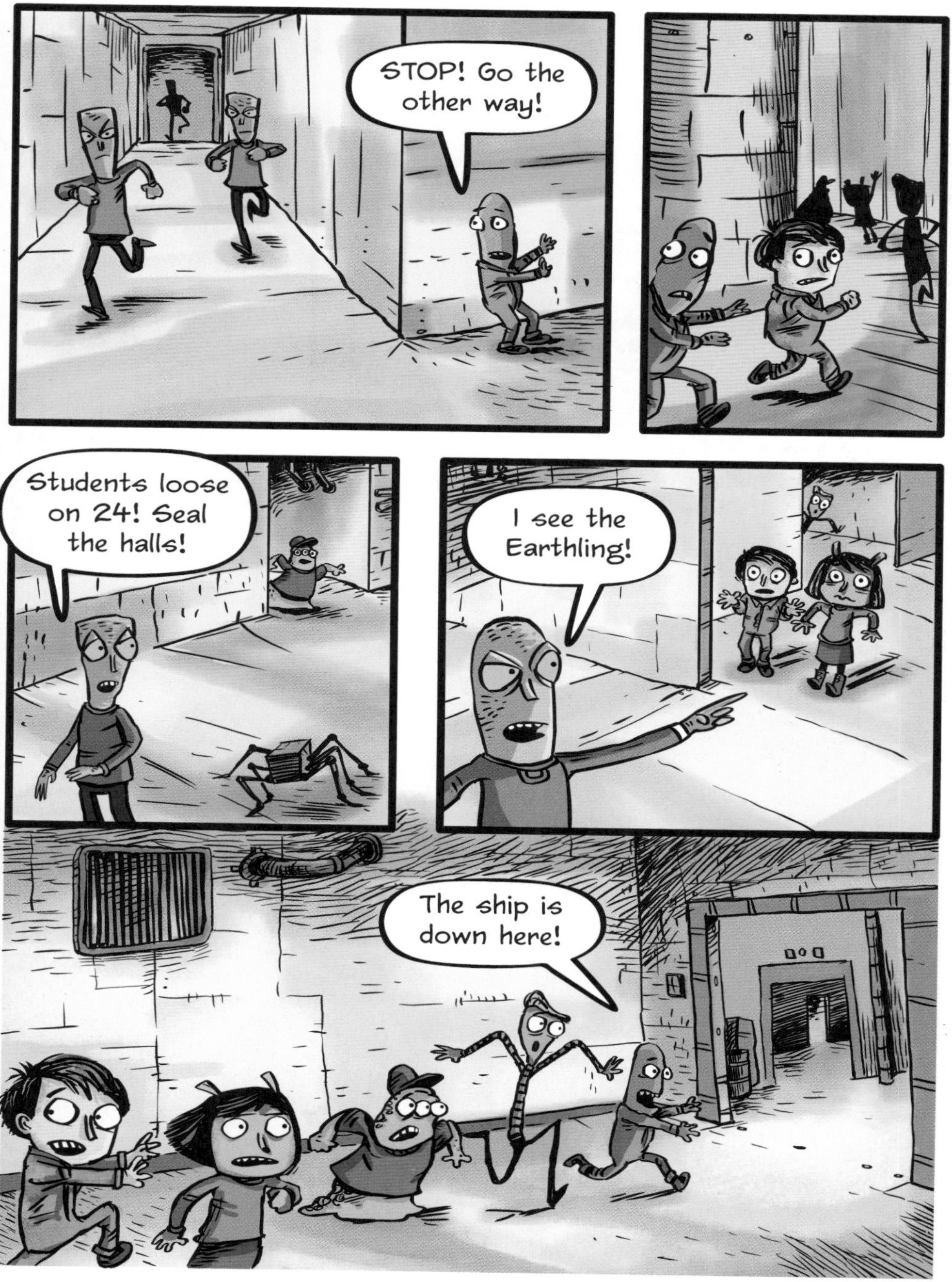
STOP! Go the other way!
Students loose on 24! Seal the halls!
I see the Earthling!
The ship is down here!

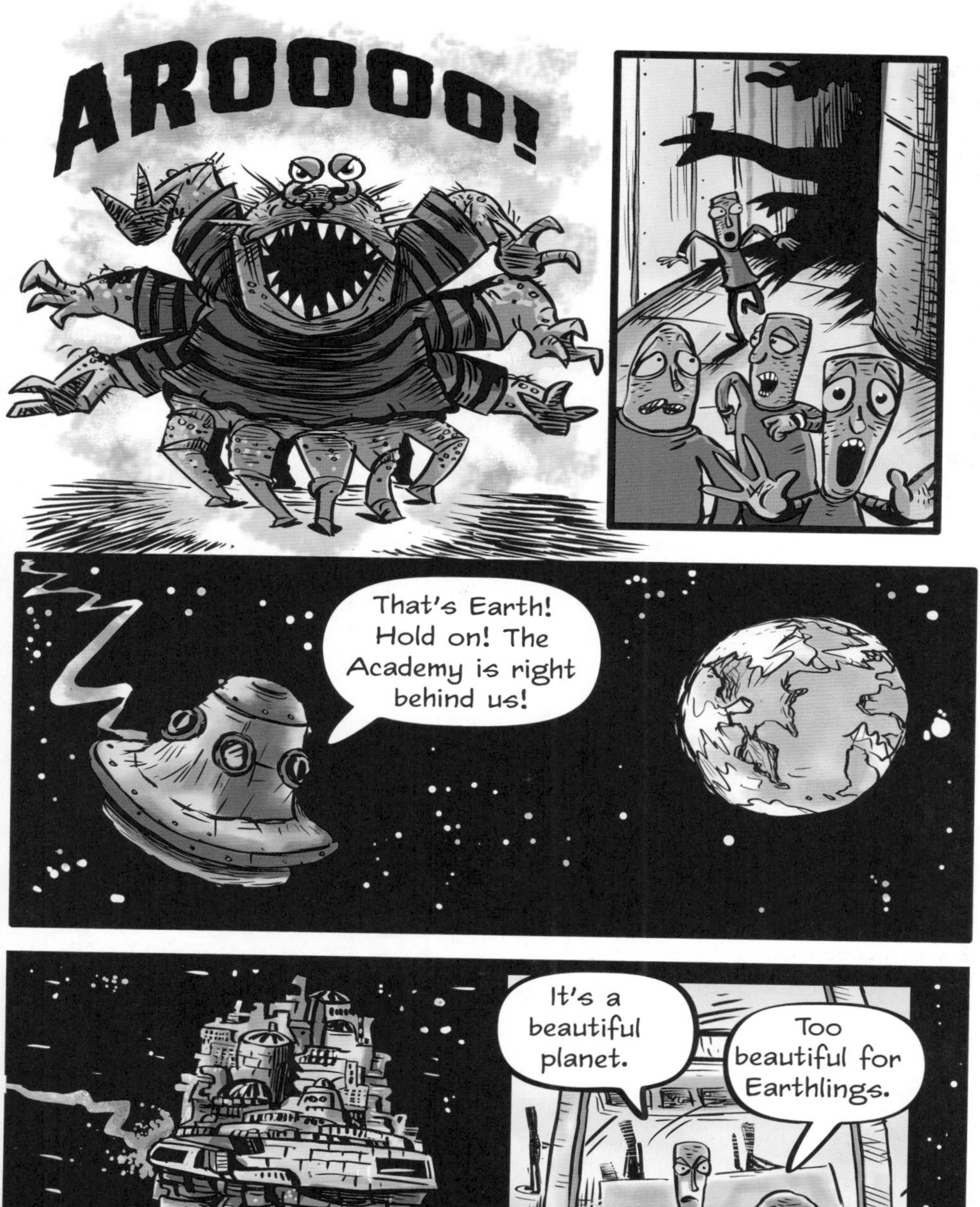
AROOOO!
That's Earth! Hold on! The Academy is right behind us!
It's a beautiful planet.
Too beautiful for Earthlings.

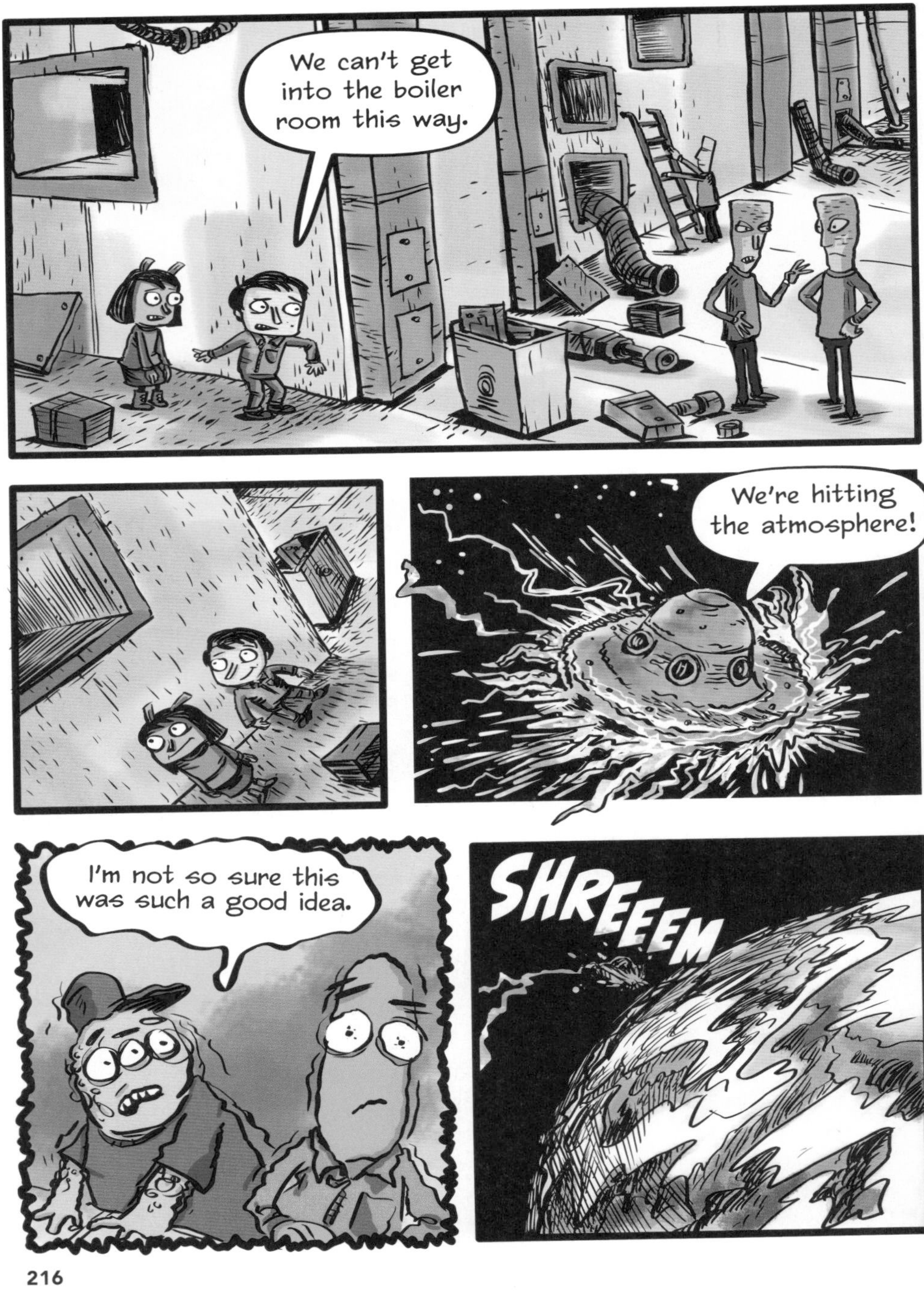
We can't get into the boiler room this way.
We're hitting the atmosphere!
I'm not so sure this was such a good idea.
SHREEEM

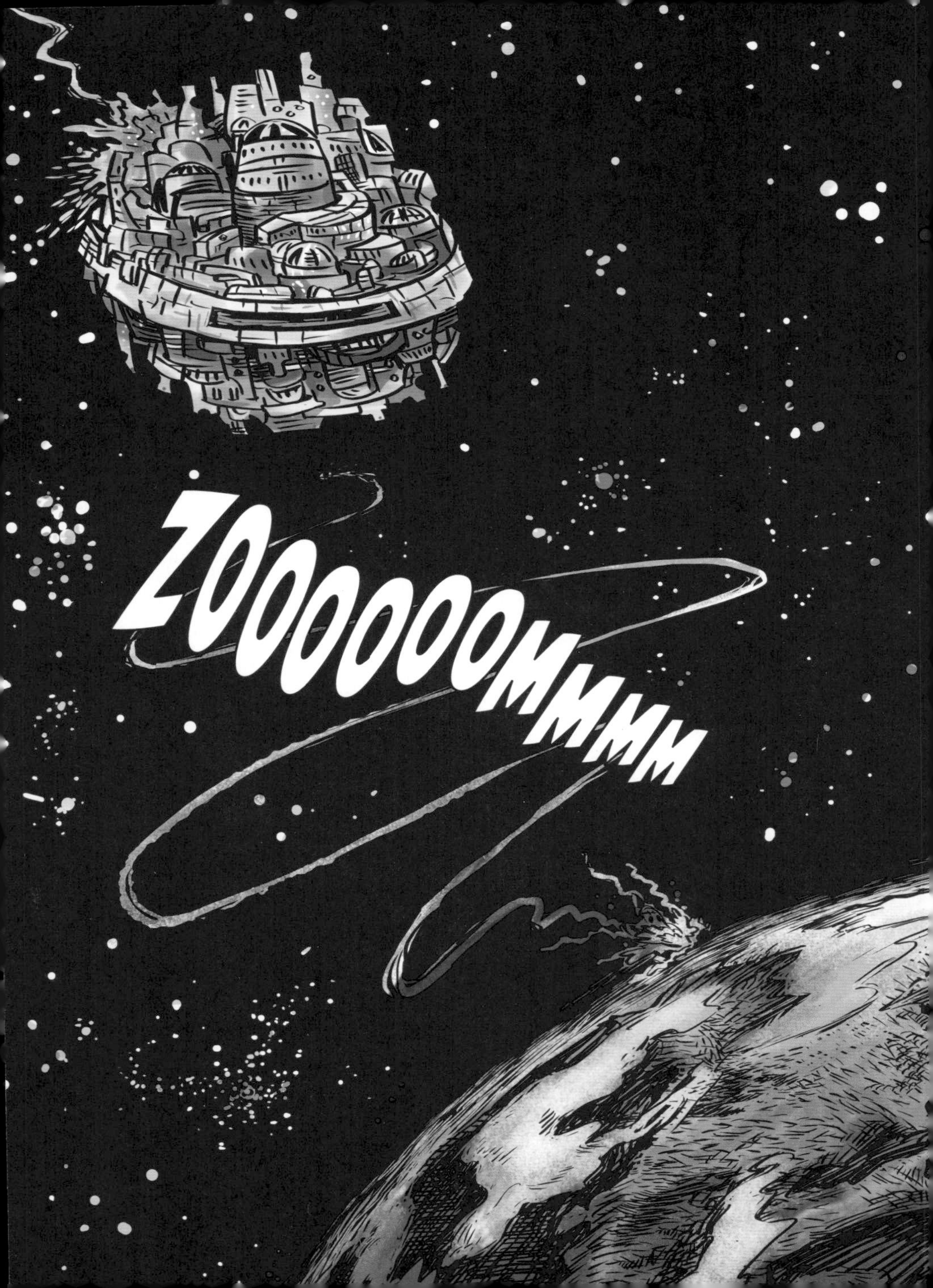
ZOOOOOOMMMMM

CHAPTER 9

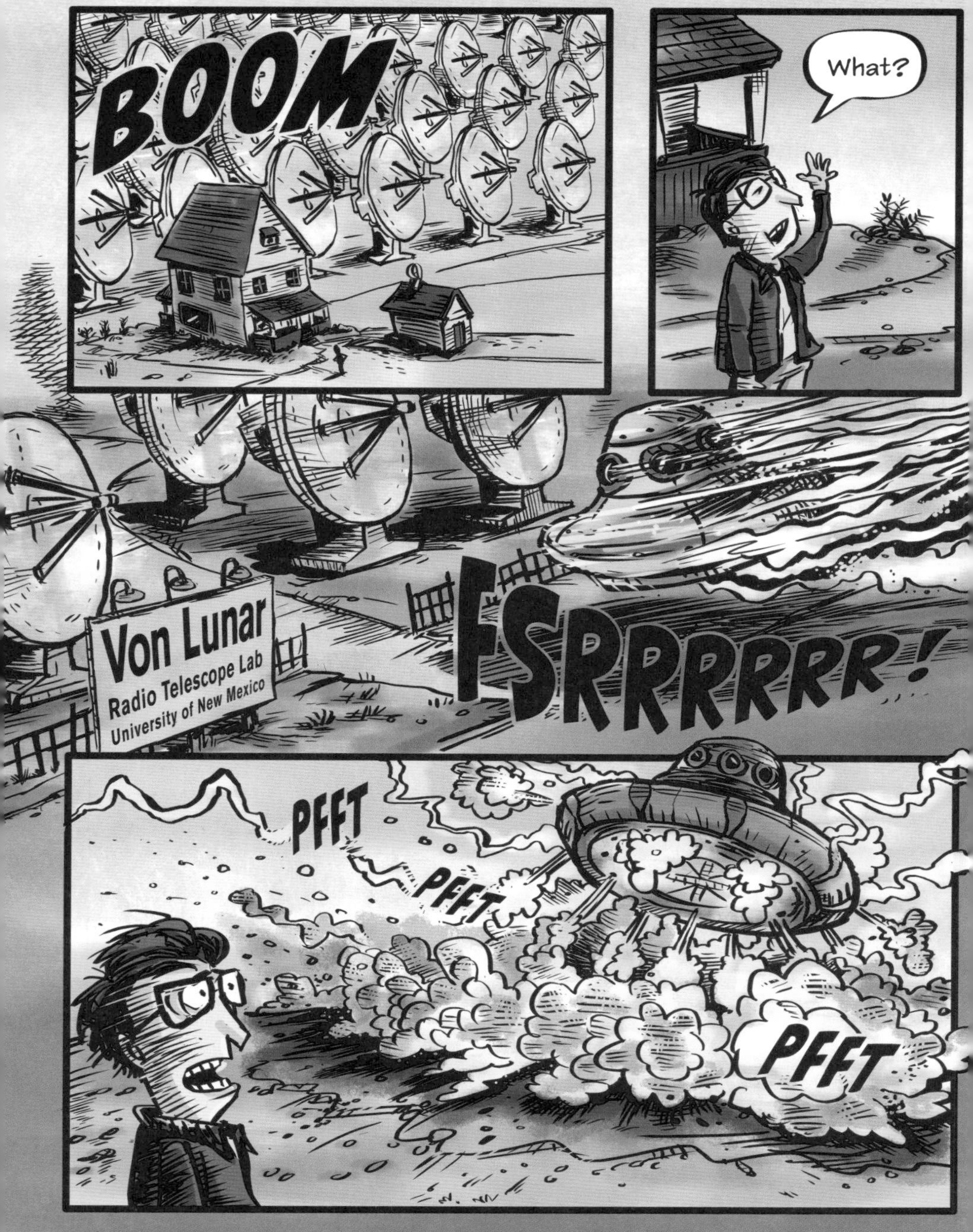
BOOM
What?
Von Lunar
Radio Telescope Lab
University of New Mexico
FSRRRRRR!
PFFT
PFFT
PFFT

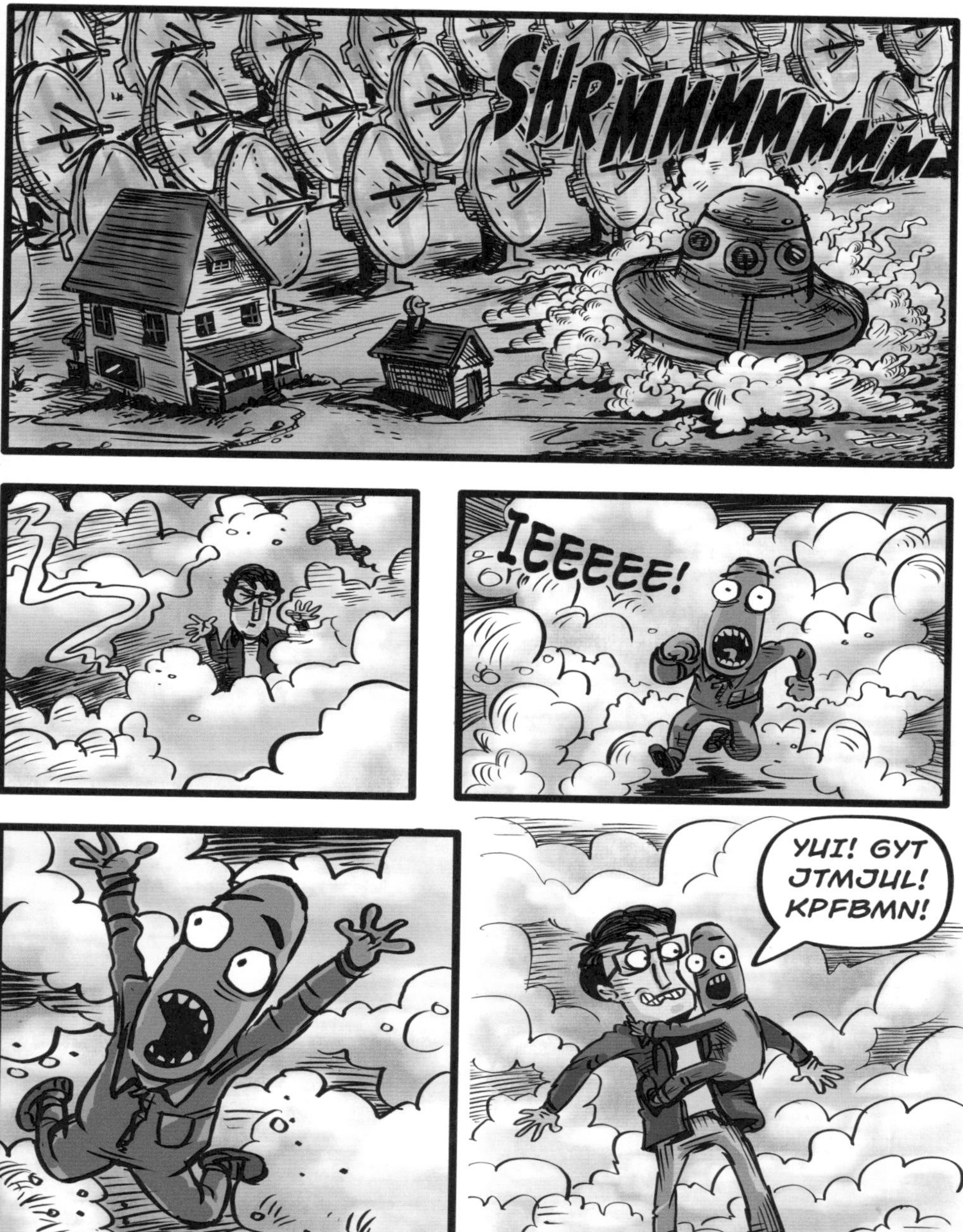
SHRMMMMMMMMM
IEEEEEE!
YUI! GYT JTMJUL! KPFBMN!

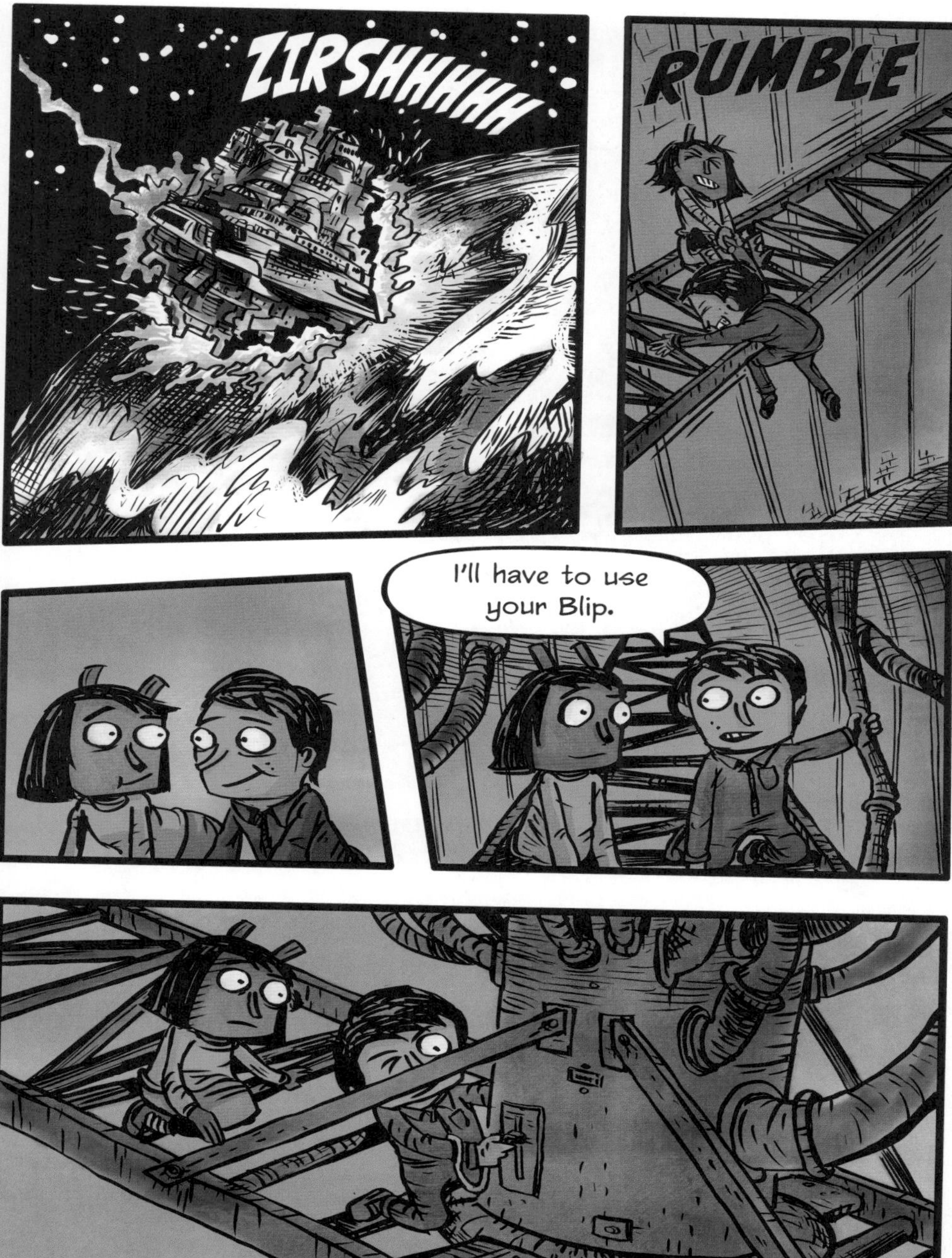
ZIRSHHHHH
RUMBLE
I'll have to use your Blip.

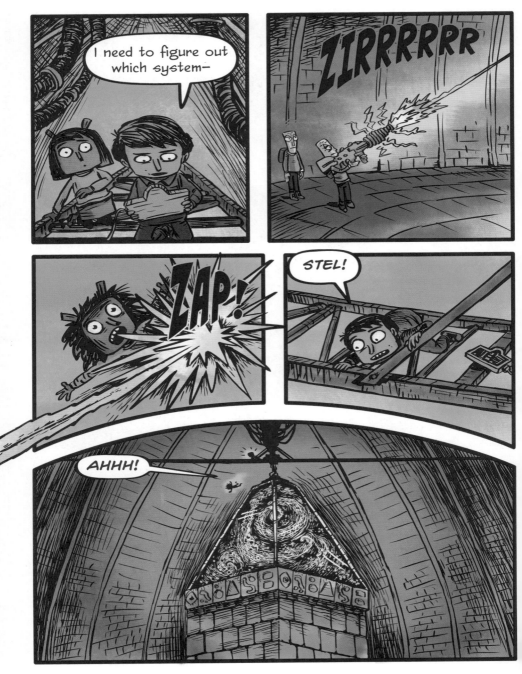

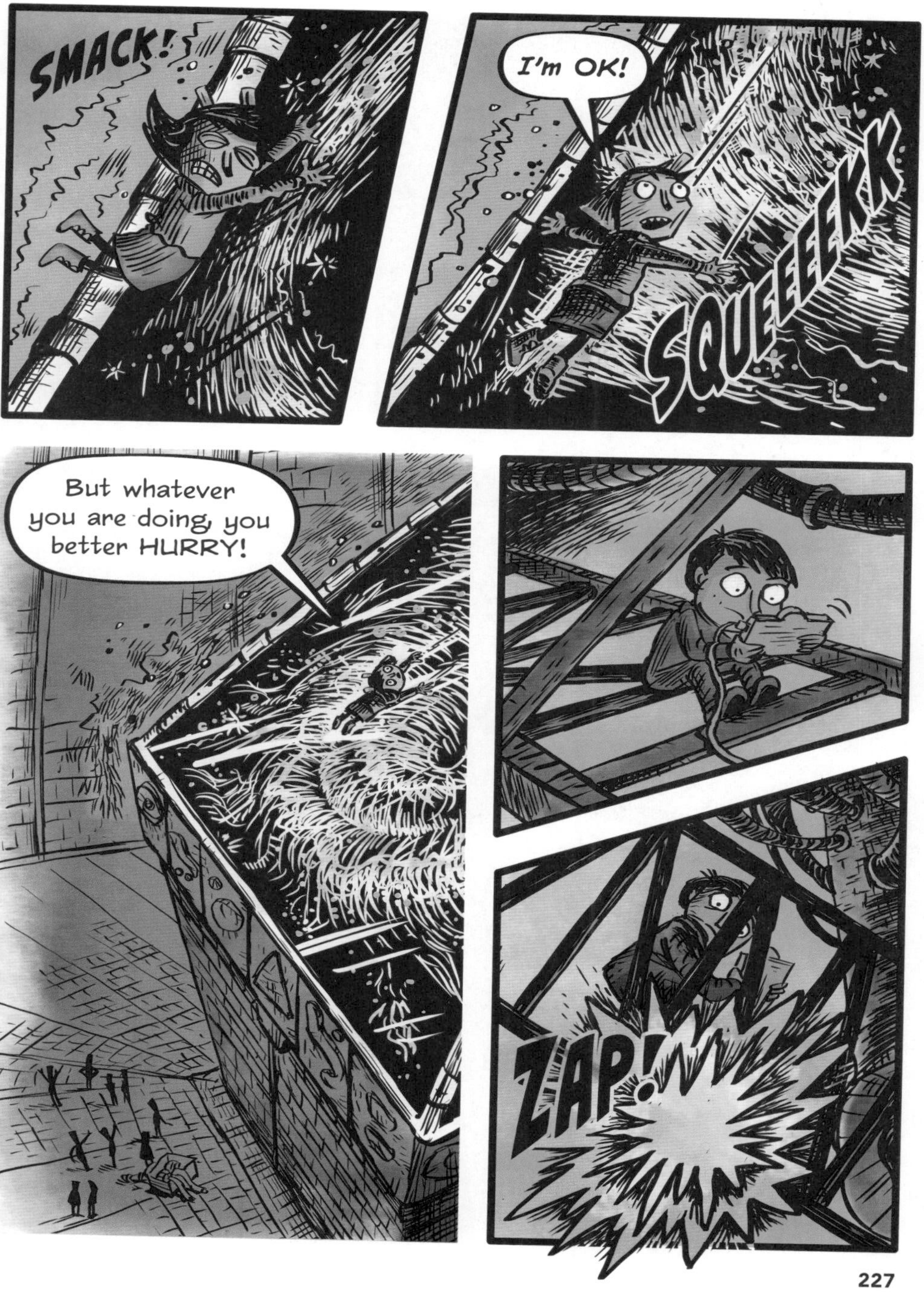
SMACK!
I'm OK!
SQUEEEEKK
But whatever you are doing, you better HURRY!
ZAP!

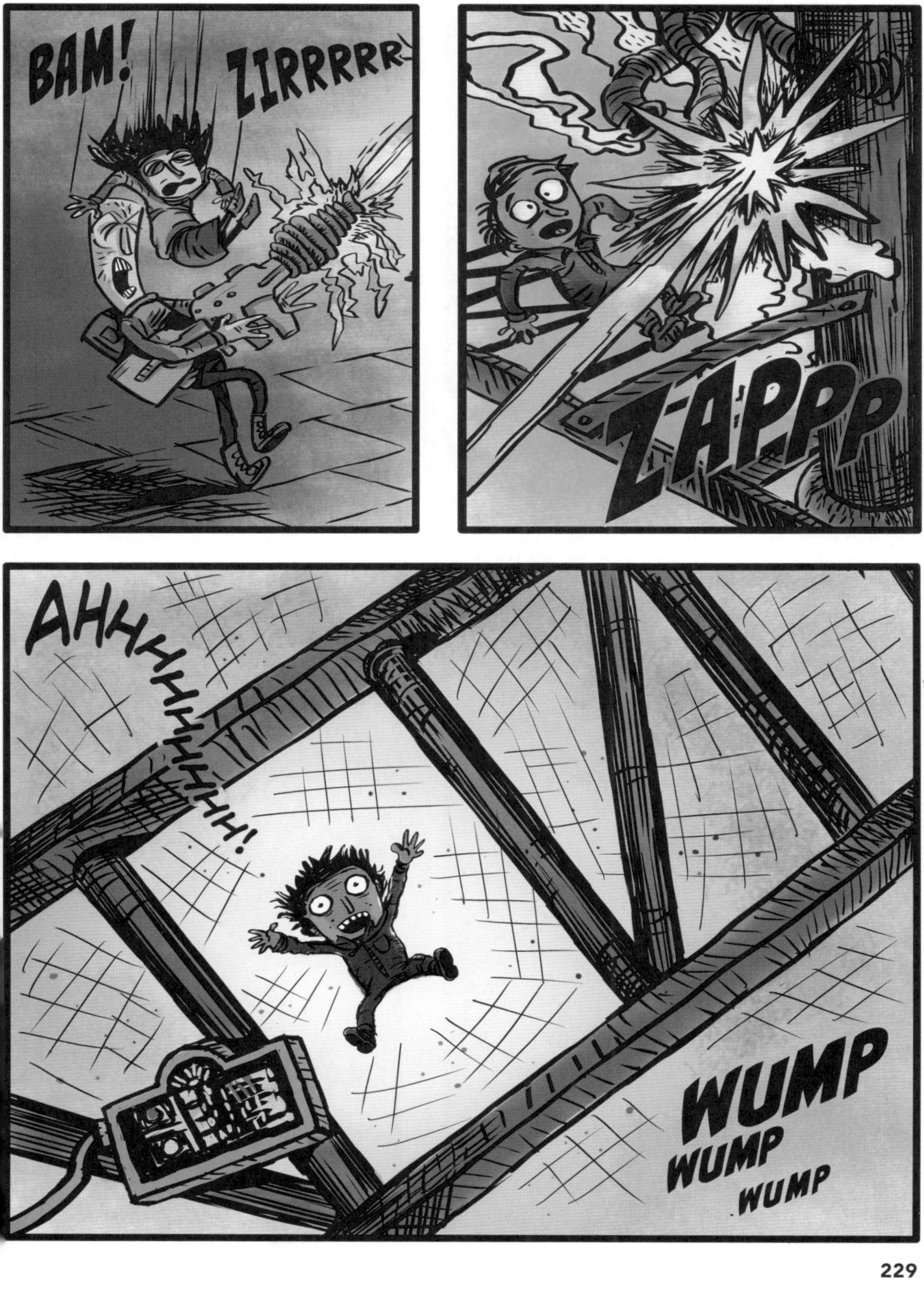
BAM!
ZIRRRRR
ZAPPP
AHHHHHHHHHH!
WUMP
WUMP
WUMP

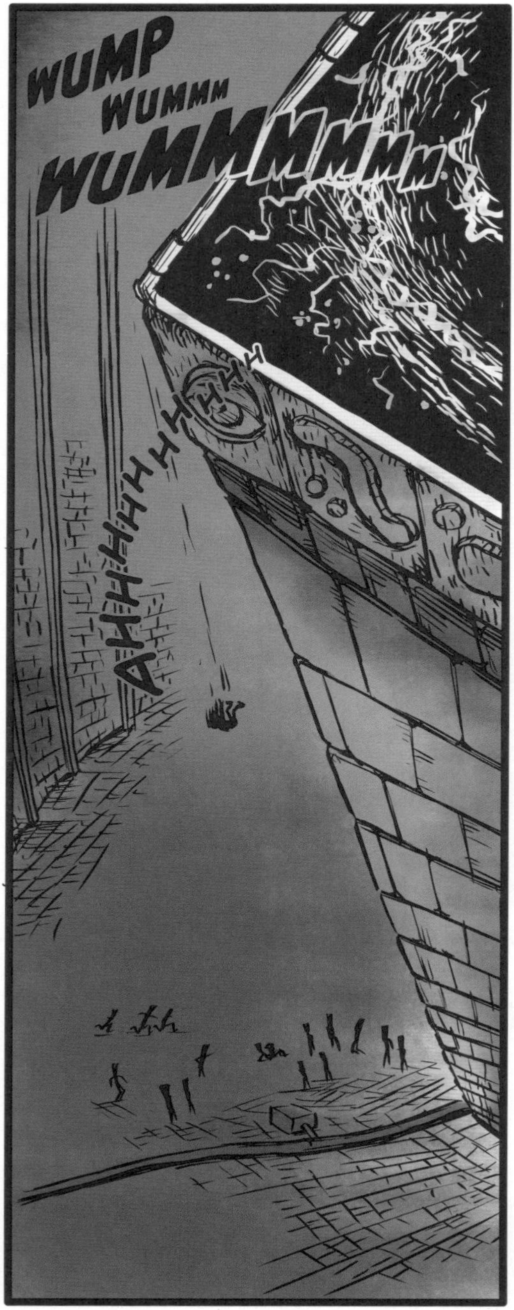
WUMP
WUMMM
WUMMMMMMM
AHHHHHHHHH

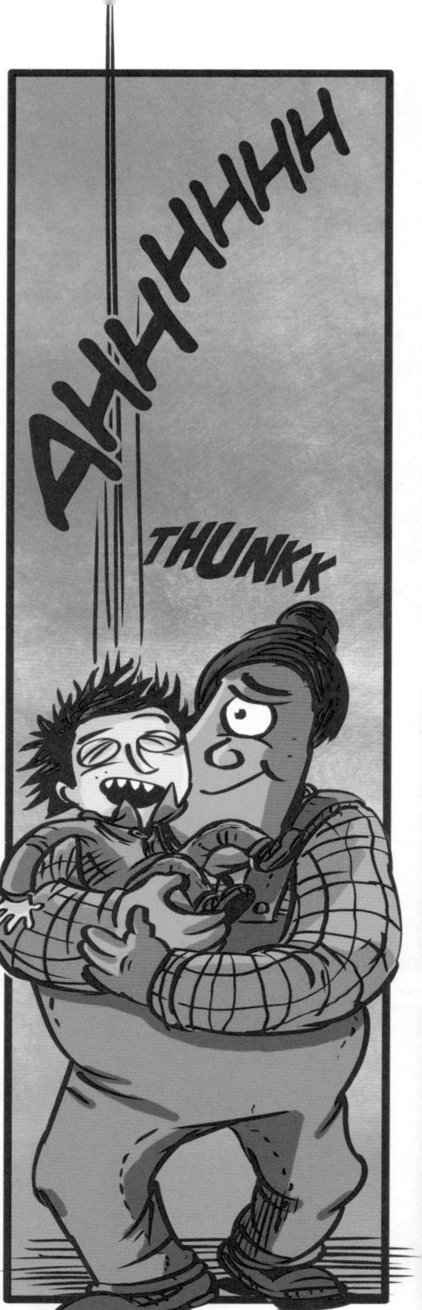
AHHHHHHHH
THUNKK

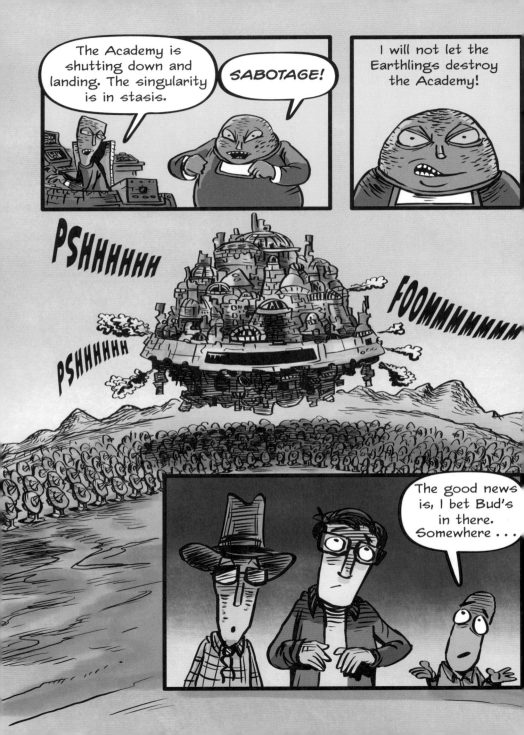

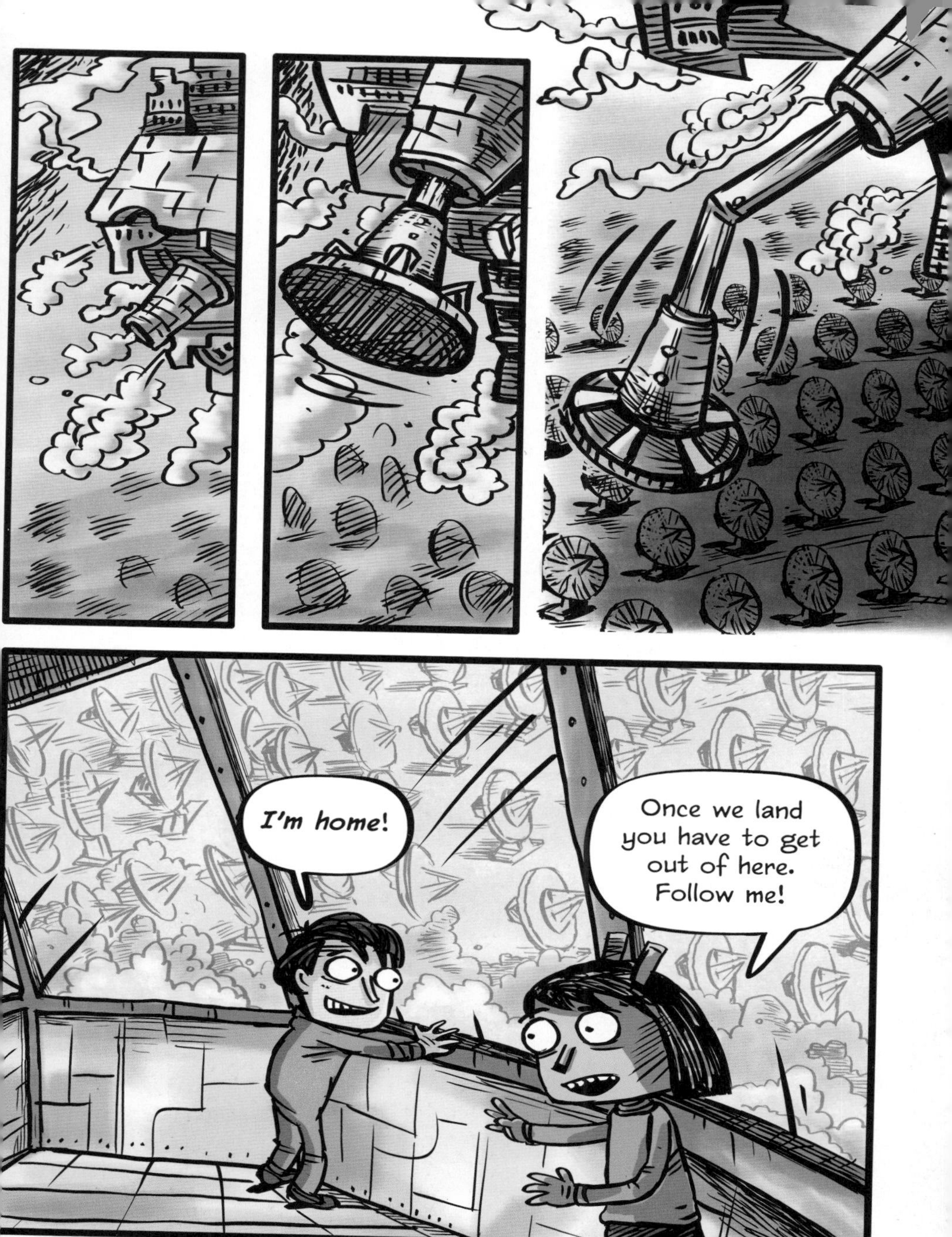
I'm home!
Once we land you have to get out of here. Follow me!

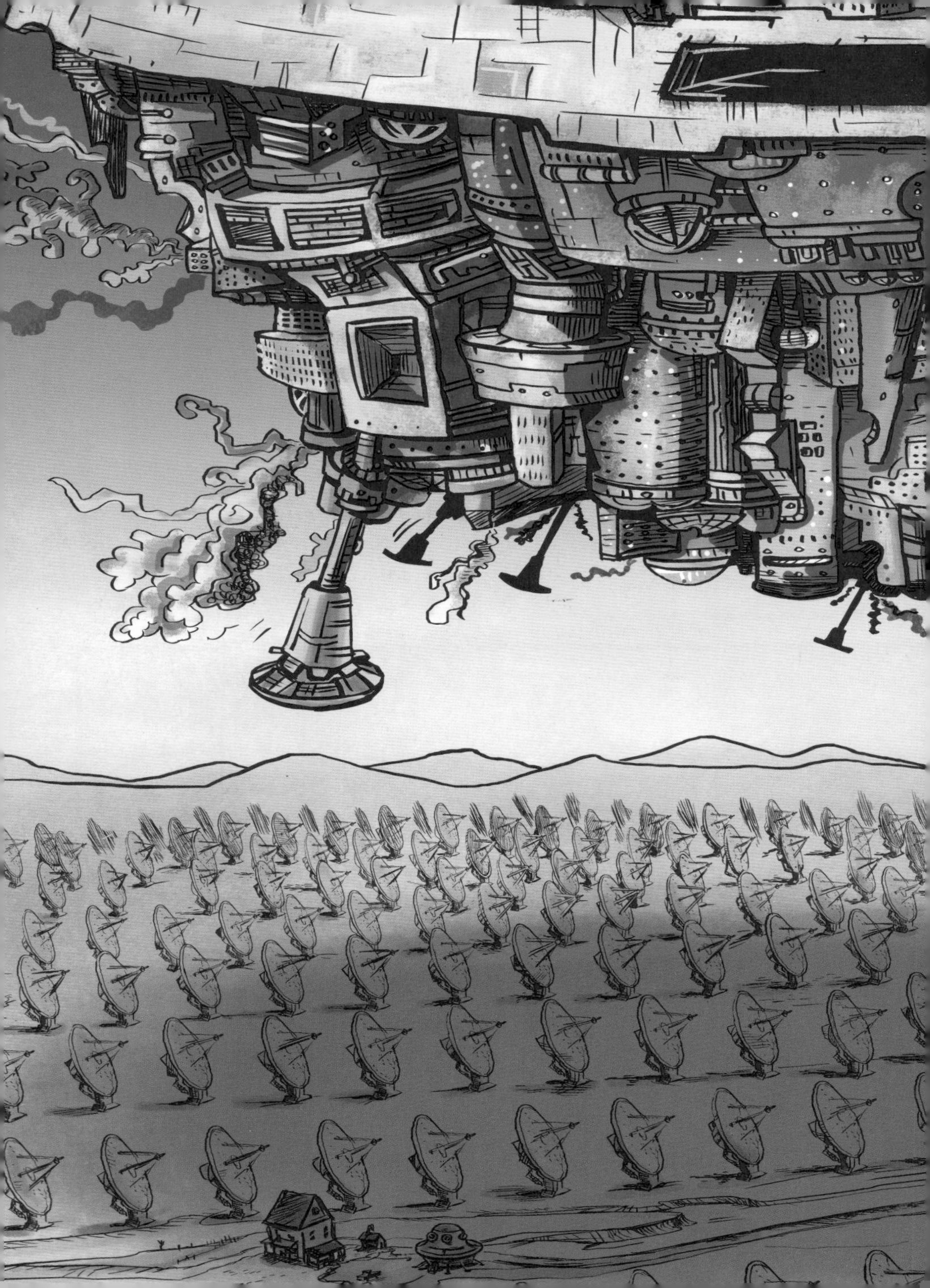